TASK
FORCE
BAUM

TASK FORCE BAUM

JAMES D. SHIPMAN

KENSINGTON BOOKS
www.kensingtonbooks.com

KENSINGTON BOOKS are published by

Kensington Publishing Corp.
119 West 40th Street
New York, NY 10018

All Kensington titles, imprints and distributed lines are available at special quantity discounts for bulk purchases for sales promotion, premiums, fund-raising, educational or institutional use. Special book excerpts or customized printings can also be created to fit specific needs. For details, write or phone the office of the Kensington Special Sales Manager: Kensington Publishing Corp., 119 West 40th Street, New York, NY, 10018. Attn. Special Sales Department. Phone: 1-800-221-2647.

Kensington and the K logo Reg. U.S. Pat. & TM Off.

Library of Congress Control Number: 2019944528

ISBN-13: 978-1-4967-2386-4
ISBN-10: 1-4967-2386-4
First Kensington Hardcover Edition: December 2019

ISBN-13: 978-1-4967-2387-1 (e-book)
ISBN-10: 1-4967-2387-2 (e-book)

10 9 8 7 6 5 4 3 2 1

Printed in the United States of America

I dedicate this book to my wonderful wife, Becky, who puts up with my continuous brainstorming, editing, fidgeting, and writing at all hours of the day and all days of the week.

Prologue

The Ardennes Forest, Belgium
December 19, 1944

He tasted chocolate and blood. The frozen edge of the D ration lanced his gums. He sputtered and spit, a crimson froth staining the white blanket of snow at the edge of his foxhole. He bit again at the icy bar, more carefully this time. A chunk broke away, and he chewed greedily, wrestling the bitter flavor. He scanned the horizon through the darkness, his eyes walking the hundred yards to the woods. Nothing.

"Captain Curtis"—the voice jolted him, and he half-rose, his hand cradling an M1911 .45 automatic pistol. Second Lieutenant Tim Hanson materialized through the misty blackness, gingerly balancing two steaming tin cups. Hanson labored through the snow, his lean legs stabbing the icy dust into his knee with each strenuous step.

The lieutenant extended a bony hand, and Curtis gratefully grasped a mug, tipping the fluid to his lips. The coffee was scalding hot, and he burned his tongue with the first sip, but he relished the fiery liquid as he swallowed. His throat and stomach embraced the river of warmth. He was freezing. Colder than he could ever remember. The winters in Indiana were harsh, but there was always shelter waiting nearby. A warm fire or the heater of his pickup. Since they'd arrived a week ago, he'd stood, sat, and slept in an icy world with no escape. He pulled his jacket closer, fighting down anger. Where were the winter clothes the army had promised them? He took another sip, a deeper one. He removed his glasses and ran a cloth over them, wiping away the frost. His eyes scanned the trees again, an endless futile vigil.

"Anything out there, sir?" asked Hanson, drawing a handkerchief up to his nose between hazy breaths.

"I told you, you can call me Jim when it's just the two of us around. And, no, nothing but trees and frost."

"Any word from the outpost?"

Curtis nodded. "Half hour or so ago. They report the same. Course, this is supposed to be a quiet sector."

"Maybe it's more than that," speculated Hanson, taking a sip of his coffee. "Rumor is the Germans have had it."

Curtis grunted. "Figures. Two years of training, and we miss the whole show by a week. Let's hope not. We can't send these boys home empty-handed."

"You're not supposed to be this far up, sir," said Hanson, his cobalt-colored eyes narrowing in concern.

"No choice, Lieutenant. I can't make out a darn thing back at the command post. I need to see." Curtis tipped his cup back, gulping down the rest of the coffee. He wiped his lips with a frozen glove.

"Guess it doesn't matter," said Hanson, shrugging. "Nothing going on anyway."

"How are the men?"

"My platoon is fine. I can check on the rest of the boys, if you like."

"Do it. Track down the sergeant major too. He can help. I

want to make sure everyone's getting some coffee and has sufficient rations. Any word on the hot food I requested?"

"Not a thing."

Curtis grunted. "Check our ammo too."

The lieutenant laughed. "Why, sir? Ain't nobody that's shot a thing since we got here."

"Just do it. If anything comes our way, I want everyone prepared."

"Roger that."

"And get on the radio to battalion; ask about the food. And the clothes. Tell them we're freezing our tails off up here."

"Yes, sir." Hanson climbed awkwardly out of the foxhole and shambled through the thick blanket of snow. The captain watched him until he vanished in the night.

Curtis pulled his jacket closer, searching for any scrap of warmth. He glanced at the single bars on his shoulders and smiled. Not even time to sew on the doubles. He wasn't supposed to be running a whole damned company. He shook his head. What lousy luck. His CO came down with dysentery the night before they shipped out, and Curtis found himself in charge of 140 men. He spat into the snow, his gaze racing along the tree line again. Always nothing. He yawned, and his eyes watered. The forest in the distance shifted in and out of focus.

Red streaks ripped past him. The woods exploded in light. He watched in disbelief before he recovered. He opened his mouth to scream a warning, but a wave of thunder engulfed him, dropping him to his knees. Curtis blinked and strained to focus his eyes among the flashes in the distance. He couldn't see a thing. Snow kicked up, washing over him. He fell to his stomach, closing his eyes, his hands covering his ears. He couldn't move, yet his whole body shook in terror. What the hell was happening out there?

A moment passed, and another. He clutched the snow as the staccato barking of machine-gun fire shattered the air above him. He felt hot humiliation. *I'm a coward, not fit for command. No!* he shouted to himself. *Get up! Take charge.* He willed his hands down on either side and pushed himself to his knees. He drew his pistol and raised his head above the lip of the foxhole until he could see.

The flashing flickers from the tree line continued. He scanned rapidly to his left and right. His men were returning fire up the line of foxholes. He breathed deeply in relief. They were holding their position. He thought about the boys in the outpost, set just inside the trees a hundred yards toward the attack. They were probably dead. The snow exploded in front of him again, and he ducked down. Something hard slammed into him. He whipped his pistol around but held back on the trigger just in time. Lieutenant Hanson had returned.

"What that hell is going on!" Curtis demanded.

"Germans. I don't know how many. A company at least. Maybe a battalion."

"Tanks?"

"Not so far."

"Are they advancing?"

Hanson shook his head. "They're firing from the trees. Could just be a patrol. What do we do, sir?"

Curtis didn't know. His mind whirled. He tried to reach back to all his training, but he drew a blank. His heart threatened to tear through his chest. He concentrated, striving to calm himself. Slowly the drilling crept back to him. He turned to the lieutenant. "Get back to the CP double quick! Call for reinforcements and any air support. And get our damned mortar crew working those trees!"

Hanson nodded. He turned and rose, scrambling out of the hole. Hot liquid washed over Curtis, and he couldn't see. He spit some of the salty metallic solution out. It wasn't water. What the hell had happened? He cleared his eyes and stared down in shock. Hanson lay against the foxhole; a gaping hole in his back spurted out frothy red bubbles. Curtis reached into his jacket and pulled out his field first-aid kit. He ripped open a packet and poured white powder all over the wound before pressing a bandage against it. The lieutenant writhed and groaned beneath his hands. Curtis drew out a morphine syringe and plunged the needle into Hanson's shoulder. The lieutenant shuddered and lay still.

Curtis wound his arms around his wounded friend, rocking back and forth. Tears ran down his face. Around him, explosions mixed with screams of terror and pain. Where were the mortars? When would the reserves arrive? A new sound punctuated the darkness. The ominous rumble of diesel engines. Terror sprinted up his spine. Cannons cracked, and explosions rocked the line. He raised his head, and he saw them: German tanks rumbling through the field, stopping to fire before streaming forward. In fascinated horror, he saw white figures like ghosts darting among and behind the tanks. It felt like a dream, a nightmare. There were thousands of them.

Curtis turned back to Hanson, holding his friend and closing his eyes. Soon, he heard sharp barking behind him. He rolled over. His foxhole was surrounded by Germans, towering over him in their winter white camouflage. They screamed in their clipped, barking language. He didn't understand. He drew his hands into the air. One of them raised his rifle and drove it down toward his face. He saw a sharp flash of light as the wooden stock crashed against his head, and all was darkness.

Chapter 1

First Lieutenant Sam Hall ran a bored finger down the map, tracing the farthest point of advance. He marked the spot with a heavy black pen and double-checked the information to make sure the coordinates were correct. Pointless, since by the time anyone bothered to read his report, the front would have advanced a half-dozen times. He set the papers down and rubbed his eyes, yawning and leaning back for a moment. He checked his watch. Twelve hours. Didn't the major ever sleep?

He scratched the dimple in his chin and looked up and down the narrow hallway outside Stiller's office. His desk filled most of the space, forcing the endless line of staff members to pass single file around him. His legs were crammed against the metal surface, almost to his chest. He had to be careful. He reached down and ran his hand over his ankle, lifting the hem of his trouser. He looked around. Nobody was coming. Hall pulled a flask out of his sock and drew it to his waist, sitting up straight with his hands concealed. He methodically unscrewed the cap, keeping a lookout down the hallway. He glanced quickly one more time behind him and lifted the metal rapidly to his lips; tipping the brandy down his throat, he pulled a deep gulp, letting the fiery liquid drizzle down inside him. He coughed and sputtered. He'd drunk too much too fast. He recovered and took another swallow. He smiled to himself. Nobody had seen a thing. He hastily screwed the cap back on and returned the flask to its hiding place.

Hall closed his eyes and let the liquid fill him. The brandy warmed his insides, a drawback, as it was already too damned stuffy in here. He shook his head in disgust. Such intolerable conditions. He made sure the hallway was still clear and opened a drawer, retrieving an envelope containing a letter from his father and a magazine. He pulled out the journal and smiled: it was a periodical about Washington State College, his alma mater and his father's too. He opened the page to an article about the school football program. There'd been no games in 1943 or 1944, but the college was hopeful that the war would end this year and the team could return to the gridiron the coming fall. He hummed the fight song of WSC as he read, the brandy tingling in his fingertips.

"Hall, what in the hell are you doing?" The Texas drawl of Major Alexander Stiller rumbled over him. He jolted upright and hastily covered the magazine with his report. His commander stood in the doorway like a chiseled granite statue. *Sneaky bastard.* Hall hadn't heard him open the door. Must be the brandy. Stiller reached out a stone finger and slid the report aside, exposing the reading material beneath.

"Just what in the Sam Hill is this, Hall?"

"Nothing, sir."

The major scowled. "It don't look like nothing. It looks like some personal trash covering up my operational map." He reached down and picked up the magazine, thumbing through the pages before flinging it to the floor. "You know better than that, Lieutenant. That dog just ain't gonna hunt. We got important work to do and no time for daydreaming over football."

"I know sir, but I was just—"

"I hope you were finishing my ready report." The major's eyes bored in on Hall, as if to burn through him. The weathered leather of his face creased into a frown resting beneath a short-cropped crown of salt and pepper hair. "Is that what you were doing, Lieutenant? Finishing my ready report?"

"That's exactly what I was completing. I just needed a little break before—"

"What the heck is that smell?" The major took a deep sniff, moving his head closer to the lieutenant's face. Hall stiffened. If he was caught drinking on the job . . .

He stood up quickly, turning away from Stiller and reaching down for the magazine. "Let me just put this away, sir." He stuffed the periodical into his desk drawer. "I was looking at the tactical situation, and I had a couple of ideas."

Stiller watched him closely, taking another deep breath. His eyes narrowed further. "Come in my office. I want a word, boy."

Hall reluctantly followed his commander into the hotel room that currently served as the major's headquarters. He took in the space rapidly with his eyes as Stiller bent to examine some papers: a folding table and chair, clothes rumpled on an unmade bed, the ever-present brass spittoon at the foot of the mattress. The major stomped around the table and tipped the chair back, crashing into the seat as he reached for some documents. He appeared to find what he was looking for, a brown leather pouch. He unzipped the wallet and drew out a plug of chewing tobacco. Stiller stuffed the wad into his mouth until a lump formed in his cheek. He swished the substance around for a few moments and leaned forward, hawking an auburn glob of liquid through the air to land violently against the side of the spittoon. The major smiled in satisfaction and turned his attention to Hall.

"How long have you been here now, boy?"

Hall cleared his throat. "About three months, I guess."

Stiller grunted. "Seems longer to me." He rested his hands on the desk, his eyes boring into the lieutenant again. "Well?"

"Well what, sir?"

"The report, damn it!" A scarlet storm crossed the major's brow.

Hall drew himself up and began. "Not too much new since the crossing on the twenty-fourth. The krauts didn't expect us in boats, and they weren't prepared. We suffered far fewer casualties than expected. Across the board, we're now rolling through Germany with little more than localized resistance. Same with the British up north as well. The Russians are hitting hard in the east. Only a matter of weeks, I'd say, before we link up with them, somewhere in the south, I'd wager."

"Your assessment of the Germans?"

"Not much life left in them, but when they organize, they can still hit hard. To be honest, I think they're about ready to call it quits, but after the Bulge, nobody knows for sure."

Stiller nodded. "That was a goat rodeo. Damn krauts don't know when they're beat. Should have given up months ago. Instead, they hit us hard with our pants down and damn near drove us back to Antwerp."

"That's why I recommend caution, sir. I think we've got them this time, but who knows what they'll pull out next."

"Anything you think we should be doing differently?"

Hall was surprised by the question. Stiller never asked his opinion. "I don't know. I could come up with some ideas if you want me to."

"I'll let you know." The major still stared at him, his face a stone scowl.

"Is there anything else, sir?"

"No, you're dismissed, Lieutenant."

Hall breathed in relief. He'd delivered his report without incident. He'd expected to be chewed out about the magazine. He saluted crisply and turned to go.

"Oh, Lieutenant."

He froze, still facing the door.

"I guess there is one more thing."

He turned slowly around. "Yes, sir?"

"You want to tell me about this?" The major held up an envelope, tapping it a few times against the desk.

Hall felt his heart racing in his chest. *Oh no.*

Stiller opened the package and pulled out a letter, making a great show of scanning the contents. A crease crossed his forehead and deepened as the crimson flush returned to his cheeks. "Imagine my surprise when Patton handed me this. My own aide writing directly to the general to ask for a transfer."

"I can explain, sir. I told you what I wanted—"

"And I told you that you'd damned well stay right where you are!"

"But, sir, the war is almost over, and I've got to get some combat time. If I don't—"

The major leaned forward, pointing a finger. "I don't give a damn about your combat experience, Lieutenant. I care about finishing this war. Now, you asked me direct about finding you a patrol or something, so you could get some exposure. Do you think you're the first little shirttail lieutenant that's asked? What did I tell you?"

"You told me that you'd find a chance sometime."

"That's right. I told you I'd take care of it," said Stiller, his voice rising an octave. He rang his spittoon again, the force almost knocking the container over.

"That was months ago. I've asked a few times, and you always give me the same answer. Now it's almost too late."

"So you went over my head to the general!" Stiller was screaming now. "Who the hell do you think you are?"

"I . . . I just thought he might help. He knows my father—"

"I'm aware of that, Hall! I know your father too. Trust me, you are *not* your father! He might have landed you this staff position, but that don't give you any special rights to go over my head!" The major stood, his eyes still looking up at the lieutenant. "Now you listen here, you little shit. You are gonna keep your mouth shut from now on, do you hear? You are gonna get your work done and do as you're told. You can forget a combat patrol after this bullshit. The closest you're going to get to the action is your damned desk! Do you hear me? Stand at attention, boy!"

Hall stiffened and stood rail straight, staring ahead.

"One last thing."

"Yes, sir."

"If I catch you drinking on duty ever again, you'll be out of the army so damned fast you won't know what hit you. And I don't give a shit who your daddy is. You got that, boy?"

Christ, he knows. Hall saluted again. He willed himself to stay calm.

"Now get out of my sight!"

Hall turned to go, but the door opened before he reached it. A corporal stepped through and saluted nervously.

"What is it?" snapped Stiller impatiently.

"Orders from headquarters, sir," said the corporal.

The major waved the man over and retrieved an envelope. He lifted a bayonet from the table and deftly sliced open the packet. He scanned the note, his face creasing into a frown. "I've been summoned to see the chief. Hall, you stay here and take any incoming messages."

"You're both supposed to come," said the corporal.

"What are you talking about?"

"Look at the envelope, sir; it's addressed to both you and the lieutenant."

Stiller pulled the paper up and read the front. "That's fine, Corporal; you're dismissed." The enlisted man saluted and rapidly retreated from the room. A slow smile creased over the corners of the major's mouth.

"Looks like Patton wants to address you direct, Hall. I wondered why he sent me your letter." Stiller shook his head and gave a whistle. "Oh boy, that's not too good, Hall. I figured he'd have me chew you out one-on-one, but if he's summoning you to an interview, he must want a little bite of you himself." The major chuckled. "Maybe you shouldn't get too used to your desk job after all. It might be the slow boat home for you. Get yourself cleaned up. That tie is a mess, and your shirt is wrinkled. You know how Patton feels about that stuff. I'll meet you in five minutes, and we'll head over together." Stiller rubbed his coarse hands together. "I don't want to miss this. Dismissed."

Hall saluted again and was finally allowed to depart. He fled the major's office in dismay. The brandy sat heavy in his stomach now, burning like acid. His mind reeled. He'd been so sure the letter would get him what he wanted. Patton was a friend of his dad's, after all. He wasn't asking for much. Just a few hours of combat and maybe a medal. He'd seen plenty of other staff officers get the same treatment in the few months he'd been there. What was the point of connections if you couldn't get a promotion and a citation out of it? He'd thought Stiller was keeping him down, but now it looked like the old man was gunning for him too. What the hell? Why'd he join in the first place? His dad said it would be easy. A commission, a position on Patton's staff, a promotion or two, and then a civilian future in Spokane when he came home a hero.

He scrambled to his room, throwing on a new tie and dusting off his clothes. Patton was a notorious stickler for uniforms. When he thought he was presentable, he made his way back toward Stiller's office, waiting for the jeep that would take him to his destiny.

* * *

Hall and Stiller maintained an icy silence during the short ride to Patton's headquarters in an adjoining villa. Two GIs snapped to attention as the officers scurried into the building. An aide sitting at a desk in front of the lieutenant general's office waved Stiller past but motioned for Hall to wait. The lieutenant looked around at the walnut-paneled walls of the entry room, filled with oil paintings depicting landscapes from the countryside. He thought about quizzing the aide for information about the meeting, but the sergeant was busy with a pile of papers and the telephone, which seemed to never stop ringing. Hall sighed and found himself a seat to wait for the impending chew-out.

He wondered if Stiller would tell Patton about the drinking? He didn't have any proof, just the major's word against his. Still, who would the general believe? Drinking on duty was a serious offense. If Patton chose, he could court-martial Hall. He would never do that to his friend's son, though, would he? His dad had served with Patton in World War I. They had stayed in contact even after his father left the army and started a law practice in Spokane. His dad knew Stiller too, although not as well. Surely these men would not take drastic action against him.

No, he'd be fine, he decided. A slap on the hand at the worst. It would be no different than at the college. He remembered with an internal chuckle the test questions he was caught with at Washington State. They'd threatened to kick him out then too. A lot of yelling and posturing until his father stepped in. He'd get out of this okay.

Still, what if they wouldn't let him into combat? He just wanted one mission. One glorious action yielding a Bronze Star or, better yet, a Silver One. Promotion to captain would surely follow, and he would go home a hero, well positioned to rise high in his father's firm, if he chose law school, or commercial real estate with his uncle. From there, Congress always beckoned. His father talked about it often enough, that was for sure.

He couldn't come home with nothing, though. That's what Stiller threatened now. Returning as a staff lieutenant with no combat experience at all? There would be scores of young men with medals and glory. Too many fish to swim with, even in little Spokane. He couldn't allow it. His father had made that clear, and Patton had promised. Safety and position, mixed with just enough controlled combat experience to win his laurels. They had to give him a chance. This was his future! He felt his blood rising. Who did they think they were?

The door opened, and Stiller stood in the entryway, beckoning to Hall with a stiff flick of his head. The lieutenant tried to read the expression on the major's face, but he showed nothing. *Damn him.* Hall rose and walked past the aide, still busily poring over his documents, and into Patton's office.

The lieutenant general was perched behind a massive mahogany desk at the far end of the room. Maps and charts filled the wall space behind him and most of the surface in front. He was dressed impeccably as always, his three silver stars gleaming brightly from a starched collar. His jaw worked furiously at some gum. Patton watched the lieutenant with hawkish eyes nesting beneath a gray crew cut. Hall's breath quickened, and his hands shook. He'd met the general twice before, but they'd spoken only a few words to each other. He stood at attention and saluted. The gesture was crisply returned.

"At ease, Lieutenant."

"Thank you, sir."

"Do you know why you are here today?"

Hall hesitated. He could guess, but he didn't want to admit it. "No, sir," he lied.

"Major Stiller has communicated to me about you for some time now. A little of this, a little of that. Laziness, bad attitude, a sense of privilege."

Hall glanced over at Stiller, who stared into space with a sat-isfied smirk cresting his lips. *The bastard*.

"Pay attention, boy," growled the general.

Hall went rigid again and returned his focus. "Sorry, sir."

"I told Stiller to have patience. After all, we all were young once, and most of what he described didn't seem too unusual for a young college graduate with a powerful father. I figured it would all work out in the end. Then I received your letter." Patton leaned forward, his countenance clouding. "I don't play games, Lieutenant. We don't break the chain of command in the Third Army. Worse than that, I'm not sure I've ever read a correspondence more filled with entitlement." Patton's eyes bored into him. "Just who the hell do you think you are? You figure just because your dad ran a tank under my command in the Meusse-Argonne that I owe you something?"

"No, sir, I—"

Patton jabbed a finger at him. "I didn't tell you to talk, boy. Now listen up. I told your father I'd get you some combat time. I informed Stiller of the same. But it's his damned deci-sion when and how. I don't have time to grease the wheels for every damned kid with a father that served with me somehow or somewhere. If you'd worked your ass off and followed the major, you'd already have what you wanted. Instead, you've sat back, half-assed, and demanded what you could have achieved if you'd just shut your mouth. Then when you don't get it fast enough, you have the balls to try an end run around, directly to me!" Patton was shouting now, and a speck of spittle frothed at the edge of his mouth.

"I'm sorry, sir, it's just that—"

"I told you to be quiet!" The general rose out of his chair, his arms crossed. "I thought I had enough to chew your ass out about. Now I find out you've been drinking on the job."

"I wasn't drinking, sir. That's a lie."

Patton's face flared an angry scarlet, and a speck of spittle frothed at the edge of his mouth. "So, Stiller's a liar, is it? Do you want to go home right now?"

Hall hesitated again, his cheeks hot and his eyes on the floor. "Okay, sir, it's true, I took a little nip. I'd been up twelve hours—"

"*I'd been up twelve hours,*" Patton repeated in a mocking tone. "The boys in the field are up for days at a time! And their buddies are blown up, shot, and stabbed! No shower, no food, no sleep! Death stalking them every minute! You don't know a damned thing about being tired! You're the biggest pile of shit I think I've ever seen. What do you think, Stiller?"

The major grunted in agreement.

"I'm sorry, sir," Hall began again. "I just wanted a chance to serve in combat. I wanted to do more—"

Patton's eyes narrowed. "I know what you wanted, Hall. You wanted a cushy half hour in pretend combat somewhere near the line so you could bring home a decoration to daddy. Well, I've got something different in mind for you."

"You can't mean . . ." interjected Stiller.

"I mean exactly that."

The major stuttered in protest. "I don't want that *boy* with me. That's the last thing I need."

Hall didn't know what they were talking about. He looked from Patton to Stiller.

"He's going," said the general. "If anything is going to make a man out of this pile of horse manure, this will."

"Sir, what are you talking about?"

"Shut your mouth before I change my mind."

"Yes, sir."

"I'm sending you with Stiller. You're going to be his bodyguard. I'm authorizing a task force to break through enemy lines and liberate a POW camp near Hammelburg. You're going with him."

Hall was shocked, Hammelburg was fifty or sixty miles behind the front. "But, sir, that city is—"

"I know damned well where it is, Hall. You want combat experience? You're going to get it. But you won't get a soft patrol in a safe zone. You're heading balls deep into the shit. If you come out of this thing alive, we'll talk about a medal. If you've done everything Stiller tells you, without question, without hesitation. Do you understand me?"

"Yes, sir."

Patton stepped right up to Hall, standing an inch away from his face. "But you listen here, you little maggot," he said, jabbing a finger into the lieutenant's chest. "If you step a toe out of line. If I hear one thing you failed to do. Then I will run you through the wringer for drinking on duty. You'll go home without a commission, dishonored, on the slowest ship I can find. You'll have a tough time finding a job sweeping the damned streets in Spokane. Do you hear me!"

"Yes, sir!"

"Now get the hell out of my office!"

Hall saluted and retreated from the room. His face was flushed, and he was hot with humiliation and anger. He'd never been talked to like that before. His whole life, nobody had dared. That shit Stiller was responsible for this. He'd get his revenge when the time was right. He smiled to himself. They'd be going where accidents sometimes happened. He'd be smart and play the game. He would do everything asked of him on this mission. No matter what, he would get his medal and his promotion. And if there was a chance for some payback as well, all the better.

The stupid aide still sat at his desk, fumbling through papers. Hall looked down at him. "Sergeant, on your feet!" The soldier looked up in surprise and confusion. He hesitated for a moment and then rose, coming to attention. "Salute your superior," said Hall, keeping his voice low enough so that it would not be heard in the office next door. The sergeant saluted crisply. Hall looked at him for a moment, then turned and arrogantly swept out of the office, already feeling a little better.

He decided to walk the short distance back to their headquarters. Stiller hadn't expressly ordered him to wait. He smiled to himself. Despite all this, he was getting his way. He had his mission. He would show those bastards and get what he wanted in the end.

Chapter 2

Captain Jim Curtis stared out at the frozen fields beyond the barbed-wire fences. There was freedom there, just out of reach. The towers looming above the fence line bristled with guards wielding automatic weapons, MP 38s, and a smattering of the new STG 44 assault rifles. Any attempt to cross that fence, day or night, was instant death for the prisoner. He knew this from firsthand experience. He'd seen men killed here.

He took a couple of feeble steps toward the wire. His legs shook, and he shivered in the cold. He glanced down at his skeletal frame. How much weight had he lost in the past few months? Thirty pounds? Maybe more. He couldn't weigh more than 150 now. There was never enough food. Even with the occasional Red Cross package, they were all starving. In the last month, the Germans had cut their meager rations in half. Rumor had it the guards were getting less food too. Further proof, if any was needed, that the war would soon be over.

He turned and headed away from the fences, nodding here and there to other forlorn scarecrows standing silent vigil in the camp. As he stumbled on, a figure caught his attention, approaching with an arm waving to attract his attention. Curtis looked over. It was Goode's aide.

"What is it?" the captain asked, wiping a hand through his greasy brown hair.

"The boss wants you."

"Do you know why?"

"Search me," said the messenger, his broomstick of an arm almost folding over itself as he pulled it down.

Curtis breathed in deeply. He didn't feel like going just now. It meant a long walk, and he was already exhausted. Why had he volunteered in the first place? Well, at least it was something to do. He nodded by way of acknowledgment, and the man shuffled off to pass the message to others.

Curtis turned and headed toward the POW headquarters, his breath coming in rapid spurts from the effort as he passed row after row of Allied barracks looming over him to his right. The buildings were rectangular and brick. The sturdy structures had served as a German training camp before the war. After a few minutes, he entered the headquarters building, a larger structure set off by a courtyard from the rest of the housing. The front of the building consisted of a forty-by-forty room with a couple of card tables and a scattering of folding chairs. The room was inadequately heated by a single woodstove shoved into the corner with a crude pipe jutting upward through the roof. There were already quite a few officers milling around when he arrived, some of the representatives of the various barracks, he realized. The prisoners called themselves "kriegies," after the German word for war.

In the middle of the room, facing each other and talking quietly, Curtis recognized the commander of the POWs, Colonel

Paul Goode, and his executive officer, Lieutenant Colonel John Waters.

Curtis had come to know the executive officer since he and Goode had arrived in the prison camp in early March 1945, when their POW camp at Szubin, Poland, was evacuated. Goode and Waters were the real deal, not volunteer flunkies like Curtis and the rest of the 106th. They were Regular Army types who'd served in North Africa in the thick of the fighting back in '42 and '43. As Curtis watched him, Waters glanced in his direction with his hawkish blue eyes and gave him a friendly nod, beckoning with a tick of his head for the captain to join them.

Curtis hustled over, waiting a moment for the commanders to finish their conversation. Waters turned and greeted him. "What's up, Jim?"

"That's what I was gonna ask you," said the captain. He shook hands with the two officers. "Anything new?"

Waters shook his head. "Not too much. We got a sniff of news, but nothing earth-shattering. For now, we're still shining nickels."

Curtis felt disappointment creep over him. He'd hoped there might be something exciting. But it looked like Goode had summoned them to the regular daily briefing.

The POW commander lifted his fingers to his lips and gave a short whistle. The dull muffle of conversation faded, and the officers turned their attention to the colonel.

"What do you have for us today?" called out one of the majors from the 21st Division, another of the green formations hit hard on the first day of the Bulge. "Are we rescued?" The comment brought a chuckle from the crowd. There was much talk of freedom, and yet the sun set each day with all of them still living behind the barbed wire and the towers of the Oflag.

"Now, now," said Goode, raising a hand to silence them. "None of that. I've got news, but not quite *that* news. Not yet anyway."

"What is it then?" asked the major.

"Something pretty darn close. You all know Lieutenant Stevens, right?" There were some grunts and murmurs from the assembled men. "He's developed a little bit of a relationship with Sergeant Himmel. Seems the sergeant is a smoker, and he's tired of that ersatz garbage they issue the guards. He wanted himself some good old Virginia tobacco." Again, some laughter and a few cheers.

"The lieutenant came to me about things, and I cobbled together a carton out of some of our Red Cross reserves. Our boy gave them to the sergeant yesterday in exchange for a war update. Now I don't know how accurate this is, but ole Himmel said that Patton isn't but sixty miles hard drive from this very spot. Not only that, the sergeant said there isn't but a batch of old men and little boys from the *Volkssturm* and maybe a chewed-up regiment or two between them and us. He thought they could be here in two days, maybe three."

Curtis cheered with everyone else. Waters had slow-played his hand to him. Liberation in a few days? Could it be true? He didn't want to get his hopes up. He'd been disappointed so many times.

"How do we know this isn't more of the baloney they are always feeding us?" This question came from a captain, one of the North African vets.

Goode shook his head. "No way to know for sure. Still, why tell us that? Most of what we've heard direct from the Germans has been lies about them winning the war, not the other way around. I think we can consider this reliable."

"Could we verify it with any of the other guards? What about Knorr?" asked the Captain. He was referring to Sergeant Knorr, "the Ferret," a German who had spent a few years in the United States before the war.

"I wouldn't ask that bastard for anything," said Goode. "He's the worst of the lot."

"Even if it's true, it won't do us any good if they ship us out of here before our boys arrive," said Curtis, voicing a common fear.

"Yep, that could happen," said Goode, nodding in response. "So far, though, I haven't heard a thing from the *Kommandant* about moving us. Last time around, in Poland, we had a bunch of advance notice, so we could get ready. A couple weeks. I may just be whistling, but I figure they've got bigger fish to fry now. Besides, where would they move us? The Russians are out there somewhere to the east, closing in. They can't be far behind us either. No, my gut tells me they won't touch us this time. Course, I've been wrong before."

"What do you want us to pass on to the men?" asked Waters.

Goode lowered his voice, drawing them in for his instructions. "We've got to be careful. This liberation deal could be tricky. The guards are going to get plenty antsy. I hope they'll just run off, but they might do the opposite. Could lead one or two to have a quick finger on the trigger. I want everyone on their best behavior, away from the fences, no lip, even joking. And keep an eye out for the Ferret. He'll be up to his old tricks when the shooting starts.

"Besides that, we need to be ready for the fight itself. Now, there's no sense getting directly involved. We don't have weapons, and we'd be as likely to be shot up by the Americans as we would by the Germans. I want everyone prepared to hunker down in their barracks until the bullets die down. Have a plan for stacking bunks. Try to give the boys a little extra protection wherever we can fish it up."

"What about food?" asked Curtis.

"When we know they're close, I want someone from every bunk to come get some. We could be sitting in those barracks for a day or more while the fighting goes on. We need food and water in every building, along with whatever medical supplies we can spare.

"When you go back and tell the boys, have them keep their mouths shut. No celebrating! No talking in the yard. Last thing we need is for the Germans to find out we are on to them. Any other questions?"

There were none, and the men started to disperse.

Waters stopped Curtis as he passed by. "How you holding up, son?"

"I'm doing okay." Curtis tried to inject a little spirit into his response, but his emotions warred inside him.

"I know you better than that, Captain. What's wrong?"

"This whole damned thing is wrong."

"Aren't you happy about the news?"

"I am. I'm grateful. But at the same time—"

"At the same time, you don't feel like you ever fought? Is that it?" Waters watched him with shrewd eyes.

How did he know? He nodded, not responding.

"Is that all?" said Waters, chuckling. "Hell, Captain, we hardly did any better in North Africa. I zipped out with a few tanks, and the next thing I knew we were up to our armpits in panzers. Before you could snap your fingers, we were all blown up and surrendered. Damn Germans swatted us away like a bunch of annoying flies."

"Yes, sir, but it's not the same. You did fight for a while. Besides, that's when the Germans were still really in the war. Back in forty-two. By the time we arrived, the whole thing was supposed to be over. Instead, we were clobbered and wound up here . . . or dead."

Waters put a granite hand on Curtis's shoulder. The lieutenant colonel was as emaciated as the rest of the kriegies, but he retained an iron strength.

"Now, don't you worry yourself about that. Nobody is going to say a damned thing to you when you get home about this war. If they do, to hell with them. You fought the Germans, and you did your best. You served your time in this camp. The war is over for us. What we need to worry about at this point is surviving, and getting home to our families. You go back to the barracks and put your best face on things. We'll get through this and get you home."

Curtis nodded again and shook Waters's hand. He left the building and started back to his barracks. He did his best to lift his spirits, but he couldn't shake the feeling that had haunted him over and over these past months. He'd failed to protect his men, and he'd never fought the Germans, never had a chance to prove his mettle in combat. Now he'd run out of time.

Curtis briefed the barracks, answering questions and assigning tasks to the men. He passed on the warnings too, although he was worried the Germans would know everything they planned. There were stoolies somewhere in the camp, and the Ferret was never far away. The men had flushed out a couple of these spies and taken care of it quietly—just another dead body found in a bunk. However, there still must be more out there. The Germans always seemed a step ahead of them.

After he was finished, the captain left the barracks and headed to the hospital building, another larger rectangular structure, a football field past Goode's headquarters, toward the German portion of the lager. Before he entered, he pulled a wrinkled cardboard box out of his pocket and drew out his last cigarette. He looked down at the paper cylinder wistfully. Should he have it now? Once this one was gone, how long before he could find another? *Screw it, I need this.* He fired the stick up and took a deep drag, closing his eyes and steeling himself for what would come next.

Stepping into the hospital ward, he found Lieutenant Hanson in a cot halfway down the row of beds. His friend was covered by a sheet and a coarse brown woolen blanket. Curtis stifled a shiver. The temperature in the room was barely above freezing. Men moaned and coughed, surrounded by the drab stone walls of the hospital. A couple of male orderlies and a doctor filtered among the beds, checking wooden charts as they went.

The lieutenant was propped up by a couple of pillows, reading a wrinkled letter. His dark hair swam across his eyes, a bushy roof protecting his gaunt features from the bare bulbs above. Hanson looked up and smiled grimly, a pale ghost.

"How are you, Tim?" he asked, forcing his own artificial grin.

"I'm alive."

"What are you reading?"

The lieutenant looked down. "The same thing I've looked at every day since the Bulge. My last letter from home."

"You haven't had anything since we were captured?"

"Have you?"

"Nope, not a one." Curtis chuckled. "But don't complain too much. At least you have something. The damn krauts took everything off me when I was captured. Letters, pictures, rations. Worst of all, my smokes. I had a carton of Lucky Strikes, and they didn't leave me a pack. Waters gave me a few he salvaged out of a Red Cross parcel, but overall I've had a bare handful the whole damn time I've been here. Just finished my last one before I came to see you. I'd give my soul for a letter from home—and some tobacco. Frankly," he said, chuckling, "I'm not sure which one I'd take over the other."

Hanson nodded but didn't respond. His eyes were glazed over, and he was staring up at the ceiling, not really listening.

Curtis knelt down and leaned near his friend's ear, keeping an eye on the German guard at the end of the hallway who was looking his way. "Hey, buddy, I got some news," he whispered. Hanson still didn't respond.

"Freedom," whispered Curtis. "Rumor has it we might be out of this place in the next few days."

"Freedom," said Hanson, repeating the word mechanically. His lips pressed upward a fraction, but then a darkness seemed to envelop him. "Don't see how that's going to do me much good at this point."

"Nonsense, Tim. Think about it for a minute. Hot food and showers. New uniforms to replace these lice-ridden rags. Hell, no lice. Medals, promotions, and a boat ride home to our families. No more war, no more camp, no more army. Just life in our hometowns with our families again."

His friend smiled a little. "At least it's nice to think about those things. I'm happy for you."

"It's not just for me," he said, his heart wrenching a little. "It's for you too. It's for all of us."

Hanson didn't answer.

Curtis put a hand on his friend's chest. "Think about getting home for a second. What will you do first? When I walk through the door, I'm gonna kiss my wife like she's never been kissed before. Then we can sit down to a homemade dinner of fried chicken, mashed potatoes and gravy, biscuits and warm apple pie. To the end of my days, I swear I'll never be hungry for a minute again."

"Tell me about your wife's pie again." Hanson closed his eyes, listening.

He was getting through to him, at least a little. He spent the next half hour describing in minute detail each moment his wife spent preparing her pie. The flaky crust, hand-kneaded and brushed with generous strokes of liquified butter, browned to perfection. The fresh apples, sugar, and cinnamon composing the filling. The homemade ice cream scooped on top of the piping-hot pie. He never could wait for it to cool. He could taste every bite as he told the story to his friend.

"Thank you," said Hanson. "I needed that. That's something I'm still good for. I can still eat pie."

"There's a hell of a lot more to home than just food. Baseball and football will be starting up again—what with the war over. Who do you follow on the diamonds? My family is split right down the middle between the White Sox and the Reds."

"What about the Cubs?"

"Hell no." He was about to ask Tim about his own team, but he was interrupted. An orderly had stepped up behind him. "Could you help me, sir?"

"Sure," said Curtis.

The orderly moved around the cot until he was directly across from the captain. "Put your arm back here," he directed, placing his own hand behind Hanson's back. Curtis nodded, mirroring the orderly's movements. When they both had a firm grip, he pulled up, dragging Hanson upright. "Now hold him," said the orderly, who reached down and pulled the blanket and sheet back; he drew up a sponge and cleaned the lieutenant's legs. Curtis was shocked at how withered they'd become. So soon.

Hanson laughed, staring down at his feet. "It's funny. I'm so surprised to see my legs there. Every damn time. There they are—ankles, knees, thighs—but at the same time, they're gone forever. What I wouldn't give to wiggle a toe one more time. Anything. Just a flicker."

"At least you've got 'em," said Curtis, not sure he was on safe ground. "A lot of boys are missing them entirely."

"I'd trade both legs if I could still use my . . ." He looked down at his waist.

Curtis patted him on the shoulder, not knowing what else to say. He helped the orderly move Hanson back down until he was resting again above the pillows. "Don't think on that right now, my friend. Think about what I told you."

A few minutes later, Curtis stepped out of the hospital, his breath coming in harsh gasps. He bent over, trying to force the bile back down his throat. He gagged and spat, waiting for the nausea to pass. It never got any easier. In the Ardennes, 140 men had depended on him to protect and guide them. Instead, they'd died or were captured before they'd even had a chance to fight. How many of his men were crippled like Hanson? How many more would never see home? He would never know. His capture had denied him even that.

"Curtis, you okay?" He heard the booming voice of Waters. He reached up and wiped the tears from his face, forcing himself to calm down and face his XO.

"Yes, sir. I'm fine."

Waters scrutinized him for a moment. He opened his steely eyes as if he would say something, his stern countenance softening. He motioned for the captain to step away from the door and join him.

"What is it?" asked Curtis.

"Bad news."

Curtis felt a lurch of anxiety. "The rumor was false?"

"Nope. I'd say it's true. That's the problem."

"That can't be negative, can it?"

"They're moving us," said Waters.

"Where?" Curtis felt his stomach churn.

"Who knows. East somewhere. The *Kommandant* told Goode to expect trains tonight. We're supposed to line up with all our things by nineteen hundred hours."

"What do you want me to do?"

"Let the boys in the barracks know."

"What else? You want me to get things rolling for the evacuation?"

Waters sniffed, considering the suggestion and shook his head. "Sit tight on that. I don't want us jumping the gun. Once Goode knows it's a done deal, we'll start moving things into action. But be prepared. Everyone should make a sack to carry a little food and clothing. Any contraband has to be well hidden or destroyed."

"How will we deal with the food?"

"Same as liberation. When we know it's gonna happen, we'll distribute what we have equally to each barracks, and then split it out among the men. The stronger boys should carry more, but they can't keep it for themselves. Everything has to be divided up fair."

"Yes, sir." A thought occurred to him. "How do we handle the hospital?" he asked.

A strange expression flickered across Waters's face. "Don't worry about that, Captain. Focus on your group."

"Tell me."

Waters hesitated again. "We don't deal with them."

"What?"

"In Poland, we had to leave them behind. Don't worry, they should be okay. Patton will be here in a few days."

"Should be?"

"It doesn't matter." Waters looked away.

"Say it."

"At the old camp, we had some rumors. That's all."

"What kind of rumors."

"We heard stories that the Germans at some camps liquidated the wounded."

"You can't be serious?"

Waters turned back to him. "Would that really surprise you, Captain. Don't be naïve. You've heard the stories of the Eastern Front. Mass killings. Atrocities everywhere. The krauts don't play by the rules. This is a different kind of war."

"It can't be true." Curtis said it out of revulsion, rather than conviction.

"Doesn't matter. True or not, our hands are tied. We can't take them with us if the Germans won't let us."

"Hanson's in there."

"Who?" asked the XO.

"Lieutenant Hanson. One of my boys. Platoon commander in my company."

Waters shook his head. "I'm sorry. I hope the stories are lies. But what can we do? It's in God's hands."

Small comfort, thought Curtis. God had abandoned him long ago.

Chapter 3

Near Headquarters, Combat Command B,
4th Division, US Army
Southwest Germany
March 26, 1945, 1600 hours

An icy silence blanketed the jeep ride to 4th Division. Stiller and Hall sat side by side like stone statues, bouncing along the potholed back roads without exchanging a word. They passed miles of forested hills, dotted occasionally by picturesque villages cluttered with gingerbread houses. Hall noted that these little towns, straight out of a fairy tale, were marred here and there by the carnage of war. Windows blown out by bombs and artillery. The whole side of a house missing, the interior floors starkly exposed to the world. After six long years of aggression, war had come home to Germany.

He was glad Stiller was silent. He'd expected a chew-out the whole way. Not that he deserved it. It was the other way around. The major was the one with the problem. Hall rubbed his chin, feeling the coarse hairs and the trademark dimple of his chin. He'd hated it as a boy, but the girls felt otherwise, so he didn't mind so much now. He smiled to himself, thinking about all those ladies at college. They were so beautiful and innocent. All wanting a husband. He loved the time with them, the compliments and the insults. Always keeping them a little off guard. Filling their empty heads with his promises. They all wanted to be Mrs. Hall. They ended up like these little villages. Still beautiful but with a few scars.

He ached for a drink. Why did that prick have to catch him? When he returned from Patton's office, he'd hastily tossed his flask in a corner and covered it with a coat. Now he had nothing to sip on. All these months, and nobody'd seen a thing. He'd done his job just fine. The drink helped keep him going. Now the bastard had caught him, and he was out in the field with nothing. Still, these GIs were famous for boozing, weren't they? He'd read the reports. He should be able to scrounge something up. He just had to get away from the Lone Ranger sitting next to him. That shouldn't be a problem once they got out on the road with the combat group.

They rounded a corner, and a checkpoint materialized: three GIs with rifles ready and a fourth mounting a thirty-caliber machine gun trained on their vehicle. A sergeant raised his hand and ordered them to stop.

"Who are you?" he asked, when the jeep was close enough.

"Major Stiller with a message for HQ," explained the driver. He handed some paperwork to the sergeant, who read it and turned to scrutinize Stiller and Hall. Satisfied, he saluted and waved them past. The jeep jolted into motion, and they jingled along the last few hundred yards to the HQ command tent.

Hall followed the major out of the jeep and into the structure. The interior was full of a smoky fog emanating from the cigarettes held in a dozen hands. The men surrounded a card table covered in maps and paperwork. As they entered the tent, the light from outside sprang across the table, and the officers collectively looked up, straining their eyes to see who had entered.

"Alex, is that you?" a deep voice grumbled.

"Sure enough," said Stiller. "How you doing, Creighton?"

Hall realized Stiller must be talking to Lieutenant Colonel Creighton Abrams, commander of Combat Command B of the 4th Division, US Third Army. He stood like a khaki sequoia, bulging boulders for arms resting below a child's face, as if God had assembled spare parts to play a joke on the man.

"What the heck you doing here, Major?" asked the colonel, his eyes flickering in mirth. "You finally grow tired of all the pencil pushing and come down here for a toss-up?"

Stiller chuckled. "Something like that, Creight. I've got a job from George. Can I have a private word with you?"

Abrams's eyes narrowed, and his face grew thoughtful. "Sure thing, Alex." He turned to the group surrounding him. "Give us a few minutes, boys. Why don't you get a little coffee? And bring me some too, and a bit of grub if you can scrounge it."

The men filed out, and after a few moments, only Stiller, Abrams, and Hall remained. The colonel glanced over and pointed at Hall. "What about that one?"

Stiller pulled out his pouch of tobacco, drawing a wad of oily leaf and shoving it in his mouth, his eyes boring into Hall. "Guess he better stay," he said finally.

"What's this all about, Alex?"

"Orders direct from Patton."

"What kind? Since when are you his errand boy? Why didn't this just come down the usual way?"

"It's a special deal."

Abrams dropped some paperwork he'd been half-perusing and turned to Stiller. "Now you do have my attention. Tell me about it."

"He wants you to punch through the German lines and liberate a POW camp around Hammelburg."

"Hammelburg?" asked Creighton, staring down at the map for a moment. "Jesus, Alex, that's fifty miles back. That's a mighty big leap. What the hell for?"

Stiller's eyes shifted, and he paused before answering. "He

didn't give me all the reasons. What I do know is, there's an officers' POW camp somewhere around there. He said he's worried about the Germans carting those boys off again—or, worse yet, killing them."

Abrams's eyes narrowed. "Now that don't make no sense. How many camps are there out there, up and down the line? Fifty? A hundred? What makes this camp special? We can't stop the war to deal with all of them. That's been the gospel from George since we landed in France."

"I told you, I don't know every reason. Maybe he's sore at MacArthur. He don't like anyone else getting the limelight."

Hall knew what Stiller was talking about. General MacArthur had famously liberated two POW camps from the Japanese this past January. The exploit had made all the headlines and created quite a stir. That was just the sort of thing to get the fame-seeking Patton's ire up.

"Well, it don't make any sense to me," said Abrams. "We'll be there in a few days if we follow current plans. Can I tell him no?"

Stiller shook his head. "No chance. I've already gone through it with him. He's dead set on this."

Abrams chewed his lip. "Well, orders are orders. When do we get started? I'll need at least a day to plan. Pretty big change in orders."

Stiller shook his head and spat a trail of brown liquid on the ground. "Not you, Creight. Patton wants a reinforced company. That's it."

Hall was shocked. This was the first he'd heard of that. Combat Command B numbered in the thousands, many times larger than a company. He'd assumed they'd all be going. A reinforced company would be a few hundred men at most.

Abrams clearly shared Hall's surprise. He scratched his cheek, his eyes on the map. "You've got to be kidding me, Alex. We send in a tiny force like that and all they'll bring back is a batch of bodies. If they even get back. Hell, there might be ten thousand Germans between us and Hammelburg. I've got to talk to George. No way he's thought this through."

"I argued about that with him too, Creight. I told him we should take the whole command. He's insistent it's just a few hundred men."

"Well, I won't do it. He's just not thinking straight. I'll get him on the phone, and we'll get this flushed out." Abrams shouted, and a head poked into the tent. "Get me General Patton on the phone."

"When, sir?"

"Right now, damn it!"

The head disappeared as quickly as it had materialized, returning a few moments later with a field telephone. He carried the enormous green box over and set it down gingerly on the table. A moment later, the phone started to ring. Abrams lifted the receiver. "George, is that you? Hey, I got Stiller here, and he's giving me the story on your request. Now, George, I'm not sure I understand why you want to do this, but that's not my job. It is my role, however, to make sure we get the thing done. I can't do it with a company. I want to take the whole command." Abrams stopped, listening to the response on the other end.

"But, George, we can't get guaranteed success with that few men . . . no, I know it's not a general breakthrough but . . ." He listened for a few more minutes. "If I do this, it's under protest, George . . . yes, sir." He hung up the phone. His face flushed an angry scarlet.

"A reinforced company it is. George doesn't want too much attention on this. He thinks a small group can get in and get out before the Germans even know they're there." Abrams shook his head, pursing his lips, his forehead furrowed. He exhaled deeply. "Perhaps he's right. If you'll excuse me for a few minutes, boys, I'm going to get the ball rolling on this. I'll be back in a half hour, and we can talk logistics."

As the colonel left, Hall stood in shock. This was not at all what he had in mind. It was one thing to ride along in the middle of a massive armored column, with a thousand or more men all around him. It was another to dash behind lines with a few hundred, not able to put up any real resistance, and with no guarantee they would ever make it back. This wasn't what he'd signed up for at all. He felt the panic rising. He had to get out of this.

"Sir," he said, addressing the major for the first time since Patton's office.

"What is it, Lieutenant." Stiller was facing away from him, chewing away at his tobacco, arms folded. His voice was terse.

"Do you want me to take any messages back to HQ when I leave?"

Stiller turned slowly, his eyes burning a hole in Hall. His leathery cheeks creased and crackled as he sucked on the plug. "What was that you said, Hall?"

"I was asking if you wanted me to take anything back to Patton?"

The major's lip curled in a knowing grin. "I thought you were balls in to see combat, boy?"

"You told me you weren't going to take me with you. I figured you were just waiting to get away from Patton before you sent me away. I want to follow orders, sir. You . . . you were right all along."

Stiller's cracked lips pressed in a tight grin. "Oh no, little Hall. You're not going anywhere. You want medals and promotions. This little trip will have plenty of both . . . assuming anyone makes it back alive. I wouldn't deprive you of the chance to be a hero."

"But, sir—"

"There's no argument, Hall. You're going into the shit, and I'm going with you. Three hundred men against ten thousand?" He spit on the floor. "Our own personal Thermopylae. We oughta be just fine." He took a step forward; his forehead furrowed, and he raised a finger. "Now, you listen to me, you little shit. This is the real deal. I'll be watching you every step of the way. You'll do your duty, and you'll do it up right, or I'll run your ass out of this war, and you'll go home to daddy with your tail between your legs. You got me?"

Hall nodded, too stunned to answer.

Stiller spit again, eyeballing the lieutenant as if deciding something. "I'll tell you what, though, I'll give you a little carrot to go with the stick. You do this right, and I'll forget the past. Show me you got some guts, boy, and I'll see to it you're taken care of. You got me?"

"Yes, sir." Hall turned away, unable to face the major for a second more. What was he going to do? He might well die out there on this suicide mission. He stood there, staring at the tent walls, while men scrambled in and out, preparing for a suicidal storm.

Over the course of the next hour, there was a hornet's nest of activity. Hall watched the frantic movements unfold around him as he recovered from his disbelief. A stampede of officers and men came and went, reporting to Abrams as he scrambled to assemble the scratch task force. Stiller stood with him, chewing and chatting, poring over maps of the area between the Combat Command and Hammelburg.

Hall ached for a drink. Anything to take his mind off this ridiculous mission. He wondered if he could excuse himself long enough to track down something before Stiller checked up on him again. After some consideration, he decided he couldn't risk it. The major kept flicking his eyes up and glaring in Hall's direction, daring him to try something stupid. No, now was not the time.

As the planning continued, Hall noticed a figure marching in lanky strides across the tent. His crew cut was jet black with flecks of gray dotted through it. The man moved to within a few feet of Abrams and stood silently, apparently waiting for the colonel to notice him. Abrams looked up and smiled. "Captain, you're here." He clapped his hands together and turned toward Stiller. "Alex, I don't think you know Captain Baum. Baum, this is Major Stiller." The two men saluted briefly and shook hands.

"Abe's a hell of a go-getter," said Abrams. "Just the man you want to lead this thing."

Baum's eyes narrowed. "Just what do you have in mind for me, Creight?"

Abrams shook his head. "Not me. Orders from up top."

"From Hoge?" Hall knew Baum was referring to Brigadier General William Hoge, commander of the 4th Division.

"A little higher than that even. These came straight down from Patton."

Baum whistled. "What does he want with me?"

"Hang on to your seat, Abe. The chief wants a task force to break through the lines and liberate a POW camp."

The captain whistled again. "What for? Where is it?"

"Right here." Stiller jabbed the map with a leathered finger.

Baum stepped closer and examined the map. His eyes widened. "Fifty miles? You're kidding me, right?"

Abrams shook his head. "That's the deal."

The captain paused for a second, as if considering the order. "How many you gonna send in with me?"

"Not sure yet, but pretty small. Figure two, three hundred."

"Can't be done," said the captain, shaking his head firmly.

"How many would you need?" asked Stiller. "Minimum."

Baum put his hand to his chin, stroking it for a moment. "Absolute bottom line? Figure a reinforced battalion. Seven hundred men with fifty tanks and a shitload of support. A thousand would be better yet."

Abrams grunted "I can't get you that, Abe. I wanted to send the whole combat command, but Patton already shot me down."

"Maybe you should try it again with Baum's numbers," suggested Stiller. "Give the old man some options."

Abrams nodded in agreement. "Can't hurt. Already had my ass chewed once today. Why not try for twice?" He ordered a staff member to connect him with Patton. The men stood silently for a few minutes until the general was patched through. Hall watched, holding his breath, hoping their commander would authorize a substantial increase in the force he was accompanying. However, this call was a repeat of the first one. Abrams could hardly get a word in, and after a short conversation, he hung up.

"No dice," Abrams said. "A reinforced company is all he'll authorize." He turned to Baum. "I'm sorry, Abe. Want me to find someone else to do it?"

The captain scratched his chin for a moment and shook his head. "No, sir. I've never disobeyed an order, and I won't start now. I don't think it can be done with three hundred, but I'll give it a run. Can you get me at least that many? I need a batch of tanks too, and some self-propelled guns."

"I'll get you everything I can."

"You know how many prisoners are in that camp?"

"Maybe two or three hundred," said Stiller.

"Better rustle up some half-tracks too then. At least a dozen."

"Can't they ride on the tanks?" asked Stiller.

"Some can, but not three hundred, no matter how many Shermans we have with us. Plus, we'll be fighting, maybe all the way back. The back of a tank is a nasty place for infantry to ride out an armored fight."

"Don't worry, Abe. I'll get you everything I can." Abrams looked at his watch. "It's almost seventeen hundred. Let's meet back here at nineteen hundred, and we will roll out. Is that enough time for you?"

Baum nodded. "It will have to be." The captain turned and started to stride out of the tent.

"Oh, Captain, one more thing," said Abrams.

"What's that?"

Abrams jabbed a thumb toward Stiller. "The major here is going along with you. He and Hall over there."

Baum looked Stiller up and down. "He outranks me. If you want a different leader for this, it's more than fine with me."

"Not on this deal. You'll still be in charge. He's just along for the ride."

"With all respect, sir, I don't like it," said Baum. "In my experience, when a fellow rides along who outranks the commander, it mucks up the works. It's confusing to the men. We have enough problems on this trip as it is."

"Don't worry captain," said Stiller. "I know my place. I won't interfere with your job. Patton wants me along."

"Why is that?" asked Baum, raising a suspicious eyebrow.

Stiller hesitated. "He didn't authorize me to say. This is a pet project for him. Real important. He told me he'd recommend the commander for the Medal of Honor if he pulls it off. You'll be a hero if you can swing it."

Baum grunted dismissively. "I'm not interested in medals, Major. Just in my duty. I don't like the smell of this one bit," he said to Abrams. "Still, it's not my job to like everything I'm ordered to do. I'll see you back here at nineteen hundred." The captain strolled out of the tent.

"Alex, I don't like this any more than Baum does," said Abrams. "Why is Patton dead set on this raid? Why the hell go after some POW camp with such a small force? Something doesn't add up."

"Like I said, Creight, he's got his reasons. He doesn't explain everything, even to me."

Abrams shook his head. "Well, Baum is top-notch, the best we have. If he can't get it done, nobody can."

"Thanks for that. Is the mess open where we can grab some chow before we take off?"

Abrams nodded.

Stiller looked over at Hall. "My lieutenant will need to play escort. Can you find a Thompson for him, and a little ammo? Maybe a couple grenades also."

"Sure thing, Alex. Anything else?"

"Maybe a clip or two for my forty-five?"

"I'll get it all together. Go get some grub, and we'll see you back in a few."

Alex beckoned for Hall to follow him. They left the command tent and made their way to the mess, walking through the chow line and piling up a couple servings of creamed chipped beef on toast and some canned vegetables.

They found a table and sat across from each other in silence. Hall ran his fork back and forth across the pasty substance, unable to take a bite. His stomach was a churning cauldron as fear lashed through him.

"Eat it up, Hall," said Stiller. "That's the last hot food you're likely to see for a long time coming."

"I'm not hungry,"

"I didn't ask if you were hungry. You're going to need your strength. Now shovel that stuff in, Lieutenant. All of it. That's an order."

Hall dug into the substance, forcing a slimy bite down his throat. He hated the stuff and nearly choked, but he wasn't going to give the major the satisfaction. As he mechanically worked through the plate, his mind raced, trying to figure some way out of this disaster. He couldn't come up with a damned thing. He thought about feigning illness. Certainly, the food was enough to make him throw up. Would Stiller order him to remain behind if he had the stomach flu? No way, he realized. The major was on to him and watching him like a hawk. The reality was he was stuck. He was heading into combat in an ill-defined, under-armed raid that nobody seemed to believe would succeed. What in the hell was happening?

They eventually finished the meal and lingered over their coffee, letting the minutes drag by. The two-hour wait was interminable. Finally, Stiller motioned for them to rise, and they cleared their trays, heading back toward the command tent. Hall was surprised to see how much things had changed outside in the past couple of hours. A dozen or more tanks were disbursed in the open ground in front of HQ, along with a few 105mm self-propelled guns and a batch of half-tracks. There were also a few jeeps. Men milled around in every direction, loading ammunition and rations. Mechanics climbed over and under the tanks, working away on mechanical issues. Hall did a quick count of the assembled men and came up with around three hundred.

Captain Baum approached Stiller with a few men in tow. "Major, I want to introduce my commanders." He motioned to a lieutenant standing directly behind him. "This is William Nutto. I've worked with him a few times before. He's in charge of the Shermans."

Stiller saluted. "Nice to meet you. How many do we have?"

"Ten, sir," answered Nutto, wiping his dirty chin with the back of a gloved hand. He was approximately the same height as the major but outweighed him by at least twenty pounds.

"I was hoping for more," said Stiller.

"We've been banged up pretty good the past few days, sir. Frankly, we need a rest badly. We were just settling down for a break and a refitting when we received orders for this little expedition."

"Sorry we're interrupting your breather," said the major.

Nutto laughed. "Hell, isn't the first time by a far stretch."

Baum turned to another of his men, a handsome young, blue-eyed soldier who looked even younger than Hall. "This is Lieutenant Weaver. He's in charge of the light tanks. We've got five of them. Watch out for this kid; his dad's a West Pointer, so he's Regular Army through and through." Weaver nodded, a sheepish grin on his face.

"Last but not least, we've got three one-oh-fives that Tech Sergeant Chuck Graham will run for us. This here is Major Stiller and his aide, Lieutenant Hall." The men all shook hands.

"So, what's next?" asked Stiller.

Baum opened a map he was holding in his hand and moved over to the hood of a nearby jeep. The men gathered around him. "We are right here," said Baum, tracing an elongated finger along a line depicting the headquarters. We will be departing in the next few minutes. Our first objective is Schweinheim. That's the front line at this point."

"How do we get through?" asked the major.

"B Company of the 37th Tank Battalion and B Company of the 10th Armored Infantry are going to punch a hole through for us. That shouldn't take more than half an hour. They are starting their attack any minute. Once we get through, we will head east until we reach Gemünden. There's a bridge there crossing the Main. Once we hop over that, it's east/northeast on the highway to Hammelburg. The Germans won't be expecting us. With luck, we'll break through the camp just after first light tomorrow and be back through our lines by early afternoon."

"What if we encounter resistance?" asked Stiller.

Baum shrugged. "Welcome to our world, Major. That happens most of the time. If we do, we fight or we run around it. Don't worry about that stuff. You're along for the ride. We know our business. We'll get you in and back. Any more questions?" There were none.

Even as they finished the discussion, the vehicles were lighting up, the steely rumble rising to a thunderous roar all around them.

"Stiller," shouted Baum, so he could be heard over the noise. "Here's your ride. Everything is in it, and we're ready to go."

Hall followed Stiller over to an open-top jeep where a

sergeant waited in the driver's seat. In the back rested a Thompson submachine gun nestled against an ammunition satchel, as well as the extra clips for Stiller, a radio, and two days of K rations.

"You need anything else?" shouted Baum.

Stiller shook his head.

"Okay, sir. We are heading out. Stick tight to the sergeant," he said, pointing at the driver. "He's a trooper. I'll see you on the other side." Baum turned and walked briskly away. Stiller motioned to Hall, and they both took a seat in the back. Hall lifted the Thompson and checked the safety. He'd trained with the weapon before but had had very little time with it. He hoped he'd have no need to use it.

They sat in the jeep for a few minutes as the tanks started slowly into motion. They took their place in the long line of vehicles heading toward the front. The dull crash of artillery already thudded on the horizon.

Chapter 4

Rieneck, Germany
March 26, 1945, 1900 hours

*H*auptmann Richard Koehl glanced at his watch again. She was late. He looked around the restaurant, but he couldn't find her. Had something happened? He lifted his glass of whiskey and drained the remainder with a quick flick of his wrist. The liquid burned as it went down, but he hardly noticed. His mind raced through a dozen scenarios. An accident. A bomb. Anything could have happened. He fumbled for his wallet, drawing out a few notes and crumpling them on the table. His hands shook. He couldn't just sit here; he would go find her. He whispered a *Hail Mary* . . .

"Richard."

The musical voice released all his fears, and he exhaled a river of relief. She was here.

"Gerta," he said, hastening around the table to greet her. She was taller than he remembered, blond braids swinging against his shoulders as he held her tight. He released her and stepped back to look her over. She was a young woman now. A scattering of freckles climbed the bridge of her nose. Blue eyes crowned pale features. "You're beautiful. You must be driving the boys crazy."

Her cheeks flushed, and her dimples deepened. She laughed. "What boys? Everyone's at war. Besides, big brother, you're a priest; you're not supposed to notice earthly beauty."

He laughed. "I'm hardly one these days. Except perhaps a warrior priest."

"It's been so long," she said, suddenly serious.

"I wanted to come home when we were transferred west, but I couldn't swing it. The Americans won't give us a minute's rest."

"How much longer can it last?" she asked, taking a seat at the table. He ordered her some wine and another whiskey for himself before he answered.

"No way to tell, but I wouldn't think much longer. Maybe summer at the latest." He whispered the words. Even now, at the end, it was dangerous to utter defeatist words.

"Oh, Richard, what will we do? Will we be safe?"

He thought about that for a moment. "When it's over, I think we will be. If the Americans take us, or the British. It will be terrible for a time, but things will get better again eventually."

"What about the Russians?"

Koehl shook his head. "You mustn't be captured by them. They're animals."

"They can't be as bad as the rumors."

He leaned forward: "They are worse. That brings me to why I set up this dinner, besides wanting to see you, of course."

She started to ask what he meant, but they were interrupted by a waiter who asked what they wanted. Koehl ordered a whole chicken and some bread for the two of them to share. There were no butter or potatoes available.

When the waiter left, they resumed their conversation. "All right," she said, her eyes twinkling a little, "why has my big brother summoned me all the way to Rieneck?"

"I've arranged a transfer for you to my unit."

Her eyes narrowed, caught by surprise. "What do you mean?"

"I want you to move over to my headquarters."

"In what role?"

"I need a typist."

She sat back, her cheeks flushed again, but not with pleasure this time.

"What's wrong?" he asked.

"I won't do it," she muttered stubbornly.

"What do you mean?"

"I'm serving the fatherland in my flak crew. I'm a soldier, protecting our people against enemy planes. You want me to leave that to become a typist?" she asked, her voice rising.

"Keep it down," he said.

"I won't," she said. "I can't believe you, Richard. All these years I've worshiped you. I've hardly had a brother in my life. You were always gone. But I've had an idol. Richard Koehl, German officer and tank destroyer. Our own family hero. You've served, and you've fought, and now it's my chance to do the same. I'm not going to give all that up to type up your messages like a common secretary!" She was shouting now, and other customers in the restaurant were gawking at them.

"I said, Lower your voice." His words were calm and measured, but they were edged with a hint of steel.

She looked around for a moment before she continued; then she shrugged. "What difference does it make? We won't ever see these people again. I'm so confused," she said, wiping tears from her eyes. "I thought you'd be so proud of me. Instead, you want me to quit and become some stupid clerk."

"I am proud of you, but I also want to protect you." He reached out, running a finger under her eyes to wipe away the tears. She pushed him away.

"Stop it," she demanded.

"No," he said, grabbing her by the wrist. "You don't understand. You still think this is a game. You haven't seen war, Gerta. You've had the newspapers and the schools filling your head with fantasies about glory and serving the fatherland." He looked around and lowered his voice. "It's all a lie. War is dirt and blood and death. I've lost so many comrades. Everyone close to me is gone, except Schmidt." He softened his grip. "I can't lose you as well."

"You're not going to lose me, Richard," she responded, her voice softening. "Besides, I'm in a flak crew, not on the front lines."

"You think you'll be safe? What do you believe you're shooting at? Those are fighters and bombers. They have their own sting. You think a flak crew is safe? Antiaircraft crews have died in the thousands. Besides, the front line changes every day. You'll be caught up in the whole mess before you know it."

"By my choice," she said, eyes flaring. "That's what I want to happen. I want to serve Germany before it's too late."

He shook his head. "You don't have a choice. The orders have already circulated. You're coming with me now." He removed the transfer papers he had tucked in his tunic and shoved them across the table.

She gasped, her eyes widening. "You can't be serious."

"I put this in process a few weeks ago. Your commander approved the transfer. I can drive you back to pick up your things." He looked at his watch. "We'll eat and then head over there straightaway. Do you have a lot to bring?"

"I'm not going with you."

"Oh, come now—"

"I refuse."

He hadn't expected this. He thought she'd be relieved, grateful. He was on unsure footing. "You don't have a choice," he said, using his sternest voice. "It's an order."

"Orders can be changed."

"You *will* go."

She stood, scraping her chair across the wooden floor. He rose also, his hands spread out, willing her to calm down. "You're not my father, Richard," she said. "You can't make me do what I don't want to do. I'm going to go back to my unit. I'll talk to my commander. He'll straighten this out. I'm sorry. I know you're trying to do what you think is best, but I don't want this."

"You don't understand. It's not a choice."

"*Hauptmann* Koehl." A strange voice interrupted him. He looked over, and there was a sergeant standing near him, paperwork in his hand. He didn't recognize the man. *Not now, damn it.*

"Stay," he pleaded with Gerta. "I just need a minute." He turned to the messenger and ripped open the envelope, scanning the contents. An attack was in progress. Another one. Didn't the Americans ever stop? He was wanted back at headquarters immediately.

"Thank you, Sergeant, you're dismissed." The soldier saluted and turned to depart.

"What's in there?" Gerta asked.

"New orders. The Americans are at it again."

"Good," she said. "Then you'll have something to do instead of trying to chase me down."

"I told you: you have to come with me."

"No," she said. "I'm sorry. I love you, but I won't go with you." She stepped forward and kissed him briefly on the cheek

and fled swiftly toward the door. He started to go after her but
stopped himself. He would let her calm down and think about
things. She couldn't change the orders. He would visit headquarters and then swing by to pick her up. Yes, a few hours
would calm her down. He took a final pull on his drink, closing
his eyes and taking a few deep breaths.

All would be well. He'd pick up his sister later tonight and
take her to the safety of his headquarters. For now, he would
report to his commander and find out what the damned Americans were up to.

Hauptmann Koehl arrived back at his regimental headquarters
in Hammelburg at about 2000 hours. As he jumped out of the car
sent to bring him, he strained his ears for the sound of artillery.
He couldn't hear anything but the revving of diesel engines as vehicles passed behind him. He was a little surprised. If the message was as urgent as it seemed, he'd have expected an anthill of
activity. He puzzled over this as he stepped through the front
door of a small hotel serving as the command center. At the
desk, instead of a manager, two privates lounged against the bar,
their Mauser 7.922mm rifles and other equipment laid out to
dry as they spread cheese out of a tube on some crudely cut
slabs of bread. Koehl recognized one of them and nodded. The
man started to rise, but the *Hauptmann* motioned for him to
stay put.

"Where's the *Oberst?*" Koehl inquired after the regimental
colonel.

"Upstairs," said the soldier, taking a bite of the bread and
cheese. The gummy golden paste gave off a pungent stench akin
to unwashed feet. The soldier noticed Koehl's crinkled nose.
"Want a bite, sir?"

"I'll pass," said Koehl, laughing, "tempting as your offer
might be."

The soldier chuckled in return. "It's better than smelling corpses."

"Amen, *mein freund*."

Koehl nodded farewell and hopped up the first few steps.

"Sir, are we heading back into action?"

Koehl stopped, looking down at them. "I hope not, at least for now. But something is barking out there."

"Is it that *schweinhund* Patton?"

Koehl grunted. "Looks like it. But I'll know more in a few minutes. You gentlemen get some food down, then catch a nap. Understand?"

They nodded, returning to their bread. Koehl kept tromping upstairs, a smile on his face. He loved the privates. Their only worry in the world was staying alive and when their next meal would be. Oh, if it could all be so simple . . .

He climbed the narrow wood-paneled stairway and turned the corner to a long, dimly lit hallway dotted with numbered rooms. He walked along, trying to remember where the colonel had his staffing quarters. He'd been here only a couple of times since the last retreat had required them to relocate yet again. *How many times have we had to move?* he mused, his mind walking through the hotels and villas in Russia, France, and now Germany. *And all in the wrong direction.*

He paused at a door. Room 214. He thought he recognized the number. He knocked sharply and heard a muffled reply. Now he was sure. Nobody could mistake the colonel's booming voice. He turned the knob and entered.

Oberst Helmut Hoepple lay on his hotel bed, feet crossed and a pipe puffing out prodigious columns of smoke. The room was clouded with the thick, sweet smell of the pipe tobacco that reminded Koehl of his father. Was that why he'd always appreciated the colonel? Perhaps, although there were other reasons as well.

"*Ach, guten abend, Hauptmann,*" said Hoepple, smiling between puffs. "Come on in. I've got something for your rather specialized talents."

Koehl was puzzled. What did the colonel mean? "I assumed when I received your message there was a breakthrough."

"*Ja.* I think so. But I don't know yet for sure."

"Where?"

"Come over and I'll show you. Don't mind the smoke. It's the fog of war!" Hoepple laughed jovially, and his voice thundered out through the room, threatening to knock the pictures from the walls.

Koehl stepped to the bed, standing over his colonel. He'd never seen him lying down before, and the sight felt unnatural for some reason. The colonel pointed a sharp finger on the map.

"Schweinheim," noted Koehl.

"Just so."

"Makes sense. Use the highways. We have anything there?"

"A sprinkling of *Volkssturm*. They won't last long."

Volkssturm. Koehl thought of the old men and boys Hitler was calling up to fight in the last defense of the fatherland. No training, little equipment. The children died in droves—the elderly deserted at the first sniff of danger. They were virtually useless. "What do we have to bring up?"

"Not much more. I've been on the phone to Division for the past hour. They tell me we're it for now. They can't bring anything else up to stop them."

Koehl was shocked. Was it really that bad? "Surely that's just talk. Where are the reserves?"

"Apparently *we are* the reserves, *Hauptmann.*"

"That's insane. I've got six tank destroyers left. I don't even have the four they've promised to replace for me. I'm down to half ammunition, and I don't have the petrol to maneuver. What do you want me to do?"

"Don't worry about the petrol. I have enough here to get you by. I can get you some shells as well."

"And my replacement vehicles?"

The colonel shook his head. "You'll have to make do, *Hauptmann*."

Koehl wanted to protest, but he knew it wouldn't do any good. "Where do you want me to go?" he asked.

Hoepple traced his fingers down the map. "We are here. The Americans are probably heading toward the Main, *ja*? No point in trying to catch them in the open before the river. You'll either be exposed by fields or find that the roads are too narrow with the hills and trees. Too much or too little. I think you should set your defenses up here," he said, pointing to the map.

Koehl looked at the location and the terrain, the river, the bridge. He nodded. "That's a good spot. What do you want me to do when I get there? I can't stop a whole damned army."

"I don't expect you to. Just delay them. Do what you can. Nobody wants you dead, *Hauptmann*." He looked up. "As a matter of fact, I want you to do everything you can to avoid significant casualties. This war is almost over, and I want to visit you at your parish for years to come."

Koehl was surprised. He'd never heard him talk like that before. Still, there was business to attend to. "What are my orders then, sir?"

"Take out the lead tanks. Blow up this bridge. Slow the bastards down for a day or two. If we don't, the *Führer* will have us all up against a wall. We've got to make a fight of it."

"If we stop them too well, the damned Russians will be here. We should be joining the Americans and fighting the Bolsheviks," observed Koehl.

"I agree with you, *Hauptmann*, but orders are orders, and one war at a time. The Americans don't understand our communist friends yet. They will learn soon enough."

Koehl studied the map again. "You want me to take out the bridge? I don't have explosives or the men to do it."

"Don't worry. I'll get a company of infantry down to support you. They'll have a few engineers with them."

"Any air support?"

The colonel laughed. "You are optimistic, my friend. When's the last time you saw one of our friends in the *Luftwaffe* overhead."

Koehl smiled in return. "One can always hope."

"If you hear an airplane, you better duck. I might get a spotter plane up there to track the advance, but no fighters or bombers. They're all trying to stop the damned Eighth Air Force from wiping out what's left of our cities. That assumes there is anything left of them that's worth hitting."

"If the Americans get air support over our little trap, we won't last a minute in there."

"We can't help that. Pray for clouds and skilled engineers, my friend. And you'd better come home safe!"

Koehl saluted and turned to leave.

"Just a second, *Hauptmann*. You seem to be missing someone. Where is this mysterious sister of yours? I was expecting to see two people enter my room tonight."

"She refused to come, sir. I was going to stop her, but your message came at the same time. I'll collect her when this thing is over."

The colonel chuckled. "Another stubborn Koehl. I'm sure she'll be an asset in our office."

"I'll report back when I've stopped the advance."

"*Gott* protect you, *Hauptmann*."

"*Danke, Herr Oberst.*"

Koehl saluted again and left the room. He would have to hurry if he was going to get his tank destroyers in position before the Americans arrived. He wanted to go after Gerta, but there wasn't time. He'd have to arrange for transportation for the petrol and the shells. He also had to track down the infantry company. A school of details swam through his mind. One object dominated everything else. Survival. *I must survive. I must protect my sister and my crew. It's almost over. This is no time to die.*

Chapter 5

They waited in the darkness, a long line of vehicles and men parked helter-skelter, illuminated periodically by the flickers and flashes ahead of them. Hall strained to check his wristwatch: 2300 hours. He swore under his breath. They were already far behind schedule. The task force, according to the plan, was to break through the front crust of the German line by 2200 hours. Abrams had designated two armored companies to blow a hole through for them. Resistance was anticipated to be light or nonexistent. Yet here they were, sitting back in the darkness, waiting in vain for a signal that the way was clear.

"What's taking them so long?" he asked finally, frustration and anxiety churning up the hot cauldron of his emotions.

"It takes as long as it takes," said Stiller, motionless beside him in the darkness.

The bastard, thought Hall. *How can he sit there so calm?*

Must be too stupid to have an imagination. Besides, who would miss him if he was killed? Hall strained his eyes again, trying to make out any progress in front of them, but all he could see was the occasional flash followed by a distant booming, dancing with the staccato rattle of small-arms fire. Why didn't they get a move on? The longer they were stuck here, the more time the Germans had to prepare for them. Damn this whole operation!

"Something's wrong, sir," he said. "Do you want me to check with Baum and find out what the hang-up is? We should be long out of here. If we don't hurry, the Germans will be waiting all along the route."

Stiller chuckled, turning to Hall. "Nerves a little on edge, boy? I forgot this is your first time in near combat. Don't worry, we'll have plenty of the shit on this little trip, no matter when we get through here. And, no, I don't need you bothering Baum. I promised we'd stay out of his way, and the last thing he needs right now is a snotty-nosed lieutenant asking him questions. Just sit tight. We'll be out of here soon enough."

As if summoned by the mention of his name, Baum material-ized out of the darkness. The lanky captain was striding rapidly up to their jeep, helmet in one hand and a map in the other. He exchanged a brisk salute with Stiller.

"You got everything you need?" he asked.

"Just like you promised. What's the deal up ahead?" asked the major, nodding toward the front.

"We're delayed. There's more resistance than we figured. A couple companies maybe, spread out in the buildings. A tank or two also, or artillery. We haven't figured it out yet."

"How long do you figure before we bust through?"

"I'm not sure. Could be at it all night. That's what I came to let you know. I don't want to wait. I think we'll force the issue."

"What do you mean, sir?" asked Hall.

Stiller jabbed a finger at the lieutenant. "He wasn't talking to you."

"That's all right," said Baum. "I'm talking about lighting up our machines and storming right through town. The two companies Abrams sent are already well in. It's the last few blocks that are giving them trouble. If we rip through right now, we should make it just fine . . . except—"

"Except it may get a little messy," finished Stiller.

"You got it, Major. Figure we're gonna lose a few boys that way. I hate doing it right out of the gate, but we got to get this show moving before we call half the German army down on us. You all right with that?"

"I told you, Baum, I'm just along for the ride. This is your ball game."

"Can't we wait a bit longer?" asked Hall.

"You'll have to excuse the lieutenant," said Stiller. "He's a greenhorn. Never tasted any combat before." The lieutenant flushed with anger at the comment. *Shove it in my face all you want, you bastard. I'll show you.*

"Don't worry, Hall," said Baum. "We aren't taking much of a risk. You'll get used to it anyway, before we're through with this little trip." The captain pointed down at the Thompson. "I'd get that loaded and ready to go. Never know what might come out at you, and we can use all the covering fire we can get. You know how to use that thing?"

Hall nodded.

"Good. When we get into town, spray the second-floor windows as we roll by. You don't have to worry about hitting anything. I just want those krauts ducking as much as possible. But one clip only, okay? We're going to need all the ammo we have on this hike."

"Yes, sir, one clip only."

"Get ready then. We're moving out in the next few minutes." He turned to the driver. "Just gun it when the Sherman in front of you takes off. Stay on his ass; you won't want to give them a chance to spot an unarmored target. Good luck, boys." Baum turned and disappeared rapidly into the blackness.

Stiller turned to the lieutenant. "Well, Hall, this is it. Get that Thompson up and ready to go. When we get into the town, keep your cool. Hit those second-story windows, like Baum said. You'll see. It's all easy enough once it gets started. It's the waiting that's the problem."

Hall reached down and pulled the Thompson up. He jammed a clip into the submachine gun and locked it into place, flipping the safety open with his thumb. He kept his finger off the trigger and the barrel pointed out of the vehicle at a forty-five-degree angle, as he'd been trained. He was thankful to have the weapon to cling to, and he hoped the major couldn't see how much his hands were shaking.

A new sound erupted in the night. Rolling back from the front of the column came the rumbling of engines as first the lead Sherman, then the others fired up their engines. Hall heard the jeep start, adding its buzz to the thunderous roar of the task force as it prepared to move.

"We're heading out," shouted their driver. "Be prepared for a bumpy ride." They sat there for a few more minutes before the Sherman directly in front of them roared into motion. Their driver lurched forward, keeping the front of the jeep pressed up and almost kissing the rear of the lumbering tank.

They jolted and banged along the road, the flashes and thuds of artillery growing ever closer as the town drew into sharper focus. Hall gripped his Thompson, his heart echoing the racing rattle of machine-gun fire.

"Hang on," said Stiller. "We're almost there." The major drew his .45 pistol and lowered the lip of his helmet. He reached into his mouth, pulling out his wad of tobacco and tossing it into the night.

The column entered the first row of houses. Hall was shocked up close by the damage to the buildings. While the frames of the outer structures still stood in most places, the walls were pitted with machine-gun bullets interspersed with the gaping holes of artillery and tank shells. Fire raged through one of them, the flames licking greedily out every window. A German soldier lay facedown in front of the front door, surrounded by an angry red pool, arms stretched out and fingers gripping the pavement in twisted claws.

The roar of explosions in front of Hall clattered thunderously. His ears rang, and he felt concussive spasms overwhelming him wave after wave. The detonations erupted rapidly now, and he could see the horror unfolding in front of him by the light of the shells and the raging fires.

Flashes flickered from the windows of many of the houses. A Sherman a few ahead of him jerked, and its cannon belched fire. A house a hundred yards away erupted from the shell, the whole structure collapsing in on itself. Hall saw in terror the outline of a man writhing in flames among the rubble.

"Hall, what the hell are you doing!" demanded Stiller. "Fire your weapon at those windows!"

The lieutenant had forgotten his orders in the chaos. He drew a deep breath and raised the Thompson to his shoulder. Sighting down the barrel, he depressed the trigger. The weapon bucked hard against his shoulder and flayed wildly in his hands as a spurt of bullets flew out, crashing against one of the houses.

"Keep it up, boy!"

He fired the Thompson again and again, aiming for the windows. His arm was nearly ripped from the socket by the violent recoil. He had no idea if he was hitting anything, but Stiller kept shouting, and he continued pressing the trigger. He pulled down again, and nothing happened. He looked at his weapon, wondering what was wrong. *Out of bullets.* The thought amid the fog of his emotions. He reached down to the satchel between him and Stiller and drew out another clip, but the major grabbed his wrist, shaking his head.

"One only, Hall. Besides, look," he said, pointing out of the jeep. "We're nearly through it now."

Hall glanced around and realized the major was correct. They were passing the last line of houses and submerging into the darkness again. They were through. He was still alive. The thought struck him intensely, and every fraction of his body coursed with this one miraculous thought. *I am alive! I survived!* He slumped back into his seat, dropping the Thompson to the floor of their vehicle. He felt a hand on his shoulder. He was surprised to see the major leaning toward him.

"Good job, Lieutenant," said Stiller in his gruff Texas drawl. "I wasn't sure you had it in you. You done good, boy."

Hall closed his eyes, breathing in as the jeep bounced along and the sound of battle faded away. They'd broken through. He'd made it. He felt superhuman. He'd faced combat, and he'd done his duty. Even Stiller said so. Maybe he was going to make it through this and get his ass home as a hero after all.

The night still deeply covered the sky as Task Force Baum rolled along, Schweinheim fading away behind them. Hall watched the eerie claws of tree branches as they passed overhead, blotting out the stars above the winding road. Next to him, Major Stiller worked away, pouring hot coffee out of a tin container into his mug. He tipped the opening in short spurts, trying to time the movements with gaps in the jarring bounce of the jeep. He finished and screwed the top back on, took a sip, and offered the cup to Hall. The lieutenant took the warm liquid gratefully, sipping from the cylinder and letting the heat restore his body against the frigid air of the early-spring morning. *Too bad it wasn't something stronger.*

"How you doing, Hall?" asked Stiller.

"I'm okay, sir," said the lieutenant. "Thank you for the drink."

"You did good back there. You see how it goes now, right? When the shit's hitting the fan, it's not so terrible. You just stick your nose in it and keep your cool."

Hall took another sip. The major's charms didn't affect him, but they could be used to his advantage. He decided to play the convert. "Where do you think we are?" he asked, his voice affecting interest.

"I was just thinking on that. Did you study the map Abrams had?"

"Not well enough."

"Well, we are traveling about due east right now. Not too long up here, we'll come across a couple little villages. Not much, a few houses. Shouldn't be anything to worry about—hopefully, at least. After we clear those, we'll arrive at Rechtenbach and Lohr. A little more to them. Then we get to Gemünden. That's the big one. We must cross the Main River. Only one bridge up across the damned thing. Once we're over, we make our way northeast to Hammelburg." The major looked at his watch, grunting. "We're a few hours behind schedule, close as I can figure it. We still should be damned close to that Oflag by dawn, if we keep a move on."

"Do you think we'll make it through without any more trouble?"

"Tough to say. It'll take the krauts a while to figure out what we're up to. But that don't mean we're in the clear. Depends on what's up ahead anyway. We don't have great intelligence all the way there. This camp's just too far back from the front lines. I'd say we better figure we'll hit a rough patch or two. You never know what's brewing ahead. A couple tanks in an intersection or a barracks we don't know about. Shouldn't be nothing we can't handle. It's the trip home that's gonna be a solid-gold bitch. After we nab those POWs, you better hold on to your ass."

Hall felt a surge of fear pierce him again. He hadn't thought much about the return journey. Just getting through the front lines seemed difficult and traveling fifty miles to the POW camp damned near impossible. Now that he considered it, of course, the major was correct. The Germans wouldn't be on full alert on the way in, at least if they were lucky. But the more time they spent behind the lines, the more the enemy would organize and pinpoint their position. Could this group of three hundred men and a few tanks stand up to what the krauts would throw their way? He didn't know.

"Look," said Stiller, pointing, "houses ahead."

Hall peered into the darkness. He couldn't see anything at first, but eventually he made out a few buildings in the distance,

"Better get that Thompson ready, just in case."

Hall reached into the satchel and pulled a clip out. His fingers walked over the remaining metal sticks, counting his reserves. He had five, six with the one he was loading now. He would have to be careful.

Still, they had broken the crust of the German line. He felt the power of the Shermans in front of him. Mobile steel fortresses bristling with weapons. They rumbled along, shielding him from harm.

The village loomed higher on the horizon. A few heartbeats, and the first tank clambered onto cobblestone streets ahead. The houses were bathed in the oily darkness of the night. As they rolled through the town, first one light, then another flickered on. Hall saw a head pop out to stare in surprise at them. A few moments more and they were through. The lieutenant breathed with deep relief. A half hour later, they passed another sleepy village without incident.

They traveled on through the endless winding roads, the trees and hills blocking out the stars and the rumbling of the tanks guiding their driver in the inky blackness. Hall wasn't sure how long they jounced along, but Stiller went through several cups of coffee. The sky spoke a further story. At first, the lieutenant thought it was his imagination, but minute by minute he saw the early kiss of dawn perforating the onyx blanket above him. Soon the eastern heavens were mottled with the faint promise of morning.

"Are we almost to the camp?" he asked Stiller.

"Not close," said the major. "But I'm not sure how far. Damn it, I should have asked for my own map. But we left late, and we're supposed to be crossing a pretty big river at some point. Unless I missed it in the dark, we haven't hit a bridge yet."

"Maybe this town has got one," said Hall, noticing some houses in the distance. "Looks like a bigger one. The kind of place that might straddle a river."

"We'll find out. Look sharp, Hall."

Hall swung his Thompson over and flipped the safety off. He felt a hot excitement coursing through him. He'd never experienced such exhilaration before. Not in sports, or in training. Not even when he'd toyed with the girls in college. He hated and loved the sensation.

In a flash of time, they were inside the town. His impression of a larger place was borne out as they streamed down the main street. Instead of simple houses, there were buildings here, shops with signs and side streets packed with structures fading away into the distance in both directions. The pre-dawn light played havoc with Hall's sight. The shadows below were impenetrable as his eyes strained against the brightening sky on the horizon, glaring directly into his eyes.

A burst of fire erupted somewhere to his right. Bullets rattled off the Sherman in front of them like hot rain. Hall raised his Thompson and blindly fired a few rounds. Stiller put his hand across the barrel, pulling it down. "Save them until you know what you're looking at," the major ordered.

Shots rang out from several directions now. The firing was sporadic and seemed to do slight damage to the column. Hall slumped down lower in his seat, aware of how exposed they truly were in their unarmored, open-air jeep. The task force rolled on, plowing through the town, machine guns blazing away.

The sky opened back up, and they were through. Hall thought perhaps the column would stop to check for casualties, but he was wrong. The tanks kept rumbling as they moved into the fields and farms beyond. The landscape changed here. During the night, they'd traveled through a hilly, forested landscape; now the horizon flattened out, exposing fences, farms, and fields.

"You okay, Hall?" asked Stiller. The major pulled out another huge plug of tobacco, offering his pouch to the lieutenant, who declined.

"Fine, sir. Think anyone was hit?"

"Doubt it. The Germans put up a pretty piss-poor fight back there."

"It gets worse?"

"Hell, yes, it does. When the krauts are serious, you'll know it."

Hall felt a flicker of fear. How much worse would it be? As he thought through this, he noticed a cluster of buildings coming up on the right. He could see much better now. The structures were squat and square, more functional than aesthetically pleasing. There was something familiar about them that he couldn't quite place. He watched them closely as they passed by.

The jeep cleared the buildings. Behind them was a large concrete square, and that's when Hall realized what he was reminded of. The buildings were barracks. The courtyard beyond was full of at least a company of soldiers, lined up in neat rows for morning inspection. Even as he watched, he could see surprise register on the enemy faces and fingers pointed in excitement toward the column.

"Look at that, sir!" shouted Hall.

"Shit!" shouted Stiller. "Turn that Thompson on them!"

Hall flipped the safety off and aimed his weapon at the line of soldiers. He hesitated. They were unarmed. He couldn't just shoot them like that. The Shermans didn't hold back. He heard the machine gun fire ahead of him, and a row of soldiers toppled over. The enemy scrambled as the tanks poured fire into them, killing some of the Germans and sending others tumbling for cover.

"Shoot them, damn it!" shouted Stiller.

"No point," said Hall, turning to the major. "The Shermans have this. I need to save my ammo, don't I?"

Stiller stared at him hard for a minute. "Good thinking," he said finally. "No point wasting bullets on those boys. They don't have anything to shoot back with."

The machine gun fire continued. Hall kept his eyes on Stiller. He didn't want to watch the slaughter any longer. His brain tried to process what he'd seen. He heard the screams of pain and fear through the firing. Thankfully, the column was still moving, and soon it was over. He did not turn around but kept his eyes fixed firmly on the tank in front of him.

The major seemed to understand, and he patted the lieutenant's hand. "That's tough stuff back there, Hall, but it's part of war."

"They weren't even armed."

"Don't matter. They would be by the time we came back, that's for damn sure. That's a whole batch of kraut bastards that won't get a chance to kill more Americans. I know it hardly seems fair, but remember, this whole war is a mess. If there's any good news, it's that it's almost over. For now, we've got to keep our eyes on the ball. Just remember what's ahead. A bunch of our boys locked up. If we don't help them, they may be shipped away or even worse."

"What do you mean?"

"There are rumors the Germans are shooting prisoners."

"That can't be true," said Hall.

"You don't know the Germans. Don't worry about it, Hall. You're doing fine." Stiller put his hand on the lieutenant's shoulder again. "Just keep rolling, and we'll get through this thing."

Hall sat back as the barracks faded away in the distance. He felt sick to his stomach. He couldn't drive the images of those dying unarmed Germans out of his mind. He wished he'd stayed behind, that he'd never pressed for a combat mission in the first place. Still he was here, and it was almost halfway over. A few more hours and he'd be done. With the war almost finished, he'd be rid of Stiller and the army.

Another hour passed as they moved along the German countryside. Hall could see farmhouses dotting the highway, and even a farmer who stopped what he was doing in the middle of a field to watch the long column pass him by.

The sun poked above the hills in the distance, although Hall could see the clouds rolling in above him. They were in for an overcast day, perhaps even rain. Hall saw that the task force was approaching a small city. The highway here was dotted with trees lined row after row on each side of the road. Stiller rose to his feet, holding on to the driver's seat in front of him and staring out around the Sherman directly in front of them.

"That's a big one up ahead," he said. The column rolled along a little farther and then rumbled to a stop. "Looks like something's blocking the road. We're gonna be here for a bit. You want some more coffee? I'll see if I can find—"

A metal cylinder ripped through the air and struck the Sherman directly in front of them. The tank shook, bouncing a few inches above the ground, and came to rest in a cloud of smoke and fire. The hatch opened, and Hall heard agonized screaming. A figure emerged through the turret; he was on fire, and the flames licked his arms and his back. The lieutenant watched in horror as the man almost calmly pulled himself out of the tank and stood for a moment, as if scanning the horizon, before he slumped over and fell sideways off the tank, landing in a ditch near the road. He didn't move, but the fire engulfed his body, licking the flesh to charcoal.

Hall saw the outline of a German soldier through the trees. He was holding a spent *panzerfaust*, an anti-tank weapon like their bazooka. The lieutenant realized with horror that there were dozens of enemy soldiers out there, rifles raised and fire flashing from the barrels. He started to aim his weapon, but he couldn't fire in that direction without endangering the driver and Stiller. He turned his head to the right and saw other Germans closing in from that direction as well. He twisted his Thompson around, trying desperately to respond to the fire and death closing in on them.

Chapter 6

Oflag XIII
Near Hammelburg, Germany
March 27, 1945, 0700 hours

Captain Curtis lay in his bunk, his eyes half closed. He'd had the dream again. Most nights, he experienced the same vision. He was back in the Ardennes—the cold, the snow, his men spread out in well-prepared positions, with nothing to guard. The night exploded. The ghostly Germans were there among the trees, between the tanks, belching fire as the peaceful landscape erupted in metal, fire, and death. Lieutenant Hanson crouched in the foxhole with him. He reached to protect him, to take the shrapnel in his place, but he was too late. His friend, the officer under his protection, was wounded, near death, paralyzed forever.

He shook his head awake, glaring at the pine-knotted surface of the top bunk. Why couldn't he ever reach his friend in time? Even in his dreams? It was always the same. No matter what he did, how hard he tried, his company was lost, all of them, wounded, dead, or captured. He felt the anger boiling in him.

Why hadn't the brass warned them? Where were their tanks, their planes? Who was the bastard that placed them there, only to die without a chance to ever even fight? The answer came back to him as it always did. *You were the officer in command. Headquarters didn't fail the company; you did.* He felt the despair overwhelm him. *I am at fault. And only me.*

He heard the artillery again in his head. Now his dreams were haunting him when he was awake. As the thudding continued, he realized it wasn't in his mind. Curtis strained his ears until he was sure. There were explosions out there in the distance somewhere. Far away, for sure, but close enough that he could hear them. He rose out of his bunk to see dozens of men standing, their faces peering out the window intently, listening to the sounds of war. There was a collective, palatable joy in the barracks. The thunder spelled freedom. Their comrades were coming for them after all.

Would they get there in time? The Germans were evacuating the camp. They'd waited for hours last night for the orders to come. Miraculously, there were delays. But they could be moved out any moment. Now, with the Americans on their doorstep, the excitement and dread rose to the highest pitch. If they could just hold on for a few hours, the army might rescue them in time.

Curtis moved away from his bed, sprinting past the others, who stood like statues, listening to the battle waging somewhere in the distance. He had to find out what the plan was. He left the front door and winced at the bright sunlight filtering through the crisp morning air. He'd left his jacket by his bunk. No matter, he couldn't really feel the cold in his joy. He marched as rapidly as his weakened legs would allow, joining others who herded in a collective mass toward the headquarters barracks. The distant rumbling was distinct in the camp yard.

Curtis stormed into the command building and found most of the messengers already assembled. There was an electric charge to the atmosphere, and the men laughed and clapped their hands like joyous children on Christmas morning. Colonel Goode and Lieutenant Colonel Waters walked among the men. Waters's face was lit up with an enormous grin, and he shook Curtis's hand when he saw him.

"It's happening," he said.

"Do you think so, sir?"

"Definitely. Nothing else that thunder could be. Patton's coming for us."

"Any idea how long?"

Waters shrugged. "Doesn't matter. He'll be here soon enough."

"What if we aren't around to greet him?"

Waters's face darkened a shade. "What will be will be. We have to be prepared . . . either way."

As he said that, Goode clapped his hands a few times, drawing the group's attention to their commander. He was beaming, his face giving off a light of its own.

"Okay, boys. This is it. The big day we've all waited for. It's also a day of danger, from a batch of directions. We can't do a damned thing about that. But we can be prepared. Now here's what I want you all to do. First, go back to the boys and give them the plan. Second, it's the same drill we discussed yesterday. I want each barracks to send a runner to the canteen. We're going to divide up our Red Cross packs and all the grub. An equal amount for each group."

"Why divide the food if we're going to be rescued today? That sounds like we're going to be marched away," observed one of the officers.

"We have to prepare for a last-minute evacuation. But even if that doesn't happen, we also must be ready for liberation. The front-line troops will be moving fast. They won't have a batch of backup rations and supplies. It could be days until we're properly supplied. We need to hope for the best and prepare for the worst."

"What about the battle itself?" someone shouted.

"If it comes to a scrap for the camp, we need to hunker down in our barracks and stay the hell out of the way. We can't fight these bastards without weapons. We wait for the shooting to stop. Trust me, our boys will recognize a POW camp when they see it. They'll be careful."

"What about the wounded?" asked Curtis.

Goode looked at Curtis. "Yes?"

"If we're shipped out, we're taking them with us, aren't we?"

Goode considered the question. "I don't know that. They didn't let us in Poland."

"And they killed them, didn't they?"

Goode's face flushed. "We don't know that, Curtis. We just know they wouldn't let us bring them along. Hell, the wounded would have died for sure if they'd come along with what we went through. Snow and ice, miles of hiking without shoes. They wouldn't have lasted an hour out there."

"Better for all of us to die than to leave them," said the captain.

"Nonsense," responded Goode sternly. "We don't have control over everything. If they do take us and they do it by train, we might be able to arrange something. I'll have a talk with the *Kommandant* and see if there's anything I can do. But I'm sorry, captain; if it's by foot, we don't have a choice."

Curtis nodded in response. Goode was going to talk to General von Goeckel, the camp commander. If there was any chance to save the wounded, the colonel would do his best.

"Now, if there aren't any more questions, boys, we've got a batch of work to do. Get going, and let's get things organized."

There was a smattering of cheers and clapping, and the officers shuffled out of the command headquarters, hurrying back to their barracks to organize everything according to orders. Curtis moved as quickly as he could and was soon back in his own building, explaining everything to the excited men, who could barely contain themselves at the prospect of liberation at last. A lieutenant volunteered to pick up the food and left to retrieve it, a makeshift bag slung over his shoulder. The rest of the men set to work pulling down the plywood from the upper bunks and stacking sheet after sheet into a barricade near the center of the room. They worked with excitement but as quietly as they could. If a guard came in and saw what they were doing, there was no telling how he might react. They crafted a square shelter with boards stacked six thick in each direction. Curtis hoped with luck it would stop a stray bullet. He knew what would happen if they were hit with an artillery shell.

As they worked, Curtis realized the sound of explosions in the distance had faded and then stopped completely. What did this mean? Was it a pause before another attack? Had the Americans passed any German resistance? Or, he thought with a sinking heart, had the Nazis stopped them cold out there somewhere? Now that he had sipped the possibility of liberation, he didn't think he could stand another day of waiting.

The lieutenant returned with their food. They had a sack of sugar, three complete Red Cross packs, and a dozen biscuits. The men looked at the food ravenously. They'd had hardly anything to eat lately as the rations had dwindled to practically nothing.

"Can we eat the biscuits now?" one of the men asked. There were grumbles of ascent from the assembled crowd, who had dropped what they were doing and were crowding tightly around the food packs.

"No, we can't," said Curtis. "We need to keep what we have for now."

"Who put you in charge?" asked the man.

"I'm the runner. I took the orders."

"That doesn't make you in charge of us. You're not even the top-ranking man in this barracks." The man took a step forward and grabbed a biscuit. "I say these are ours. There's plenty left for us to have later."

Curtis tried to stop the men, but it was too late. The ravenous POWs stormed the center, grabbing the biscuits and tearing at the bread, shoving the bites into their mouths. One officer struck another in the face, knocking him back so he could get at the bread. Other hands seized the Red Cross packs, tearing them open with greedy hands, cackling maniacally. The men scrambled in, tearing and fighting as they battled for any food they could get ahold of. Curtis screamed at them, but they were starving, and the lure of the ready food was too much. They stuffed their faces, grunting and groaning in pleasure like a pack of animals. Curtis shuffled away, powerless and dejected. He had failed again.

The captain sat by himself, his eyes closed. He could hear the joyous grumbling of the men around him, but he tried his best to ignore them. He felt a tug on his shoulder. He looked up, and the lieutenant who had started the stampede was standing over him. He was holding out half of a biscuit and three cigarettes he'd retrieved from a Red Cross pack. "Here, captain, take these."

Curtis looked down, refusing to answer. The lieutenant pushed forward. "Come on, sir. It's not your fault. We've hardly had a thing to eat for days. Don't take it so hard. Have a little."

"We won't have anything now if we have to march out of here."

"That's not true, sir. We'll have full stomachs. First time in I don't know when. That's worth a hell of a lot to everyone."

Without responding further, Curtis silently reached out and took the cigarettes and the half-eaten biscuit. He turned the hard, grayish roll over a few times, then bit down on the stale, flavorless bread. At first, he chewed methodically and without reaction, but soon his body took over. His mouth watered, and his stomach rumbled. He shoved the rest of the biscuit in his mouth, chewing it quickly and swallowing the first food he'd eaten in nearly a day. The biscuit barely stanched the cascading wave of his hunger, and he looked around greedily for more. But there was nothing for him. Each man was an island, hoarding his tiny cache of remaining food. If he wanted some, he'd have to fight for it. He wouldn't sink to that, not yet anyway.

Still, there were the cigarettes. He looked down at the three precious sticks, his hand rolling them delicately between thumb and fingers. He drew them to his nose, breathing in the rich tobacco, his body tingling all over in trepidation and excitement. He tucked two of the cigarettes into the inside of his shirt pocket and then fished a match out of his trousers. He flipped the head against a rough patch of his bunk, and the stick exploded in flames.

Curtis lifted the fire to the tip of his cigarette and pulled his breath luxuriously in, drawing the smoke deep into his lungs. He closed his eyes, hunger leaving him, enjoying the rapture of the tobacco. He leaned back into the bunk, sucking in the delicious smoke, forgetting about the war for a moment, that his stomach was empty and his future uncertain. For a few minutes, he was alone in the here and now.

Too soon he was finished. He drew the last few breaths, trying to pull every ounce out of the cigarette. No matter, he had two more. They should get him through until Patton arrived. If they were taken away by the Germans . . . well, he would have bigger things to worry about.

He decided he'd better report his failure to Colonel Goode. Another disaster to chalk up in his long line as a so-called commander of men. He smiled to himself again at the irony. He'd shown nothing but promise during the training, winning promotion and the praise of his commanders. Oh, how disappointed they would be in him now. He wasn't fit to lead after all. *Well, so be it*, he thought. Did it really matter anymore? The end was near.

He left the barracks and headed out into the still-frozen air toward the headquarters. He was one of the few POWs allowed out of the camp, and he felt the eyes of the guards watching him as he tramped toward Colonel Goode's office. He tried to keep an even pace, not wanting to arouse suspicion. Soon he'd made it without incident, and he entered the building, which, for once, was practically empty. Colonel Goode was not present, but Lieutenant Colonel Waters sat at a desk filling out some paperwork.

The colonel looked up, smiling in recognition. "Curtis, how good to see you. How are the preparations going?"

"That's what I'm here to talk about, sir. I regret to inform you that I failed."

"What do you mean?" asked Waters, his eyes alert and a frown creasing his face.

"It's the food, sir. We gathered it like you said, but when I got to the barracks the men rushed in and consumed it. I tried to stop them, but there was nothing I could do. We have nothing left."

"You too, aye?" said Waters, pushing back in his seat. "That's a story I've heard a lot this morning."

"What do you mean?"

"I mean you didn't screw up, Curtis. Goode and I did. We didn't think about how hungry the men have become. Right after we dismissed you, there was a run on the canteen. Boys started grabbing not only their fair share but anything they could get their hands on. I'm surprised your man even made it back with anything. He must have been one of the first ones there."

"You mean—"

"I mean we tried to give a little bit of food to a pack of hungry wolves. I don't think there's a scrap of food left in the whole camp, at least that the general population knows about. We should've seen it coming. We could've brought everything here and held onto it." He looked up at Curtis with a knowing expression. "You blamed yourself again, didn't you? It's always the same story with you, Curtis, but this one wasn't your fault. I told you we're a long way from perfect. We're all just men."

The door slammed open, and a POW stood there panting, doubled over.

"What is it?" demanded Waters.

"You gotta come, sir! Right now."

"Let's go, Curtis," said Waters, rising and running out the door. Curtis followed him, amazed at his swiftness. He caught up to the colonel just a few steps from the entrance. He stood, unable to move, frozen in horror.

Less than a hundred yards away was the hospital. A truck had pulled up nearby, and there were at least a dozen Germans standing nearby, rifles and submachine guns at the ready. As they watched, the Germans moved as one toward the infirmary door.

Curtis started toward them, but Waters grabbed his arm, holding him back. The captain tried to fight free, but the XO held him in an iron grip. "Stay put, son," he ordered harshly. "Whatever is about to happen, there's not a damned thing we can do about it."

A shot rang out, then many, ripping through the crisp air. Curtis fell to his knees, tears washing over him. After months of protecting his friend, keeping his spirits up, promising him a future, all his worst fears were coming true.

Curtis fell to his knees, vomiting in the frozen dirt. His head spun. He struggled to rise, but Waters kept a firm hand on his shoulder, keeping him down. "Stay down there, son."

Curtis tried to fight the colonel off, but he was too strong. A memory flashed through his mind of when they had first met. The camp was in chaos at that time. Nobody seemed to be in charge. The Oflag was full of the dejected members of Curtis's division and other green troops captured at the Bulge. A collection of misfits who'd failed on their first day of combat. He'd felt ashamed for them and for himself. They were unkempt and unwashed; there was no discipline and no purpose. Curtis and the others hadn't cared whether the war was won or lost.

Then Waters and the others had arrived from Poland. Curtis remembered them shambling into the camp. They were dirty too, frozen and half-starved. The new arrivals were for the most part in worse shape than the original prisoners. With a notable difference. They walked with their heads held high. They stared defiantly at the guards and marched to their assigned barracks in disciplined order. In a matter of hours, they seemed to take over the camp. Waters himself had confronted Curtis, sitting on the stairs of his barracks, staring listlessly at the fence line.

"What are you doing, Captain?" he'd demanded.

Curtis had ignored him.

"On your feet, Captain! I'm Lieutenant Colonel Waters, and when I talk to you, you listen!"

This had drawn his attention. He struggled to stand and gave a half-hearted salute.

"Again!" Waters demanded.

Curtis repeated the gesture, this time delivering a crisp salute.

"What's your name?"

"Curtis."

"That's better, Curtis! What division are you from?"

"116th, sir."

"What happened to you?"

"Captured on the first day of combat, at the Bulge," explained Curtis, his gaze darting back down to the ground.

"Eyes up, Captain. Now you listen to me," said Waters, pointing a finger. "I heard all about that battle. A swarm of Germans caught Eisenhower with his pants down. Nothing to be ashamed of. What were you, two divisions against twenty? A mess of tanks too? You're lucky you're even here."

Curtis shook his head, refusing to listen. "My fault. The responsibility is on me."

"Nonsense, Captain."

"It's the truth."

"Look at me, Curtis." The captain lifted his eyes again, although he found it hard to meet the colonel's iron glare. "I don't give a damn what you think you did. I don't care who you blame, but the past is the past, and it won't do you or anyone else any good to dwell on it. This camp is a shit hole. I'm embarrassed to call myself an American after touring this mess. But all of that is going to change today, and you're going to help me. Do you understand?"

"I'm sorry, sir. I don't think—"

"I didn't ask you, Captain. I told you. Now, we're taking charge of this FUBAR situation starting this minute. Colonel Goode and I will set up headquarters and start organizing an escape committee, inspections, and everything else that should have been done here months ago. You're going to be a designated runner for your barracks. Get it?"

Curtis nodded, and Waters had stomped off. He'd felt hot anger then, and resentment. Nobody had talked to him like that in months. At the same time, there was a different feeling rising inside him, something deeper. He felt a spark of hope, something to hang on to.

And so now he clung to Waters as the shots rang out in the hospital, ending the lives of the wounded, of his friend. He didn't know how he would survive this, but he knew that in the deepest moment of desperation, Waters would be there, an iron pillar to cleave to.

Chapter 7

Lohr, Germany
March 27, 1945, 0800 hours

Bullets flew everywhere. Hall fumbled with his Thompson, trying to move the weapon into position. Even as he watched, a line of holes ripped across the hood of their jeep, breaking the window just short of their driver. He aimed his weapon to his right and pulled the trigger, the sharp buck of the recoil driving the weapon up so that the bullets whizzed harmlessly into the air above the enemy.

Stiller was screaming next to him, shouting something undecipherable. Hall could hear the sharp bark of the major's .45 banging away at the Germans on the other side of the road. Another metal flash ripped through the air, passing right by his head. He could hear the whistle and feel the heat as the projectile ripped by, crashing into the trees on the other side of the road. He depressed the Thompson again, aiming lower this time, and saw with satisfaction bullets kicking up the dirt near the tree line, forcing one of the Germans to dive to the ground.

He glanced in front of him. The Sherman still smoked and bellowed, but he was shocked to see that the tank was rumbling forward. Was it possible some of the crew had survived? The vehicle steered to the left and rolled at an angle into the ditch. Hall looked more closely and saw that the next Sherman in line was towing the disabled vehicle out of the way.

An explosion erupted to his right. Another tank fired into the cluster of Germans near him. He watched a mangled torso fly fifty feet up before crashing in a bloodied mass in the field behind the trees. As he tried to process this, his jeep lurched forward, and they were moving again, pushing through the barricade and storming into the city. The Germans were pulling back, fleeing from a trail of metal and the blazing cannons of the Shermans. Bullets still whizzed through the air, but the fire was dying, and soon they were well into the town and away from the ambush.

Hall was sure there were other Germans waiting for them, and he scanned the windows with his weapon, but the town was silent, and the task force moved through without further incident. As the jeep bounced over the stony streets, Hall checked his weapon, realizing he had expended another clip in the firefight. He ejected the metal stick and tossed it out on to the sidewalk, drawing another of his precious reserve into the submachine gun and clicking it into place.

"You all right?" asked the major.

"I'm okay," said Hall, not sure that was true. His mind kept racing over the shell explosion, the flying limbs, the blood.

"How you set for ammo?"

Hall fumbled through his satchel, counting the clips. "Still four sticks, sir, plus the one in the chute."

Stiller grunted. "I'll have to see if I can get you some more. This thing's a little hotter than I expected. I used up everything for my forty-five." He patted the grenades lying between them. "Still have the pineapples, though."

The task force sped through the last of the streets and back out into the countryside. Hall sat quietly, trying to calm down. He closed his eyes, breathing deeply. He felt his whole body shaking. His nose was filled with the acrid smell of gunpowder. His ears rang so loudly he could hardly hear the roar of the engines anymore. After a few minutes, he felt a lurch, and he realized the column was slowing to a stop. He pulled the Thompson around, expecting another ambush. He realized that they were in the middle of some empty fields and there were no threats. He breathed deeply, willing himself to relax.

Stiller looked around. "Wonder why we stopped? Hall, come with me. Keep a sharp eye." The major jumped out of the jeep, walking toward the command jeep, a few vehicles behind. The lieutenant followed, his Thompson out—ready, if need be.

They reached the jeep and found Baum there, his command team clustered around him. They were poring over a map. "What's the situation?" asked Stiller, interrupting the discussion.

Baum's eyes flashed a flicker of irritation. "Trying to figure that out right now, Major," he said. "I'll be with you in a second."

The captain returned to his huddle. "Where are we?" he asked.

Lieutenant Nutto leaned in, jabbing a sharp finger at the map. "We just came through here. That's Lohr right there. We have about seven miles until we hit Gemünden, then about ten more to Hammelburg."

"Not too bad," said Baum. "Considering the delay. Any idea where the hell this camp is supposed to be?"

"Nope," said Nutto. "Not for sure at least. But to the south of the town is an old barracks. See, it's marked on the map. If I was gonna set up a POW camp, I wouldn't start fresh; I'd put it right there."

Baum nodded approvingly. "Good thinking. When we get there, we'll try the old camp first. If that's not it, we'll do a sweep in a circle five miles around the city. We should hit it eventually."

"There's going to be a shitload of Germans there if we have to play ring-around-the-rosy," observed Nutto.

"Agreed. Let's hope your instincts are correct, Lieutenant."

As they debated, a sergeant appeared and approached Captain Baum. The commander looked up. "What is it?"

"Casualty reports are in, sir."

"Give it to me straight."

"It's not too bad. Got six wounded in the half-tracks. Nobody in the jeeps."

"What about that Sherman? Anyone get out?"

The soldier shook his head. "They're all goners. The thing lit up like a Zippo."

Baum rolled his shoulders as if trying to shake off the news. "Well, I guess I didn't expect to get through this for free. What's the condition of the vehicles?"

"Everything looks good, sir. We took some bullets, though. A radiator on one of our half-tracks is torn up pretty good. But the boys are looking into it. We should be good to go in a few."

"Gasoline?"

"I don't know, sir. Haven't checked. We were full up heading out. Some jerry cans in reserve. We should be fine if we go straight in and out."

"I don't want to assume anything, Sergeant. Go find out. I want an exact report. We won't get anywhere if we run out of juice. I don't want to be limping out of here with my tail between my legs while we have half the German army breathing down our neck."

The sergeant nodded and turned, heading back down the line to check in with the vehicles.

"Okay," said Baum. "Where were we?"

"We were starting to talk about resistance, sir," prompted Nutto.

"Well, we can expect plenty more of that as we go. I was hoping we would make it all the way to the camp without any problems, but it looks like that's not gonna happen." Baum shook his head. "Damn delay. Well, can't be helped. We're gonna have to do our best with what we have." He looked around, searching for somebody. "Any way we can drum up some reconnaissance?" he asked.

"I'm trying, sir," said one of the men. "But the clouds rolled in nice and low. Gonna make it rough on the planes."

"Do what you can. Be helpful to know what's up ahead." Baum turned back to the huddled officers. "Listen up now, boys; we've got to make a little change in the plans. Because I'm expecting more resistance, I'm going to shove all the Shermans up front. That way, if we get into another scrap, we can hit them hard and fast. Let's wedge the jeeps in right behind them, then the half-tracks. The one-oh-fives and the light tanks can bring up the rear. Any questions?"

The men nodded, accepting the orders.

Baum dismissed his commanders, and they hurried to their assignments. Vehicles started moving to the side of the road and shifting their positions. The Shermans could not turn quickly, particularly in reverse. The maneuver would take a few minutes. Baum watched the progress of the jerky, unwieldy tanks for a time, then walked over to Stiller, wiping his forehead with a rag. "Okay, Major, you had some questions?" His voice was terse.

"I think I heard just about everything I needed," said the major. "Any idea when we might make the camp?"

"God knows, but if I had to guess, something like midafternoon."

"That late? I thought we were almost there."

Baum's eyes flickered in anger. "This isn't exactly what you'd call a walk in the park. We're already late as hell, and the

Germans are on to us. That'll slow us down some. Plus, walking into this camp won't be free. We'll have to fight our way in and probably again on the way out. When we do make our escape, that's when the real fun will start." He turned and looked the two of them over. "How are you holding up?"

"Not too bad," said Stiller. "Out of ammo for my pistol, though."

Baum pursed his lips. "I'll fetch you a clip or two. Don't use it again unless we're in a real close-up scrap, though. Let the Shermans do their job. Hall should be able to handle things with the Thompson. Can I get you anything else?"

"Any more Thompson ammo available?"

Baum shook his head. "I can't spare any; we're low already."

Stiller shrugged. "We'll get by. Good job incidentally, Captain."

Baum scoffed. "You can tell me that when we're out of this. Good enough so far." He turned and marched swiftly away, barking additional orders.

Stiller and Hall returned to their jeep, sitting in the back and waiting, with nothing to do while the vehicles jostled in and out of position around them. The nauseating exhaust of the engines was thick in the air. Hall used the few minutes to try to calm himself after the stress of combat. Stiller pulled out a K ration and cracked open the can of pork, digging in with a spoon. He took a few bites, then handed the can to Hall. "Hungry?" he said.

Hall didn't really feel like he wanted something to eat, but he appreciated the distraction. He took the can and scooped out some of the pink substance, scraping aside the clear jelly. He hated the stuff, but he needed to keep up his strength. He choked down a couple of swallows as they waited in silence with the tanks rumbling around them. They were miles behind enemy lines now, but still with a long way to go.

* * *

After a half hour, Task Force Baum resumed its journey on the road, still heading east/northeast toward Hammelburg. Hall gradually felt more like himself. He was proud he had survived and faced combat, but he felt a new determination that the next time they found themselves in the fighting, he would perform better under fire with his Thompson. He didn't want to give Stiller any excuse for not recommending him for a commendation. He still desperately wanted a drink. He'd thought there would be more stops, a chance to get to know some of the boys a little, sniff around for some booze. But so far, it was all balls in and rumbling down the road with the major's eagle eyes always watching.

Eventually, another town loomed on the horizon. Hall prepared himself for an encounter. As they drew closer, he heard the buzzing of an aircraft. *Finally, some reconnaissance*, he thought. He looked up and made out the plane following above them in the sky. The aircraft passed directly overhead, and he was shocked to see the German Cross on its wings as it banked away and headed east. An enemy plane gathering information about the task force, he realized. Soon the Germans would know everything about them. The approximate size of the column, the number of tanks, their direction. He felt the trap closing in on them.

They approached the town cautiously this time, the vehicles slowing down and guns trained on the sides of the roads, searching for an ambush. They were in luck. There were no trees here to hide the Germans, making any attack more difficult for the krauts to manage.

They rolled into the first streets of the town. Hall was surprised to see white sheets hanging from the windows. These Germans were ready for the war to end. Still, he kept his Thompson at the ready. This could be a trap. As they passed street after street, he saw some civilians even standing on the sidewalk, arms in the air. The task force ignored them. They were not here to fetch German prisoners or to capture towns. They had a distinct mission and no time to waste. As they left the streets and returned to the countryside, the vehicles rolled to a stop again. *What now?*

A soldier ran back from the front of the column, passing their jeep and heading to Baum's command vehicle.

"What is it?" Hall heard the captain ask.

"German column coming this way," was the answer.

"Armor?"

"No, sir. Looks like regular trucks."

"How far away?"

"About a mile. They don't look like they're traveling too fast. Figure two or three minutes away."

"Anyplace for us to turn off?"

"Noplace and no time, sir."

"They spotted us?" asked Baum.

"No way to know, but they aren't doing anything unusual. I'd say at this point they think we're a column of panzers."

"Well, let them come on," said Baum. "When they're astride us, we'll hit them hard. Wait until the lead truck gets to me before anyone shoots. Pass the word."

Men ran back and forth along the column, passing the information down the line. In less than a minute, the vehicles were lurching back into motion, heading down the road toward the convoy.

Stiller looked over at Hall. "You heard the captain. Get that thing ready." Hall removed the safety and made sure his weapon was loaded. He moved his Thompson over to the left, aiming at the space between the driver and the major.

"That's no damn good," said Stiller. "I don't want you clipping me in the excitement. Switch spots." Hall nodded and rose. It was difficult, but they managed to wiggle their way past one another in the tight confines of the jeep until Hall was sitting on the left-hand side directly behind the driver. In the distance now, he could see the column drawing ever closer. A line of five gray trucks covered in the back with canvas, looking quite a bit like their own deuce-and-a-half vehicles.

The convoy drew closer, a few hundred yards away, then a hundred. Hall waited until the first truck passed him. He saw the surprise in the German's face as the man looked closely at Hall.

Task Force Baum erupted in flame. Hall joined in, pumping rounds into the back of the nearest vehicle. The Germans jerked and jolted as they struggled to recover from the shock of the attack, but there was no chance. The last truck in line exploded in fire from a point-blank tank shell. Machine guns raked the enemy with fire.

Hall added his rounds to the melee. In short seconds, the Thompson was empty. He groped for another clip, but Stiller held him back. "That's enough, Hall. They're cooked."

The lieutenant turned to watch the last moments of the fight. The nearest truck rolled to the right, angling sharply as it skidded down the embankment and twisted over on its back, wheels still turning. Hall wasn't sure he had heard a single return shot. The entire enemy column was crumpled either on the road or in the ditch. He felt adrenaline coursing through him. Before Stiller could stop him, he slammed another clip into his weapon and leapt out of the Jeep, scrambling down the embankment and sprinting toward the smoking opening of the truck. He wouldn't miss this time. He turned the corner to fire into the back but stopped short, his jaw dropping.

Golden braids spilled out of the back of the truck. A young girl stared out at him with lifeless eyes. Her white shirt was smeared with angry blood. He stared in horror inside the truck. He could hear the moans of wounded women. *We're killing girls.* He turned, raising his hands, screaming at the column, but nobody could hear him. The firing continued, shell after shell ripping through the trucks. Hall fell to his knees, retching. He flung his Thompson aside, staring up at the smoking ruins filled with flaxen braids and death.

Chapter 8

Hammelburg, Germany
March 27, 1945, 0800 hours

He listened in the receiver to the endless ringing on the other end. Koehl hung up on the thirteenth chime with no answer. He stared at the phone and then glanced at his watch. He couldn't wait any longer. He'd called Gerta four times with no answer. *She's ignoring me*, he realized. He'd hoped she was seeing clearly this morning and would head over to regimental HQ on her own. No matter. He'd swing by and pick her up later, assuming he was alive at the end of the battle. He chuckled to himself. What a strange world he lived in where plans depended on whether you died before you could implement them.

He pulled on his boots and strapped his belt into place, then pulled on his tunic and buttoned the heavy black wool jacket. He'd had time to launder his clothes, with the break in the fighting, but the fabric was worn and fading. He'd made an order for a new set, but the tailor informed him there was no fabric available. Another shortage that whispered ominously of the end.

Koehl stepped out of his room and on to the busy streets of

Hammelburg. The winding road teemed with vehicles and personnel stomping hurriedly up and down the narrow sidewalks. There were few civilian pedestrians, he noticed, and no private vehicles of any kind. The sharp stench of diesel belched from gray and green leviathans lurching past. He turned to his left and walked a few hundred yards, weaving through the crowded mob, everyone seemingly convinced that *their* individual task was the most important. He arrived a few minutes later at an open, paved parking lot on the edge of the city. Waiting for him there were his machines and his crew—his family.

Six Panzerjager Tiger tank destroyers, nicknamed "Ferdinands," were lined up in a neat row against a barbed-wire fence at the end of the lot. A massive 88mm main cannon jutted out of the rectangular fixed turret of each of them; its shells were made to crush the massive Russian armored tanks on the Eastern Front. The enormous, armored bodies of the machines were painted a green-and-brown camouflage. An MG 34 machine gun mounted in a ball casing in the front of the destroyers added an anti-infantry punch to these rolling weapons. The medium-sized, medium-armored Shermans used by the Americans were no match for his tank destroyers, which could punch a hole through the enemy vehicles with one well-aimed shot.

Still, gradually over time, he'd lost four of his beloved crews while fighting in France and Germany. Two had fallen to mechanical failures, and two succumbed to attacks by multiple Shermans at the same time. He'd pushed his regimental commander for replacements. His colonel did everything he could, but there were no new machines available. Perhaps in the spring there would be something, but for now, he would have to make do with his dwindling force.

As he walked toward his machines, his command sergeant stepped out to meet him. *Feldwebel* Heidrich Schmidt gave Koehl a welcoming grin, looking up at his commander with eyebrows raised knowingly behind thick glasses. The *Hauptmann* grasped his hand, and he pulled Schmidt away from the group.

"Is everything ready?" asked Koehl.

"Everything but the petrol."

Koehl frowned. "Hoepple told me he had enough for us here."

"That may be, but I haven't seen it yet. Did you reach Gerta?"

Koehl shrugged. "No answer."

"Don't worry, my friend. I'm sure she's fine. She's probably put out with you over your little surprise last night. By the time we're done with our little party, she'll be ready to come. If not, I'll go with you, and we'll nab her right out of her bed."

"She won't appreciate that," said Koehl, laughing.

"We don't get everything we want in life."

"Can you do me a favor?"

"I suppose so, but you'll owe me." The sergeant's eyes twinkled.

Koehl sighed dramatically. "A million NCOs in the Wehrmacht and I get landed with you."

"I told you how lucky you are. That's why you've survived so long."

They shared a laugh. Koehl appreciated the chance for humor. If they truly let everything they'd seen and done get to them, they would have only room to despair.

"You're pulling me off track. I need you to go check on the petrol. I thought it would be here."

"Fine. I was going to enjoy one of our delicious supply of field rations, but I suppose it can wait. I'll check in and find out what I can." He finished his statement with a grossly embellished bow.

"You're impossible. Just go find my fuel."

The sergeant departed, and Koehl spent the time waiting,

huddled over a map, double-checking routes in and out of the ambush zone he and Hoepple had selected. He liked what he saw. Good highways in and out, and an excellent place to delay the Americans, at least for a time. If they had petrol, that is. And if his infantry showed up as promised, with engineers and explosives. A lot of uncertainties. More than he liked for an operation under his control.

A half hour later, Sergeant Schmidt returned. Koehl could tell by his reluctant gait that he carried unwelcome news. "What is it?" he asked.

"There's no more petrol. Hoepple says he is sorry, but the rest of his reserves were taken early this morning by Division. Something about needing more stockpiles. It was done without his knowledge."

"What the hell for? The war is here and now!"

"You know those bastards at Division. No rhyme or reason for what they do."

Koehl was exasperated. How could he do his job without petrol? What did the bastards at headquarters need it for? To warm their asses? He felt the anger burning through him.

"Well, damn them all. They tell me not to get killed out there, then rob me of what I need to survive." Koehl shrugged. "Well, we have to try." He turned to Schmidt. "Do we have enough petrol to get to the ambush site at least?"

The sergeant nodded. "Yes, sir, but that's about it. We'll be coasting in on vapors."

"Nothing to help it. Let's get rolling. Before we leave, let Hoepple know we won't get far once we get there. See if he can pull some fuel from somewhere, somehow."

"Yes, sir," said Schmidt doubtfully, and he turned, running this time, back toward the headquarters hotel.

Koehl turned and waved for his company's attention. "All right, folks!" he shouted, making his voice loud enough so all could hear. "We are heading out. I'll be in the lead. Keep your eyes and ears open. I don't know what we are heading into, but you can be sure it's going to be a lot. Maybe a whole division. We must get to the ambush site before Patton does. If we do, and if our brilliant strategists deem it wise to reinforce us, we will blow the bridge over the Main, wipe out their lead tanks, and stop them cold! Are you men ready for battle?"

The company roared in response. He raised his hand, pumping it in the air. He loved all of them. He looked from face to face, trying to burn their eyes into his memory. He did this frequently and always before a major engagement. He knew that, for some of them, this was the last time he would see them alive.

Koehl rumbled along, his head sticking out of the top of his tank destroyer as he rolled down the highway. He closed his eyes, letting the crisp March wind rush past his face. He looked out again to the horizon, to his left and his right. The woods and hills were so beautiful, fresh from the melted snow and with all the promise of spring. He loved the time before battle. Most people felt terror or a strange numbness when they knew they were heading into combat. Not Koehl. Perhaps it was the years of religious training, or the discipline. He knew death was but a step on a better journey. He loved the little moments when the end of life loomed near, when he could taste eternity.

They were already a half hour out of Hammelburg, rumbling along to the southwest at ten miles an hour. They were making excellent time. He didn't have updated intelligence on the enemy, but he sensed they were going to make it to the ambush in time.

Would it be in vain? He had no information on the infantry company or its precious explosives and engineers. If they failed to materialize, like the petrol this morning, all he could do was score a few hits on the lead Shermans before his force was overwhelmed by whatever the hell was coming down that road toward them. In that case, he was likely to be dead before noon. *Well*, he thought, smiling to himself, *in that situation at least I can avoid another meal of our awful field rations.*

He stepped down into the belly of the Ferdinand. Immediately an overwhelming stench of diesel and sweat assaulted him. Despite the smell, he drew a deep breath. This was the familiar comfort of war. He was safe here, among foul air and fair friends. He watched their progress from a slit and consulted his map again. He didn't really need to see where they were going. He'd long since memorized the route, but the map was as comforting as the confined space. Old habits sustained him.

Schmidt sat just below him to his left. He ran a cleaning rod down the end of his MP 38 submachine gun. The sergeant was a calm, cold killer with the short-range weapon. No matter that he couldn't sleep from the nightmares that tortured him. He did his duty.

Koehl placed both hands on the sergeant's shoulders. "You ready for this?"

"Sure, sir. I love getting shot at. Particularly when we're terribly outnumbered."

Koehl laughed. "Same as always, isn't it? We haven't had good odds since the early Russia days."

Schmidt smiled. "Ah yes, the Soviet Union in '41 and '42, streaming along the steppes with nothing to stop us. Those were the days. Too bad the damned communists got so serious at Stalingrad."

"Well, I'd rather be here now than on the Eastern Front."

"Who wouldn't? At least the Americans play by the rules. There are no good endings in Russia."

The *Hauptmann* stared out of the viewing slit. "How much farther up?"

"Ten minutes, I'd say."

"We going to beat them?"

Schmidt shrugged. "We'll find out soon enough. Sir, when

we're done with this, would you mind saying a Mass for some of the men? It's been weeks."

Koehl smiled, "I'd be happy to."

They rode along for a few minutes without talking. Koehl was mulling over the map in his mind, and the logistics of dealing with the bridge. Assuming the infantry showed up. Schmidt interrupted his thoughts.

"Town's coming up, sir."

Koehl strained his eyes and saw buildings in the distance. He lifted his radio. "All right, men, we are coming into the town. The bridge is on the far side. Look sharp; it's possible the Americans are already here. If so, it's going to get very hot, very quickly. If I spot any armor, I'll fire. If you hear a shot, begin a retrograde movement immediately, cannons ready. We'll back out of the town and get the hell out of here."

They rolled into the buildings. Koehl popped his head back out of the turret and looked around. He spied the occasional face in a window, but that was about it. There were no vehicles on the narrow streets or even pedestrians. He strained to hear the sound of enemy vehicles, but his own Ferdinand was so loud there was little chance of making out anything else. He felt the tension. A Sherman could be waiting around any of the narrow, winding corners. If there was one, the first he would know would be a shell crashing down on him, potentially killing them all in an instant.

He rounded another corner, and he could finally make out the river in the distance, along with the iron girders of the bridge. His eyes leapt to the far side, looking for men, tanks, anything. He saw nothing. He breathed in deeply, the relief washing over him. They'd made it. They could take defensive positions and prepare, no matter what happened with the infantry company and the engineers. The first part of his mission was a success: beating the Americans to the river.

They cleared the buildings and moved into an open area just

short of the bridge. A small park with an elegant lawn under the shade of some hardwood trees spread out for a hundred yards to the left and the right in front of the crossing. Koehl ordered his tank destroyer forward onto the grass. The treads ripped up the turf, flinging sod and soil behind them. He felt a flicker of sadness at wrecking such a pleasant scene, but he repressed the emotion and moved on with the solemn preparations for death.

Koehl climbed out of his Ferdinand. He drew his binoculars to his eyes and scanned the other side of the river, searching as far down the highway as he could see and into the adjacent countryside. There were no Americans in sight. He had a few minutes to set his men.

He leapt down to the ground and led individual tank destroyers to the positions he wanted them in. He placed one down each of the converging side streets, a few yards back from where the roads ended into the park. He then placed the two remaining Ferdinands behind the trees near the front of the park. He now had some cover for each of the vehicles, both as camouflage and to block some of the incoming shells. They were also spread far enough apart, at least thirty yards at the minimum, so that they would not take collateral damage if a stray round missed.

The preparation of his positions took scarcely five minutes. He checked his watch. The infantry still wasn't here. That was unfortunate. Without the equipment, he could not blow the bridge. Well, at least he would take a few Shermans with him, and if there was time, they might make a fighting retreat and escape. It was the most he could hope for. He had just finished making his dispositions when he heard the first sounds of engines in the distance.

He was surprised and delighted. The rumbling was not from American tanks, but rather a column of German vehicles rumbling up from behind him. His infantry company was here. The small convoy stopped behind one of the tank destroyers, and the engines sputtered to a stop. Men tumbled out of the trucks like so many industrious ants, and they passed him rapidly, spreading out among the Ferdinands and the trees, rifles already drawn and ready. A captain approached Koehl, saluting.

"Welcome."

"Thank you," said the captain. "What do we have coming in?"

"No idea, but plenty of whatever it is. Do you have any engineers with you?"

The man nodded. "A group, with explosives. Is that what you want us to take out?" he asked, nodding at the bridge.

"*Jawohl*," said Koehl. "Is there time?"

"I don't know. But let's find out." The captain turned and whistled. The men ran up, carrying satchels and charges. "That's the bridge," said the company commander. "The Americans will be here any minute. Get busy!"

The soldiers saluted as one and took off at a fast jog toward the bridge. In a matter of minutes, they were unloading charges and wires, and setting to work both above and below the bridge. Koehl scanned the highway again with his binoculars, expecting any moment that the Americans would appear. But so far, he was fortunate.

Fifteen minutes passed and then a half hour. The engineers climbed all over the bridge, a metallic anthill of activity. It seemed impossible, but minute by minute, they continued their work uninterrupted. Then, as quickly as they had started, they were scrambling away from the bridge, arms waving the signal that all was prepared.

Koehl pulled his binoculars up again. In the distance, he could see a column of green armor advancing toward them at rapid speed. They had finished just in time. He was elated. Everything had fallen into place. They were ready, and he was going to stop them cold right here at the river.

"*Hauptmann!*" He heard the shout from behind him. It was

Schmidt. He raised his hand for silence; he needed to get a fix on how big the force was.

"Sir, I need you." It was the strange quality of Schmidt's voice that pulled him away. He turned, and the sergeant was there, his face a mottled red, tears streaming from his eyes.

"What's wrong?" Koehl asked.

"I just heard from headquarters." Koehl was confused. He'd never seen the sergeant look like this before, except perhaps after a battle with terrible losses. A creeping fear washed over him like a rising tide.

"What is it, Sergeant?"

"It's Gerta."

Koehl felt his blood freeze. "What about her?"

"She's gone."

Chapter 9

Oflag XIII
Near Hammelburg, Germany
March 27, 1945, 0900 hours

Curtis stared at the hospital building in stunned silence. Lieutenant Colonel Waters held his arm tightly. He wasn't sure if the XO was holding him up or still restraining him. Perhaps it was both. The gunshots faded, and an eerie silence settled over the camp. Curtis didn't know how long he'd stood there now, waiting, praying, hoping for some miracle.

After an eternity, the doors to the infirmary swung open. Several soldiers came out first, men Curtis did not recognize. They were followed by Sergeant Knorr, who was coughing into a red handkerchief before he wadded the cloth up and shoved it in his pocket. He yawned and checked his watch, apparently making a great show of it. After a few moments, he looked up, staring directly at Curtis. Their eyes met and held. The sergeant's mouth curled into a cruel and knowing smile. He nodded slightly to Curtis and turned and walked away.

The captain felt the anger boil up inside him. The bastard did it! He'd killed Hanson and every other wounded man in the hospital. What was more, he'd wanted Curtis to know it. He'd relished it. The captain was surprised by the look. He'd had a run-in with the sergeant a few months ago, but that had seemed long past.

He remembered the first time he'd met Knorr. Curtis had arrived at the camp in the early winter. They were exhausted and disoriented. The Germans had shoved and prodded the POWs through the gates, screaming in clipped, barking language as they forced the prisoners into smaller groups and pushed them through the snow to form wretched lines for roll call.

Knorr was in charge of Curtis's group, and the captain was surprised to hear the German greet them in English.

"Greetings," he'd shouted out, a compassionate grin on his face. "I trust your trip here was pleasant."

There were murmurs from the men in line. Knorr's forehead creased in concern. "What happened?" he asked. "Please tell me. Any mistreatment must be immediately reported. You may have heard rumors to the contrary, perhaps even from your commanders, but I assure you they are nothing but lies. We strictly follow the Geneva Convention here. Any deviation from those rules must be reported immediately, and we will swiftly punish the perpetrators."

Nobody had answered.

Knorr looked around. "Please, comrades. Help us do our job."

"We've hardly had anything to eat for days," responded Curtis, deciding something had to be said. "They marched us hour after hour with no breaks and little water."

Knorr looked over at Curtis, shock registering on his face. "This cannot be true."

"I swear to it."

Knorr shook his head. "What is your name?"

"Captain Jim Curtis."

"Everyone else is dismissed to the barracks!" the sergeant

commanded. Knorr gestured to Curtis. "Come with me. The *Kommandant* will want to hear about this immediately."

Curtis followed the guard. His feet were frozen, and he struggled in his exhaustion to force one step in front of the other, but perhaps his luck was finally going to change. They had walked through most of the camp, and Knorr had turned toward a building near the hospital. The guard removed some keys from his pocket, whistling as he did so, and tried a number of them on a lock until he found one that opened the door. He stepped inside and flipped on the switch, gesturing for Curtis to follow him.

"Here's our waiting area," he explained.

Curtis had stepped in and looked around. He was surprised to find a small, bare room with a single light bulb. The space was barely six feet by six, with no furniture. He could feel a pinprick of fear on the back of his neck, but he realized there was nothing he could do.

"Just wait here for a few minutes, Captain. I'll be right back with our commander."

Curtis could still remember the slight twisting grin on the sergeant's face. The German closed the door behind him and locked it. He'd been gone only a few moments when the light flipped off, obviously from outside. Curtis fumbled in the blackness until he located the interior switch, but it would not turn the light back on. He shouted and beat on the door, but nobody answered. Finally, after several hours of futile resistance, he'd given up and slumped to the floor. He'd sat that way for God knew how long, with no water, no food, shivering in the cold. Days passed. The slightest crack in one wall near the ceiling helped him distinguish between night and day. The thirst burned his throat, the agony endless. He thought he could not take a moment more, but time crept relentlessly on. He was sure he would die.

The door opened, and Knorr was there. Curtis could barely

lift his head. The light turned on abruptly, and the captain blinked and groaned, fighting to see. Knorr had stepped up to Curtis, examining him closely.

"You're still alive, I see. I checked with the *Kommandant*, but he was not able to see you just yet. Would you like to continue to wait?" His voice was silky and full of innocence, as if he'd just left.

Curtis managed to shake his head.

"Well, then. I must assume you consider the matter closed." Knorr chuckled to himself before reaching down to drag Curtis from the floor and shove him sprawling out the door. As the captain tried to recover, the sergeant had upended a canteen of ice-cold water over Curtis, before he was half-dragged, half-carried to the barracks.

That was the captain's first experience with Knorr. Since that time, he had avoided the sergeant, although he had witnessed other prisoners suffer from his sadistic cruelty.

Months had passed since then. Curtis had hoped Knorr had forgotten him. But had he? Had the sergeant known about Hanson? Did he observe the daily visits to the hospital? Would Knorr actually lie in wait all these months just for another opportunity to toy with the captain? He felt the anger well up again, and he started toward the building, but Waters held him back.

"Let me go!" demanded the captain.

"Quiet now! Stop struggling!" Waters's whisper was a hiss. "They'll kill you!"

"I don't care anymore! I want them to!"

Waters spun him around, backhanding him even as he kept his grip. Curtis reeled from the sharp pain, and he tasted blood in his mouth. "Now listen to me, boy. You're going to knock it off right now! I haven't kept my eye on you all this time for you to just end up dead. You're going to shake it off, and we're going to walk away."

"I can't do it. I can't let them get away with it," Curtis said through gritted teeth. He spit blood on the frozen ground.

Waters refused to release his iron grip on Curtis's arm. "You can't save Hanson. He's already dead. Think, boy! What did we hear this morning? The army is almost here. You can't go and get yourself killed right now. In a few hours, we may be free. If the camp is liberated, what do you think is going to happen to that son of a bitch Knorr? We'll take care of him ourselves, or the army will. I'll make sure of it. But if you screw this up and do something stupid, you'll never see it happen."

Curtis closed his eyes, taking a deep breath. His mind spun with images of the bloody interior of the hospital, of Germans shooting and laughing amid the screams and agony of the dying prisoners. He willed himself to calm down. "You're right," he said. "There won't be any revenge if I'm dead."

Waters released his tight grip, but he didn't let go. The colonel's eyes softened. "You sure?"

Curtis nodded.

Waters released him. "Let's get the hell out of here then. I want to tell Goode and the others what just happened. Did you recognize any of the other men?"

He shook his head.

"They must have brought a special unit in for the dirty stuff. All except Knorr. That bastard would be up for anything."

"Sir. I can't do it anymore. I can't make it." Now that the anger had left him, Curtis felt the doubt and humiliation envelop him. The feeling was intensified by Hanson's murder in cold blood. He felt impotent, futile. After years of intense training and preparation for leadership in combat, everything had fallen apart in that foxhole at the Bulge. His confidence and pride died that day, and although Waters had restored a spark of his spirit, there was no flame.

"You're doing fine," said Waters. "You hold tight. We're hours away from this thing being over."

"And if they take us away?"

"Then it becomes days. Either way, this whole thing's about to collapse on top of these krauts, and God have mercy on them because I'll have none."

"Thank you, sir. Thank you for everything."

"No sweat. Now you've got to excuse me. I'm going to go collect the colonel. You get the hell out of here and head back to the barracks, you hear?"

Curtis shook Waters's hand, and the colonel turned, heading off toward the cluster of barracks. The captain watched him for a few moments and turned away.

"Captain Curtis," said a familiar voice, laced with a thick German accent. He felt his blood freeze. He turned slowly to face Sergeant Knorr.

"How are you today, *mein freund?*" asked the guard, his piercing blue eyes twinkling with sadistic mirth.

Curtis did not answer.

"I started the day out with a cloud over my head and a snuffle in my nose," said Knorr. "I decided I needed to check myself into the hospital for a little while. Then bang!" he said, slapping his hands together, "I suddenly felt so much better. Do you know what I mean?"

Curtis could feel his anger burning. He wanted to rush the sergeant and throw him to the ground, wrap his hands around his thin, long neck, and choke the life out of him. But he stopped himself. He knew he'd be dead the moment he touched him.

Knorr watched him closely. He pulled his handkerchief out and ran his fingers through it. "By the way, I saw your friend Hanson in there. You should check on him. He doesn't seem to be doing very well."

So he did know? The sergeant had waited months for this opportunity to take revenge on Curtis. He'd targeted other POWs along the way. Curtis remembered the last delivery of Red Cross parcels. Knorr had led the members of the International Red Cross through the camp, answering questions and playing the tour guide. After the delegation left, he had lined up all the prisoners, and while they watched, he'd stacked up the food into a large pile and set it on fire. He'd stood behind the conflagration, that same twisted grin on his face, watching with delight as the Americans groaned and swore in frustration.

Now he was apparently playing another of his games. Curtis was losing control. He took a step forward. Knorr braced himself, an ever-widening smile wrapping its way across his face. The captain held back. "You say what you want, Sergeant. You'll be captured or dead in a week."

The sergeant's face flushed red. He approached the captain, inches from his face. Curtis could feel his hot, fetid breath. "The war isn't over yet. The *Führer*'s miracle weapons will end it in victory for the Reich."

"Fat chance."

"Do you think your friends are coming for you?" the sergeant asked, his voice a whisper. "We will stop them."

"Like you've stopped them so far?"

Knorr lunged at Curtis, throwing him to the ground. The impact knocked the wind out of the captain, and he lay there for a few moments in agony. The sergeant stood over him. "Don't you worry; we will stop them. Besides, you'll all be long gone before they get here. The trains are coming for you, Curtis. You're going deep into Germany, where nobody will ever find you again."

"Even if they take us away, we'll be free in a week."

"Good luck with that, my friend," said Knorr menacingly. "They're shooting more than the wounded where we're sending you. You'll never see your friends again, or your home. You're going to die, Curtis, like your little coward friend Hanson."

Curtis didn't answer. He knew the sergeant was baiting him, trying to prod him into physical action that would lead to his death. He closed his eyes and rolled over into the fetal position, refusing to move or to acknowledge the sergeant.

"What do you have to say for yourself?" shouted Knorr.

Curtis refused to answer. There was a pause, then he felt exploding pain in his back as Knorr kicked him. He struck once, twice, then again and again. Curtis rolled over, groaning with the pain.

"That's a little taste of what's to come. I'll leave you to your fantasies for now. Unless you want me to escort you to the hospital?"

The sergeant's boots crunched on the hard ground as he walked away. He heard the laughter, and it filled his mouth with bitterness to mix with the blood already swimming there.

He lay there on the cold ground for long minutes. He was afraid to rise, worried that Knorr might return and pounce as soon as he showed any sign of recovery. After what seemed an eternity, he finally rose cautiously to his knees and turned his head slowly all around him, making sure the sergeant was gone. He didn't see the man anywhere. He breathed a sigh of relief that immediately sent sharp pains down his back and upper legs. He still felt the stabbing throb where the boot had kicked his back. He was worried he might have internal damage. No matter, he couldn't go to the hospital. That was certain death. He lifted himself to a squatting position, one knee still down, but the other foot on the ground. With a gagging groan of anguish, he drew himself up to a hunched, semi-standing position and shambled toward the nearby entrance to Goode's headquarters.

He reached the door and slowly pulled it open, leaning against the frame, trying to find an angle where the fire in his back didn't burn so deeply. He fell into the doorway and hit the wood floor hard, the blow sending flashing lights through the darkness of his mind.

"Hell, Curtis!" He heard Waters shouting. "What on earth happened to you?"

"Knorr," whispered Curtis, with clenched teeth. He felt close to passing out. There were hands on him in an instant.

"Where does it hurt?" asked Waters.

"My back. He kicked me over and over."

The colonel ran his hand down the captain's back, probing gently. He touched a spot, and Curtis screamed out in agony.

"Get a doctor," said Waters to someone else in the room, "and be quiet about it."

Curtis lay there for a while, Waters talking to him and holding his hand. The captain heard boots on the wooden floor and a new voice enter the room.

"What is it?"

"Curtis was badly beaten by Knorr. I need you to look at it."

The captain felt prodding again. He squirmed and called out again when the fiery pain grew too intense.

"He's got some bruised ribs," said the doctor. "Perhaps some damage to his kidneys as well. No way to tell for sure right now."

"What can we do about it?" asked Waters.

"He needs rest and watching. Let's get him to a cot, and I'll keep an eye on him. He will need to stay put for a few days."

Curtis heard Waters giving the order and felt hands on his shoulders and legs.

"Careful now," said the doctor. "We don't want to hurt him any more than he has been."

The captain was lifted as gently as possible. He screamed again as the slight twisting sent scorching fingers of pain up and down his back. He opened his eyes and saw Waters and the doctor above him, along with the lights and the bobbing of the ceiling. They moved him into a separate, smaller room. In a few moments, it was over, and he was lying down on a cot, a pillow under his head. Waters quickly brought him a blanket and tucked it around his feet and up to his chest. He smiled down at Curtis. "There you go, son. Now you just lie there and rest."

"But what about the liberation, the evacuation? I've got to get back to my boys."

"Don't worry about that now. I'll send someone else to deal with your barracks. If Patton gets here, we won't have a thing to worry about. If they evacuate us, well—"

"Well what?"

"We'll worry about that when we need to. Now get some rest."

Waters departed, leaving Curtis alone. The colonel turned the light off and closed the door. The captain lay in the darkness, a flicker of light poking through cracks in the rafters far above. The pain in his back was almost unbearable. He lay that way for a long time, the sound of murmured conversations in the next room too low for him to understand. Finally, he fell into a fitful, tortured sleep.

He was jolted awake by the lights and a loud voice. He tried to sit up before he remembered his injury and wrenched his back anew. He was trying to recover from the shock when he heard Waters's voice, thick with urgency.

"Curtis, wake up!"

"What is it?" he asked, the pain still throbbing through his back, his head groggy from his half sleep.

"They're taking us away. We have to line up for roll call. Word just came down to Goode."

Curtis shook his head. "I can't move. There's no way."

Waters bent down on one knee, his hand reaching out to grasp the captain's arm. "You have to. If you don't, they'll kill you where you lie."

"Maybe it doesn't matter anymore."

"Nonsense. Look at me, Captain!"

Curtis opened his eyes. Waters had leaned in now, and his face was close. "You're going to get off of this cot, and you're going to walk out that door. You'll stand good and straight for that roll call. I don't care how damned long it takes. And you're going to walk out of this camp with the rest of us and survive. You got that?"

Curtis nodded. He steeled himself against the agony and

reached his hand out for Waters. The colonel grasped his hand and slowly pulled him to a sitting position. Fire lanced his back. He shouted out again, but he ground his teeth and continued to pull himself up until he was standing. With Waters's help, he limped slowly out of the room and into the front of the headquarters building. A few other men were there, including Goode. They watched Curtis limping out with sympathy and fear in their eyes.

This was a joke. There was no way he could stand on his own. He was going to tumble over the second Waters let him go. He might as well just stay in bed and wait for Knorr to track him down. Even as these thoughts ripped through his mind, another part of him steeled himself and demanded that he continue, that he try to survive. He stared grimly at the other men as he stumbled past them. Goode came to attention and saluted. The other men, as one, did the same. Buttressed by this show of solidarity, he stumbled on.

By some miracle, he made it out of the front door and into the POW yard. He could make out the large cluster of men as they milled about, slowly putting themselves in position according to their barracks for the roll call. Curtis scanned the nearby German guards, trying to find Knorr, but he couldn't see the blond serpent anywhere. Perhaps he would be lucky, and the sergeant would be off duty or called away. If he was absent, Curtis knew he had a far better chance of surviving.

"You have to straighten up now," whispered Waters.

"I can't."

"If you don't, you'll be dead. Suck it up, Captain."

Curtis focused on his back. Slowly, with Waters's help, he drew himself upward. He gasped at the hot pain, but he kept pushing until he was standing more or less erect.

"Now walk with me. Not too fast. I'll help you."

The captain took one step, then another. Each movement was burning agony, but he kept going, moving toward the mass of men. His barracks was several hundred yards away. They would never make it that far, so Waters was leading him to the nearest group, trusting to luck that the Germans would not notice he was out of place and order him to the proper group. The journey took long minutes, and Curtis was sure with each step that he could not make another. Somehow, he managed to reach the lines of POWs, and Waters pulled him into place, explaining to the nearby men what was going on. Several of the taller kriegies moved quickly to surround Curtis, in front, back, and on each side, attempting to shield him from the prying eyes of the guards.

"All right, Curtis. I have to leave you," said Waters.

"Sir, I can't stand here for long by myself."

"You have to. Don't think about the pain. Think about getting out of here. Whether it's today or a few days from now, we are going to be free. You look at me, Curtis!" ordered Waters.

The captain stared into Waters's hard blue eyes.

"You will survive. That's an order."

Waters was a brave officer, and his resolve inspired the captain. "I will, sir. I'll find a way."

The colonel saluted him, his eyes maintaining a bridge for another moment before he hurried off. Curtis breathed deeply in and out, trying to force back the crippling sting in his back. He couldn't stand straight. His left shoulder was crooked, down a few inches lower than his right. Still, by concentrating and fighting back the pain, he was able to maintain his position.

Guards were walking up and down the rows now, counting out the men and checking the numbers against a clipboard. Curtis knew with mounting apprehension that the numbers in his group would not match up. There would be one too many, and then the Germans would scrutinize the men more carefully to figure out why. He turned his head to the left, scanning the long lines toward his barracks. He knew he would never make it there.

By some miracle, the krauts completed the count without any commotion. Perhaps the guards were just going through the motions. As the Germans, in line after line, completed their task, they seemed to lose interest in the POWs and grouped up, standing nearby, laughing and joking, enjoying cups of coffee while the kriegies continued to stand there, shivering in the freezing morning air.

Minutes turned to an hour. The Americans stood at attention, moment by agonizing moment, shaking in their inadequate clothing, waiting for the Germans to take them farther into captivity. For Curtis, the interval was unbearable. The pain mounted with each passing second, as fire burned up his back and down his legs. He was sure he would fall, crumpling in the dirt. He kept Waters's last words close. They were a cross he clung to in his agony.

Curtis saw a movement to his right. He glanced with his eyes and made out the *Kommandant*, General von Goeckel, stepping to the front accompanied by a few other officers and trailed by Sergeant Knorr. The general walked along the line of men, looking up and down the rows and chatting with his officers. Curtis could not make out what they were saying. Finally, he turned to address the POWs.

"*Guten tag!* I trust you've had a good morning," the general shouted in his thick accent. "I apologize for the wait, but our trains are running behind schedule. I've just been informed that they will be here within the hour. I will need you to be patient for just a little longer, and then we will walk to the station. The march will be several of your miles. If you believe you are unable to walk that far, please inform one of the guards, and alternative arrangements will be made for you. I will not be accompanying you to your new camp. I encourage you, as I have here, to follow orders, respect your guards, and we will all get through this together. As soon as the German victory is complete, you will be sent home. Until then, good luck and *auf wiedersehen!*"

The men murmured but did not protest. The guards would react violently and swiftly to any overt reaction. Curtis stood in shock. What was he going to do? He would never make it two miles to a train station. He was desperate. Perhaps he could group himself in the middle of many men, and a few of them could help him walk. He would have to talk to Waters.

"Herr Captain, I'm surprised to see you in line." Curtis recognized Knorr's silky voice immediately. The fear closed in around him. He turned to see the sergeant standing a few feet from him, an ironic grin laced across his face again.

"I'm fine," Curtis muttered.

"Oh, I'm sure you are, but I must make sure you are a suitable candidate for so arduous a journey as the train station. I'm sure you understand."

"I can make it," Curtis said through gritted teeth.

"Well, let's make sure, shall we? Come here, Captain."

Curtis, turned, limping through the men, holding himself as upright as possible, trying desperately to keep his face expressionless as he battled internally to push down the pain. He made it out of the line and over to the sergeant. "See, I'm able to walk."

"*Ach*, so. But this is just a little distance. I would worry if you had trouble on the longer march. Let's do some calisthenics to make sure you are fit." The sergeant tapped his cheek with his finger, as if giving the matter considerable thought. "I know, some deep knee bends should get us started. I'd like twenty. Now, Captain!"

Curtis knew there was nothing he could do to resist. He had to try. He kept Waters's words close in his mind. *I can do this*. He put his arms out, stared hard at the sergeant, and dipped his body down, bending his knees. The agony was crippling. He felt dizzy and thought he might fall over. Somehow, he pushed through the fire and pulled himself erect again. Struggling, he bent again, repeating the excruciating cycle.

The sergeant called out each with glee. "*Eins, zwei, drei . . .*"

Curtis continued, but twenty seemed impossible.

"No, no, Captain. That won't do," said Knorr, shaking his head in mock disapproval. "I need you to do a proper knee bend. All the way down. Let me show you." He stepped forward, placed both of his hands on the captain's shoulders, and shoved him down hard. Curtis tried to recover, pushing upward at the last minute, but he was too weak and there was too much pain. He felt the rippling agony tearing through his back; he tried to rise, but it was all too much. He toppled over, screaming in misery.

"Oh, no, *mein* Captain," said Knorr, leaning over him and shaking his head. "This simply won't do. I'm afraid you are not fit for this journey. How sad. I was cheering for you this whole time. I wish there was an alternative, but I'm afraid I have no choice." Knorr smiled, winking. He reached his right hand over and drew out his pistol, lowering it until it rested against Curtis's temple. "As the general said, *auf wiedersehen*, Captain."

Curtis closed his eyes, waiting for the darkness to come.

Chapter 10

"Hall, get up!" He heard the order and knew it was Stiller. He tried to rise, but his stomach still burned, and he hunched over again, retching on the grass. He could hear the screams and the pleading of the wounded girls just a few feet away from him.

"Damn it, Lieutenant! We don't have time for this bullshit! Now get your ass up and moving. We've got to go!"

"We have to help them," he muttered, wiping his mouth and spitting the remaining bile out.

"No time for that. We have to leave now."

"But they're dying. They're women."

"This is war, Hall. It's messy, bloody, awful shit. Now get your ass up, and let's get out of here!"

He felt the major's hands on the back of his shirt. Stiller jerked him, and the lieutenant allowed himself to be pulled to his feet. He turned around to face his commander's fierce features, etched in creases of stern countenance.

"Hall, I know that's some tough stuff down there. But you

got to remember, nobody knew it was full of women. Besides, the damned Nazis use females in their army." He pointed to the truck. "Look at their uniforms. Those are soldiers. Now I'd love to stop here and help them. Every part of what makes me a man wants to do that. But we can't, Hall. We're on a mission. We don't have the troops, and we don't have time to stall here. We've got to get moving. We're already late."

"What's the holdup?" asked Captain Baum. The task force leader had stepped down the incline and was standing with fists tucked against his sides, clearly impatient with the delay.

"Nothing," said Stiller. "The lieutenant needed a minute. He's ready now, though, right?"

Hall nodded, not able to answer. The major turned around and started up the hill. He had no choice but to follow him. His mind still reeled from what he'd just seen. He'd never dreamed of anything like it. He could still hear the moans as he moved away from the girls. That bastard Stiller. How could he have brought him along? The major knew it was going to be like this. He had set him up, and now he was reveling in the shock. Hall spat again on the ground, his eyes burning into his commander's back. No matter.

He climbed back into the jeep, and soon the column was on the move again. Hall turned back once, watching the smoke waft lazily up from the burning trucks. An explosion rocked one of the vehicles, the entire truck immolating into fire. He kept his eyes on the broken convoy until the task force rounded a bend and they were finally out of view.

Stiller was looking at a map he'd secured from Baum. The major took a few minutes to find their position as the jeep jarred along, bouncing the small chart up and down. "Only a few miles to go until we cross the Main," he said. "I hope those bastards left us a bridge. I don't feel like swimming today."

Hall didn't respond.

Stiller turned to face him. "Lieutenant, I need you to focus. I know that was a shock to you, but that's how this shit works. Now pull it together. Pick up that Thompson, and get it ready. We're a long way from getting out of this, and I can't have you staring out in a daze when the bullets start flying again."

Hall pulled his Thompson back into his lap. He tested the safety and made sure the weapon was ready. Focusing on something else helped slightly, and he started to feel himself coming out of the funk. His stomach still felt raw and twisted, but he breathed the air in deeply and tried to think of something else, anything.

"Another town coming up," said Stiller. "Look sharp, Hall."

They approached a cluster of buildings in the distance that was partially obstructed by a hill rising to their right. As they drew closer, Hall realized this wasn't a town at all, but rather a cluster of commercial structures, long, rectangular, and covered with corrugated sheet metal on the walls and the roof. He pulled his Thompson around to his right, preparing to spray the windows with fire if any enemies appeared. No threats emerged as they started passing the buildings.

When they cleared the hill, the entire complex came into view. Hall realized this was a train marshaling yard. Beyond the buildings were five sets of tracks, all narrowly clustered in front of the buildings before spreading out in ever-widening directions behind the hill they'd just passed. On the two nearest tracks sat engines, steam up, and trailing long lines of cars.

Even as Hall watched, he saw a massive explosion strike the closest engine. A moment later, the thunderous sound of cannons reverberated in his ears. One of the Shermans had fired on the train, scoring a direct hit. The air filled in an instant with chaos. Detonations sounded one after another as the whole line of tanks poured fire into the waiting trains. The yap of machine-gun fire added to the scream of metal. Hall could see a rifle flash here and there coming from the trains.

Now the buildings came to life as heads appeared at windows

and soldiers attempted to defend the train depot. Hall lifted his Thompson, taking a jouncing aim at the buildings and firing off a few bursts. He couldn't tell if he had hit anything, but the act of shooting steeled his courage. A door flew open, and a German burst through, an MP 38 at his hip, spraying bullets toward the convoy, impervious to or ignorant of the terrible violence awaiting him.

Bullets ricocheted off the hood of the jeep. Hall jerked his weapon and sprayed in the direction of this irritating gnat. To his surprise, he watched bullets tear across the German's chest. The body jerked back and forth for an instant, his weapon flung to the side; then he toppled backward, hitting the ground hard while his legs kicked up and down in a fit of agony. Behind him, the trains belched fire and rocked with explosions as the Shermans swiftly completed the destruction of the nearby trains.

The convoy rolled to a stop. Hall flew out of the jeep, swinging his Thompson into position. He kept his weapon aimed at the windows, but the enemy either were all dead or had retreated. He moved quickly forward and knelt next to the German, who still writhed back and forth. Angry holes gaped in his chest, covered with a mass of blood and fragments of uniform. The man's eyes were wide open, but he looked past Hall, consumed by pain and confusion. Hall tried to get the German's attention, but he was in his death throes, beyond him. He quickly scanned the German's waist, finding what he was hoping for. His hands scrambled for the man's belt, unsnapping a holster and removing a Walther 9mm pistol. The perfect souvenir. He stuffed the weapon into his jacket and was starting to turn away when he felt a lump. He pressed with his fingers and wrapped them around hard metal. He drew the object out and glanced down. He couldn't believe it. He'd found a flask. His heart throbbing with excitement, he quickly drew the object up and shoved it inside his jacket.

"Hall, what are you doing there?" Stiller was standing behind him. He turned, hoping the major hadn't seen what he'd done.

"I was checking on this soldier," he said. "And look, I found a pistol." Hall showed the weapon to the major.

Stiller stared for a moment, a flicker of disapproval running across the leathered features; then his shoulders gave the slightest of shrugs. "I guess it don't do no harm, you taking home a keepsake. But let's get going, boy. The whole convoy's about to move out."

Hall moved immediately, following the major. He felt the flask with his fingers, a smile creeping across his face. He stared at the back of Stiller as his commander tromped toward the jeep. *Take that, you, bastard*, he thought. He jumped into the vehicle next to his commander, all thoughts of dead girls behind him.

Task Force Baum started moving again, heading down the highway due east toward the Main River. Hall knew there was a bridge to cross there, and that this structure was critical to the mission. If they were unable to find a way across the Main, they would not be able to reach Hammelburg or the POW camp. Hall was of two minds about the bridge. He was fascinated by the mission, and the idea of blazing into a POW camp excited him, particularly for the prospects of credit the rescuers would receive. On the other hand, they'd already done enough. If they were blocked, they could head home, and certainly he would receive the commendation and promotion he richly deserved. That simpleton Stiller had said as much, and he'd played the game perfectly since they'd had that little talk. He smiled to himself. People could be so stupid. He liked the idea that he was playing this stern war veteran and Texas Ranger like a little puppet. He imagined moving his hands and dangling Stiller back and forth on strings. He couldn't stifle a chuckle.

"What's funny, Hall?"

"Nothing much, sir. Like you've told me, this war stuff is pretty terrible. I just figured if you can't laugh at it a little—"

Stiller put a hand on Hall's shoulder. "I understand. You've done good stuff out here, Hall. You've grown. You'll make a man yet."

I'm already three times the man you'll ever be, you ignorant piece of shit. He smiled ingratiatingly at the major. "Thank you, sir. That means a lot to me."

"You better reload your weapon. We're getting close to that bridge."

Hall nodded and reached into his satchel, removing another clip. He had three remaining, including the one he slammed into place. He picked up one of the grenades from between them, looking over the weapon. He'd practiced only a couple of times with dummies in basic training, but he decided he might want to brave one. He ran his hands over the pineapple-textured cylinder, his thumb resisting a momentary temptation to rip out the pin. He tucked the grenade into the front right pocket of his jacket, snapping it into place.

They rode along in silence for a half hour, the fields and trees passing them on both sides as they rolled along toward the river. They hadn't encountered any Germans since the train station, and they'd caught those krauts totally by surprise. Hall was starting to hope that the Germans this far back hadn't received notice of the raid. If that was true, they should be able to bust in and out of the camp before anyone was the wiser. He imagined arriving back at headquarters, a couple of POWs stuffed into the Jeep, newspaper reporters snapping pictures as he waved and smiled. Hell, that might be good enough for a Silver Star. Maybe it was better if the bridge was still up after all . . .

It looked like they were about to find out. Hall could see the outline of a city in the distance. He knew that Gemünden was the next town ahead and that the bridge was on the near side of town.

"There it is!" shouted Stiller, pointing excitedly. "It's still there!"

Hall followed the major's finger down the road. Straining his eyes past the Shermans, he could see the very top of some steel girders in the distance. The structure seemed intact. Hall felt his excitement rising. They were going to make it.

An eruption ripped down the column, nearly knocking Hall out of the jeep. A pillar of smoke belched into the sky. The task force ground to a halt. In the distance, the city vomited fire. Explosions rocked the column up and down the line. Bullets tore across armor, clanging loudly as the shells bounced off the steel and crackled into the air.

Hall froze, shocked by the sudden violence that poured over him. Their driver jerked, and his head snapped back. The sergeant's hands flew to his forehead, blood spilling down the digits.

"Hall, help me, damn it!" shouted Stiller. The major grabbed their driver and pulled him down over the other front seat, so he was laying down with his face up. The major jumped out and moved quickly around the front of the vehicle, and bent over, pulling back the soldier's hands so he could examine the wound.

"I need a cloth, Hall!"

The lieutenant ran his hands over his jacket, but he didn't have anything.

"Where's your aid kit?"

Hall hesitated for a moment. "I'm sorry sir, I forgot to bring it."

"Damn it! Go get one from somebody fast! I need it now! And find a medic!"

Hall stared at the inferno around him. Was Stiller out of his mind? He thought of refusing but knew that would be the end of his medal. He drew a deep breath and jumped out of the jeep, turning and sprinting back down the line of jeeps. He reached Baum's vehicle in a half-dozen heart-pounding seconds, and the captain looked up from directing the battle.

"What is it, Hall?"

"I need an aid kit, sir!"

Baum fumbled with his belt and pulled up his kit, handing it to the lieutenant.

"We need a medic too!"

Baum shook his head. "No time right now."

Hall rushed back toward the jeep. Bullets kicked up in the dirt, and he threw himself behind their vehicle, hitting the ground hard.

"Hall, I need that damn kit!"

The lieutenant closed his eyes. He was frozen with terror. He drew himself to his knees, then reached down and removed the flask from his shirt. Keeping it close to his chest, he quickly removed the cap and took a deep drink. He nearly choked on the liquid. He hadn't expected the sweet, cloying flavor of schnapps. Still, anything was welcome. He took another quick drink and then screwed the cap back on. Waiting a second more, he rushed around the jeep and up to Stiller, handing the kit to the major.

"Where's the medic?" his commander asked, already ripping open the box.

"Baum said there isn't time."

Stiller grunted and turned to the soldier. He drew a smaller white box out of the package and pulled the little ribbon on the end, ripping the container open and pulling out a field bandage. He immediately pressed it against the wound, trying to clear enough blood to see what had happened. Hall watched over the major's shoulder. The driver's forehead belched a fountain of scarlet liquid. The soldier rocked back and forth, moaning from the pain.

"Stay still, son," said the major. "I'm trying to see what the hell is going on here." Stiller finally cleared away enough of the blood. "I've got good news for you. Looks like it just grazed the skin. Probably bounced off something first. You're going to feel like hell for a few days, but you're going to be okay, son. Now listen up. I don't know what I'm doing. I'm going to bandage you up and give you some morphine. We'll put you in the back, and Hall and I will jump in the front. As soon as we can get you a proper look-over, we'll do it. Do you understand me?"

The soldier nodded, his eyes closed and his teeth gnashing from the pain.

"Okay, good. Hall, get over here and give me a hand."

The major seemed impervious to the explosions and bullets flying all around him. He was obviously too stupid to feel fear. Hall stepped forward, hunched over as much as possible. He took Stiller's position on the left side of the driver, while the major stepped around to the right, exposing his back to the incoming fire. Stiller placed a large bandage over the soldier's forehead, then held it in place with one hand while he taped it down with the other. When he was finished, he removed a morphine syringe and jabbed it into the driver's arm. A few seconds later, the soldier went limp. "I sure hope I did that right. Haven't had any cause to use one of these before."

Stiller reached down and ran his hands under the soldier, nodding at Hall to do the same. In one motion they lifted, pulling the sergeant to their chests. The man was dead weight. They pulled him out of the jeep and then stepped backward, feeding him into the back seat. Every moment, Hall expected to be hit by gunfire.

"Okay, Hall, jump in!"

The lieutenant headed around the back of the jeep to the driver's side, but Stiller waved him off. "I'll steer. You need to use that Thompson!"

Hall ran back around and jumped into the passenger seat. He reached back and grabbed his weapon, prying the ammunition satchel out from underneath the wounded driver. He turned back around while Stiller put the jeep into gear, edging it closer to the Sherman directly in front of them.

Captain Baum materialized next to Stiller. He had his pistol out, and he was trailed by two GIs in close support. "I need you both to help with covering fire. Leave the jeep!"

"You heard him, Hall. Let's go!"

The lieutenant hesitated. Now that they were in the shadow of the tank, he felt a little safer. He didn't want to go back out there. There was nothing he could do; he steeled himself and jumped out, carting his Thompson with him, and followed the major as he tried to keep up with the brisk strides of the task force commander.

The small group walked along the line of Shermans. The tanks were actively engaged, firing their cannons at the buildings on both sides of the river. Machine-gun fire sprayed out of the front of the armored behemoths. Baum kept low, darting from tank to tank, heading toward the front of the column. Bullets whizzed and ricocheted all around them. One of the GIs in close support of the captain was hit, toppling backward with a bullet to the chest. Baum kept moving, ignoring the wounded soldier. Hall looked back as they passed. A comrade was already rushing to the soldier's side.

They finally reached the front of the column. The lead tank was a smoking husk. Hall could smell the sickening aroma of burned flesh. He felt his stomach wrenching again, but he somehow gagged down the bile and kept his place behind Stiller. Baum knelt on the side of the Sherman, using the tread as cover. He pulled out a set of binoculars and scanned the bridge and the houses on the other side of the river. He turned, waving behind him. Lieutenants Nutto and Weaver raced up, pulling in behind Hall and squatting down behind a Sherman.

"Okay, here's the deal," said Baum. "That bridge is still operational, but I don't know for how long. We've got a batch of resistance up there. A company maybe of infantry and some anti-tank cannon. I'm not sure if it's armor or what. I can't see a damn thing."

"What are we going to do about it?" asked Nutto.

"Same thing as at Schweinheim. We roll right the hell through it."

Nutto nodded, although Hall thought he could see doubt in the lieutenant's face.

"We're going to push this Sherman out of the way," explained Baum. "Then I want the tanks to go across, guns blazing. I'll bring up a platoon of infantry for close support. Let's get a tank across with the infantry and form a little bridgehead. When we see what reacts, then we hit them hard and roll across with everything we've got."

"Yes, sir," said Nutto, wiping the dirt from his face. "I'll go over first."

"Negative," said Baum. "Can't risk it. Send one of the boys."

Nutto shook his head. "I want to lead it, sir. That's a hell of a gamble. I'd rather go myself."

"I said no," retorted Baum, a hint of steel in his voice. "I told you, it's somebody else. Now make the orders and let's go."

Baum moved back a few yards and found cover behind a copse of trees near the road. Stiller and Hall joined him to watch the attack unfold. The firing seemed lighter from there, and Hall wasn't sure if that was because they were out of the line of fire or if the German resistance was beginning to break.

As he watched, the Shermans ground forward. The second tank rolled slowly until it bumped into the lead. Then the driver gunned it. The treads rumbled over the pavement and dirt, kicking up a storm of rock and concrete behind it. The lead tank remained in place for a moment and then rolled forward and slightly to the right. The two vehicles moved together for a few yards before the lead tank rumbled off the side of the road and out of the way. The new lead Sherman stormed on, firing from its cannon even as a platoon of infantry sprinted past Hall, spreading out and firing as they went.

The Sherman surged toward the bridge, picking up speed and leaving the infantry behind. A soldier fell and then another, hit by the fire from across the river. The tank made it to the bridge and started across, slowing now so that the infantry could catch up. The first dozen men reached the bridge and stormed on, catching up to the rear of the advancing Sherman.

The bridge evaporated in an instantaneous pillar of fire. The force of the explosion threw the infantry still on the shore back like rag dolls, flinging them high in the air. Hall watched in horror as the bodies shot through the sky before raining down hard to the ground a hundred yards or more from the river. The Sherman and everyone on the structure when it blew were vaporized. The steel structure screamed as it bent and bristled, plunging in a shrieking rip and tear of metal into the waiting water below. The Main belched up a frothy chaotic hiss of steam that sent circlets of waves out from the crash. The water churned and coughed for a few angry moments before resuming its current as if nothing had ever happened.

"Shit!" shouted Baum. He removed his helmet and threw it to the ground. "Sons of bitches blew my bridge. Killed a bunch of my boys, too!"

"What are we going to do now?" asked Stiller.

Baum looked up through his grief. He narrowed his eyes. "Not much to do, Major. This is the only way over the damned river. I don't have bridging equipment."

"There has to be another way."

"I had intelligence up and down this river. This is it. We have to turn around."

"We can't!" said Stiller, his voice agitated. "There's got to be another option." Hall was surprised by the vehemence in the major's statement.

Baum shook his head again. "Can't be done, Major. Now I

don't have time for a long discussion. I've got two tanks down already and a batch of men. All dead for this foolish damned mission. So, if you'll excuse me, I need to attend to my boys. I suggest you make your way back to the jeep, and let's get the hell out of here."

The captain started to leave, but Stiller grabbed his arm, holding him back. Baum turned sharply, his eyes flashing a dangerous anger. "What the hell are you doing, Major? Get your hands off me!"

"I can't. We've got to go on. We can't return empty-handed."

"What do you mean, Stiller?"

"Patton's son-in-law is in that camp."

Hall was frozen with surprise, and so, clearly, was the captain.

Baum stared at Stiller for a moment, his lip twitching. "Christ, is that what this is all about then?"

"That's right," said Stiller. "And we can't come back with nothing but our dicks in our hands. We've got to go on, and we've got to grab him. No other choice."

Baum looked at Stiller for a moment, shaking his head and whistling. He stared at the river, then looked the other way at his battered column. He shook his head. "All right, Stiller. We'll see what we can do up north." He pointed a finger at the major. "But everything from here on out is on you. You and that son of a bitch general of yours."

The captain turned and scrambled off, starting to shout orders. Stiller turned to Hall, as if realizing all at once that the lieutenant was there as well. "Now listen here, Hall. That's a secret between you, me, and the captain. You're gonna carry that one to the grave. Do you understand?"

Hall nodded, too stunned to answer out loud. He stared out at all the dead men, the burning vehicles. *That bastard sent us all in to die, just to save his daughter's husband. If I get a chance, I'll make him pay too.* The lieutenant spat and turned to follow Stiller back toward the convoy.

As he moved, a steel cylinder ripped past him and crashed into the ground at Baum's feet. The metal exploded, knocking the captain and Lieutenant Nutto to the ground. Hall stared in horror. Neither of them moved.

Chapter 11

Gemünden, Germany
March 27, 1945, 1000 hours

Koehl sat on the pavement with his face buried in his hands. Hot tears seeped through his fingers and ran down his arms. She was dead. Gone in an instant, like so many thousands he'd watch disappear in the past six years. But this was his flesh and blood. He'd tried to protect her. She'd refused him, but he could have forced her. Why hadn't he gone after her? Required that she leave with him for headquarters immediately? With all his experience of the unexpected tragedy of war, why had he allowed himself to be lulled into a false sense that she would be safe for a day or two without him?

"*Hauptmann.*" He heard Schmidt's voice, a distant echo through the fog of his grief.

"Leave me alone," he sputtered in response.

"I cannot, sir. I'm so sorry. You know I'd never willingly violate your grief, but right now I don't have a choice. The Americans are coming. They've been spotted in the distance. We need your attention to this."

A burning flame of anger tore through his sorrow. The Americans were here. The ones who killed his sister. His fury tore him from his grief. "How many are there?" he asked, the torrent of his anguish swirling around him.

"New intelligence from our spotter planes suggests it's a modest force," said Schmidt. "It's a raid, not a general attack. Figure five hundred or less."

Five hundred. The number rang through his mind. A force that size was more than he could handle, unless he hit them just right. It was a long shot, but he might pull it off with some luck. He would need to let them cross the river in force if he were to have any chance of wiping them out. Hit them a little to draw them in, then let the armor cross and blow the bridge after everything was on this side. In the narrow streets of Gemünden, his company and the six tank destroyers would have the force surrounded and bunched up in a tight space where each round would do massive damage. *His own Cannae.* He didn't want to delay the Americans any longer. He wanted to destroy them, every last one. His mind whirled through the details as he adjusted to this new possibility.

What about the colonel? His instructions were specific. Koehl was to delay the enemy force and blow the bridge. Everything was prepared already. Could he ignore his commander's express order? He made his decision.

"New plan, Schmidt. I want you to find those engineers. Tell them to wait until the column is across the bridge. We will hit them with some light fire when they come into range, then draw them over. Once they reach the park, we'll blow the bridge and wipe all of them out." Koehl delivered the command with a shaking voice dragged raggedly over the coals of his sorrow.

Schmidt's eyes widened in disbelief, and he took a step back as if struck physically by the order. He shook his head, and his voice was measured, quiet, almost pleading. "Sir, there are way too many of them. Shouldn't we just blow the bridge and take a few of them out? Wasn't that what the colonel asked us to do? We can turn them around here or keep them at bay with long-distance shots." He took a step forward, his eyes full of under-standing. "Don't you worry, sir. It won't be long before the colonel can pull in more reinforcements. That will be the time to hit them hard. We will make them pay for what they did to Gerta."

"You heard me!" snapped Koehl. The sergeant flinched. He came to attention, saluted, and stomped away. Koehl felt a tinge of guilt. He couldn't remember the last time he'd chastised Schmidt. They'd been through so much together. He was al-most family himself. Almost.

A few minutes passed. Koehl watched the approaching Amer-ican column through his field glasses. Around him, he heard the muffled scurrying of men and equipment, as his force hastened to move into position in time to ambush the enemy formation. He relished the preparation for combat, the tense minutes before the attack that kept the haunting churn of emotions about his sister at bay for at least a little while. Schmidt eventually re-turned. "Everything is ready, *Hauptmann*." The sergeant's voice was flat, tinged with disapproval. Koehl ignored the im-plied reproach.

"Excellent. Hit them with small-arms fire early. But nothing too much."

"They'll know we're here, sir," protested the sergeant.

"I want them to. We need to draw them in if we are going to get the whole force across the river."

The sergeant shook his head. "I wish you'd reconsider. I've rarely questioned your judgment, sir, but I'm worried you're not thinking clearly. Not that I blame you. Look out there," said Schmidt, pointing to the advancing column. "We're going to take some licks before they get over. They've got a batch of

Shermans out front. If we're not careful, it's going to get out of control fast."

"Take the lead out. That will confuse their fire. They will have to regroup, then they'll storm across all at one time."

Schmidt nodded. He turned to the nearby Ferdinand and shouted instructions to the commander. Koehl kept his eyes on the enemy force. The lead tanks were just a few hundred yards from the bridge now. "Hit them!" he yelled.

The town around them exploded in fire. Koehl winced, embracing the concussive force and struggling to lift his glasses again, straining to see the effect of the attack through the smoke and fire erupting across the Main. Small-arms fire sparked and sputtered on the enemy armor. As he watched, the lead enemy tank turret turned slowly to the left, an irritated monster searching for the insect that annoyed it. The Sherman never struck back. An 88mm shell struck the tank near the seam between the turret and the base. The tank bounced and shuddered. Fire and smoke belched out of the interior as the vehicle ground slowly to a halt. Behind it, men scurried for cover.

Koehl watched with growing excitement. The Americans moved across the far side of the river like pieces on a chessboard. The plan was evolving exactly as Koehl had foreseen. The trap was set; now to spring it.

"Keep up the fire!" shouted Koehl. "But no more cannons! I don't want to pin them down on the other side!" To his left and right, the *Hauptmann* heard his commands followed faithfully by his men. The Ferdinands slacked off, instead adding their machine-gun fire to the infantry attack on the Americans. The enemy was immobile now, preparing its next move, a spring set to violently snap. Koehl just hoped the commander was aggressive enough to storm the bridge. If he waited for reinforcements, they would accomplish nothing, and he would have brought death down on his unit. He had to destroy this force.

He wanted it more than anything he'd ever desired in battle. He willed the American commander to strike them.

He thought of his sister for a moment. He remembered the day he'd left for the war. She'd been a girl then, scarcely twelve. He'd taken her for a pastry and explained why he had to depart from her and their parents. She'd cried, begging him to stay. He'd smiled, wiping away her tears. She'd asked him to pray to God that he would be spared, that he would come home to her. He'd done so, holding her hand, both on their knees. He'd never thought of praying for her life as well . . .

Now he imagined her dead somewhere in a field. A disturbing image rocked his mind. He saw her blond hair amid the wreckage of a smoldering vehicle. One body among many. He smelled the blood and heard the cries of pain. He shook his head, the grief threatening to overwhelm him again. He forced himself to return his attention to the battle.

A Sherman rumbled forward, driving the burning husk of the lead tank out of the way. American infantry shadowed the armored hulk, scrambling ahead like so many green ants. The enemy vehicle fired. A shell ripped into a building to Koehl's left. The American infantry were alternating in small groups, with a few men firing while others darted forward from cover to cover. These were veterans, Koehl noted. The new men always came on in a rush. All balls and no brains, but the experienced ones were cautious and lethal.

The Sherman advanced on to the first part of the bridge, a dozen GIs following close behind. They were going to establish a bridgehead, Koehl realized, a tight smile on his face. The enemy commander was skilled, but he was acting according to the book, and his actions drew his men into the *Hauptmann*'s carefully orchestrated trap.

"Schmidt, it's working!" he shouted, clapping the sergeant on the back. The sergeant smiled grimly in return, his shoulders hunched, and his head braced against the shrapnel and the stray bullets whizzing around them. "Make sure the Sherman makes it!" yelled Koehl excitedly. "I want everyone to pull back fifty yards. We need to give them some room. If we wipe this group out, the rest won't follow!"

The sergeant moved out, giving orders on the run and gesturing violently backward. The first Ferdinand ignited its engine and reversed, backing slowly down the street. As Koehl watched, the others followed, deepening the trap, giving the Americans room to maneuver on this side of the Main. The captain was playing a dangerous game. He remembered Schmidt's words, which seemed now to echo with vivid colors in his mind. If he misjudged the enemy force, he would have more than he could handle on this side of the river. If he failed, he would have to explain to his commander why he had disobeyed orders and allowed a powerful American force over the bridge without resisting them. Assuming they even survived such a mistake. He thought about it for a moment. He didn't care. He wanted to destroy them all. Besides, he knew what he was doing. He'd faced worse odds before on the frozen plains of Russia . . .

The Sherman crawled along the structure. The advance squad of infantry followed tightly behind. He could see the helmets bobbing here and there behind the grinding treads. A bullet ricocheted near him. Koehl jerked his head down, shaking it. He had to be more careful. The tank kept moving, now three-quarters of the way across. He turned his binoculars back to the shore, hoping the other vehicles were starting to move forward. He felt a surge of adrenaline. The plan was working. They were coming.

An enormous eruption shook the ground around him, nearly knocking him over. He jerked his field glasses to the left and dropped them in shock. The bridge was a mass of fire and smoke. At first, he thought the Americans must have blown it. Why would they kill their own men? With horror and rising anger, he realized one of the idiot engineers must have done it.

The fool had disobeyed his orders. He picked up the binoculars again, scanning the span, praying the damage was incomplete, that the Americans could somehow still make it across. Even as he watched, a huge section of the roadway spilled downward into the Main, followed by a tumbling girder from above. Finally, with one fluid motion, the entire mass of the bridge dropped into the river, churning and coughing before it disappeared.

Koehl gawked in amazement. How could his orders have been ignored? He stood in silence as the echoes of battle faded and the Americans slowly withdrew. He'd accomplished his mission, at least the one assigned by the colonel, but he tasted bitter ashes in his mouth. He wanted to make this American force pay in full for the death of his sister. Now, because of the stupidity of one of the engineers, he was losing his chance for vengeance. The stony silence continued, as tears of frustration ran freely down his face.

He had failed, but he was damned if he was going to let this go unpunished. He stormed forward toward the bridge, seeking out the engineers who hid among the bushes and trees of the park. He drew his pistol. He would show this bastard for ruining his plan. He felt a tug at his conscience even as his fury raged through him. He was a man of God, trained in the cloth. *Not anymore*, he whispered to himself.

He was halfway across the park. Jumbled steel smoked and crackled on both sides of the river. The remaining portions of the bridge, he realized. He glanced across the Main at the fleeing Americans. The column was nearly out of sight. They'd moved quickly for a thousand, he thought. Perhaps their intelligence was wrong. Not that it mattered anymore.

He saw a flash across the water and looked up in surprise. A single Sherman had remained behind, nestled in some trees on the side of the road. He braced himself for the incoming shell. An explosion rocked the park nearby. He felt the concussive blow from the detonation even as his legs were swept from beneath him. His ears rang, and he felt the tearing scrape of metal ripping across his chest and face. He hit the ground hard. He felt his heart tearing at his chest. He breathed fire and gunpowder. The sky above him hoved to and fro in a circular daze. He closed his eyes, and the blackness overwhelmed him.

Chapter 12

Hall stared in horror at Nutto and Baum. Stiller tore forward, rushing to their side. Hall growled for a medic even as the major set to work on the two commanders. Hall stood frozen, unable to move, watching the scene unfold. His mind was in a daze. The attack had materialized out of nowhere. *It could have been me.*

A medic and several infantry men rushed to the scene. The soldiers huddled over the commanders. Hall saw with relief that both men were moving—legs and arms rocking in pain. They were alive at least. But could Baum still lead the task force?

As he watched the medic work away on the wounded, his mind reeled. Patton's son-in-law was in the camp. What the hell? The bastard had sent three hundred of them on a secret, personal mission to save a family member. Hall whistled softly to himself. There were a half-dozen dead already and a lot more than that wounded. For what? To rescue one man? Patton had to be out of his mind. If word leaked out about this, Hall was sure the general's career would be over. He'd been in enough trouble with the brass already.

The medic finished his work on Baum and Nutto. Both men were able, with assistance, to get up and move around. Nutto was the more seriously wounded, with multiple bandages on his chest and stomach. Miraculously, both men were heading back to their vehicles and apparently proceeding with the mission. Nutto needed the assistance of a GI to help him walk. What was wrong with these people? Hall wondered. Were they out of their minds?

Within a few minutes, they were all back in position, and the task force was pulling out. A quarter hour later, they'd left Gemünden behind them, heading north. Hall sat silently next to Major Stiller as his commander drove the jouncing jeep along narrow, curving roads. The Main was to their right, poking in and out of view among the heavily forested banks. The task force was crawling along the constricted road. They had no idea where they were headed. The mission was likely a failure with the loss of the bridge at Gemünden. Hall knew they should be turning back now. The Germans were on to them, and there was no plan now except to try to find a bridge that was still intact across the Main. A slim chance. They should be heading back to American lines while there was still a possibility of making it.

Instead, they were pushing forward. Thanks to Stiller and Patton. Hall turned his head and spat. He was disgusted. Men dead, equipment destroyed. Worst of all, his life was in danger with this ridiculous mission to rescue Patton's son-in-law. What if he was wounded or killed? Over this?

"Sir, shouldn't we reconsider?"

"What do you mean, Hall?" asked the major, keeping his eyes on the road and the Sherman just ahead of him.

"I understand how important this is to Patton, but we don't have a way across the river now. There's no way he foresaw that before he ordered us in. Shouldn't we turn around and get out of here while we still can?"

Stiller shook his head. "No chance. You don't really know Patton, do you?"

"Not really, no."

"He doesn't take failure as an option. If we returned now, he might well court-martial the lot of us."

"There's no way he'd do anything to you. You've been friends for years."

"Like I said, Hall, there's no chance. Only thing we can do is keep rolling along this river until we find a way over. If Patton calls us back, that's one thing, but unless we hear from him, we're liberating that camp, or we die trying."

Hall didn't respond. He wracked his brain for any way out of the situation. There was none. He was miles behind enemy lines, and the major was watching him like a hawk. He had to hope that there was no way over the Main and the task force eventually turned back. There was every chance that would be the case. The Germans had left very few bridges over any of their defensive rivers. They'd been lucky to get to Gemünden with that structure still intact. He leaned back and closed his eyes, praying for a miracle. The old Hall luck had never failed him yet. Whether it was a suspicious professor or the angry parents of some college girl, he'd always found his way out of trouble. He'd find a path out of this mess too. He ran his fingers over the flask hidden inside his jacket. He wanted another drink desperately. He should have snuck one during the fighting at Gemünden, but he hadn't thought about it. Damn this bastard Stiller. Sitting there smug in the driver's seat.

The Sherman ahead ground to a halt. Stiller pulled the jeep over but left the vehicle idling. "Stay here, Hall," he ordered. "I'm going to find out what's going on." The major jumped out of the jeep and headed back toward Baum's command vehicle.

Hall wasted no time. Taking a quick look around to make sure nobody was watching, he drew the flask out of his pocket and unscrewed the top. He tipped the metal back and took a deep drink, gulping down about half the remaining schnapps with a few intense swallows. He almost coughed as the fiery liquid burned his throat, but he held it down and quickly returned the flask to his pocket. He breathed deeply, relaxing, enjoying the sensation. He felt the excitement rush through him too. He was thumbing his nose at Stiller. He relished the feeling of deceit and the control it gave him over the witless simpleton of a major. A few minutes passed before his commander returned.

"What's going on?" Hall asked, assuming a cheerful mien.

"Baum grabbed a prisoner. Some paratrooper out here all by himself. Bet you anything he's a deserter."

"So what?"

"So," said Stiller, his voice tense with irritation, "he's a local. He knows the area. He told Baum there could be a bridge a few miles north. If it's still there."

"How can we trust him?"

"Do we really have a choice? It's that or continue to grope along blindly until the Germans finally catch up to us."

Hall heard a buzzing overhead. He looked up and saw the same German plane as before, slowly passing the length of the column before turning off east. He felt his skin crawl. "What if he's just helping that guy?" he said, nodding off toward the aircraft.

"I doubt it. That pilot don't need anyone on the ground to tell him where we are. I wouldn't have believed a German would desert a few months ago, but we've seen plenty of 'em lately. I think we can probably trust him."

Baum walked up to the jeep just then. His face showed signs of fatigue, a leaf's vein of lines scrawled across his forehead and temples. He limped slightly, and his jaw flickered in apparent pain as he came to a halt in front of them.

Stiller nodded to the captain. "Learn anything?"

"Yep. If it's true. The kraut says there's a good bridge just up a ways, and a highway leading right to Hammelburg from there. If he's telling the truth, and it's still there, he said we'd be there shortly. What's more, he knows where the Oflag is. He verified it's the former barracks just southeast of the town."

"He know anything about likely resistance?" asked Hall.

"Nah. He hasn't been back here in a while. Just ran off a few weeks ago, and he's been making his way home. Lucky we picked him up."

"What if he's lying?" asked Hall.

"I don't see why he would. If he is, he's going to get a bullet in the brain. I told him as much. We're only a half hour or so from where he said the bridge is. I don't think he'd gamble with his life when we'll know the truth of it in a jiffy."

Stiller grunted. "Good point. When we moving out?"

"Ten or less. The poor sap was practically starving. I gave him some grub so he stays alert, at least until we get to the bridge."

"What are you going to do with him after?" asked Hall.

"We'll hold on to him until we get to the Oflag. If he's been honest, I'll let him go. If not," Baum made a pistol shape with his fingers. "Anyway, sit tight, and we'll be out of here in a few."

Stiller nodded, and Baum went up the line to give orders to the Shermans out front. Hall returned his direction to the sky, but the German reconnaissance plane was nowhere to be seen. "How long you figure before he comes back with some friends?" the lieutenant asked.

Stiller shrugged. "No way to know. This whole thing went to hell in a handbasket when the bridge blew. But Baum knows what he's about. If we can find a way across, I'll bet you we make the Oflag in a couple hours."

"Then what?"

The major scowled, spitting brown liquid on the ground. "Then we see."

The column rumbled back into movement, faster this time

with the apparent guidance of the German paratrooper. Hall was surprised the Shermans would move so quickly on such narrow roads, with the right-hand side jutting precariously downward a hundred yards or more to the river. At times, the tank in front of them was a mere foot away from the edge. If it tumbled over, everyone inside would assuredly be drowned if they weren't killed by the impact of the fall.

The minutes rolled by. Hall felt relaxed with the schnapps coursing through his body. His toes and fingers were warmed, and he was calm. He understood why most of the armies and navies in world history had kept their men half-drunk most of the time in combat. He thought it a stupid decision to take the daily ration away, as most had done in the nineteenth century.

In the distance to his right, Hall thought he could make out the sharp, bony outline of iron through the trees. He strained his eyes, and after a few moments, he was sure. His heart trembled. A bridge. The damned paratrooper was telling the truth. There was an intact span over the Main.

"Hall, do you see that?" shouted Stiller, nearly coming out of his seat in elation. "A bridge. Damn it, if that kraut wasn't right. He's the hero of this whole expedition." Stiller laughed. "If we make it through this thing, hell, I'll recommend him for a Bronze Star!"

Hall nodded without response. Stiller might be thrilled they were going, but the lieutenant was far from it. They were turning away east now, heading directly in the direction that German plane was heading. There wasn't a damned thing he could do about it but hang on and hope for the best.

In twenty minutes, Task Force Baum completed their traverse of the Main River. The bridge was undefended and intact. The structure was narrow and a little rickety, requiring the armored vehicles to pass one at a time. Hall could scarcely breathe when they crossed, but the structure served its purpose

well, and soon the column was back on the road to Hammelburg.

They passed a small town just after the bridge. Hall kept his
weapon trained on the windows of the little gingerbread houses,
but there were no shots. There weren't even attempts at surrender.
The Americans must have caught the village totally unawares.
The citizens hadn't even had the time to react to the violent
green monsters grinding past their homes. They were blissfully
unaware of the danger. For them, Hall thought, the war was
nearly over. Unlike Spokane, though, and the rest of victorious
America, what would peace look like in Germany? He thought
of the women. The older girls and the young widows. How
desperate they would be. Begging for favors. They would do
anything for a little chocolate or some cigarettes. Perhaps he
should delay his return home for a few months after all . . .

Stiller rode along silently next to him. Hall wondered what
thoughts, if any, went through the simpleton's head. He's probably humming "The Star-Spangled Banner" to himself. Or perhaps "The Yellow Rose of Texas." What would it be like to live
your life like that? A loyal, hardworking sap. Content to lick
the boots of his betters. Hall could taste the bile in his throat.
What a repugnant thought. His father had taught him to look
beyond all of that, to watch each person and every moment.
Look for their weaknesses, their hopes, addictions, dreams.
Then file all of that away and wait like one of the rattlesnakes
they had come across now and again on their hikes near Mount
Spokane. Lie in wait, coiled, and at the right moment, strike,
your bite a pinprick of pain, but deadly.

For all his simplicity, Stiller had been a conundrum for Hall
from the start. He wasn't subject to the kind of flattery and attention that most women and men responded so well to. He
couldn't be persuaded or bought. Hall had had the feeling from
the very first day that despite Stiller's dim-wittedness, he could
read the lieutenant like a book. But now finally he had the

major where he wanted him. He'd shown the bastard that he could handle himself in combat. But there was more fighting ahead.

That thought reignited his anxieties. He decided to engage Stiller in some conversation, both to assuage his fears and to answer his apprehensions directly. He already wanted another drink of the schnapps, but he knew he would have to wait for that.

"Sir, I have a question for you."

"Shoot, kid."

I'm not your kid. "What is actually going to happen when we reach the camp?"

"What do you mean?" Stiller looked over at him for a second, and understanding filled his face. "Oh, you're wondering what kind of shit are we getting ourselves into?"

Hall nodded.

"Well, I don't rightly know for sure. A bit more than what we've seen so far, I suspect. Course we won't likely be riding into battle either."

Hall hadn't expected that. "Why not?"

"We'll need to support the tanks and the infantry. There will probably be an MLR. You can't roll into one of those in an open-air jeep. Not if you want to stay alive, you don't."

"MLR?"

"Main line of resistance. So far, we've been plowing through towns. There's been a road right through the middle, and the krauts haven't really had any time to prepare. Even if they barricaded it, the Shermans just drove on over. This camp will be different. There'll be trenches maybe. Sandbags and machine-gun nests. Even artillery and tanks. If the Germans know where we're going, and they're prepared, it's going to be a hell of a lot hotter at the camp. But that's okay; we'll be going in fast and on foot."

"Sir, I don't have any experience in infantry assaults."

"Bah. Don't worry about it. I do. We'll be hugging the Shermans close and moving fast. Just stay behind the tanks and stick close to me. We should be able to get in there just fine without taking a hit."

"What about once we are in the camp?"

"Simple. Gotta find Patton's son-in-law."

"How?"

"Shouldn't be too tough. There's only supposed to be a couple hundred people in there, remember? We'll ask around and nab him. Once we have him, though, we must avoid any combat on the way out. We sit tight until the camp is secure, then we walk him out together, weapons drawn. Nobody gets near him. It won't do us any damned good to get all the way there and then find him dead. You got it?"

"Sure, sir. What about the rest of the prisoners?" Hall didn't give two shits about the POWs, but he felt the need to keep the conversation going just now.

Stiller nodded his head behind him, pulling out a chewed-up plug of tobacco as he did so and flinging it in the back seat. "That's what all the half-tracks are for. Should be able to get everybody. Patton's not a selfish son of a bitch. He's not just after family. We'll get our boys out of there."

Hall didn't ask any more questions. Now that they were over the river, the column was making rapid progress. There was no resistance at all. Hall thought of that plane that kept stalking them. He'd expected an ambush already. He wondered if the Germans were too weak or too far away? Was it possible they would enter a lightly defended camp and then get out before any meaningful enemy arrived? Stiller seemed to think so, but then again, what did he really know?

"Hall, what the hell are you doing?" Stiller's sharp question drew him out of his reverie.

"Nothing, sir," he responded somewhat lamely.

"Keep eyes sharp. This is no time for daydreaming."

"Yes, sir," said Hall. He wondered if anybody would know

or care when Stiller got home. He imagined the major arriving in his hometown alone. Some dusty bit of Texas nowhere. The thought warmed him immensely.

"How many clips you got left for that Thompson?" asked Stiller.

Hall checked. "Three left."

"Shit, kid. I guess it can't be helped, but you can't use any more until we get to the camp. We may need it."

"What if we have to defend ourselves before we get there."

"Duck," said Stiller. "And let the Shermans do their work. You just hold on to those bullets until we hit the Oflag . . . Damn it!" The major's voice jumped several octaves.

Hall looked and followed Stiller's eyes, trying to figure out what had so rattled the major. Then he saw it, and cold fear froze his heart. The convoy was just rounding a bend, and the lead vehicles were already grinding to a halt. The road ahead and the hills on both sides were crawling with Germans. Thousands of them. Ignoring the major's order, Hall whipped his Thompson around and raised the site, taking vague aim at a thick cluster of the enemy. There were far too many. The lieutenant waited for the chirping flashes of the enemy rifles and the bullets that would end his dreams.

Chapter 13

Gemünden, Germany
March 27, 1945, 1000 hours

The sky. Koehl blinked, his eyes examining the gray cloud cover. Something was important about the heavens, but he couldn't think just now what it was. He heard a screeching ring in his ears, the volume rising and ebbing with each beat of his heart. A head appeared above him, staring down with eyes and forehead creased in concern. It was Schmidt. The sergeant mouthed something to him, but the *Hauptmann* couldn't hear the words through the drowning hum.

The explosion. Images flooded him. The trap, the bridge, the failure. The Americans fleeing away and the lone Sherman belching fiery death across the Main. Then the darkness. He'd been hit. Or had he? His entire body felt squeezed and pulverized as if he'd been pressed through a serrated tube. He moved his legs, his arms. Everything seemed to be working. Schmidt still stood over him, mouthing away. Koehl blinked and shook his head, trying to drive the high-pitched song from his brain. He raised a hand and waved it, gesturing for Schmidt to help him up. The sergeant shook his head. Koehl motioned again, more insistently this time. Schmidt shrugged and extended his hand, grasping his commander and pulling him with one motion to his feet. The *Hauptmann* fought a wave of dizziness. He stumbled, taking a couple of steps, and then found his balance. After a moment, he felt stable on his feet, although the terrible ringing would not recede.

"Are you all right?" shouted Schmidt.

"Where is the Sherman?"

"Gone, sir," Schmidt shouted. "Left with the rest."

Koehl nodded to show he understood. "Bring me the engineer."

The sergeant's face registered surprise. He shook his head again. "Time for that later, sir. You need a hospital."

"Bring him," Koehl repeated, his voice tinged with iron. He was probably screaming through the roar in his ears, but he didn't care. "Now, Schmidt."

The sergeant hesitated for a second and then nodded. He turned and gave commands to another soldier, who took off toward the infantry position. Koehl stepped over to his Ferdinand. The armored vehicles had rumbled back into the park with the Americans' departure. He leaned both elbows on the base, resting and fighting against the vertigo. A few minutes later, he saw the messenger returning with an NCO in tow.

The sergeant for assault engineers stood at attention before Koehl. The man was papier-mâché with a hard veneer; the captain was sure he could crush him with a single downward swing of his fist. The soldier's face was pale and his eyes wide. *He must have been forewarned.*

"You are the man who blew the bridge?" the captain asked, trying to control his brimming fury.

"*Jawohl*," the sergeant answered without looking up.

"Did you receive my order to leave the structure intact?"

"I did sir, but—"

"Speak up! I can't hear you!"

"*Jawohl.*"

"Then why didn't you do it?" screamed Koehl. "I gave a direct order, and you disobeyed!"

"Did you see the force they had, sir? Let me explain—"

"I don't care what you think they were going to do!" shouted Koehl. He fumbled for his holster.

"No, sir!" interjected Schmidt. He stepped forward swiftly and placed a firm hand on the *Hauptmann's* wrist.

"Let me go!" ordered Koehl.

Schmidt tightened his grip, pulling the captain's hand away from the holster. Koehl turned, his eyes blazing, focusing on his command sergeant. "Get your damned hands off me!" he insisted.

Schmidt shook his head. "Sir, you can't. He screwed up. He thought he was doing the right thing. You can punish him, sir, but not that."

Koehl still struggled, but Schmidt would not release his grip. He felt the blood rushing to his head and the dizziness returning.

"Please, sir, you've never done that before—even with everything that's happened to us."

"He disobeyed a direct order!"

"I know he did, sir." Schmidt leaned in. "But he didn't kill your sister." The sergeant pleaded these last words.

Koehl reeled at the statement, his anger draining out of him. He fought his sergeant half-heartedly for another moment, then dropped his hand. He couldn't take much more of this. He needed medical treatment and a little rest. "You're right," he admitted.

He turned to the engineer. "I want you out of my sight and out of my unit. You are relieved immediately and will return to the regiment. You will wait there in arrest until I've had time to submit a report. Do you understand?"

"Yes, sir. I'm sorry—"

"I don't want to hear it! Get out of here now before I change my mind!" The sergeant gave a vigorous salute and retreated swiftly from the *Hauptmann*. Koehl breathed in and out, leaning against his Ferdinand. He was exhausted from anger and frustration.

"We've lost them. Those bastards killed Gerta, and I won't be able to revenge her now."

"You got some of them, sir."

"A handful. I had them all. If that *Schweinhund* had followed orders. I'll peel the skin of his body when we get back to HQ."

"It's going to have to be enough. I can't imagine they would try to cross the Main again." Schmidt placed his hand on the captain's shoulder. "You did your duty, sir, as always. We stopped them. Now let's go home and take care of Gerta."

Koehl thought about his sister. He would have to claim her body and assist with the burial details. Assuming he could even get to her now that the Americans were battling through on the front. He tried to imagine what she would look like. He'd seen so much death, none of it pretty. No, he couldn't deal with that. When the time came, he'd let Schmidt assist him. The dependable sergeant could take care of the details—would make sure his sister was honored.

"Should we mount up and head home, sir?" asked his sergeant.

Koehl hesitated. He wanted to say no, but what was the point? They weren't doing any good sitting here. Schmidt was right. It was time to return to headquarters. If nothing else, he could make sure that this insubordinate engineer got his due. He'd got some of those bastards. It would have to be enough. He felt the hole in his stomach. It tasted like an unfulfilled promise.

The *Hauptmann* climbed up onto his Ferdinand and, with both hands on the top turret, lowered himself into the hatch. The behemoth was ambling backward, away from the river, within seconds.

Soon the column of anti-tank vehicles rumbled down the highway out of Gemünden, as heads poked out of windows to wave. Koehl saw the solemn expressions of the inhabitants. They probably realized this would be their last celebration of the war. He raised his arm in salute, the traditional military one, not the preposterous Hitler gesture they were all gradually discarding. His eyes met with a middle-aged man who returned the gesture. His face wore the battered creases of World War I. He'd already known defeat. A nation crumbling in flame. Now Koehl's generation would join them. Twice destroyed in the century, Germany must find some way to survive, he realized sadly.

Koehl felt a tug on his trousers. Schmidt was huddling below him, handing the radio up through the portal.

"What is it?" asked the captain.

"It's the colonel."

Koehl nodded and took the radio receiver. The ringing in his ears had largely subsided. He drew the instrument upward. "*Ja?*"

"*Hauptmann*, I've heard reports you blew the bridge at Gemünden. Is that true?"

"*Jawohl. Das is richtig.*"

"Congratulations. Did you destroy any enemy units?"

"Two Shermans and a squad or two of infantry."

"Excellent. You've done well, my friend."

"Thank you, sir. It doesn't feel like enough."

"Yes. I heard about your sister. I'm so very sorry."

"Thank you, I appreciate it," said the captain, fighting to control his voice. "Is there anything else?"

"We have some more intelligence on the enemy attack. It's a bit of a puzzle really."

"How so?"

"I thought we were facing a general advance, but the attack was on a much narrower line than we originally suspected. I managed to extract a reconnaissance flight from our stingy friends in the *Luftwaffe*, and the mystery grew from there."

"What do you mean?"

"I mean there's no more than five hundred of them. A smattering of tanks and some half-tracks. The whole situation makes no sense to me. Why, with a hundred thousand men in spitting distance, would they send a tiny speck of dust at us?"

Koehl was as surprised as the colonel. The attack was totally out of character with everything else the Americans had done. Their friends from across the Atlantic liked everything big. Massive armored attacks with fast-moving infantry and plenty of ground-support aircraft. Patton was an artist who painted with a sledgehammer.

"That's peculiar, sir," Koehl said finally. "Still, it matters little at this point. They can't get to us, and we can't get to them. Unless you have some men tucked away on the west side of the river that I'm unaware of."

"How I wish I did, Captain. But all hope may not be lost. They aren't returning to their lines."

Koehl's ears perked up at this. "Where are they going? There aren't any more bridges across the Main."

"Not so, captain, there's one at Burgsinn. It's not much of a structure, but if they're a little patient, they can get across one by one. If they don't give up and if they can find it."

Koehl's mind focused. "How far away is that?"

"Less than ten kilometers, due north from your present position."

The captain calculated the distance and the likely speed of the enemy force. "I might be able to make it there in time if I proceed at full throttle. Do you have anything else to throw at them?"

"I'm sorry, *Hauptmann*. I'm trying to pull some resources together, but they won't get there in time. If you go, you go it alone. Now that I know the size, I've changed my mind about these Americans. I don't want you to take the bridge down. I want you to blow the bastards to hell. And Koehl . . ."

"*Ja?*"

"If you do catch up to them, give them a few rounds for me. For your sister. But I want to stress this, *Hauptmann*, I'm not ordering you to take them head-on. If you can get up there in time, and if the situation presents a reasonable risk, do it. I'm leaving it to your judgment."

"*Jawohl!*" Koehl dropped the headset down to Schmidt. The sergeant looked up at him with an expectant expression.

"Are we going, sir?"

"Yes. We will roll up there at full speed. We have the inside cord of the arch, and they will be feeling their way along, looking for a way across. That will cause a delay. We should be able to beat them to the crossing and crush them with the same ambush I planned last time. Spread the word, Sergeant!"

Schmidt turned to the headset and began barking orders. The Ferdinands jerked as they accelerated almost immediately. Koehl stared out over the wooded fields as the column turned north, grinding along the twisting road that followed the Main. He felt his blood surge. He would avenge his sister after all.

Koehl's column rumbled north at full speed. The captain felt the jarring vibrations of the Ferdinand in his teeth. He was sitting down inside the vehicle now, leaning against his command chair as they jounced along, bouncing and jolting over the pavement, rushing to win the race to Burgsinn.

Schmidt sat below him to the right, his eyebrows furrowed in concentration as he strove to pour some coffee out of a container into his tin cup. He finally managed to half-fill it, spilling as much as he was able to land in the mug. The sergeant took a deep sip, then another, before handing the drink toward Koehl. The captain shook his head.

"Take it," ordered the sergeant. "You need to revive, sir."

The captain smiled to himself. Just who was in charge here? He knew the answer to that question too. Without further comment, he took the coffee, pulling it up to his lips carefully and then taking a deep drink of the lukewarm liquid. The flavor was sharp and foul. God knew what it was made of. Certainly not real coffee. They'd run out of that years ago, the ocean routes cut off by those bastard English.

"Sir, maybe we shouldn't pursue this."

Koehl looked down at Schmidt sharply. "What are you talking about?"

"You heard the colonel."

"Yes, I did. It's not a main attack. Just a small force."

"That *small* force outnumbers us five to one."

"What does that matter?"

The sergeant hesitated, glancing up with understanding as he placed a hand on his commander's knee. "Because as difficult as it might be to admit it, sir, it might be a blessing that bridge was blown."

"We have orders from the colonel to get up there and stop them."

"That's not quite true either, sir," Schmidt said gently. "He gave you the option, but he didn't order you to do it."

Schmidt was correct, and not just about the order. They were heavily outnumbered. He was putting his entire force in danger for highly personal reasons. For the first time in six years of war, he was operating out of emotion instead of out of the cold, rational intelligence that had kept him and his crew safe throughout the conflict. Even worse, his desire for revenge was against everything he'd learned and practiced as a priest. He tried to think clearly, to grasp the truth, but he couldn't manage it. The hot fire of sorrow burned his intellect away. Just this once, regardless of cost, he was going to follow his burning passion. Gerta deserved it. *I should have forced her to come with me.*

"Sir?" He realized he hadn't answered the sergeant.

"Someone has to stop them. You heard the colonel. He doesn't have any other resources to throw at this. If they get across the Main, they are a knife aimed at the heart of Germany. We don't know for sure what is coming up behind them. We can't allow them a bridgehead." He knew the lie of his words, and he delivered the speech in a wooden, hollow tone.

Schmidt nodded without challenging him further. Koehl saw the understanding again, and he was terrified by the loyalty and sacrifice he saw behind the look. "You're right, sir, of course. We'll get there and do our best. We'll get those bastards, every last one of them. That's what your parents would have wanted."

Koehl jerked slightly. More pain. He forced it down until it simmered in the tired place. He wouldn't think about that now. Gerta had joined his mother and father and most of his companions. Perhaps he would see them soon. He would welcome it.

He reached his hand out and grasped Schmidt. The sergeant knew him better than anyone alive. He was a substitute brother, father. He was life. He turned to his friend. "You keep your eyes sharp when this starts," he warned. "If you let something happen to yourself, I'll never forgive you."

Schmidt laughed. "Speak for yourself. You were standing in the open like a wounded gazelle in Gemünden. I think for the next fight you can conduct the battle inside our machine as well as strolling around in the open like you're taking a midday walk."

Koehl laughed. "Fair enough. Let's both be careful when we get there."

The radio chimed just then, and Schmidt turned, pulling the headset out and fiddling with the switches. He spoke quietly for a few moments. When he was done, he turned excitedly to Koehl. "That was headquarters. We have positive intelligence on the column. They are parallel to us on the other side of the Main. But they've been delayed a bit. We're at least a kilometer north of them. We should be able to get to Burgsinn with plenty of time to set up the trap. We've done it, sir."

Koehl clapped his sergeant on the back. "Great news. Let's step it up and beat those bastards!"

The Ferdinand, already rumbling mightily, coughed and jerked as it lurched forward at maximum throttle. Koehl closed his eyes, beginning to map out the trap they would set for the American column. He didn't have a map of Burgsinn, and he cursed his lack of planning for this eventuality. If he'd only known this other bridge was there, he would have ordered a local chart so he could study the potential tactical situation. He was unlikely to be as lucky as he'd been in Gemünden. So many of these small towns contained narrow, winding streets and houses that kissed the river's edge. He assumed Burgsinn was the same. He made mental adjustments, planning out killing zones and lines of retreat. Given the overwhelming su-periority of the Americans, the lack of an open shooting field near the river might actually be an asset, as each Ferdinand could protect an individual street, along with a sprinkling of in-fantry. How could they maximize the firepower and destroy as many enemy Shermans as quickly as possible? If he couldn't take out the armor, he would fail. As the minutes passed, he knew what he would do. He could taste the trap as if it had al-ready sprung.

The Ferdinand jerked and sputtered. Koehl opened his eyes in surprise, afraid they'd been hit by a shell. "What the hell was that?" he demanded.

The driver was silent for a second, setting his controls. Then he responded, "We are out of petrol."

"No!" screamed the captain. He drew himself out of the tur-ret, climbing the ladder until his head and chest poked out of the top of the vehicle. The Ferdinands behind him were all rumbling to a stop. He turned to motion to them, but he was interrupted by Schmidt.

"Another one just called in, sir. He's out of fuel as well. The rest are on reserve. We're not going to make it."

Koehl shrieked in anger and frustration. He turned to the north, where he could just make out the tips of the tallest houses in the distance. They were out of petrol. Their object was a half kilometer away. He closed his eyes. All he could see was the silent, lifeless face of his sister frowning down on him in disappointment.

Chapter 14

Near Burgsinn, Germany
March 27, 1945, 1100 hours

Hall slipped the safety off his Thompson submachine gun and slung it toward the enemy. He hardly had to aim. They filled the entire horizon, not only the road but up the hill on both sides. His heart exploded in his chest. He fought to catch his breath. He winced even as he moved, expecting any moment the bullet or shell that would end his life. His finger pressed the trigger.

"Hall, no!" screamed Stiller, reaching over, jerking the barrel of the Thompson into the air.

"What the hell?" Hall shouted in response, trying to jerk the weapon away from the major, who had clearly lost his mind. "Let me go!"

The major kept his iron grip as the two of them pulled the Thompson back and forth. "Damn it, Hall, those aren't Germans."

The lieutenant slackened his grip, and Stiller ripped the submachine gun out of his hands. Hall breathed deeply for a few moments, fighting the adrenaline down. He looked out again at the packed mass of men with new eyes. The major was right. The mass of huddled figures did not wear the grey of the *Wehrmacht*. Who were they? They weren't wearing GI uniforms either. "Do you recognize those—"

"Russians," Stiller finished for him.

Russians. That didn't make any sense. "Have they come this far west?"

The major shook his head. "Prisoners. Look at them. They're half-starved, and they have no weapons."

Hall stared at the men and realized the major was correct. "If they're prisoners, where are their guards?"

Stiller turned the jeep off, slinging the Thompson over his shoulder and stepping out of the vehicle. "Let's go find out."

Hall hopped out and stalked cautiously around the front hood to join Stiller. Even as he reached him, Baum was limping up, surrounded by his command team and a squad of infantry, weapons poised. The captain stopped to talk to Stiller.

"What do we have up there?"

"Looks like a batch of Russians," said Stiller, reaching into his pocket to pull out another brown plug of tobacco. The major stuffed the oily leaf into his mouth, gave the wad a couple of gnaws, and spit an amber ball of liquid to the ground.

Baum's eyes flickered with wary interest. "Where are the Germans?"

"I was just going to find out. Would you like to come along?"

The captain bristled a little. "You are welcome to accompany *me*, if you wish." With that, the lanky commander strode past Stiller, moving around the next Sherman in line, trailed by his support team and their fire support.

Stiller stood by the jeep for a moment as if he was not going to follow. Finally, he grunted and turned to the lieutenant. "Let's go."

Hall followed the major past one Sherman, then another. He felt naked without the Thompson, and he wondered if he should ask for it back. He'd neglected in the rush to even grab one of the grenades sitting on the seat. The major was striding after Baum with a determined look on his face. Hall decided to leave the situation alone for now. After all, if the Germans fired on them, they'd likely go after the one holding a weapon first.

They passed another tank as they caught up with Baum. The Americans had spread out, trying to protect their commander but also to space out the enemy's targets as much as possible. The Russians were less than fifty yards away now and starting to move toward the halted column. They were grouping up in a great mass, and Hall could see the excitement on their faces as they waved wildly. A great din rose from the crowded Soviets. But the same question passed through his mind again. *Where were the Germans?* Hall glanced nervously up to his right and his left, the thought occurring to him that this would be the perfect place for a trap. He couldn't make anything out in the hills above him on either side, but that didn't mean the threat wasn't there. If they were hit now, the whole force could be decimated in a matter of minutes. There would be no escape.

"Careful now, boys," said Baum, his caution mirroring Hall's. "We don't know what's ahead of us. Eyes sharp for those krauts."

The gap closed. The Russians were swarming past the lead tank now. Hall saw the turret flip open and Nutto pop his head out, staring in amazement at the mass swirling past him as if the tank was a boulder jutting out from a strong river current. As the Soviets spotted Baum's group, several of them broke into a run, sprinting forward to embrace the captain. The task force commander grimaced from the contact, the pain of his wounds affecting him.

"You are American, no?" asked one of the men, speaking broken English with a thick Slavic accent.

Baum nodded, and the man embraced him again. "We are prisoner here many months. You are army coming to rescue?"

The captain shook his head. "We are a task force on our way

to Hammelburg. The main American army is fifty miles behind us. Where are your guards?"

The soldier made a cupping gesture with his hand, then twisted it violently. The men around him laughed. "They are *kaputt*, as Germans say."

"You killed them all? When?"

"As soon as we saw you coming around bend."

"How many were there?"

The Russian shrugged. "Not so many for us. But you say you are not American army. Still, you must take us with you."

Baum shrugged helplessly. "We can't. I'm sorry. We don't have any room. We're on a mission."

A flicker of disappointment flashed across the Russian's face. He turned and spoke rapidly to the men behind him. Hall could hear the groans coming up from the crowd, growing in power in a reverse wave that traveled violently away from them as the men realized they were not here to help them. The soldier turned back to Baum.

"Do you have food? Weapons? Anything for us?"

Baum didn't respond. He turned to Stiller and Nutto, who had joined them. Nutto was pale and leaned against one of the tanks. "What do you think?" asked the commander. "I hadn't planned for this." Hall could tell that Baum was deeply moved and frustrated by the unexpected situation.

"We can spare a bit of both, sir, can't we?" asked Nutto. "We gotta do something."

"I agree," said Stiller.

Hall was shocked. They were already low on ammunition and nowhere near their destination, let alone on their way back. How could they spare anything for these Russians? The American army would be here any day. There were at least a thousand Soviets here; they should be able to take care of themselves until then.

Baum rubbed his chin for a second. "Let's give them ten

Garands and a hundred K rations. That won't solve their problems, but it will give them a bit to eat and let them at least put up a fight if the krauts come calling again. Besides, they'll have some weapons from those guards."

"Can't we do more?" asked Nutto.

"I don't see how. It's too much already," said the commander. Baum turned around and gave the order. A few men broke off to comply. The captain returned to the Russian soldier.

"We will give you some rifles and a little food. It's all we can spare."

The Soviet brightened. "That is very generous, comrade. What should we do now?"

Baum turned to his left, pointing above his shoulder. "I'd head up into those hills. Find a good position and defend yourselves. Our boys should be along in a few days, and they'll liberate you proper."

The soldier stepped forward and shook Baum's hand. "Thank you."

Baum returned the gesture. Stopping the man as he turned to leave, Baum drew out his own .45 and handed it to the Russian. The man's eyes widened.

"For me?" he asked.

"Yep. You take it. You'll need it as much as I will, maybe more."

The Russian embraced Baum again. "Thank you. Thank you much. You are great man."

"I need you to clear a path for us now. You should get out of here anyway, before the Germans come back."

The Soviet nodded toward the hills. "We going now to find good spot to wait. *Proshchay, tovarishch.*"

Hall and the other Americans stood quietly as the supplies and rifles were brought forward. The Russians quickly passed out the weapons, hefted the rations, and began their trek up into the hills. The Americans watched them in silence for a few minutes, until the road was finally cleared. As they faded away in the distance, Baum went rigid at attention and saluted their allies. The rest of the Americans did the same. All except Hall. What did he care for a bunch of Russians? The captain finally turned back to them. "I wish we could have done more for them, but we've got our own job to do, and it's about time we got back to it. Let's return to our vehicles and roll out."

The Americans turned and headed quickly back to the column and the highway to Hammelburg.

The task force was moving within a few minutes of the last Russian clearing the road. Hall sat in the passenger seat of the jeep, the steel barrel of his Thompson bringing him relief as he held the weapon with red knuckles. He was still recovering from the potentially fatal confrontation, and from the sight of twenty or more gray-clad bodies twisted in cruel angles and sprinkled up the hill. The German guards, he realized, and he thanked God he was not a target of the Russians' wrath.

Stiller drove along next to him, his face set in a perpetual half frown. He could have been a statue except for the occasional flicker of his jaw as he worked away at a plug of tobacco. Hall wondered if the bodies had affected the major—if indeed anything could bruise the iron composure of the Texan. *Too stupid to feel much*, Hall realized, thanking God or whatever higher power might exist out there for the gift of his birth and his intelligence. Perhaps that wasn't charitable, but who gave a damn? Besides, he desperately wanted a drink, and there wasn't a thing he could do about it right now.

"Where are we, sir?" he asked, more to pass the time than from any genuine interest.

"I don't know for sure. Maybe five miles from Hammelburg, ten at the most. If those bastards don't have any more surprises for us, I'd say we'll make the town in the next half hour."

"If they do?"

"One problem at a time, Hall."

He hadn't realized they were that close to their target. He hoped the camp was scantily defended. With any luck, they could have the POWs loaded up within an hour and be back to the American lines before nightfall. Without luck, well . . .

As if in answer to that thought, he heard a familiar buzzing, first at the edges of his consciousness and then growing in intensity. He looked up, knowing already what he was going to see. Sure enough, the German scout plane was back, circling high above the formation a couple of times before darting away.

"It's that spy plane again," said Hall.

Stiller grunted. "I know it. Not much we can do about it, though. I don't know why the hell we don't have any air support ourselves. Damn krauts haven't hardly had a plane in the air since D-Day, and now the only thing up there's got a swastika for a tail."

"Should we try to shoot it down?"

"That's up to the captain. You ever taken aim at an airplane? Particularly out of a moving truck? That's like threading a needle while riding a wild bull. Ain't gonna happen unless you get damned lucky. We don't have much ammo left for that peashooter of yours. We're not wasting it pissing in the wind."

Hall nodded. He didn't like the answer, but he didn't have any choice in the matter. While Stiller had babbled on, the plane disappeared anyway. The Germans would know exactly where they were headed.

The minutes ticked by slowly as they rumbled along. Hall checked his watch over and over, counting the minutes against Stiller's estimate of when they would come across their destination. They finally hit the number, and he looked up, straining his eyes to make out if he could see anything. Sure enough, there were spires in the distance, a church or two sprinkled over a fair-sized town. *The old bastard was right, of course.*

Stiller reached over and slapped Hall's arm. "Look out there, son. Just like I told you and right on time. Get that Thompson ready. We're headed around the south part of the town, but who knows what's waiting for us inside. Best be prepared."

Hall pulled the Thompson around and slipped the safety off. He felt oddly at home with the weapon now after he had had it in his possession for three-quarters of a day. He liked the bucking power of the weapon when he fired. He could grow used to combat, he realized, as long as it wasn't too close at hand and assuming the monster never turned and bit him back.

The town grew closer, the buildings taking shape in the distance, the details materializing into view. A minute passed, and then another. Hall braced himself, waiting for the first shells to rain down on them. Miraculously, there were none. The town seemed quiet, without any vehicle traffic or even pedestrians nearby. As Hall watched, the road turned to the right, and they bent slowly away from the town. A few more minutes passed, and Hammelburg was behind them.

"How far to the Oflag?" he asked.

"A couple miles at the most, I think. Up some hills. They built the damn thing at the top, according to the prisoner. Hell of a place for a great defense if there's a batch of krauts up there."

Hall lowered the Thompson, but Stiller grabbed the barrel and pulled it back up.

"Best keep that in place for now. No time to relax until we get back to the Main. It's in and out time, boy."

Hall bristled but kept his mouth shut. He was a *man* with a college degree and a pedigree. He pushed his anger down. It didn't matter, they were almost there. A few more hours . . .

The column reached the end of the valley and moved slowly up a narrow, winding road that rose steeply among the dotted pines of an enormous hill. The entire area was surrounded to the southeast by a series of prominences rolling back one on another. The landscape, rife with evergreens, reminded Hall of the hills to the northeast of Spokane. He thought back fondly of the hikes he took with his father. The long talks about the family future and his role in building their empire. He smiled to himself, enjoying the memories and thinking of the future.

The Shermans were laboring now, pushing the engines to drive the armored giants up the hill. The task force slowed to a crawl. The fumes nearly overwhelmed them in their open-air jeep. Hall coughed and sputtered, taking out a handkerchief to cover his face.

"Don't do that, Hall. It's good for you," joked Stiller. "A little exhaust won't hurt you none. Make a man out of you."

Hall had had enough. He turned to the major, a hot retort on his lips, but the words never left him. A rapid and thunderous string of explosions rocked the column in front and behind them. The concussion nearly drove the jeep off the road. Stiller struggled to maintain control while the spit of machine-gun fire raked the Sherman in front of them. They were ambushed on all sides, with nowhere to hide.

Chapter 15

South of Burgsinn, Germany
March 27, 1945, 1100 hours

"I don't care how you get it, just get the damned petrol here now!" *Hauptmann* Koehl screamed into the receiver. The town of Burgsinn was a scant half kilometer off. The Americans would be there at any moment. If he could get his fuel immediately, he still might cut them off in the cramped streets of the city and annihilate the enemy column. Instead, he was arguing with this *schweinkopf* on the other end of the line. He'd called the colonel, who had patched him through to supply. He'd spent five minutes trying to prove to some dim-witted sergeant on the other end of the line that he wasn't an enemy spy, only to learn, after the man finally decided that Koehl was in fact a German, that they'd located some petrol, but there was no way to get it to him.

"Our refueling truck is up on blocks right now, Captain. I'm sorry. We had to change the oil. You can't let these vehicles go without their regular maintenance, you know. Particularly with all the wear and tear in the field. If your ground troops were a little more patient and gentle with our equipment, we would be able to get—"

"I don't give a damn about your problems!" shouted Koehl. "If that truck isn't on the road in ten minutes, full of petrol for my company, you'll be the one up on blocks! Do you hear me!"

"*Jawohl, mein Hauptmann*," said the sergeant, hanging up quickly. Koehl hoped he'd scared the bastard enough to get some movement out of him. He needed that fuel, and he needed it now.

A half hour of agonizing waiting later, the truck rolled into view. Koehl stared at his watch, calculating the distance from Hammelburg. As frustrating as the delay was, the sergeant had moved quickly to get the refueling vehicle back into operation and all the way to the Main. Now it would be another twenty to thirty minutes to fuel the vehicles. A wasted hour.

"Fill them halfway only!" he ordered. He was taking a gamble, but if they reduced the intake, he could save ten minutes or so in the process. He only hoped the Americans were delayed. The truck filled one Ferdinand, then the next. He watched the process, keeping a close eye on his watch and shouting orders to move down the line when he felt the behemoths had enough petrol. Finally, the last one was done. The driver of the truck saluted. "I'll be heading back to Hammelburg if that's it, sir."

"No, you will not. You will be coming with us. I may need you again before this is over."

"But, sir," the soldier protested, "I have orders."

"You have new ones now. Get your vehicle to the end of the line. We are leaving immediately. *Schnell!*" Koehl looked down at his watch. Seventeen minutes to refuel. Well, there was nothing he could do. The anti-tank vehicles rumbled back into operation and lurched down the road toward Burgsinn. He kept his head out of the turret, eyes darting between the town and the opposite bank of the Main, searching for any sign of the enemy column. They were a few hundred meters away now.

They were going to make it. He stepped down into the belly of the steel beast, tugging on Schmidt's jacket. His command sergeant looked up, ready for orders.

"Pass the command now. We won't have time to set this when we get there. I want our machines to fan out, one per street, and roll down toward the Main. Put a few infantry on the back of each vehicle. When we get to the Americans, they can spread out and provide support fire. If we get into position before they are across the river, we can look at what else we might do to prepare." Koehl paused. "And put that engineer on our turret. He can ride out front."

"But, sir, that's suicide."

"We need a good spotter. If he makes it through, and if we bag those Americans, I might consider dropping the report at headquarters." He felt a twinge. The order didn't feel right. *To hell with it. He ruined my plans!*

The sergeant nodded, but Koehl could tell he didn't approve. The captain struggled with his feelings for a few moments. "Fine, Schmidt, he can ride on the back. But he better do his job and do it well!"

The sergeant smiled. "Yes, sir. You're a good man, sir."

Koehl grunted. "I just don't want him to get in the way of our cannons."

"Of course not. That is wise thinking." The NCO was grinning now from ear to ear.

"Enough. Make the orders."

Koehl lifted himself back out of the top and looked toward the town. He lifted his field glasses. The narrow streets were crowded, and it was difficult to see. He could not make out any American vehicles. He looked to his left and examined the far bank. Again, he saw nothing. He felt an electric tug at his heart. Was it possible they had beat the Americans, even with the delay? Yes! *Unless they were long gone.*

As if in answer to that thought, Schmidt's voice echoed up

out of the Ferdinand. "Sir, it's HQ on the line. They have an update on the Americans. I'm afraid it's bad news, sir."

Koehl took the receiver with as much calm as he could muster. "Is that you, Colonel?"

"Koehl, what's your position?"

"We're half a kilometer from town. Where are the Americans?"

"Well past you. Our reconnaissance plane flew over the column fifteen minutes ago. They are halfway to Hammelburg."

"*Scheisse!* Is that their target?"

"There's no way to know. I'm preparing our defenses in case they come into the town."

"I'm on my way."

"No way you can get here in time, Koehl. You're a half hour behind at least."

"If you can hold them, we will hit them from behind and crush them. I'll be there as soon as I can."

"Negative."

"What do you mean?"

"My instincts tell me they are after the POWs. That's the only thing that makes sense. If so, they will have to cut in near Hammelburg and then turn into the hills. Look at your map, *Hauptmann*, there is a straight road from your location. With any luck, you can be ready and waiting for them on the road to Oflag XIII."

"And if you're wrong."

"If I'm wrong, then we will handle them here, or they will handle us. But I'm not wrong. Now get moving."

"I will, sir. Good luck."

"You too, Koehl."

The captain paused for a moment and then gave new orders, sending his column on a sharp right toward the hills beyond Hammelburg. He knew the area well; he'd been training with his company here for more than a week, preparing for the defense of the area when the general attack from the Americans came. He wondered whether the colonel was right. What if the Americans were after the town instead? Why would they be? With such a small column, what would be the purpose of capturing a town? No, the colonel was correct, as he always seemed to be. They were after the POW camp. He was still puzzled about the size of the force. Why send less than a thousand men this far behind enemy lines with no support? The Americans seemed to have unlimited men and resources. The decision made no sense. Well, thinking at that level was not his problem. He was a tactical leader, and this force was enough of a problem for him. He just hoped he could get there in time and punish the column for his sister. Even as he contemplated that event, his vehicle was turning sharply, rolling down a bumpy side road toward the steep hills of Hammelburg.

The Ferdinand vibrated terribly on the gravel road. Koehl pushed his driver, laboring to eke out every ounce of his machine's performance on the narrow, pothole-ridden road. They were moving due east toward the cluster of hills to the southeast of Hammelburg. Even now, the ground was beginning to arc upward.

Schmidt was on the radio with headquarters constantly now. The Americans had not materialized at Hammelburg yet and were past due based on the calculations of the reconnaissance pilot. Koehl felt the first prick of panic. Had they turned off somewhere along the way? The colonel assumed their target was the city or the Oflag, but what if they were wrong? Schweinfurt, the center of Germany's ball-bearing industry, was just a few kilometers farther east. What if this was a daring gamble to smash that industry? Certainly, the American air force had tried and failed to do the same. If so, the column might have rounded Hammelburg to the north and could already be far out of his reach. He consulted his map, trying to find a route the Americans might be taking. Was there any way, in such a scenario, that he could still get in on the kill?

He heard Schmidt talking below him. There was a rapid exchange, and then the sergeant lowered the headset. "The Americans have been spotted again, sir," he said.

"They've turned north, haven't they?"

"No, they're headed straight for the town."

"Then they are attacking Hammelburg? Not the Oflag?"

"No way to know that yet, sir. The highway heads straight toward the city before a branch road heads up into the hills. We won't know for a few more minutes."

Koehl checked his map, trying to pinpoint the location of the Americans and his own column. Even if the enemy force was coming to the Oflag, he wasn't sure he could be in position in time. If they weren't headed toward the camp, the Americans could hit Hammelburg long before he would reach the position. He felt his frustration mounting again. Why hadn't the colonel allowed him to proceed directly toward him, where they could have caught the GIs in a double-sided trap, hammer to anvil.

"Step it up," he ordered. "We've got to get there in time."

"Sir, any faster and we may lose the engine," reported Schmidt.

"I don't care. Push it."

The sergeant put a hand on Koehl's leg, looking up with understanding eyes. "I understand, sir, but do you want another delay? If we lose a vehicle or two, we might not be able to go on at all. A little caution now will pay dividends."

Koehl wanted to lash out at Schmidt. As much as the sergeant was his friend, he could not feel the emotions ripping through the captain right now. He held back. They'd served together for years. Seen and done things nobody would possibly believe. "You're right," he said finally. "Get as much speed as you can, but get us there intact."

"Don't you worry, sir, we'll beat those bastards to the Oflag, and we'll give them a nasty surprise when we do."

Koehl hoped the sergeant was right. Images of his sister kept flaring up in his imagination. He saw her sitting across from him at dinner, smiling, laughing; then the scene changed, and she was in a field, eyes wide open, blood smattered over her delicate cheeks and pale skin. Surrounded by laughing GIs. He shook his head, trying to drive the nightmare away. There was only one thing he could think of to atone for her loss, for his hesitation, his weakness.

The column was entering the hills now, winding up steeply through the trees. He consulted his map, trying to determine where to go. The area was crisscrossed with small roads, zigzagging through the sharply inclining landscape. He traced his finger along the probable routes from Hammelburg toward the Oflag and compared the two-dimensional lines with his recollections of their recent training here.

As he did so, he recalled an area that would be perfect for what he had in mind, a clearing halfway up a hill, behind a line of trees that hovered over the main road from the town. He would be able to line up his entire company and hit the column in a massive broadside. If he placed his infantry on the other side, he would have the Americans in a cross fire, and with any luck, he could wipe out the whole force in a matter of minutes. If only he could find his way there. He'd never approached this area from the west. He didn't know the roads from this side, and he was unsure of exactly where to go. In the bumping, rumbling vehicle, he could barely concentrate on the map. He felt a terrible frustration, but he would have to stop the column and spend a few minutes mapping out their route.

He gave the order to Schmidt, and the line of Ferdinands stumbled to a halt. He pulled the map up closely and traced the routes, trying to find the meadow on the chart. It wasn't marked, but he thought he could see in his mind the approximate location. If he was right, they were not far, less than a kilometer. They would have to cut over to another road, but he saw an area that would allow them to get there. He gave these new instructions to Schmidt, and soon the anti-tank vehicles were moving again, headed toward the ambush point.

They arrived at the crossroads in less than five minutes. The force took a sharp right and lumbered up another road, this one a little bigger and paved. To his left, right on cue, was the line of trees. Koehl could see the clearing popping out through the maze of branches and pine needles. He'd led them straight to it, he realized with elation.

"We're here, Schmidt," he said.

"We're where?"

"The ambush point. There is a small road leading up into that clearing in about a hundred meters. I want all the Ferdinands up there, lined up downhill, spread out ten meters apart. The infantry should be on the other side. We don't have much time, so everyone must get into position as quickly as possible."

Schmidt started giving orders but was interrupted by headquarters. The sergeant listened for a few seconds, then turned to the captain. "The colonel was right. They didn't hit Hammelburg," he said, his voice trembling with energy. "They're coming this way."

Koehl could barely contain his excitement. The Americans were heading toward the Oflag and right into his trap. He'd arrived first, and he was in position to hit them. He turned back to Schmidt. "You heard it, Sergeant. Get them up there quickly."

Schmidt barked orders, and the Ferdinands turned off the road, rumbling up through a narrow gap in the trees and into the open meadow beyond. The anti-tank vehicles bumped and jarred their way into place, one after another, leaving a gap that would hopefully prevent a shell from destroying two of them at a time. In less than ten minutes, the vehicles were all in position, their 88mm main cannons reaching out toward the road, waiting like the eager claws of some terrible monster to rip and render the Americans. In the distance through the trees, Koehl could see his infantry scrambling into their positions. The ground troops would be terribly exposed once the fighting started and stood in danger of taking a stray round from the Germans in the coming cross fire. They were brave men, all of them. He thought of the engineer. A good man, perhaps, who'd made a mistake. He would make amends when this was over.

Minutes passed. They were in position now, but if anything, the tension elevated with nothing to do but wait. He looked through his field glasses again and again, straining to make out the first American Sherman. Fear nagged him. He remembered the map. There were so many roads. He'd covered the most direct route to the Oflag, but what if the Americans chose another route? There were a half-dozen ways to get to the camp. If they didn't pass this way, he still might miss them. He looked through the glasses. Still nothing. He checked his watch. It was past time.

"Schmidt," he said, "get HQ up again. We need that plane to give us an updated position. I think we've missed them."

The sergeant started on the radio communication, but Koehl stopped him. "Delay that order," he said, his eyes focusing on the first green hint of movement. "They're coming. Everyone should be prepared to fire once the lead Sherman is all the way past our line."

Schmidt gave the order. Koehl was full of excitement. He watched the column progressing slowly up the road. He spotted three Shermans, then five. They were lined up before him like ducks in a pond. The captain was worried the Americans would spot him, but they rumbled by tranquilly as if they were out on a peacetime exercise. The force continued, the lead tank approaching the leftward track toward the meadow. Koehl closed his eyes for a moment, whispering a prayer of thanks. "Fire!" he screamed, and the world exploded around him.

Chapter 16

Oflag XIII
March 27, 1945, 1230 hours

The thunder in the distance rattled the camp. Knorr hesitated, his pistol to Curtis's head, then he reversed the handle and brought the base down on the captain's temple. Curtis felt fire and streaks of lightning-hot pain rip across his forehead; black dots flashed in and out of his vision as he fought to stay conscious. Nausea welled up, and he retched into the frozen dirt of the yard. He scarcely noticed the rumbling of artillery in the distance.

He felt hard hands pulling at his arms. He waited for the bullet that would end his agony. He almost welcomed it amid the wrenching pain of his back and head.

"Curtis"—he heard the familiar voice of Lieutenant Colonel Waters. The hands on him were not German.

"Yes, sir," he managed to say through the pain.

"We've got to get you out of here. Can you stand?"

The captain struggled to rise. Waves of dizziness drove him back to the ground. He closed his eyes, trying to shake off the unbalanced forces tearing through his brain. "I can't."

The hands readjusted, taking a firmer grip. "Up," said Waters, commanding the men to pick up Curtis. The captain felt the hot, tearing pain lance through his back as they jerked him upward. "I can't," he repeated, panting for breath. "Please, just leave me here."

"Won't do it, Curtis," responded Waters. "Knorr is after your hide. The artillery distracted him for a minute, but he'll be back. We've all been ordered to our barracks. We've got to get you out of here and hidden, in case that bastard comes looking for you."

Curtis shook his head. "I'm too dizzy to get up."

"Don't worry about that. These boys will help you along. Just don't fight 'em."

Waters gave the command, and the men with him pulled Curtis's arms around their necks. They stepped forward, half-carrying, half-dragging the captain. Curtis tried to open his eyes to see where they were going, but the blinding streaks of light and darkness still gripped his eyes, and he could not see. Each step, each moment was a torment almost beyond measure. He gasped, choking and chewing on the anguish. But they were making progress. Although it seemed an eternity, Curtis heard a door squeak open; he felt the ground beneath him change to the wooden floor of a barracks. A bright, bare bulb flashed above his eyes for a few moments, then he was pulled into darkness. Carefully, the men laid him back onto a cot, and Curtis realized they had returned him to the room just off the command center of the POW camp.

"You stay here now, Curtis, and try to keep quiet," said Waters. "But be ready; we might have to move you if Knorr comes calling."

"What is that noise?" he asked.

"You mean the rumbling. Artillery, I figure, but I don't know if it's ours or theirs. Could be just some training going on, but it sure seemed to rattle the Germans. I'd guess our boys are close, a hell of a lot closer than the krauts thought. If we can sit tight for a few more hours, I think we're liberated."

"I'm not going to make it," said Curtis, feeling a surge of shame as he said it.

"Nonsense. You're just fine. A little bruised, but you ain't broken yet. You sit tight and keep your mouth shut. Get some rest. I intend to keep you in one piece."

The door closed, and Curtis was there by himself. Through the blur of his pain, he thought about liberation. Could it truly be just a few hours away? This nightmare would finally come to an end. He thought of his dead friend Hanson, and a terrible sadness overwhelmed him. Just twenty-four hours longer and he'd still be alive. He'd failed him, as he'd failed in everything. Everything he touched was a disaster. They'd selected him for officer training because he was supposed to be a leader—someone who could shepherd his men through combat. He'd excelled in training, winning promotion to platoon leader and then company commander. He'd looked forward to testing his mettle against the Germans. Then the moment had come, and he'd done nothing. The Germans had swarmed his position, and all his training had come to nothing. He hadn't been able to save his men. He couldn't even save Hanson, at the Bulge or at the Oflag. He felt the fear again—there must be something missing inside him. Something he couldn't see.

In the distance, he could still hear the faint rumbling. Was it getting closer? He couldn't tell. He wished the buzzing in his ears would stop. He needed to concentrate. He hoped the Americans had medicine with them. He desperately wanted a shot of morphine or anything to dull the pain. He felt the shame again. There would be real casualties. Boys with terrible wounds who needed immediate attention. He steeled himself. He would keep his mouth shut and wait his turn. He would not give up the last shreds of his honor.

He heard the door bang open and closed again, and he bristled, still unable to see. "It's me," said Waters, and Curtis exhaled in relief. "I've brought you a little bread and a cup of water. Sorry, it's all I've got left."

"I can't sit up, sir. Can you give me the bread?"

"Sure, son." Waters handed the plum-sized crust to Curtis. "I'll just put the water next to you on the floor." Curtis nodded, and Waters left the room again. The captain gripped the stale bun, tearing off a mouthful and shoving the coarse roll into his mouth. He didn't feel like eating, but he knew he might need his strength soon, so he forced his teeth to chew the flavorless food until he could swallow it. He nearly threw up, but he held the bite down. He willed himself to take another, then another, until he'd finished the meager ration. By the time he was done, the nausea had subsided. The flashes were receding now too, and he found that, by blinking his eyes open and closed, he was starting to see bits and pieces again.

A rumble of thunder rolled away in the distance. He tried to calculate how far away the sound might be coming from. He chuckled to himself. What did he know about combat? He'd fought for a half hour, if you could even call it fighting. More like cringing in his foxhole. He didn't know a thing about measuring artillery. Still, it kept the minutes flowing by, so he made a game of it, predicting how long between each rumble and trying to calculate whether the sounds were staying in the same general area or were getting closer.

The door flung open again, and the light above him was abruptly flicked on. Waters was there. "Curtis, we've got to go."

"What do you mean, sir? I can't stand."

"No choice. The krauts are here. They're evacuating us after all."

"Can't we stop them?"

A flicker of fire flashed in Waters's eyes. "If there was any chance, I'd fight them with my bare hands. But we don't have any weapons, and they're ready for us. They're armed to the teeth now and jittery as hell. We've got to take you with us."

"No chance, sir. My back is too badly hurt. I can barely

walk. Just leave me here. Maybe the Americans will get here first."

"They'll get here all right, and they'll find you with one of Knorr's bullets in your brain. If we must go, you're going with us."

Curtis shook his head. He didn't want to face the pain again. He felt peace here, in the solitary room, alone with his thoughts.

"It's not your call, Captain. You're going, and that's an order." Waters turned away for a moment and called to someone out of the room. A couple of POWs appeared and moved toward the bed. Curtis closed his eyes, wanting to fight them. He just wanted to give up, to take his chances that the army would get here before Knorr found him. But he knew Waters. He steeled himself even as the hands wrapped around him. Wherever Waters was going, he was going with him.

The fire in his back flamed up again as they drew him as gently as haste would allow from his bed. At least he could see now, blinking still, but able to make out the semi-blurry forms around him between the flashes of his lids. He felt a fraction stronger. Perhaps it was the bread. This time, he was able to move his legs, although much of his weight was still on the kriegies holding him on each side. Now that he was up, he knew Waters was right. It was suicide to remain behind. He'd be no better than those poor saps in the hospital wing, than his friend, dead from Knorr's bullets. They shambled out of the private room and into the main headquarters area. A few men milled about, waiting for messages from Goode. The camp POW commander looked up, nodding briefly at Waters before his eyes fell on Curtis. The colonel frowned.

"Is he well enough to travel?"

"He's going to have to be," said Waters.

"We've been through this already, John. He's better off here if he can't make it."

The XO shook his head. "I told you, I'm not leaving him behind." Waters's voice was laced with steel. Goode seemed to be thinking the matter over for a second, and then he relented.

"Have it your way. But he has to keep up. God knows what's in front of us. He's your problem. I've got to attend to the rest of the men."

"I'll take care of it," answered Waters. "Let's go, boys."

The kriegies wrapped their arms more tightly around Curtis and pulled him along again. Waters walked to the front door and opened it. The yard was bustling with POWs and guards walking frantically in every direction. The sound of the booming guns was louder outside and seemed closer to Curtis, although it could just be his imagination. His head was clearing, and his sight now seemed entirely returned to him, although he had a scorching headache. He wanted to lift a hand to the top of his head, to see if there was any blood there, but he was afraid he would lose his balance and fall.

As he looked more closely, Curtis saw that there was a pattern to the seemingly random movement. The men were being herded to his right, past the hospital building and beyond. Waters's little group groped its way into the mass and hobbled along, trying to keep up with the shambling mass of humanity as they worked their way past the infirmary under the clipped barking of the German guards. They eventually cleared the hospital and came to an area of the camp near the fence that Curtis had rarely seen before. There was a small outbuilding for the guards here, a place to warm up in between circuits around the camp. Beyond the building was the fence and a gate that led to the soldiers' quarters and the *Kommandant*'s office.

The fence here was usually closed and guarded by at least two men with machine pistols. Curtis was surprised to see the gates open wide. The guards were leading the POWs through the opening and into the German area beyond. He looked closely at the compound, afraid of a place that was forbidden, that had always meant instant death. He looked for any signs of an ambush, machine guns, or krauts poking out of the towers or windows, but for now, all seemed deserted. His back still burned, but fear was a powerful narcotic, driving down the pain as his body took over, seeking to survive.

A series of trucks lined up in single file within the German portion of the camp. They were vehicles similar to the American deuce-and-a-half, with a large canvas cover in the back supported by metal hoops. The mass of POWs jumbled up as the group neared the row of trucks. Curtis strained to see through the throng, ignoring the pain in his back. He could just make out the POWs climbing into the bed of some of the lead trucks. So the Germans were truly intending to evacuate them. He'd feared they were going to liquidate them here and now.

There were at least thirty trucks waiting. Curtis knew this would transport only a fraction of the POW population. He wondered if the vehicles would make a return trip or if the rest of the population would be forced to walk. He knew he would never make it if he was forced on a march of even a mile. He kept an anxious eye on the loading as they gradually drew nearer to the front. He prayed there was still room for him before the convoy was full.

Finally, he reached the head of the line, and he was pulled toward the last of the trucks. He searched around for Waters but could not find him. The lieutenant colonel must have been forced into another group by the push and pull of the crowd. He looked to his right and left, at the struggling faces of the kriegies who were helping him. Everyone was weak and undernourished after months in the camp. He saw the grimaces in their cheeks and the fatigue in their eyes. They were sacrificing precious energy they might need in the uncertain future on his behalf. He thanked God for them.

They reached the very last of the trucks. Curtis saw, to his dismay, that the vehicle was already full. The men shook their heads as he approached. "Please," he said, "I'm badly hurt. I can't walk." The POWs kept their eyes averted, starting at the floor of the truck.

Curtis started to turn away when a young lieutenant rose. "I'll give up my seat for you," he said. He walked past the somber faces of the other men in the back, all looking at their feet. He jumped down. The boy, no more than twenty-one, gripped Curtis's hands.

The captain was overcome with guilt. "That is kind, but it's your spot."

The lieutenant shook his head. "You need it more than I do, buddy."

The men in the back were helpful now. One of them reached out a hand and gripped Curtis. With others shoving from behind, he was drawn swiftly up into the back of the vehicle. He grimaced from the pain, but he did not shout out, and hand by hand he was drawn back to a place among the kriegies, crouched on hard benches beneath the canvas.

He tried to look into those faces, but it was difficult. The brightness of the opening contrasted sharply with the darkness within. The temperature was considerably colder inside, and his breath exhaled in a frosty cloud. "Where are we going?" he asked, hoping someone would know something, anything.

"God knows," answered one of the men, a gruff-looking major sitting in the dimness directly across from him. "But if there's any walking, you are damned for sure."

Curtis knew the man was right. He'd lost his escort when he took this spot in the truck. And there were no more available vehicles in the convoy. If they were forced to march, even a short distance, he would have to ask for help and hope that these men were as generous as the others. He didn't know if he could walk even a few steps at this point without assistance. He no longer felt the raging dizziness he'd experienced before, but his lower back still throbbed and burned, and he wasn't sure he could manage even a hobbling shamble on his own.

The artillery rumbling had ceased. Curtis wondered what that meant. Another failed attack? The Americans always seemed just a little out of reach. It made little difference at this point, at least for now. They were headed farther into Germany, and if they made it to the new camp, their liberation would wait weeks, months, or perhaps longer. He was tired of hope—that betrayer of truth. For now, he must focus on survival.

They sat that way for a long time, waiting in the cold and the darkness. The engine still rattled and coughed but provided them no warmth, no solace. The pain in his back increased on the hard seat, and he braced himself, preparing for the harsh jouncing of the vehicle on war-torn country roads.

Outside, he heard harsh yelling in German and a growing murmur. Curtis strained his ears, trying to understand what was going on. A guard appeared at the rear of the truck. He was screaming at them, his face scarlet. "*Raus!*"

What was going on? Why were they supposed to get out? They hadn't gone anywhere. The men at the end stared at the German in surprise, obviously not sure how to react. He raised his rifle and jabbed one of them with the end of the barrel, harshly repeating his command. The man rose, arms in the air, and jumped down, followed by the POW across from him.

"Help me," Curtis pleaded to the man across from him.

"What's wrong with you?"

"It's my back. I'm hurt. I'm not sure I can walk by myself."

The emptying line of men rapidly reached them. The man watched him for a moment and reached out a hand, taking Curtis by the arm and pulling him as gently as possible into a standing position. Curtis shouted at the stabbing pain of the sudden movement. The guard watching fixed him with narrowed eyes. Curtis forced himself to be silent and shambled the few feet to the end of the bed, trying to keep his face from betraying his pain.

His helper leapt out in front of him and then turned, raising a hand to Curtis. The lieutenant took it, placed his feet as close to the edge as possible, and jumped down. The impact on the frozen dirt was like on concrete, and his back exploded with stabbing needles, but he forced himself to hold back the agony under the watchful eye of the German. He looked around, trying to grasp the situation.

POWs were scrambling in every direction. The shouts of the guards increased in volume now that he was outside. After a few moments, he realized they were moving away from the trucks and back through the gate toward the main camp. What had happened? What change had halted the evacuation? He wanted to ask someone, but there was no time. He looked around. His helper had disappeared, either unwilling to help him further or swept up in the mass of retreating kriegies. He felt his panic rising. The guard was still watching him closely, ignoring the other men jumping out of the truck. He knew he only had moments before the German stopped him. He had to try to walk away.

Curtis took a shaky step. His knees buckled, and he stumbled as the pain in his back tore through him. By a miracle, he kept his balance and took another step forward, then another, shambling toward the crowd of POWs that even now was fading away from the immobile convoy of trucks. He wanted to risk another glance at the guard, but he was terrified he would fall if he did, so he kept his face forward and concentrated on the other POWs a few yards away. Fortunately, there was a bottleneck at the gate, and after another half-dozen wrenching steps, he reached the back of the line. He placed his hands on the shoulders of the man in front of him.

"What the hell are you doing?" the prisoner asked.

"I can't hardly walk," whispered Curtis. "Please just let me rest here and walk along with you. They'll kill me otherwise."

The man hesitated. "Fine, buddy, but not too much weight on me. I'm not exactly doing great myself."

Curtis was thankful. He looked around, hoping he recognized someone in the press, but while he saw a few faces he thought he knew, there was nobody from his barracks or from the command team that he could see in the immediate area. It didn't matter. The line was moving, and he was able to keep his balance now. Once they were back in the yard, he could find Waters and get a few boys to help him back to his bunk. He just hoped there were no more evacuations. If they sat tight, they should be liberated in a few days, maybe even today.

The line was moving well now, as the majority of the kriegies filtered through the gate and headed back toward their barracks. There were scarcely fifty men left in the German portion of the camp. In the distance, Curtis thought he could see Waters, standing with a cluster of men on the far side, scanning the POWs for something or someone, perhaps even for him.

"Let me help you, Captain."

Curtis's heart iced over. He tried to keep moving, but he felt a hand on his shoulder, holding him back. He turned gingerly to face the smirking countenance of Sergeant Knorr.

"Where are you heading in such a hurry, Captain?" he asked with mock concern. "*Mein Gott*, your face is white as snow. Is something wrong with you?"

"No, I'm fine," responded the captain through the pain, trying to keep his expression clear.

"Nonsense. You've been hurt somehow. *Das ist so schade*," said the sergeant, wiping his face with his scarlet handkerchief. "Whatever shall we do with you?"

"I don't need any help," said Curtis, trying to pull away, despite the pain. "I'm just going back to the barracks."

"I'm afraid I can't allow that, Captain. You are obviously far too ill for that. I wouldn't want to burden the other men with you." He paused as if considering the problem, and his face brightened into a grin. "I know the best place for you. Our hospital. I know you're familiar with it, aren't you?" he said, his eyes brimming with mirth. "I think you had a friend who was recovering from his wounds there. Unfortunately, he didn't make it."

"You killed him, you bastard," said Curtis, taking the bait but not caring. Whatever happened to him, he would not let that pass.

"Bastard? That is a bad English word isn't it, Captain?" The sergeant's eyes were dangerous now. "But, of course, you are not yourself due to your injuries. You will be much better after a trip to the hospital." He started to pull Curtis away from the gate, toward the German barracks.

Curtis was horrified. He searched desperately for Waters, but if that had been the colonel, he was no longer there. Most of the POWs were already out of sight, and he was heading in the wrong direction. "The hospital is the other way," he said, trying to buy some time.

"I'm going to take you to our German medical center, Captain. Only the best for you. I've been waiting a very long time to make sure you received the treatment you deserve."

"Help!" screamed Curtis, trying to pull away or at least get the attention of the other POWs. But they were too far away. The guards had already shut the gate to the main camp. He was trapped.

Knorr kept an iron grip on his shoulder, pushing him toward the buildings. Curtis looked around desperately, grasping for anything he could do to save himself. The barracks drew nearer, the roof filling the sky like an ominous monster reaching out to rend his soul. They reached a short set of stairs, and Knorr pulled him up them abruptly. Curtis cried out with the burning pain.

"You see, Captain. You tried to hide it from me, but you're hurt. Don't you worry; we'll get you fixed right up here." Curtis could taste the malice in the sergeant's voice.

He was dragged through the doorway into a large rectangular room. The building was filled with a long row of bunk beds.

The beds were wider than in their prisoner barracks and con-tained mattresses and pillows. After months in the POW camp, the interior looked like a luxury hotel to the captain. But it was certainly no hospital.

"Where are we?" he asked.

"This is a barracks, as you can see, Captain. I would have taken you to a hospital, but let us stop this game. We both know you won't need a doctor soon."

"Please," begged Curtis. "Please just let me go back to the camp."

Knorr reached out and stroked the captain's cheek. "Don't worry, *mein freund*. You won't even feel it." He reversed his hand and shoved down hard on Curtis's shoulder. The captain hit the ground hard, his back wrenching again in renewed in-jury and pain. He writhed on the floor even as the sergeant drew his pistol, aiming carefully at the captain's chest.

Chapter 17

Between Hammelburg and Oflag XIII
March 27, 1945, 1230 hours

Steel rained down on Hall's jeep. The thunderous detonations tore at his ears and penetrated his mind, the concussions jerking the jeep left and right as Stiller fought to keep the vehicle in control. A billowing funnel of onyx smoke ahead of him told the lieutenant that at least one Sherman was already destroyed. Hall tried to concentrate amid the chaos around him and the clanging ringing in his ears.

The lieutenant glanced quickly to his right and his left. He could see flashes emanating from above in both directions. They were in a perfect trap and could not hope to survive. He ripped his Thompson to his right and depressed the trigger, spraying the barrel wildly at the unseen targets on the incline. The weapon jerked and bucked. He pulled the trigger in a few short bursts, and the magazine was exhausted. He had no idea if he'd hit anything in the wild melee swirling around him, but firing the weapon gave him a fraction of control, the ability to do something, to fight back.

The Sherman directly in front of them continued to roll forward, jerking and shaking as shells bounced off the armor and as its own cannon screamed in fiery anger. Hall ripped his clip out and fumbled for the bag, tearing out the metal stick and shoving it into his Thompson. He pulled back the bolt and twisted the weapon out to his right, firing madly, an animal yell escaping his lips unconsciously as he fought for his life.

He emptied the Thompson in moments and fumbled for more ammunition. He shoved the last clip in and blazed away, hunched down as low as he could get as he depressed the trigger over and over. Soon the Thompson was exhausted again. He was out of ammunition. Now he was helpless and had to wait for the bullet that would kill him. Stiller drove beside him, brow furrowed, quiet and cool, pushing the jeep forward as close to the butt of the Sherman as he could. Simple or not, he was brave under fire, a natural warrior. The shells rattled in, exploding and raining over them.

Then they were through it. Somehow the column kept going. Hall counted three burning Shermans, but they were able to weave through them. The column rumbled and rounded a bend. He craned his neck, trying to make out the half-tracks that he was sure would be torn apart by the cross fire. He couldn't see them past the trees.

Minutes passed, and the fire died down. The road straightened out even as it continued upward. The lieutenant pivoted in the seat and half stood, straining his eyes to see the back of the force. To his surprise, a good number of the half-tracks seemed to have made it. Some were battered, and smoke emanated from the hood of one, but they were still there, still moving. Somehow the task force had escaped.

"Shit," said Stiller finally, spitting an enormous wad of tobacco and bourbon-colored saliva out of his mouth. "That was a hot-damned surprise. Krauts nearly had us there. You okay, Hall?"

The lieutenant couldn't answer. His tongue seemed frozen to the roof of his mouth. His hands shook, and he felt like his body had been run through a grinder. He'd never experienced such intense fear and violence. The previous day's skirmishes seemed like pleasant holidays in comparison. He merely nodded, unsure of himself. He checked his arms and legs. His fingers came up bloody. At the same moment, a throbbing, fiery pain emanated from his upper right arm. He looked down and saw a quarter-sized gash. The skin hung in a red flap, and the blood poured out of the wound in pulsing froths. "I'm hit," he managed to blurt out.

"Where?" asked the major, concern in his voice. "Let me see it."

Hall rotated his arm, showing the wound to the major, who glanced over a few times to examine it, even as he kept the jeep moving up the road. "Doesn't look too bad, Hall. Shell fragment ripped right by you, it looks like. Do you have another bandage?"

"I think so," said the lieutenant. He reached down into his jacket, gingerly pulling out the aid kit he'd retrieved earlier. His hands shook, and he felt tears coming down his face. He fumbled through the pack and retrieved a bandage. Ripping it open, he wrapped the gauze around his arm. The action was difficult to perform with one hand in the bounding jeep, but after a few tries, he managed it. He was wounded. Good lord. He might have died.

"Not too tight now," advised the major. "You'll cut the circulation off and lose the damned thing."

"I think I've got it," he said.

Stiller chuckled. "Good man. Now you're a real soldier, Hall. You did good back there. You have any ammo left?"

"I used it up."

Stiller grunted. "Can't be helped. We'll scrounge up something when we get there. We can't be far now, maybe just a few minutes. When we arrive, hold back with me, and I'll see about more ammo for you and something for me. I don't want to charge them with only my dick in my hand."

"I can't believe we made it through that."

"I've had worse and survived. You never know what will get you and what won't. In war, you've got to take each moment at a time. Smell it, taste it, feel the seconds. Each could be your last."

Despite the fear, Hall knew what the major was saying. He'd never lived like this before. The colors of the pine trees and the sky, the sharp, brisk pitch of the air, mixed with diesel, the grinding rumble of the Shermans, and the whining rev of the jeep engine. Everything was exaggerated, stretched out with diamond clarity in front of him. All his conquests and victories in school, in life, seemed dim in comparison. This was life balanced on the sharp edge of a knife. He was terrified, but he relished it.

The column lumbered on, the engines gasping for breath as they struggled up the incline of the hill. Hall expected to see the German plane, almost an old friend by now, materialize overhead, but it was nowhere to be seen. Perhaps having passed the ambush, they were in the clear. If that was all the Germans had left to throw at them, they were a feeble and tired foe indeed. They were rolling near the summit of a great hill now, the trees opening up at the top. He wondered what they would see when they crested the hill.

Then they were over it, and the wide vista of Oflag XIII opened before them. Towers and wire fencing dominated dozens of buildings arranged in neat rows. The camp was a few hundred yards off, with nothing between them but open fields that had obviously been cleared by the Germans to provide a killing field for any escaped prisoners. The space would also make the ideal platform for an armored advance against the camp.

As Hall watched, the camp came alive with activity, like a disturbed anthill. He could see the chaos caused by the appearance of the task force at the Oflag's front door. The guards in the towers rushed back and forth, pointing and raising their weapons at the task force. It was an empty gesture, Hall knew. The submachine guns, so effective against an escaping prisoner, would do nothing against the charging Shermans.

The tanks wasted no time in preparation. Reaching the clearing, the vehicles moved rapidly into a line. Stiller stopped the jeep twenty yards behind the forming group of armor and hopped out, motioning for Hall to join him. The lieutenant saw that the half-tracks were halting just short of the crest of the hill. Baum was up also, already out of his vehicle and shouting orders as the task force hastily assembled for the attack. Even as they approached the commander, the first shells were belching out of the tanks and lobbing into the POW camp.

"Infantry spread out!" shouted Baum, screaming to make himself heard over the din of the shelling. "Stay behind and low. Don't engage the enemy until we get close. We're moving fast. Let's get the hell in there and get our boys!"

The infantry spread out, small groups sprinting to positions huddled behind each of the remaining tanks. Stiller approached Baum. "What do you want us to do?" he asked.

Baum looked over, irritation crossing his face. "Just stay the hell out of the way and go get your prisoner when the camp is open."

"No way. We've fought all the way here, and we'll fight now," responded Stiller sternly. "Hall needs some more ammo. Can you spare any?"

Baum looked at them for a second, then seemed to acquiesce. "Fine. You can go in support with a squad. Don't get in their way."

"What about the ammo?"

"Check with the half-tracks. They might have something." Baum flicked his wrist behind him negligently.

"Go find out if they have some bullets for us, Hall," ordered Stiller.

The lieutenant tromped back away from the fighting. The

half-tracks were a hundred yards or so down the road. As he reached the crest of the hill, he darted to his left, stepping into the trees a few feet so he could relieve himself. His arm was throbbing, but the bandage seemed to be holding. He finished and zipped his trousers back up. Looking around, he quickly dug the flask out of his pocket and unscrewed the top, taking a quick gulp of the fiery liquid. He immediately felt better as the warm feeling spread from his stomach through his limbs. He stuffed the flask back into place and then hurried back toward the half-tracks. Inquiring of one of the drivers, he was directed to the supply vehicle. He was able to beg for two clips for his Thompson. He was soon back up the hill and returning to the command area, where Stiller was waiting impatiently for him.

"Where've you been?" the major asked, eyeing him.

"I had to take a piss."

Stiller grunted. "Did you get any ammo?"

"Two clips."

"I guess it will have to do. I borrowed this from Baum." He flashed an M1 carbine. "This peashooter's not a hell of a lot better than my forty-five, but it will have to do. Let's get moving."

Stiller turned and hurried toward the nearest tank. It was a light M5. The 37mm gun jutted out in a stubby cylinder from the turret. Four smaller wheels connected to the tread gave way to a giant fifth one near the back. A half-dozen men already crouched behind it. When they arrived, a sergeant eyed them questioningly.

"Baum said we could join one of the groups," said Stiller. "You're still in command. We're just along for the ride."

Hall could tell the sergeant wasn't thrilled. But sergeants didn't tell majors what to do. He smiled to himself, thinking of his father and their position back home.

An explosion from their tank pulled him out of his reverie. The M5 belched out a second round, and the engine roared as the vehicle surged forward, in line with the rest of the force.

"It's on!" shouted Stiller. "Stick close to me, Hall!"

The men started forward, clinging to the raised platform near the rear of the tank. Hall could hear bullets clanging off the armor in front of him. From his obscured view, he could see the Oflag drawing nearer by the minute. Already a tower and several barracks were in smoking ruin. He wondered how many POWs were dead and wounded from the attack.

The tanks continued their advance. Hall stepped around, aiming his Thompson, but Stiller stopped him, pulling him back. "No reason to waste ammunition right now, Hall. Let's wait until we're closer."

Their tank fired again, jerking and shuddering from the recoil of the cannon. Hall could hear the rapid rat-tat-tat of the machine-gun fire as the 30 calibers sprayed the camp with bullets. He peeked around again. They'd covered half the distance to the fence line. They were no more than a hundred yards from the camp.

"Not much resistance!" shouted Stiller. "They must not have expected us here, or they've nothing left to throw our way."

Hall nodded, unable to answer. He felt winded from the loss of blood and the effects of the schnapps. The adrenaline coursed in him again, burning a heightened euphoria through his body. They were fifty yards from the gate now, then thirty. He saw a German in one of the towers jerking back and forth as rounds ripped through his body. He hung against the wooden rail for a moment before tumbling over onto the ground in front of the fence.

A Sherman nearby exploded in flame, rolling forward for a few more seconds before it came to a rest. Burning fuel spewed out of the back, spilling over the infantry packed in closely behind it. The men were engulfed in flame, a half-dozen writhing figures adding their agonizing screams to the symphony of carnage.

"They must have some artillery!" Stiller shouted. "Keep your head down; we're almost there!"

The tanks hit the fence in several places, the steel monsters ripping with ease through the barbed-wire barriers. The fencing bent, then broke, snapping and curling in long, whipping swaths. A coil ripped across a nearby GI, tearing off half his face. The soldier flipped backward, his legs kicking hard against the ground as his body shuddered.

Another tank was hit, exploding in a roar of twisted steel and erupting fire. "Where the hell is that coming from?" screamed Stiller. Hall scanned the buildings, looking for any sign of the attacking Germans. All he could see were the burning barracks, a dead kraut here and there, and the occasional flash of a small-arms weapon within the camp.

White flags appeared now at the doors of several barracks. Hall strained his eyes, trying to make out the forms behind the gesture. "Those are prisoners!" shouted Stiller. "We've made it!"

Hall realized the major was correct. They were still in combat, fighting the remaining resistance from the Germans. There was a tank or artillery somewhere that they must track down and neutralize, but they were in the Oflag, and they'd found the prisoners. Now they had one job left: they had to locate Patton's son-in-law and get him safely home.

Chapter 18

Between Hammelburg and Oflag XIII
March 27, 1945, 1230 hours

The fire from Koehl's ambush rained down into the American convoy. The surprise was perfect, and in the first moments, a tank and a half-track were obliterated by the Ferdinands. Their position was ideal, and Koehl shouted and screamed in triumph as his force continued to pour a powerful and continuous barrage of steel down onto the task force. The explosions below looked like a massive fireworks display, and the *Hauptmann* gloried in his revenge as the Americans stood on the edge of annihilation.

Koehl scanned the opposite hill with his field glasses. Dozens of flickering flames illuminated his infantry unit raining small-arms fire down on the column. Although the bullets were useless against the tanks, the constant fire caused damage to the command jeeps and the half-tracks, as well as deterring any infantry attacks up either hill. But his men were exposed. A shell erupted amid the flashes of fire. He saw bodies tumble, rolling lifeless down the hill. He was taking casualties, but the infantry was spread out, and there were too many targets for the Americans to handle.

Another Sherman exploded, the tank rolling off the road to the left before rumbling to a stop with the front wedged against the base of a pine tree. The top of the hatch ripped open, and Koehl saw several men roll out onto the ground before they scrambled for cover, their bodies darting this way and that as they dodged invisible threats.

The enemy column slowed. Koehl felt the rush of elation. If the convoy stopped, they would have them trapped, and they would destroy the remaining armor in detail before turning on the half-tracks and the infantry.

A shell exploded harmlessly near the front of his Ferdinand. The thick armor made a crippling hit difficult for the enemy to achieve. He shook his fist at the Shermans scrambling below, the flames of victory flickering in his eyes. A few more minutes and the battle would be over. Already it seemed that the enemy fire was slackening. The task force was dazed and sluggish, unable to deal with the cross-fire attack raining down on it from the high ground. A lone GI raised his hands in the air in surrender. He was mowed down by machine-gun fire in seconds, and the *Hauptmann* knew capitulation was near. His revenge was in his grasp.

Koehl's Ferdinand jumped and lurched, knocking him off his perch and into the belly of the behemoth. He stared in disbelief. The interior was awash with blood. The driver had disintegrated from a direct hit. Bits of flesh and brain were strewn all around the interior. Koehl gagged, fighting not to retch. Fire licked the bottom of the steel enclosure, burning his ammunition loader as the man writhed in extreme agony. Schmidt clawed at the ladder, anguish in his eyes, reaching an arm out in silent supplication. Koehl realized in horror that his friend's legs were missing halfway down, cut off above the knee, the tattered bloody flesh melted into the fabric of his trousers.

Even as he watched, the flames rose, licking at his boots. He risked a glance at the ammunition and saw with horror that even now the fire was kissing the steel shells. When the heat reached a certain point, the ammo would explode, killing everyone inside. He had moments to save them. He reached out to Schmidt, grabbing his wrist and pulling him toward the ladder. He had to get them to safety.

To his shock, the sergeant ripped his hands away. He turned to look at his friend. His eyes were full of pain but also with determination. He opened his mouth to speak, but the superheated air seized any sound. Koehl grabbed for the sergeant's wrist again, shaking his head; he would not leave without him.

Schmidt pushed away, his face a scowl. He pointed toward the escape hatch, his gesture a command. Koehl knew his friend was right. He had seconds at most to escape. He would never make it if he tried to assist the sergeant. He must choose between life and death. There wasn't even time for last rites.

He wanted to stay, to slump down next to his closest friend and let the flames and fire take them both. Something pulled at him, though, an instinct to survive, to flee, to save the life that Schmidt was giving him in his agony and sacrifice. He hesitated a moment more, as Schmidt gestured frantically at him. He made the sign of the cross over his friend, uttering a few words in Latin.

With a heroic effort, he pulled himself up on the ladder and started to rise. He paused at the hatch and looked down at Schmidt. He smiled sadly, tears filling his eyes. The sergeant saluted, smiling in return, battling the pain. Koehl took a deep breath and climbed up into the hatch, dragging himself out with all of his strength, racing against time. Another second passed, and he was out, rolling off the hatch onto the body of the Ferdinand. With a final exhaustive effort, he leapt from the tread into the grassy blades of the meadow. As he hit the ground, his Ferdinand exploded. Hot shrapnel flew in every direction. A fragment tore across his shoulder, lancing cloth, flesh, and bone. He arched his back and screamed with the pain, twisting and turning as his mind fought the throbbing, hot wound. He crawled a few meters away, the meadow thick with explosions, before darkness overwhelmed him.

Koehl woke suddenly, jerking and fighting. Strong hands held him down, and he struggled for his life, ripping at the fingers that grasped his chest. His shoulder burned with fire. "*Hauptmann*, stop fighting." He recognized the voice. One of his men. He was among Germans. He opened his eyes and saw he was still on the hill. A young private crouched over him, pinning him down, a weary face full of grave concern.

"It's all right, Private. I'm fine now. You can let me up."

The soldier hesitated before releasing his grasp. Koehl pulled himself to a sitting position. He could see his line of Ferdinands, which seemed intact except for his own. *His own.* His machine was gone. He'd protected her through battle after battle, only to lose her here at his moment of triumph. Worse, his men were dead, all of them, even Schmidt, his closest companion in the entire world. The last person he'd truly cared about.

At least they'd destroyed the enemy force. He looked down the hill, and then even that dream was gone. To his utter amazement, with the exception of three burned-out tanks and two half-tracks, the Americans were gone. Somehow, they'd escaped his grasp again. He burned with rage.

"What happened?" he demanded through gritted teeth, addressing the private who just moments ago was trying to help him.

"The Americans were able to push through and escape."

"How could that happen?" he demanded.

"The tanks that we hit did not block the road. They were able to push on through."

"I don't understand how that is possible. We had them!" Koehl tried to lift himself, lunging at the private. The soldier took a step back.

"I'm sorry, sir. When your vehicle was hit, several of the other crews jumped out to try to assist you."

"You should have stayed at your weapons!" he screamed, his anger mixing with pain. "I didn't give that order. We had those bastards right where we wanted them! Now they've gone and killed Schmidt too. Schmidt!" The captain coughed the last words through a bloody froth spewing from his mouth. His head swam, and he nearly passed out again. He reached out, grabbing the front of the private's tunic and pulling him near. "I didn't give that order."

The private recoiled, his face filling with shame. "I'm sorry, sir. We all are. But we wanted to save you. You're our leader. You've protected us all this time. You're more important to us than a useless column of Americans."

Despite his anger, Koehl was surprised and touched by the words. "You should have done what I said."

"You're right. We should have followed your orders, but we couldn't let you die, not when there was a chance to save you. We will follow you anywhere, sir, and follow any order, but we won't give up a chance to keep you alive."

They had turned him over now, and a medic was at work on his back. He heard the man fumbling through his equipment.

"No morphine," he ordered.

"You need it, sir. Let us take care of things."

"I said no! I must be alert!" Koehl was already thinking beyond the ambush. There was still a chance. Still time to stop them, if he moved fast. "Patch me up and make it fast."

"Sir, you need a hospital. We've done enough on this. We need to get you back to Hammelburg."

"We are going forward!" said Koehl. "Do your work. The best you can do. We are leaving in ten minutes."

"There's no way I can—"

"Do it!"

"*Jawohl, mein Hauptmann.* This is going to hurt."

"You have your orders."

The medic set to work. Koehl could feel the man poking and prodding with metal tweezers. The pain burned through his entire body, and he had to fight to remain conscious. He felt the prongs digging deeper, and he bit down, his teeth tearing at his tongue as he fought the pain.

"That's one piece of shrapnel, sir. But I think there's more."

The medic continued, digging and moving the metal instrument through his back. One of his men handed the *Hauptmann* a belt, and he placed the leather between his teeth, biting down hard to endure the agony. He felt another sharp stab as the tweezers dug deeply into his back. He cried out in a muffled yell, then dropped his head, closing his eyes as he battled the pain.

"I think that's all. Now I need to patch you up. You need stitches, but I can bandage you for now. You really should be at the hospital."

"I told you, Corporal. Just get it done."

The medic continued his work. Even the simple cleaning and bandaging of the wound was almost more pain than Koehl could take. In a few minutes more, however, it was over.

"That's the best I can do, sir."

Koehl rose, twisting his shoulder back and forth. The pain lanced through him, but he drove it down. "That will have to do. Thank you." He turned to his senior Ferdinand commander, Lieutenant Jaeger. "Do we have any intelligence on the column?"

The man shook his head. "No, sir, but it's not hard to guess where they went."

"The Oflag."

The lieutenant nodded.

"How long was I out?"

"Not long, sir, maybe ten minutes."

Koehl calculated this, adding the time to the dressing of his wound. If they hurried, there might still be time to hit the

Americans before they took the camp. "Let's roll out. I'll jump in with you. We can take the lead. How far out are we from the camp?"

"Maybe a half hour at most."

"If we gun it?"

"The engines may overheat. It's an eight percent grade."

"We'll have to risk it. Let's get going right now. Call the infantry in."

"And your vehicle?" asked Jaeger.

Koehl glanced at the burning husk of his Ferdinand. Even now his friend's body burned within, along with his precious crew. He shook his head. *I can't think of that right now.* "We'll come back and take care of things later."

The *Hauptmann* climbed into his new Ferdinand, taking the commander's seat, and within a few minutes, his reduced force was rumbling down through the narrow path and back onto the road. They turned left, passing the hulk of a burning Sherman and up the steep incline toward Oflag XIII. As they moved along, the lieutenant shouted up to him. "I know a shortcut, sir. If we take the branch to the left, we have a straighter shot at things. I think we can shave off five minutes or more."

"Take your path, Lieutenant," Koehl ordered.

The column moved forward, and Koehl utilized the radio to contact Colonel Hoepple.

"What is it, Koehl?"

"We caught them in an ambush and chewed them up pretty well. They lost three Shermans and several half-tracks."

"Excellent work, *Hauptmann.* Did we suffer any casualties?"

"We did . . . I lost my Ferdinand."

There was silence on the other end. "I'm sorry, Koehl. Did anyone get out?"

"Negative."

"Schmidt?"

"He's gone." Koehl's voice trembled with the words.

"I'm so sorry, *Hauptmann*. Perhaps you should just come back."

"Not an option, sir. We're going to get them."

"I understand. Anything I can do here?"

"If you can find any reinforcements, we need them. I want to throw everything at them and crush the rest of the force."

"I've been working on that. For now, engage and keep them busy. And, Koehl," the colonel's voice softened over the receiver, "keep yourself alive, do you hear me?"

"*Jawohl.*"

As they drew near the Oflag, a dim thunder could be heard even over the roaring of the Ferdinand's diesel engines. *The attack has already commenced*, he thought. He had to get into position and stop the Americans while he still had a chance. Another few minutes passed, and in front of him he saw the camp unfolding. He could already see the blackened smoke of a half-dozen burning buildings. To his right, in an open field, he observed the enemy force charging rapidly toward the fence line, cannons blazing, followed by clusters of infantry. The half-tracks were nowhere to be seen and probably were back up the road a bit. He cursed himself for taking the shortcut, as otherwise he would have come up directly behind the unarmored troop carriers and destroyed them in detail before he mounted the attack on the remaining enemy tanks.

There was no time for such regrets. The Americans would be inside the camp in mere moments. He thought about pulling his entire force into line before he commenced his attack, but by then it might be too late. Making up his mind, he didn't hesitate. "Fire!" he screamed down into the turret.

"But, sir," objected the lieutenant, "we're the only vehicle in position."

"No time, Lieutenant. Fire!"

A moment later, the Ferdinand jerked back as the massive

88mm cannon erupted in flame. A Sherman exploded in the distance.

"Reload!" Koehl demanded.

A few moments passed. "Ready!" came a voice from below.

"Fire!" A round exploded near another tank, missing by a few yards. The process was repeated and another shot fired, striking a light tank. "Keep them coming!" he screamed. They were destroying the enemy armor without any resistance. In a few minutes, with luck, he would have them all. Even now, the Ferdinands were moving around him and up into position. Soon he would have the entire weight of his force to bring down on the Americans.

"Sir, it's headquarters," said the lieutenant.

"Not now. Tell them we're in combat. And get that next round loaded!"

His vehicle fired again. Another near miss. *Damn it!* He was used to his own gunner, who always found the mark. "Another round. Hit your target!"

"Sir, HQ insists on speaking with you."

Koehl reached down in frustration and tore the headset out of Jaeger's hands. "What is it?" he asked in frustration.

"Is that you, Koehl? It's Colonel Hoepple. I've great news: we have reinforcements coming up. Two companies of men and some Tigers. I'm setting up an ambush, and I want you to join them. Do you have your map out? Its coordinates—"

"Not now, sir! I have them in my sights!" interrupted Koehl. "I've got them right where I want them."

"Come on now, *Hauptmann*. You have a few Ferdinands against how many tanks? It's not enough. Pull back and meet my reinforcements. Remember, it's what you asked for."

"I don't need any damned support at this point! I've got them right now!"

"Koehl, listen to me," said the colonel, his voice stern and cold. He'd never heard the colonel sound like this before.

"Your judgment is clouded by grief. You're taking risks with your men and equipment that I cannot let you continue. I'm giving you a direct order. You will pull back and join the reinforcements. Do you understand me?"

Koehl could have torn his hair in frustration. The enemy was here, distracted by the camp defense, in an open field and vulnerable. A few minutes more and he could wipe them out. But he had a direct order from the colonel, and orders were orders. "Please, sir, you don't understand the situation."

"It's you who isn't seeing things clearly, *Hauptmann*. Do I need you to turn your command over?"

Koehl stared at the receiver. Had it come to that? He'd served with the colonel for years. Still, he had to try. "Sir, if you just give me a moment to explain. I have them right now in position, I only need a few more minutes and I'll—"

"Enough! You are relieved, *Hauptmann*. Hand the receiver to Lieutenant Jaeger. You will report back to base immediately. Do you understand?"

Koehl dropped the receiver down into the turret, not even bothering to tell his crew what was happening. He stared out at the battle before him in disbelief. He had them, had them here in his grasp, and now he had to retreat. Worse, he'd lost the confidence of his commander. He could hear the Americans laughing at him. He thought of his sister, of Schmidt. No matter, there was nothing he could do. Even as he watched, his Ferdinand rumbled into reverse and backed down the road until the field and the fight were fading away.

Chapter 19

Curtis lay helplessly on his back in the German barracks. Knorr loomed over him, pistol drawn. The captain closed his eyes, his breath coming in ragged, tearing gasps. He waited for the bullet that would take everything away, his pain, his sorrow, his future. He heard the slide of the bolt as the German moved a round into the chamber of his Walther P38 9mm pistol. The sergeant placed the barrel against the middle of his chest.

"So long, Captain. I hope you have a pleasant journey to hell."

Curtis heard a sharp explosion and a flare before blackness overwhelmed him. His mind ripped through images from the past; flashes of light taunted the darkness around him. He was dead, moving to another life or whatever awaited him in the abyss. Strangely, he could still feel the pain in his back and a suffocating lack of breath. He felt himself gasp, and his arms shoved up, pushing something heavy off him. He blinked in surprise, his eyes blurry again as he tried to focus on the scene around him.

Nothing made sense. He could see the sky above, the same gray, cloudy canopy he'd faced all day. Dust swirled around, brown particles floating gently down. He was covered in wood and material. He pulled himself up, looking around. He realized he was still in the barracks. The roof had collapsed. A few feet away, he saw the body of Knorr, twisted and unmoving under a pile of rubble, his face pasty white and blood running in a rivulet from the edge of his mouth.

What had happened? He didn't know, but he had to get out of there. There was fire all around him. Flames and smoke. His ears rang, threatening to split his head open. He pulled himself up, pushing off the rubble; battling through the agony of his back, he rose to his knees and pushed off in a grimacing motion, pulling himself to a standing position. He limped and shambled out of a jagged hole in the barracks. He turned to stare at the building and realized what had happened. By some miracle, the barracks had sustained a shell that brought the roof down on top of them. He'd survived the crashing wood and material. He looked down and saw he was bleeding from dozens of wounds. His hands were a bloody mess. Still, the damage looked superficial. He needed medical attention badly, but he knew he would find nothing but death here. He had to return somehow to the main POW camp.

Curtis turned away from the barracks and realized the full chaos surrounding him. Smoke billowed from numerous buildings. The *Kommandant*'s office had sustained a round and was burning out of control. He was shocked to see tanks dotting the field in front of the fence, cannons and machine guns blazing with barrels that all seemed to be aimed directly at him. Germans ran this way and that, rifles and machine pistols in their hands, screaming and firing at the attacking Americans.

Americans. The thought hit him. His friends were here to

liberate them. But how would he survive the coming minutes before they captured the camp? He was on the German side of the fence, and he couldn't run or hide. He needed help, and he had to get back to Waters and the rest of the men.

The gate. He had to get through the gate. He stared over, and to his surprise, the entrance into the POW camp was unguarded. He took a step, then another, fighting through his pain, limping and shuffling and willing himself toward the fence as bullets zipped by him and explosions rocked the camp. Yard after agonizing yard, he lumbered through the German camp. Each step was a miracle. He expected to be blown up or shot by either the attacking tanks or a German guard. Somehow, he kept going until he reached the gate itself. He rested for a few moments, leaning against a wooden crossbar for support before he lifted a rusted iron bolt and pulled open the latch. He expected to hear cries of protest, but the Germans seemed so busy with the defense of the Oflag that they were not paying attention to a lonely crippled kriegie, shuffling feebly back to his barracks.

Curtis made it through the fence and started toward the hospital building. He was still at least a quarter mile from the headquarters barracks. To his right, the tanks were looming ever closer, spitting fiery death into the camp as the Germans fought desperately to hold them back. He realized with irony that he was very likely to die at the hands of the Americans long before he made it to Waters. Still, he thought, better that than be executed by Knorr alone in the German barracks or killed by a German here in the yard. The hospital building grew larger with each impossible step. Bullets kicked up the frozen dirt a few steps in front of him, but he ignored them, concentrating on the faded red-and-white cross of the structure.

He made it to the near side of the hospital. He embraced the corner of the building, holding on for dear life, resting for a few moments to let air into his burning lungs. An explosion erupted to his right, and he glanced over. One of the Shermans was burning. The Germans had artillery somewhere and were fighting back. What if they stopped the attack when they were so close to freedom? That was beyond his control. For now, he had to simply survive.

A few minutes passed, and he felt strong enough to continue. He worked his way around the front of the infirmary, leaning against the wall and pushing himself along until he reached the far end. Now he could see the headquarters building. He'd half-expected Waters to be standing out on the porch, watching the battle, but there was nobody in sight. He was still on his own.

He gathered his courage and pushed off from the hospital, propelling himself a few steps toward the barracks. He risked a glance to his right. The Shermans were close to the fence now, perhaps less than fifty yards from it. Smoke filled the air around him, and ash fell like dirty snow. He took another step and another. He gathered his willpower. He'd never expected to make it this far. The front porch was twenty yards away, then ten. With a final gasping effort, he scurried in rapid steps, crashing against the stairs and clutching the rail, holding on as if he clutched a life preserver at sea. He lay there for a few moments and then started shouting as loud as he could.

He called again and again, but nobody came. He wasn't sure he could be heard over the crashing battle around him. He would have to pull himself up and into the building. He was gathering his strength when the door opened. There was Waters, staring at him for a moment before recognizing the captain and rushing to his side.

"Curtis!" he shouted. "I thought you were dead!" He turned back toward the door. "I need help!" the colonel screamed. Several men scrambled out of the front door and rushed to his assistance, grabbing the captain's arms and pulling him upright, walking him into the building. The door slammed behind them, scant protection from the shells and the bullets, but still, Curtis had made it. He was alive.

"Get him some water," ordered Waters. The men led him to a nearby chair and lowered him carefully. "Do you want to lie down?" he asked.

Curtis shook his head. He'd been alone too long. Regardless of the pain, he wanted to be here with his people. "I'm okay for now, sir." He was handed a cup of water, and he took it with shaking hands, gulping the dusty, lukewarm liquid. He hadn't realized how thirsty he was. He finished the cup in an instant and was handed another. He drained that one too, and then he leaned back, shifting his position to try to minimize the pain in this back.

"Where the hell have you been?" asked Waters.

Curtis explained what had happened—Knorr, the roof collapse, the impossible journey back to the barracks. Waters listened, his eyes widening.

"Christ, son, it's a miracle you made it back. Is Knorr dead?"

"No way to know. He wasn't moving. I pray to God he's gone."

"Won't make much difference one way or another now," said the colonel. "We'll be free any minute." Waters spit. "If Knorr is alive, we'll see who gets a bullet in the chest."

Colonel Goode came over, bending down to look closely at Curtis. "You okay, son?"

"Just great," answered Curtis, gathering a flicker of humor.

The POW commander chuckled. "Yeah, you look it." He turned to Waters. "I think it's time we do something, John."

"What do you have in mind?"

"I think we need to send someone out with a white flag. The Americans need to know where we are, and I think the Germans might surrender if we give them just a little bit to think about."

Waters stroked his chin, considering the idea. "You might be right."

"Let's put a group together. You have anyone in mind?"

Waters shook his head. "I'm not sending others. If anyone is taking the gamble, it will be me."

"Can't risk you. You know that. Pick a few of the boys, and I'll see if I can scrounge up a white sheet to wave at them."

Waters stepped closer to the colonel. "I'm going or nobody is," he said with slow, measured words. Goode stared at his XO for a few moments.

The POW commander shrugged. "So be it, John. But you're not going alone. Get a couple men together and get out there."

Waters nodded. "Fetch me a sheet, and I'll put together a little group."

Goode gave the orders, and Waters moved through the officers, asking for volunteers. Everyone raised their hand. Waters selected a couple of men. Goode returned minutes later with a large gray handkerchief. "Best I could do," he said.

"It will get the job done."

The door ripped open, and Curtis was surprised to see General von Goeckel there, flanked by a couple of guards. He strolled into the building and approached Goode, saluting crisply to the POW commander.

The men were silent, not sure what was happening. Goode saluted cautiously in return. "What can we do for you, General?"

"The situation outside is hopeless," the German said. "I am surrendering the command to you, and I will take no further responsibility for casualties. You need to get ahold of your friends and call a cease-fire."

"We were just thinking the same thing, General. Only problem is your men won't be too keen on us waltzing out of this building."

"You can take Zimmerman here with you," he said, pointing to a sergeant. "He's a translator, and he'll give the orders to my men."

Goode nodded. "Much obliged, sir." He turned to Waters.

"Get hustling out there, John. Let's shut this thing down before anyone else gets killed."

Waters nodded, taking the handkerchief and motioning for his men and the translator to follow.

"Be careful out there," said Goode, and he saluted.

Waters returned the gesture and opened the door, taking in the scene around him for a few moments before he stepped out into the maelstrom. Men huddled at the door, watching the lieutenant colonel and his small party heading out toward the fence to try to shut down the battle.

Curtis wanted to see. He lifted himself from the chair, gritting through the pain, and hobbled over toward the door. He reached the group of men clustered at the threshold and placed his hands on the shoulders of one of them, holding on so he could keep his position. His view was partially blocked, but he could see Waters marching toward the fence line.

On the horizon, he saw burning tanks. Tracers zipped past, walking along the edge of another barracks. Guards, gray ghosts outlined against the fields beyond, ran this way and that, pausing for a moment to fire before moving again.

Curtis felt the old panic. He flashed back to the snow, the panzers, death raining from above. His breathing came in rattled gasps, and he fell against the threshold, laboring to maintain his balance. The fighting was all around him again. Last time, he'd lost Hanson—along with his entire company. What might he lose now?

He looked up in terror, realizing with wretched pain who was in danger now. He screamed for Waters, trying desperately to call him back. But it was too late. With the battle raging around them, there was no way the colonel could hear his words.

As Curtis watched, Waters's little group approached a German guard. The man whipped his rifle around and pointed it at the colonel. Curtis could see the translator talking, arms waving, frantically pointing back at the barracks and then at the attacking Americans. The guard shook his head, raising the rifle again.

Curtis stepped forward, calling, trying to attract their attention. The sky spun, and he tumbled to the porch. Desperately he tried to crawl, his arm extended, trying to stop what was unfolding in front of him. There was nothing he could do. The rifle belched flame. Curtis heard the retort a fraction of a second later, one shot among thousands. Waters flew backward, hitting the ground hard a few yards away. Curtis shouted and screamed. He buried his head in his left forearm, his right hand clutched in a fist, beating the wooden porch. Not again. He'd failed again. The tears fled down his cheeks. He lay there as bullets and shells crashed in among them, helpless and impotent—as ever.

Chapter 20

Hall and Stiller pressed hard against the back of the light tank. Bullets ricocheted off the armored skin, and explosions rocked the force. Where was the damned artillery coming from? They were losing tanks, and if they didn't stop the Germans soon, they wouldn't have a force to bring the men back out.

Then miraculously, the shelling stopped. It took long moments for Hall to realize it, but while the small-arms fire continued, the artillery had ceased. The tanks must have located the enemy and wiped them out. They were able to advance again now, the Shermans rumbling forward and spewing their cannon fire into the camp. A tower was hit as Hall watched, exploding in fire from a round. Bodies tore through the air, arms and legs separated to land in gray lumps in the prison yard beyond. The firing was hot. A GI near Hall was hit, then another. He didn't bother to look at them and concentrated on remaining near the center of the tank, pressed close, out of the line of fire as much as possible.

As they pressed into the camp, Hall looked down the fence line. A half-dozen Germans were kneeling in a line, firing their rifles at the tanks and infantry beyond. He whipped his Thompson over and took aim, then depressed the trigger, firing a volley. His bullets hit the mark, felling two of the guards. The others turned to face this new threat, raising their rifles, but were driven off by thirty-caliber machine-gun fire by the tanks pressing in front of them. To his left, a group of POWs were pulling a wounded man back toward what looked like a barracks. Behind them, several Germans raised their hands in the air. Even as Hall absorbed this information, the firing slackened. Within a few minutes, it was over. The Oflag was theirs.

Baum bounded up, surrounded by a press of men. He was smiling a tight-lipped grin, surveying the conquered POW camp. Germans were approaching, arms raised, and the infantry were already taking the enemy into custody.

"Great job, Baum," said Stiller, walking up to shake the captain's hand. "You got us here." He motioned for the captain to step aside, and they huddled together. Hall was the only other person in earshot.

Baum nodded. "Now I have to get us back. You came here for a reason, Stiller. How much time will you need to find Patton's son-in-law?"

"Shouldn't take long. There's what? Two or three hundred POWs? I'd say five minutes tops."

"Okay, that's fine. We've got to hump out of here as quickly as possible. I don't know where that artillery came from, but there could be more out there, not to mention any other reinforcements closing in on us. I'll get the rest of the POWs loaded up while you find your target. What's his name? I can spread the word."

"I'd rather we didn't do that, sir. I'm not sure Patton wants his intentions for this raid known. If we tell everyone why we're here, there's no way it stays a secret."

Baum grunted. "I guess I can see why. The whole thing stinks like dead fish to me. We've lost a batch of men already to rescue some POWs that would be free in a month. All for one man."

"Orders are orders. I don't second-guess the chief. You'll do well to do the same. I'll get going." He turned to the lieutenant. "Let's move, Hall. Keep that Thompson handy just in case. The krauts are surrendering, but I don't want to run into any heroes."

Even as they moved past the Shermans, they saw the prisoners. Scores of men emerged from a dozen buildings nearby. Almost an endless stream. They stepped out tentatively at first, but soon they were rushing forward, arms in the air, laughing and shouting. The first of them reached some of the infantry and threw their arms around them, kissing their cheeks, tears running down their faces.

"Jesus Christ," said Stiller.

"What is it?" asked Hall.

"Look at them."

"What? They're happy?"

"Not that, boy, look at the numbers. There's gotta be a thousand or more."

"So?"

"So we have transport for a couple hundred, maybe three at the most. We can't take more than a quarter of them."

Hall realized with shock the major spoke the truth. "What will happen to the rest?"

Stiller didn't answer. He watched for a few moments, his face pale, his jaw crushing a plug of tobacco. "It's in God's hands. I've got a mission. Let's go find our boy."

"How are we going to find him in this throng?" asked Hall.

"Just stick with me. It will take a little longer now, but that's okay. Baum's got a real mess on his hands, and he's not going anywhere for a long time to come. Let's get searching."

Hall followed the major and streamed into the crowd. Stiller looked this way and that, searching the faces. They milled around with the captives for about fifteen minutes, but he didn't find who he was looking for.

"Damn it, where is he?"

"Maybe we should check the barracks, sir?"

Stiller stroked his chin. "Not a bad idea. Let's do it."

They moved down the line of buildings, walking rapidly now. They searched door after door, but the bunks were abandoned. In less than a half hour, they'd looked in every building.

The major was frustrated now. He started back toward the POWs. "I don't understand it. We know he's here. Where the hell is he? I must have missed him the first time around."

They searched back through the POWs again, Stiller turning men around now to look into their faces. Another twenty minutes passed, but they didn't find him. Finally, he stopped, looking out again over the crowd, his face showing anxiety and confusion.

"Maybe he wasn't here after all?" said Hall.

"No way that's true," said the major, but his face belied the statement.

"What if something happened to him?" said the lieutenant. "What if he died?"

"You don't know the man. I'm not sure you could kill him." He snapped his fingers. "You might be on to something, though, Hall. There's one building we didn't check. Let's head over to the hospital. He could be sick, I suppose."

They inquired about the infirmary, and an emaciated prisoner pointed out past the barracks to a solitary building. They headed in that direction and reached the door in less than a minute. Hall went first, Thompson drawn, and opened the doors.

The hospital ward was empty except for a single prisoner lying on a cot about halfway down. Hall saw what looked like splashes of dried blood on the walls in many places. He wondered what the hell had happened in here, but there was no time to consider that right now. The prisoner was on his side, facing them. When they entered, his eyes brightened, and he raised a feeble hand. They rushed to his side.

"Who are you, son?" asked the major.

"I'm Captain Jim Curtis, sir. Who are you?"

"Major Alexander Stiller. What the hell happened in here?"

"They killed all of the sick and wounded. A few days ago. Executed them. My friend was here. I failed him." Curtis's voice shook and wobbled weakly as he said this. Out of fatigue or pain, Hall didn't know.

"You're the only one in here?"

"All but Lieutenant Colonel Waters."

Stiller drew in his breath sharply. "Where is Waters?"

"In surgery," said Curtis. "In the next room over."

"What happened to him?"

"He was shot by a guard when he was trying to get the Germans to surrender."

"Damn it," swore Stiller. "Is he hurt bad?"

"Real bad, I think," said Curtis. "He was bleeding something terrible. It just happened an hour or so ago. They brought him in here straightaway, even before they carried me over."

"How do you know any of this?" asked Hall.

"I saw the whole thing happen. Waters and I were close. He's been like a father to me." Curtis looked up at them. "I know he'll be all right now that you're here. We all will be."

Stiller grunted. "You get some rest, son. Hall, let's go."

The lieutenant followed the major to the end of the ward and through a set of double doors into an operating room. This second, smaller room was as bare as the first, with a couple of uncovered light bulbs dangling from the ceiling. A single operating table rested in the middle of the room. Several men stood over a patient, working frantically, a set of bloody instruments resting near them. As they came through the door, one of the men looked up in surprise.

"Get out of here now!" the doctor demanded. "You'll expose him to germs and kill him."

"Who is that you're working on?" asked Stiller.

"It's Lieutenant Colonel Waters."

"Is he going to make it?" asked the major.

"I don't know for sure. I think so. Who the hell are you?"

"I'm Major Stiller. I'm on General Patton's staff. I'm here to fetch him."

The doctor shook his head. "He won't be going anywhere for a very long time."

Stiller nodded as if he expected the news. "Any chance he could be transported? If we kept it smooth and slow?"

"No way," said the doctor. "At best it will be weeks, probably a month before he can go anywhere, even in an ambulance. Now, get out of here before you make it worse!"

Stiller watched the man work for a few moments longer, then turned and stormed out of the operating room.

"How's he doing?" asked Curtis.

"They think he'll make it."

"Thank God."

"Yes," said Stiller. "Thank God for that at least." He turned to Curtis. "Anything we can do for you?"

"Not just now. When will we be leaving? I'll need help getting out of here."

"Sit tight, Captain. Someone will be here to help you soon." The major paused for a second and then drew a .45 he'd picked up from a wounded task force member. "Here, son, take this and hide it. Just in case."

Stiller walked out of the hospital, and Hall followed. When they reached the porch, the major began swearing loudly, stomping back and forth. He stopped for a second to shove another plug of tobacco in his mouth, then began his cursing anew.

"That was Patton's son-in-law, wasn't it?" asked Hall.

"That's real sharp of you," answered Stiller sarcastically.

"What are we going to do?" asked Hall, ignoring the statement.

Stiller didn't answer for a moment. He spat on the ground and looked up. "Not a damned thing, Hall. Not a thing to do. We can't make things worse by taking him. He'd be dead in an hour bouncing along those roads in an open-air half-track. We've done everything we can. He's going to have to wait for the real army to get here." He shook his head. "I can't believe it. After all that shit, we've failed. Well, nothing to be done about it. We're going to make the most of it. We'll grab as many POWs as we can and get the hell out of here."

"The POWs?" repeated Hall. "There isn't room for hardly any of them. What's Baum going to do?"

"Same deal as Waters. We're going to do what we can. This raid is FUBAR. We've got to grab what we can and try to make it back." Stiller shook his head. "Useless waste of men. Patton's hardly ever been wrong, but he screwed the pooch on this one, sure enough. No sense standing around doing nothing, Hall. Let's get back to the convoy and see who we can take along." The major turned and headed back toward the vehicles and the milling mass of prisoners.

Hall turned back toward the hospital for a moment, thinking of that poor bastard inside waiting to be rescued. He shrugged his shoulders, turned and followed Stiller. Not really his problem. Task Force Baum was heading home, and he was sure as hell going with it.

Chapter 21

Hammelburg
March 27, 1945, 1400 hours

Hauptmann Koehl knocked gingerly on the door.

"Come in!" Koehl took a deep breath and twisted the handle. Colonel Hoepple was sitting at his desk, reading papers. He looked up, and his stern features seemed to soften. "*Ach*, Koehl, take a seat."

The captain took a few steps into the hotel room and grabbed a bare wooden chair in front of the colonel's desk. He was quiet, watching his leader, unsure what to say. In five years together, nothing had ever happened like this. Hoepple kept his head down for a few more seconds and then sighed, as if reluctant to begin.

"You did well out there, Koehl. Better than I'd hoped."

"I had them right where I wanted them when you called us off. If you'd given me—"

"If I'd given you any more leeway, you might have lost your whole command," interrupted Hoepple. "I've interviewed several of your men, including the engineer you nearly executed while violating orders. *My* orders!"

"Sir, I was using my independent judgment."

The colonel's eyes flared, and he raised an accusing finger. "You were prosecuting a personal vendetta and, in the process, jeopardizing your entire command. You had what, one hundred and fifty men with you? You were taking on five hundred or more, including twenty tanks. I didn't want the Americans on our side of the Main. I wanted them stopped."

"You don't understand. I had them. We were going to finish them."

"Really?" said Hoepple, leaning over his desk. "You had the convoy in a cross fire and you barely stung them."

"That wasn't my fault! They took out my Ferdinand."

"Because you put your command in danger. Because you took on a force too large for you and tried to wipe it out instead of nipping at their ankles like I ordered you to do."

"They killed her."

The colonel looked up for the first time, his eyes brimming with knowing compassion. "I know they did, Koehl. That's the heart of the problem. I've served with you for half a decade now. You've lost people before, and you've never shown it. I realize this is different. I want you to have justice, but I can't let you risk your whole command in the process."

"Is that why you relieved me?"

"I relieved you to get your attention."

"Then it's not permanent?" Koehl asked, a flicker of hope rising inside him.

The colonel leaned back, stroking his chin as if considering the question. "I don't know, *Hauptmann*. I don't want it to be. Frankly, it's up to you. It depends on our little chat and whether you are going to start following orders again."

"I have followed orders. The spirit at least."

"*Hauptmann*, I'm not going to play word games with you. If I let you go back out there, will you be the cool, capable professional I've always counted on, or are you going to continue to act out of anger and personal emotion?"

"Sir, I haven't—"

"Nonsense, *Hauptmann*. Of course, you're personally involved. You're a human being, after all. Something I had to remember."

"Then let me do my job, sir. Please."

"You don't understand me, Koehl. I'm not worried about this task. I'm worried about you. I need you to think with your head, not your heart. We may only have a few weeks left in this war. I can't afford to lose you, and I can't let you kill your men recklessly."

"I'll follow your orders this time."

Hoepple's eyes narrowed. "To the letter?"

Koehl hesitated. "To the letter."

"Even if I tell you to let the Americans go?"

Koehl had to get back into the field. It would be his job to make sure the colonel never needed to give that order. He nodded. "*Jawohl*, even if you command me to release them."

The colonel rose and stepped around his desk, reaching his hand out to grasp Koehl's. "Be careful, my friend. I can't afford to lose you. When you return, we'll go out and have some drinks for your sister and for Schmidt. Many drinks."

"Thank you, sir. I won't let you down."

"You never have, Koehl. Now let's get down to business."

After the meeting, the *Hauptmann* returned to his unit. The five Ferdinands lay in the regimental motor pool, the men swarming over them, checking their mechanical condition. The fuel truck stood nearby, a hose attached to one of the armored vehicles as his men pumped petrol. Men formed chains, passing up ammunition and shells. When they returned to battle, they would be prepared for anything. So long as there was an engagement still to find. The travel back to Hammelburg and the meeting with Hoepple had cost him more than an hour. If the Americans moved quickly, they might already be out of reach.

His force would be stuck here for at least another half hour. Koehl took the time to allow his medic to attend to his wounds. He sat on a stool the man brought and watched the work on his unit. The soldier applied a needle to the area near his wound, applying a local anesthetic before setting to work to sew up the gash. He was not totally numb, and he grimaced as he felt the vague tugs and the silky grind of the thread sliding through his flesh. At least the medic was experienced and knew how to work quickly. In twenty minutes, his work was done, and he applied a bandage.

"Are you finished?" the *Hauptmann* inquired, starting to rise.

"I guess that's as much as I can do right now. You really should be in bed for a few days, sir. You're risking an infection out here."

"The infection and the rest will have to wait," he said, clapping the corporal on his shoulder. "We still have unfinished business with our American friends."

The medic frowned but didn't argue. "Well, when we get back, sir, I want you down for at least a week. Doctor's orders."

Koehl managed a smile. "Fair enough, my friend. But only when we're done."

The *Hauptmann* spent a few more minutes supervising the loading of supplies and the refueling of the armored vehicles. "Make sure they are topped off," he ordered. "We may need every liter of fuel we can get."

After he'd seen to the men, he consulted his map, reviewing the plan the colonel had laid out for him. Despite his frustration at the Oflag, he knew that Hoepple was right. His commander was a brilliant tactician, and he'd quickly formed a new ambush that included the reinforcements he'd managed to acquire. Once Koehl met up with the new forces and moved his

Ferdinands into position, they should be unstoppable. He would no longer need luck. If the Americans bumbled into their trap, they would be annihilated.

He had to get there, however. He was now almost two hours behind schedule. He needed to get his force moving and meet up with the new units converging on the ambush point. The greatest danger would come when they left Hammelburg itself. If they had unfortunate timing, they might reach the highway and be halfway through when they were met by the point of the American column retreating to their lines. If that happened, they would be skewered and destroyed in detail long before they met up with the reinforcements. Koehl studied the map, trying to find an alternative route, but there was none. He would have to risk it.

Finally, his unit was ready. He climbed into his Ferdinand and ordered the driver to take the lead. The armored vehicle lurched into motion, and soon they were rolling laboriously through the narrow streets of Hammelburg, heading west toward the highway, his borrowed infantry company following in a half-dozen trucks.

Outside of the town, Koehl was relieved to see no sign of the Americans. They found the highway and turned to the northwest, rolling toward the ambush point. He kept his eyes busy, moving up and down the landscape for any sign of the enemy, but their luck held, and they reached the turn without incident. Another half hour passed before Koehl saw the outline of roofs in the distance. They had made it. The town of Gräfendorf loomed on the horizon. They moved in among the houses until they reached a checkpoint guarded by an MG 42 machine gun and a half-dozen Germans. Koehl ordered his vehicle to stop, and he climbed out, grimacing a little at the pain from his wound as he awkwardly scrambled down from the Ferdinand.

"Halt!" yelled one of the men, pointing his machine pistol at the *Hauptmann*.

"Put that damned thing away right now," barked Koehl. "What do I look like? A GI?"

The soldier hesitated for a moment and then slung his MP 38. "Where is your commander?" the *Hauptmann* demanded.

The soldier jerked an arm and pointed behind him with his thumb. Koehl nodded and turned to Lieutenant Jaeger, who had poked his head out of the top of the Ferdinand. "Get the whole unit up," he ordered. "Keep the engines running, and I want one Ferdinand facing back down the road, in case the Americans barge in here before I'm back. I'm going to meet with the commander of the reinforcements and coordinate our plans. I'll be back in a few minutes."

Jaeger nodded and started barking orders. Koehl hurried past the machine-gun nest and down the cobbled streets of Gräfendorf in the direction the soldier had indicated. As he passed a side street, a Tiger tank materialized in his view, the sleek monster aiming its giant cannon in his direction. *He has tanks. Good.* He walked a few more meters down the street and came to another tank. In front of this vehicle, he found the commander, who looked up, saluting crisply. Koehl returned the gesture.

"You must be *Hauptmann* Koehl?" the captain inquired.

"*Jawohl*. And who are you?"

"I'm *Hauptmann* Baumann," said the tank commander. "Hoepple told me you'd be meeting me here. What are we dealing with, and what do you have?"

"A task force of Americans. Maybe fifteen tanks left and a bunch of half-tracks. They could be carrying another five hundred escaped POWs."

Baumann whistled. "That should slow them down. What do you have?"

"Five Ferdinands fully fueled and armed. I've got most of a company of infantry."

"That's it?" said the captain, raising an eyebrow. "And

you've been tangling with the Americans all day? You're as brave as the colonel said."

Koehl ignored the comment. "What have you brought with you?"

"I've got six Tigers and a battalion of infantry."

Another six 88s and five hundred men. He had them! "That's quite a command. Isn't there a major somewhere?"

Baumann nodded grimly. "There was. His head is somewhere in France. Never could find it."

"Where do you want us?"

The captain thought about it for a second. "We've got the center of the town dialed in, but if you take your Ferdinands and spread them out on the south side, we will be able to hit them from the front and the side at the same time."

Koehl nodded. "We'll do it. I'll be in position in a half hour or less." He stepped forward and shook Baumann's hand. "Glad to have you with us," he said.

"You too, *Hauptmann*."

Koehl left, moving quickly now. He returned to his force and gave swift commands. The Ferdinands lurched into motion, maneuvering around the machine-gun nest and down the narrow street. Koehl walked along next to the vehicles, steering them down individual streets until they were all in position, each facing back toward the center. His infantry spread out as well. They were now in a similar position to their ambush at Gemünden, but with four times the force. He took a moment and said a quick prayer of thanks. He felt guilty about offering praise to God for allowing this trap to form, but he was elated and happy that he was in position for his vengeance. *For Gerta. For Schmidt.*

He positioned himself so he could see out of the town and back down the road where the Americans would be coming. He scanned the fields and the road with his binoculars, impatiently watching for the enemy to materialize. Minutes turned into an hour, and then another. The gray clouds in the heavens began to dim. The first hint of darkness. He stared out with mounting desperation. They had the perfect trap, but the Americans were nowhere to be found. They had disappeared into the countryside. He had failed again.

Chapter 22

Oflag XIII
March 27, 1945, 1400 hours

Hall and Stiller made their way back toward the task force. They had to push their way through the pressing throng in order to reach Captain Baum. The commander was in the center of a maelstrom of excitement as the POWs cheered and laughed, clapping and celebrating. After a few more minutes, they reached the remaining vehicles and found the task force leader huddled with his principal officers and a few of the POWs. Baum was in a deep discussion with a colonel, and he looked up mid-sentence, recognizing Stiller.

"Colonel Goode, here is Major Stiller right now."

The POW turned and saluted. "Major Stiller, a pleasure. Baum here tells me you were looking for someone specific." Stiller looked to the task force commander and then back. Hall knew his commander was trying to work out whether Baum had spilled the beans.

"I was looking for Lieutenant Colonel Waters, for reasons that need to remain confidential," he said sternly.

Goode seemed to understand and nodded in response. "That's my XO. Unfortunately, he was wounded by the damned krauts when we tried to get them to surrender. Did you find him?"

"Yes, he's in surgery right now."

Goode's face showed his concern. "Is he going to make it?"

"Looks like it," said Stiller. "But he's not going anywhere right now. Can't move for a month probably."

Goode nodded. "That's what I expected. Damned shame. Don't worry, Major. I can guess why you're here, but your reasons are safe with me." He turned to Baum. "But one problem at a time. The captain and I were beginning to discuss the evacuation of my men. He just gave me the news that he can't take everyone, but we didn't get around to a number yet."

Baum's face lit up with discomfort. "A couple hundred, tops."

"You've got to be kidding me," protested Goode, his eyes widening. "I've got fifteen hundred men here. They've been waiting for months to be freed. You've got to do a hell of a lot better than that."

Baum shrugged helplessly. "We've lost a batch of half-tracks getting here. I'm sorry colonel, but our intelligence estimated three hundred in the camp at the most."

The POW commander spat on the ground. "Sounds like your S-2 blew it," said Goode. "What on earth am I supposed to do with everyone else? March them back to the camp? We just killed a bunch of the guards. I'm sure they'll be real happy to welcome us back. This is a hell of a situation, Captain."

Baum paused, thinking. "We could take men on the tanks. It will be a risk for them, and we'll reduce our fighting ability, but we could probably get another hundred that way."

"That's a bit better, but not much," said Goode. "I've got to give my men more of a chance than that."

"We've got some food and a weapon or two, don't we?" said

Stiller. "We could distribute some of it to those who might want to try to escape on foot."

Baum looked over at the major, his face concentrated in a frown. "You're right. It's going to stretch us awful thin. If anything more goes wrong, we're going to be in a hell of a fix. But we've started a real mess for these boys, and we can't just leave them holding the bag." He turned to Goode. "I'll get what food and weapons we can spare and have them brought here. We'll take as many as we can, but for anyone else who wants to make a run for it, we'll give them what we've got."

"Thanks, Captain," said Goode, shaking Baum's hand. "That's something at least. I still don't understand why they sent this little scratch of a force this far behind enemy lines without any support. It doesn't make any damned sense to me."

"You'll have to ask Stiller that question."

Goode turned to the major, his face thoughtful. "Don't tell me Patton sacrificed all these men and left us all in a lurch just to bring Waters out?"

Stiller shifted uncomfortably. "We're not even supposed to be talking about that, Baum." He looked around at the small group and pointed a finger. "All of you are sworn to secrecy. That's an order. If you want my opinion, the general screwed this one up. But that's between us. Bottom line, we've all made mistakes. We've lost men. We make decisions, we gamble, and in war, the errors add up to dead people. I will tell you this. No way Patton sends this force in knowing there are fifteen hundred people here. He would have sent a whole combat command for sure."

"That's what you asked for," said Hall. "So did Abrams."

"Shut it, Hall," snapped Stiller. "That don't matter. Like I said, we all make mistakes. Sitting here and bitching about it won't make anyone else alive or any more of these kriegies free. What we need to do is get our asses out of here with as many folks as we can grab, and get our butts back to the line. Once we make it, we can tell Patton the deal. He'll kick up the attack and get our main force here double quick. It's the best we can do."

Hall felt his anger rising again at the general's stupidity. How dare he send him on this ridiculous raid without sufficient resources. He'd risked the lieutenant's life recklessly. Now they would be slowed down by too many prisoners, and they weren't going to bring Waters back. Patton would be pissed and probably in no mood to hand out rewards. He'd put his life on the line for nothing.

As he thought this through, Goode climbed up on one of the Shermans, turning to address the prisoners. He raised his hands, taking several minutes to force the din of cheers down to a level where he could hear himself speak.

"Okay, boys, I've got some news."

"Three cheers for the colonel!" somebody yelled from the crowd. The kriegies erupted in shouts and applause.

"Quiet. Quiet!" shouted Goode. "I've got some *bad* news, and it's not easy for me to tell you." That brought silence to the men. Hall could see the confusion in the eyes of the POWs as they waited to hear what Goode had to say.

"I'm going to give it to you straight, the only way I know how. We thought this attack was the main American force, but it's not. It's just a small task group, a few hundred men. They came to liberate the camp, but unfortunately the information they had back at base had us numbered at a few hundred. They only brought transportation for that number, and worse yet, they've been banged up pretty good getting here." Goode looked out at the crowd, and Hall could read the misery in his face. "They can only take about two hundred of you with them, maybe a bit more."

The prisoners exploded in a ruckus of anger and complaints. The mass stormed toward the tank, fists in the air. Goode raised his arms and violently lunged his fists at the crowd, willing them to calm down. The force of his character had its effect, and after a few moments, he could make himself heard again.

"What the hell are we supposed to do?" called out one of the men.

"That's what I've been talking to Captain Baum here about. As I figure it, you men have three options. First, the captain will take as many as he can. Second, he's gathering some weapons and some food. Anyone who wants to try to escape on foot, whether individually or in groups, can see the captain and his men. They'll set you up with everything they can spare."

"What's the third option?" asked the same POW.

"For everyone else, you've got to head back to the camp. What was true yesterday is still true now. The war is damned near over. Even if they move you somewhere else, you'll likely be free in a few weeks, a month at the most." Goode looked out over the group for a moment, letting the next words hang in the air. "I'll not lie to you, boys. From where I see it, that's the safest bet. The task force has a hell of a ways to go, and God knows what's out there. On foot, you're less of a target, but fifty miles through hills and over rivers, without maps or much in the way of food or weapons, is maybe a bigger gamble yet. I know it's the hardest choice, but the best decision might be to head back to the barracks and sit tight."

At this, the crowd erupted again in frustration. Hall watched the anger as the men shouted, arguing over who would be allowed to go and whether they should just head back to the camp. He checked his watch. It was 1500 hours. He felt impatient. They needed to get going, and the fewer of the POWs they took, the better chance they had of making it back. He turned to the major.

"Shouldn't we load up and get out of here?" he muttered.

"We will in a few minutes. Look at those poor bastards. We've left them in a hell of a situation here."

"Yes, sir," responded Hall. "But isn't the best thing we can do for them to get back to our own lines?"

The major looked over at him sharply, words hanging on his lips, but he seemed to think over Hall's statement. "You're probably right. We will do the most for these poor bastards by getting the real army here as soon as we can." He put a hand on the lieutenant's shoulder. "You did fine on our way here, Hall. A far sight better than I expected. There's a man in there after all. I know Patton's going to be disappointed about Waters, but he'll be mighty happy to hear how you did out here."

Hall nodded, feeling elation. Stiller was going to speak on his behalf. Perhaps the whole raid wasn't a loss. The major was proud of him? What a schmuck. Hot damn. He was so close.

The next hour was wasted. The POWs milled around, arguing and jockeying for position. Hall stared out from his jeep, anger rushing through him. The Germans were closing in from every direction. They had to get out of here as quickly as they could. Couldn't these men make a decision? Hadn't they heard their colonel? The best choice was to go back to the camp and wait. Frankly, Hall wished that Baum had refused to bring any of them. Wouldn't they be better off if the task force escaped and brought the army back here in a day or two? That was best for all of them.

Instead, the men selfishly battled for a spot in the column. Shouting broke out and even a fistfight here and there as men scrambled to secure a precious seat on one of the tanks or in the half-tracks. Some of the infantry brought spare equipment and ammunition to their jeep, stacking the materials in the back and strapping it down, to make room in some of the half-tracks for more men. Their wounded driver was gone. The medics must have moved him to one of the half-tracks. Hall felt relief; with all these supplies, at least they wouldn't be saddled with any of the POWs in their jeep. He looked at his watch. If only they would hurry.

Finally, when it seemed they could not possibly wait any longer, Hall heard the Shermans coming to life. The tanks were covered with POWs hanging on to every corner of the turrets. Hall looked back. The half-tracks had come up, and they too were covered in men. Hall cursed silently. The column would have to move slowly to allow the weakened soldiers to hang on. If they were attacked, they would not be able to fight back quickly because the prisoners would have to clear off the tanks. He shook his head. With the significant delay and the slow retreat they would now have to make, he had no idea how they would ever return to their own lines. He thought of raising this issue with Stiller, but he knew it would merely draw a sharp rebuke. The "Lone Ranger" would never leave a man behind if he could help it. What was wrong with these people? The purpose of the mission was clearly to get Waters. They'd failed in that, so why endanger the rest of the force with these POWs crowded on the tanks? They should only take what the half-tracks could manage—or, better yet, nobody at all. Well, there was nothing he could do about it. He was along for the ride.

The tanks in front of Hall lurched into motion. The column was on the move again after hours of wasted time in the camp. As they moved out, Hall watched two distinct groups of POWs with very different intentions. Small groups of men carrying food and weapons were heading out into the hills in various directions. Hall knew they had little chance of making it to the American lines. They would have to avoid the roads, and the terrain from here to the front was dotted with hills and forests, then open farmland, where every house held a German family that might turn them in.

Regardless of the safety of the last option, Hall couldn't help but feel the collective hopelessness of the remaining group. About five hundred men were shambling back toward the camp. They either had fought for a place in the task force and lost, or simply did not have the strength or courage to try to escape on foot. These men were headed back to captivity, to hope and pray that the Americans would liberate them again soon. Hall kept his eyes on them as his jeep rumbled away from the Oflag. Soon the men and the camp were lost behind the hilltop as the convoy rumbled back down the winding forested roads toward Hammelburg.

As they rattled along, Hall's worst fears came to the forefront. The group was barely moving faster than the pace of a light jog. The men clutched any part of the tanks that they could reach or held on to each other as they bumped and jostled along in the growing darkness. As they entered the deep forest, visibility was reduced to a few feet, and Stiller hunched forward behind the wheel, trying to keep up with the nearest Sherman without crashing into the back of it.

The force crawled along that way for more than an hour, darkness growing and the stillness of the landscape broken only by the dull rumbling of the machines as they sought their way out of the crisscrossed, narrowly winding roads between the camp and Hammelburg.

Hall had given little thought to their escape route and hadn't asked Baum which way they were headed. Would they try to come out the same way they'd come in? That seemed suicide to him, but he had no idea if there was another way to reach the American lines. At this speed, it would hardly matter. It would take a full day to get back. His only hope was that Baum would reach the same conclusion and halt the column, ordering the POWs to break out into small groups and try to find their way back on their own. He was tired after twenty-four hours without sleep. He'd existed on adrenaline until now, but in the darkness, as the column crawled along, he felt weariness overcoming him. He longed for the last few pulls from his flask. He wondered in the growing blackness if he could sneak a drink without the major seeing him. He toyed with the idea but finally dismissed it. He was too close to getting everything he wanted to gamble it all for a few swigs. Opportunities had opened up several times along the way to sneak a drink. Perhaps another would appear before they reached the lines. If not, he'd have plenty to drink to celebrate his accolades. Maybe he could even get Stiller drunk, he thought. That might be amusing.

The column crept to a halt. "What the hell is it now?" asked the lieutenant.

"Not sure," said Stiller.

Behind them, they could see the flashes of a few lights. "Let's go see what's up," said the major.

Hall jumped out and followed his commander back toward Baum's jeep. The captain's vehicle was surrounded by flickering lights like so many fireflies. Baum was hunched over a map, discussing their location with Nutto.

"What's the deal?" asked Stiller.

"Just a second," said Baum.

"Captain—"

"You're not in charge, Major. Remember that."

Hall could see Stiller balking at the comment. He smiled to himself. It was entertaining to watch the proud Texan groveling before a younger officer.

The captain looked up. "What is it, Major?"

"What's the situation?"

"The situation is, we are lost. We've crossed so many of these damned roads in the past hour, I'm not quite sure where we are. We should be out of the hills by now, but all I can see in the darkness is more damned trees. I'd hoped Nutto here had seen more from the front, but he reports the same deal. Any ideas, Major?"

Stiller shrugged. "I wasn't paying attention. What are we going to do?"

"We'll keep going the same way. We've got to reach the end of this crap soon. Worst case, we'll wait until it's light."

"That's hours away," said Hall, exasperated. "We'll never make it out of here if we delay any longer."

As if confirming this comment, a whisking rip filled the air followed by the sharp detonation of an explosion. A tank up the line exploded in a fiery conflagration. Hall could see men burning, trying to escape the tank. He couldn't tell from this distance if they were POWs, crew, or both. It didn't matter. They were dead, and the task force was in peril again.

Chapter 23

Oflag XIII
March 27, 1945, 2000 hours

Captain Curtis woke with a jolt. The lights were on in the hospital ward. His back still burned with pain, but he felt refreshed by sleeping for a spell. He was surprised by his surroundings. When he fell asleep, he'd been the only person in the room. Now a dozen cots were filled with injured and wounded men, their groans and cries an agonizing symphony. A doctor and several orderlies worked with the men, hunched over and administering to their hurts. Where had they all come from?

These must be men hurt during the attack, he realized. But where were the liberating soldiers? His mind fought through the fog. Something didn't make sense. There should be new soldiers. Fresh American faces. He remembered talking to a couple of American officers from the relieving force. Where had they gone? His eyes walked down the row of wounded and stopped near the door. A German guard stood there, a machine pistol in his hands, watching over the room. What in the hell had happened while he was asleep? Why were the Germans back in charge? The prisoner next to him was unconscious. With effort, he rolled over until he faced the other direction. There was a POW here too, a bloody bandage over one of his eyes. Fortunately, he was awake. He knew the man slightly. Another of Goode's runners.

"What's going on?" he asked.

"What do you mean?"

"Why is there a German in here?"

"You haven't heard?"

"Heard what?"

"Those bastards only brought a few trucks. They didn't have room for a quarter of us, and they couldn't hold the camp. They took a couple hundred kriegies and left the rest of us to the Germans."

Curtis couldn't believe it. "How can that be? Why would they do something like that?"

"Search me, buddy, but they've left us in a hell of a fix. The Germans are hopping mad. They killed a batch of them. The krauts already marched off most of the POWs who came back. I figure the only ones left are the people in here. There's a bunch of badly wounded and hardly anyone left to deal with them."

Curtis was shocked and betrayed. How could they have been left behind again? He had been sure the worst was over. He was badly injured, it was true, but he'd expected an influx of doctors, equipment, and the safety of American troops. Instead, he was in the custody of the Germans again, and things were even worse. The enemy had been harmed, and most of the POWs were already out of the camp. Surely, the remaining guards would want to take revenge on the wounded.

He clutched his .45 under the blankets. There was only one guard in here. Perhaps he should shoot the man and take his weapon. He realized the action was desperate and would likely lead to the death of them all. He had no idea how many Germans were still in the camp. The enemy was well armed, and the only POWs nearby were medical staff and the wounded. They could never hold the hospital with a couple of weapons against the enemy. No, he would have to keep his weapon secret, a last defense to be used only in a moment of desperation.

Curtis leaned his head back, closing his eyes. Why was everything he was involved in a complete disaster? He thought of Waters. His friend and commander was not in the ward. He was probably still in surgery—or, worse yet, dead. Without his wisdom and strength Curtis wasn't sure he wanted to go on. All he'd wanted at this point was to be rescued. It was too late to fight, too late to redeem himself against the Germans. He had reconciled himself to that fact—that he would return home merely a former POW who lost his company in the Ardennes before they'd hardly fired a shot. Now even liberation was being denied him.

The Germans had killed all the wounded here only a few days ago. They might very well do the same again. There would be no home, no reprieve for him. Perhaps it was for the best. He was a failure, and he wasn't sure he deserved to live anymore. It might be for the best that he be killed here. At least his family would never know how he had let his men down at the Bulge.

Another part of him refused to accept this. He didn't want to die. He didn't want to give up. He would fight so long as there was any chance to do something. Feeling a renewed courage, he pulled himself up to a sitting position and stood, battling through his pain. He tucked his weapon under the blankets of his cot and stumbled over to the doctor, offering his assistance, such as it might be.

The next several hours passed in a blur. He worked with the doctor and the orderlies, changing dressings, cleaning wounds, holding down men while the doctor poked and prodded. He expected a squad of angry Germans to arrive at any moment, ready to spray them all with machine-gun fire. That would be the end of them. He didn't care. He was doing what was in his control, battling against the enemy in the only feeble way he could manage.

The double doors swung open at the end of the hall. Several men carried a wounded POW in on a stretcher. It was Waters. He was still alive but unconscious. Curtis moved as quickly as possible over to the XO, assisting them in gingerly moving him onto one of the available cots.

"How is he?" asked Curtis.

"With luck he's going to make it," said one of the orderlies. "He took a hell of a shot. The damned bullet rattled around all over the place inside him. Tearing up hell. The doctor thinks he patched up all the problems, but if he missed anything, Waters could bleed to death, and we'd hardly know it until it was too late."

Their conversation was interrupted by a new visitor to the ward. "Ah, Captain Curtis. I see you stayed behind for our party. How nice."

Looking up in surprise, he saw Sergeant Knorr standing near the operating doorway, a cat's grin unfurling across his face. His right arm was bandaged in a sling, and his uniform was streaked and dirty.

"Are you surprised to see me?" asked the sergeant. He walked leisurely along the row of cots, the fingers of his good arm sliding across the forehead of one of the unconscious men. He continued until he stood directly across from Curtis. Looking down, he stared for a moment and then whistled in mock surprise. "Well, well, what have we here. Is that Lieutenant Colonel Waters? The brave man of the hour is wounded? How can he protect you if he is asleep, *Herr* Captain? How can he protect himself?"

"You leave him alone," threatened Curtis in a whispered

voice. "The Americans will be back any moment. You've missed your chance."

Knorr threw his head back and laughed. "Do you think me a fool, Curtis? Your friends have come and gone. They nearly finished me off, I must admit, but fortunately I made it through. Imagine my surprise to wake up and realize that our little ceremony had been interrupted and you were nowhere to be found. I was rather miffed and concerned I would be taken into custody by the invaders. Imagine what stories you could have told them. Very unpleasant stuff, I am sure." The sergeant took a step around the cot, placing his good hand on Curtis's arm.

"*Gott*, it seems, however, is still on my side. What a parade of gifts I've been given. First, I survive, then I avoid capture. Next, the Americans leave again, assuring I would escape your justice. Finally, I find a whole new hospital full of wounded, and greatest of all, Curtis and Waters are gracious enough to remain behind." He patted the captain's arm. "Now don't you worry, Curtis. You've got a little time. I want to wait until Waters is awake. I'd hate to deprive him of the chance for a little chat before we settle all our differences."

"You'll never get away with that."

"What do you mean, Captain? Do you mean the *Kommandant*? He's already given me permission to sort out the last few details of the camp. We must tidy up, of course. We don't want any loose ends tugging at our minds while we evacuate farther into Germany." He took another step closer, whispering into Curtis's ear. "You should have escaped while you had the chance, Captain. I was going to finish you mercifully before, but now I have a more extravagant conclusion for you. Of course, I'll let you watch me finish things up with Waters first. Have you ever seen my SS knife?" He released Curtis and moved his hand down to his waist, where a black handle with intricate runes protruded from an onyx sheath. "Every SS man gets one, you know. I've only experimented a little with it, but you won't believe the results. After we've dispatched the rest of the riffraff in here, we can enjoy Waters with it. I wouldn't deprive you of the joy of watching your mentor take his leave. Then, it will just be you and me. I wonder how long I can keep you alive? We shall have to explore that together, *mein freund*. For now, I can't have you running all around."

Knorr reached out again and grabbed Curtis by the shirt. He dragged him with one arm and threw him down on a cot. The captain tried to fight back, but he was too weak, and his back burned and clawed at him as he wrenched his injury again. Knorr straddled him, sitting on his chest. He placed his good hand on Curtis's neck and started to choke him. The captain fought back, trying to push the sergeant off. He couldn't breathe, and he struggled in a panicked rage. There was nothing he could do. Knorr held him in an iron vice. He struggled, trying to free his arms, battling for a breath, but the fingers constricted his airway until he knew no more.

Chapter 24

Gräfendorf, Germany
March 27, 1945, 2000 hours

Darkness fell, and *Hauptmann* Koehl set his field glasses aside in anger and frustration. What the hell had happened to the American force? He tried to pray again, but he couldn't contain his fury, and his mind tripped on the words. Why was God doing this to him? In five years of war, he'd never experienced anything like this. His instincts for tactics were perfect. Throughout the fighting, he'd possessed an uncanny ability to predict what his enemy would do and to maneuver his forces to lie in wait for them.

But now his mind was a fog. His instincts had abandoned him when he needed them most. *They killed my sister, my best friend.* He forced himself to concentrate, to search his mind for answers, but the harder he thought, the cloudier the answer seemed to be.

Where was the task force? There was only one bridge over the Main within fifty miles of their position. The Americans knew the route in; why weren't they taking the same way out?

Had they mapped out another escape route somehow? Koehl dismissed the idea. The Americans had attacked at Gemünden. They'd traveled north to Burgsinn only when the bridge at Gemünden was destroyed. No, that couldn't be it. They had to leave by the same way they had come, and Gräfendorf was the first major town on the route back out from the Oflag. The colonel had chosen perfectly.

Yet hours had passed, and there were no Americans. Had they slipped away to the south? But where? There were no other bridges, as far as Koehl knew. No, they must be stuck up in the winding hills around the Oflag. If he had patience, they would come to him. If he moved the force now, trying to chase their shadows, he might open a route for their escape.

How to wait, though? Each minute seemed an eternity. At least while the light had held, there'd been something to do. He could scan the roads and the horizon. Now, in darkness, he could only sit idly and stew, chasing the elusive shadows of his frustration. He knew his judgment was clouded. The colonel was right. He shouldn't be here. A part of him wanted to do the right thing and inform Baumann to take charge. *No, damn it!* He would have his revenge. What happened after that didn't matter.

Darkness wormed its way across the sky. Koehl checked his watch continuously, his anxiety mounting with each tick of the clock. *Where were they?* Another hour passed. He couldn't wait any longer. He climbed out of his Ferdinand and marched out into the darkness in search of the Tiger commander.

He found the captain near the center of the town, perched on a mound of sandbags as he examined a map by flashlight. The light flickered off the mammoth tread of a Tiger and the crouching forms of a half-dozen men. Baumann was pointing out positions to his sub-commanders. He looked up and acknowledged Koehl with a crisp nod.

"How can I help you, *Herr Hauptmann?*"

"I wanted to talk about our position."

"What about it?"

Koehl glanced down at his watch. "It's almost twenty-two hundred hours. We've had no sighting of the American column."

"That's true, but they'll be coming this way."

"What if they do not?"

Baumann looked at him for a moment and shrugged. "If they do not, then a few hundred Americans make it back to their lines, and we preserve the men and equipment we have."

Koehl was shocked. What was the tank commander saying? "I'm sorry, I may not have understood you. Are you implying that we won't shift our position?"

"I'm not implying that. I'm saying it outright."

"But we have to stop—"

"No, *Hauptmann*. We don't have to do any such thing."

"You would let them get away?" Koehl's voice rose, and he fought his emotions with difficulty.

"Exactly so."

"How can that be your decision?"

"Because I'm not emotionally involved, *Hauptmann*," retorted Baumann.

"I'm not either—"

"Nonsense!" shouted the panzer commander, his face growing splotchy in the flickering light. "The colonel briefed me on what has happened to you today." The captain's voice was firm, but his eyes were sympathetic. "Listen, I understand. I've had terrible things happen to my men . . . to my family. But our duty is something else entirely." He lifted his right arm and waved it in a spreading motion from front to back. "Look around you, Koehl. We are in the perfect position for an ambush. If the Americans come here, we will destroy them. But what if they don't? It's pitch-black out there. We have no air support, no intelligence on their position. What would you have us do? Take to the roads and grope for them blindly?

They're as likely to stumble across us as we are them. I won't endanger my command with such a foolish maneuver. And neither would you, if you were thinking rationally."

"I'm thinking very clearly," responded Koehl, enunciating each of the words distinctly. "This task force has to be stopped."

"And why is that, *Hauptmann?*" The captain stared at him, hands on his hips.

Koehl didn't know how to reply. He stared back at Baumann, but he could not formulate a response.

"There is no good reason. You know it, and so do I. Good evening, *Hauptmann,*" he said by way of dismissal. "Please return to your company, and I'll keep an eye on things from here. Never fear. I'm confident the Americans will come this way."

Koehl turned abruptly and stomped back into the darkness, a hot retort leashed to his tongue. His mind was reeling. Who was this idiot who waited for the enemy to come to him? He didn't know this Baumann. Did the man have any real combat experience? Koehl might be personally involved, but he damned well knew how to fight the enemy. Combat didn't function on nice neat lines where your foe acted exactly according to plan. You had to be ready in an instance to react, to modify, to boldly charge forward on a new axis of attack. Otherwise, the enemy won, or fled. *I will not let them escape.*

He walked through the blackened streets of Gräfendorf, his mind a whirlwind of anger and frustration. He felt betrayed by Colonel Hoepple. His regimental leader had obviously spoken to Baumann, had warned him of his emotions. *My commander has lost confidence in me.* He's put another man of equal rank in charge. Nothing was said, but that's what had happened. Why wouldn't Hoepple let him have this moment? After years of service, he owed him that much. Instead, they were going to sit here in the darkness like so many logs while the Americans slipped away to freedom.

He reached his Ferdinand a few minutes later, climbing back

into the turret and resuming the terrible waiting. His anger rose with each passing minute. There was no way the Americans were still coming in this direction. He was losing his revenge. The colonel had pulled his claws and left him with only his pain and his loss.

A thought entered his mind. A crazy, reckless idea. It was a fantasy, something he'd never considered before. He dismissed it immediately, but as the time ticked by, the concept kept surfacing to bob at the edge of his emotions. He ignored it, shunned it, but finally found himself examining the notion. He started to turn it on its ends, looking at the corners, the edges, working out some of the details. He was a faithful, loyal man. A priest, used to unquestioned subservience. If he followed this impulse, he would violate everything he'd ever known.

He made up his mind. Koehl jumped back out of his Ferdinand and strolled into the night. He visited each of his armored vehicles, issuing orders in hushed whispers. He checked in with the clusters of infantry assigned to his force. Within a few minutes, he was back at his own vehicle. He climbed in and spoke to the driver. "Turn on your machine, we're leaving." The Ferdinand's ignition fired, and the engine roared into life. The behemoth lurched forward and rolled toward the end of the street, scraping with a piercing shriek against the stone façade of a house as it passed by. They reached the end of the street and turned to the right on the main avenue, rolling past Germans staring in surprise at Koehl as they moved back out of the town. The other Ferdinands were close by. As they were departing the city, he thought he could hear shouting behind him, as if someone was trying to get his attention. He ignored them. Orders or no orders, he was going after the task force.

The column of anti-tank vehicles rolled back down the highway toward Hammelburg. Koehl could see the city in the far distance to his left as they rumbled southeast. Besides the flickering lights, visibility was low, and his Ferdinand, in the lead, proceeded at less than half speed to avoid inadvertently driving off the road and into the steep ditches to the right and left.

Koehl strained his eyes in the night, struggling to pick up any movement, any sign of the enemy task force. He realized it was possible that the Americans were long gone, perhaps already over the Main again. He swore to himself, cursing the foolish orders and the complacency of Baumann. Well, there was nothing he could do about that. He was in God's hands. If the Lord intended the GIs to escape, there was nothing he could do about it. If not, then he would find them in the blackness, and he would have his vengeance.

The column skirted Hammelburg and turned to the southwest toward Bonnland, taking a further right and veering west/southwest toward Höllrich, his intended destination. Below him, he heard Lieutenant Jaeger speaking on the radio to someone. He heard his subordinate's voice rising as he was cut off over and over. He felt his anxiety mount. He could guess who was on the other end of the receiver. In moments, his fears were confirmed.

"*Hauptmann.*"

"What is it?"

"It's the colonel on the radio."

"Tell him I'm in the middle of a transfer, and I'll reach him as soon as I can." The lieutenant relayed the information.

"I'm sorry, sir, but the colonel said he must speak with you now. He said that's an order."

Koehl took the receiver and lifted it up. "*Jawohl?*"

"Koehl, is that you?" asked the colonel. "What in the hell do you think you're doing?"

"I'm ambushing the Americans, like you ordered."

"Nonsense!" shouted Hoepple through the radio. "I ordered you to Gräfendorf to meet up with Baumann."

"I followed that order."

"And then you argued with him and snuck out like a thief. Where the hell are you?"

"We're south of Hammelburg, heading toward Höllrich."

"Turn your ass around and return to Baumann now."

"But, sir, we waited there for hours. The Americans aren't coming. There's no point in sitting there any longer."

"The point of remaining is that I ordered you to. Damn it, Koehl. Are you making a fool of me? I withdrew my command that you be relieved. You promised you would follow my direction, and now you're defying me."

"Your orders were conflicting, sir." Koehl knew that wasn't true, but he had to say something.

"Return to Gräfendorf immediately, *Hauptmann*."

"Yes, sir. I will continue on and pursue the Americans. Thank you."

"That's not what I sa—" Koehl removed his bayonet and cut through the wire beneath the receiver, severing the connection. He lifted the receiver and hurled it into the darkness.

"Sir, what did you just do?" asked Jaeger anxiously, looking up suspiciously from the bowels of the Ferdinand.

"I'm following orders, Lieutenant. The orders that count." He looked down sternly at Jaeger. They'd served together for a long time. They'd been through many trials by fire. What would the lieutenant do?

"Sir, we should turn back. The colonel ordered it."

"I know what he said, Jaeger, but I'm asking you to follow me."

"I can't do that."

Koehl ignored the response. "Have I ever let you down? Does any of this make sense to you? You know the Americans will never come to Gräfendorf. They are going to get away. I can smell them out there. I've always led us to the prey. Please trust me and let me do this. I promise, I'll take full responsibility for my actions."

Jaeger seemed to consider this. "And what if you get a bunch of us killed in the process?"

"That is God's will. Have I ever been reckless with casualties?"

The lieutenant shook his head.

"I won't be now. I give you my word."

Jaeger thought about it for a few seconds. "Not a bit of responsibility for me or the rest of the command. Your word on that."

"It's all on me, Lieutenant." Koehl felt a rush of elation, and a conflicting surge of guilt. Jaeger's words ran through his mind again: *What if you get a bunch of us killed . . .*

"All right, sir, I'm with you. I trust you. But this is your responsibility."

Koehl reached down, grasping the lieutenant's hand tightly. He felt a moment of panic. *What am I doing?* He was risking everything. He could be shot. But if he succeeded, he hoped all would be well. He just had to catch up with the Americans, and stay away from Baumann . . .

The column continued, moving through the darkness toward Höllrich. A half hour passed as the force crawled along the road. The thoroughfare narrowed, and the concrete gradually crumbled into gravel. The Ferdinand churned the rocks, kicking up a cloud of dust. Koehl coughed and sputtered as he struggled for breath. He drew a handkerchief and pressed it against his nose and mouth, but he did not move down into the vehicle, where he would be more protected from the churning particles in the air. He needed to see.

Koehl checked his watch and closed his eyes, trying to visualize the countryside on a map. He estimated their speed and tried to determine when they might reach their destination. If he was right about the Americans, they'd come this way. If they'd been delayed at the Oflag, which at this point seemed likely, he should reach the intercept point ahead of them. That would allow him to set up another ambush. He hoped that, with the darkness and the enemy task force bogged down with POWs, he'd be able to make short work of them. After that, he would face the colonel and perhaps a firing squad. He smiled to himself. After everything he'd seen and endured the past six years, death would almost come as a relief. *Almost.*

As they rolled forward, he considered Höllrich as a battle-ground. He pictured the town in his mind. He'd been here a few times, and he went through the network of streets and squares, trying to pre-suppose their positions before they ar-rived. The city wasn't an ideal place for the trap. It was not laid out as well as Gräfendorf or Gemünden, but it would serve its purpose. When he was satisfied with his preliminary plan, he ducked his head back into the Ferdinand and caught Jaeger's at-tention.

"Lieutenant."

"Jawohl, mein Hauptmann?"

"We're getting close. Here's what I want to do. I want you to . . ."

His words were cut off by a thunderous detonation. The Ferdinand rocked and shuddered. Koehl was thrown against the side, crashing against the steel interior. His shoulder cracked, and he felt overwhelming pain. He shouted orders even as his crew sprang into action. The Americans were here . . .

Chapter 25

The fire from the burning Sherman flared in Hall's eyes, dimming his night vision. He expected a cascade of explosions as the ambush rained fire down on the convoy. He was surprised to hear nothing but the crackling of the dead Sherman and the rumbling engines of the rest of the column.

"Let's get rolling!" screamed Baum, and Hall followed Stiller as the major rushed back toward their jeep. They made it back just as the tank directly in front of them lurched forward. In a few seconds, Stiller swerved sharply to the right, dropping down into a shallow ditch and back out again as he steered the jeep around the burning tank.

Moment by moment, Hall expected another round to drop in among them, but still there was nothing. "What just happened?" he asked.

"Don't know!" shouted Stiller.

"Why aren't there more?"

The major spat. "Could have been a lone *panzerfaust*. Some

bastard snuck up in the dark and took a potshot at us. Brave son-of-a-bitch. I'd still like to skin him alive. We don't have enough tanks for this horseshit."

Stiller was right. They were down to a handful of armor. If they ran into anything serious at this point, they wouldn't be able to fight their way out. Again, he cursed the decision to bring the POWs along. Without them, they'd be halfway back already. Instead, they were crawling down through the damned hills and hadn't found their way out. Still, they'd been lucky. If they had faced a full attack, the Germans might have wiped them out.

They crept down the narrow pathways through the steep, heavily forested hills coming out from the Oflag. Nutto's Sherman was in the lead, followed by three more Shermans and then the command vehicles and the half-tracks. The rear of the column was made up of the light tanks. The force moved at a crawl, barely above the brisk pace of a pedestrian. Even worse, they kept inexplicably halting, sometimes for as long as ten minutes, before lurching ahead again.

Hall felt like he could burst. What the hell was Nutto doing? The Germans were everywhere. They'd spent far too long in the camp, and now they were pussyfooting down toward the valley. If they had any chance of getting out of here, speed was critical. Was he surrounded by imbeciles? He looked over at Stiller in the driver's seat. Visibility was low, but from what he could make out, the major seemed unconcerned by their situation, staring straight ahead with that blank, stupid expression on his face while he chomped away on his tobacco.

The convoy ground to a halt again. The Shermans shuddered and coughed, and then one after another, the engines died. Hall strained his eyes, trying to see what was up ahead. He was outraged that the column was stopping. Baum must be out of his mind. Finally, he couldn't take it any longer, and he voiced his frustrations. "What the hell is going on?" asked Hall. He checked his watch. They'd been almost three hours now in the hills. By contrast, they'd only spent a half hour or so climbing up to the Oflag on the way in.

"I don't know, Hall, but why don't you go find out?" responded Stiller.

That was the major's solution? To put his ass on the line again? Why didn't the bastard get out himself and check? All he did was sit there, his mind focused on God knows what. Hall thought about refusing but knew he couldn't. Swearing to himself, he climbed out of the jeep, pulling the Thompson out and moving forward. He passed a Sherman to the right. He coughed and sputtered when he walked into a low-hanging branch, the needles clawing at his cheek. He could barely see a few feet in front of him.

Hall passed the rest of the Shermans and reached the front of the convoy.

"What do you think you're doing?" A whispered voice washed over him from the turret of the lead tank.

"It's Lieutenant Hall."

"Good for you," said the tanker, his voice laced with sarcasm. "I didn't ask your name. I asked what you're doing."

Hall bristled. "I'm trying to find out why you nitwits are taking so damned long to get us out of these hills."

"We're taking our time because I say so," said another voice coming out of the darkness in front of him. Hall turned and saw Lieutenant Nutto emerging from the blackness, limping along toward him, his face grimacing in pain.

Hall turned to the tank commander. "Stiller wants to know what's going on." That wasn't technically true, but Nutto didn't need to know that.

"Stiller isn't in charge of this task force."

"I'm aware of that, Lieutenant, but he's a major, and he's trying to figure out why we're taking all night traveling a couple miles out of these hills."

"How much combat have you been in, Hall?"

"I've been in . . . some."

"I'll bet my March pay this is your first patrol." He looked carefully at Hall, watching his reaction. "That's what I thought," he said finally. "Well, I've been in the shit now for months. Let me tell you from experience, we were damn lucky to get out of that last cross-fire ambush. We won't make it out of another. We are in the worst tactical situation right now. It's pitch-black, and we're on a narrow road with wooded inclines on both sides. What's more, I don't know where the fuck we're going. So if you want to be alive in the morning, I'd suggest you go back and tell *your* major that we'll be out of here when we're ready."

Hall was furious, but he found he could not meet Nutto's eyes. If he only outranked this smug jerk, he'd give him a piece of his mind. But he didn't, and Hall had no choice but to grunt and turn around, walking back toward the jeep with as much dignity as he could command. He was fuming. He cursed the army, cursed this war that allowed men of no background or social standing to order him around. Well, they'd be out of this mess in the next few hours, and the war was almost over. When it was, he promised himself he would return home and ensure he was never in a position again to be told to do anything.

He arrived back at the jeep, climbing silently in.

"What did you find out?" asked Stiller.

"Not much. Nutto's grown cautious, and he's jumping at shadows up there. He told me it's going to take as long as it takes. He also reminded me that you're not in charge."

Stiller chuckled. "I like that Nutto."

Hall's fury increased. Of course, the major would like the tanker. They were cut out of the same bolt of cloth. *Careful, don't say anything. You're so close.*

Fortunately, the column jerked into motion at that moment, and Hall could suppress his emotions. They crawled forward for another hundred yards or so, and then, to his amazement, the tanks rolled to a stop again. He checked his watch, shaking his head.

The remaining hour of March 27 passed like that, start and stop, fumbling blindly through the darkness in the hills. He doubted they'd made it two miles. He waited for the attack that would wipe them out, the ambush that stupid Nutto was giving the Germans all the time they needed to prepare. He chewed his lip, suppressing his frustration at this impossible situation.

Midnight passed, and then one. Hall gave up all hope as the task force stuttered and stopped in the darkness. Was the bastard waiting for dawn? If so, they'd surely catch it good. He complained to Stiller again, but the major silenced him, chastising him for interfering with Nutto, an expert in combat. With each moment, he waited for a *panzerfaust* to fire and the shells to rip through the column, killing them all.

And then, miraculously, they were through. The ground leveled, the trees gave way to fields, and in the distance, Hall could make out the lights of a town, perhaps Hammelburg. He checked his watch again; it was 0130. Hall's spirits rose; they'd burned through half the night traveling a few miles, but they were in the clear now, and soon they would be back on the highway and streaming toward the Main and beyond to the American lines. Stiller chuckled as he accelerated; even the major was apparently relieved to be out of the winding hills. Hall laughed as the major clamped him on the arm. He felt a fleeting moment of comradeship with his commander. He breathed deeply of the crisp night air. Only a few hours to go. They were going to make it.

To Hall's shock, the column ground to a halt again. Was Nutto still playing his game of hide-and-seek with the Germans? Was he intentionally trying to kill them all? The lieutenant had had enough of this. He would not let himself be destroyed like this. If the idiots in charge of this were going to stay here in the dark, he would find some other way out.

Baum's appearance interrupted his panicked contemplation of escape. "Morning, boys."

"Morning," said Stiller. "What's the situation?"

"As I'm sure you can see, we've made it out of the hills."

"Finally," said Hall.

"What's that, Lieutenant?" asked Baum.

"He didn't mean nothing," said Stiller. "Sometimes he doesn't know when to keep his mouth shut."

Hall stewed, but there was nothing he could do. He tried to concentrate through his emotions on the conversation.

"Where are we headed from here?" asked Stiller. "Back to Hammelburg?"

"Negative," said Baum. "Likely too much heat up that way. That's the direction they will expect us. No. I studied the routes carefully over the past few hours as we've mucked around in those hills. I'm heading south."

"What's south?"

"Bonnland, for starters. I figure we make our way through there and on to the Main."

"But how the hell do we get across the river with no bridge?" asked Hall, refusing to keep quiet.

"We don't know what's down there south of Gemünden."

"What if there's nothing?" he persisted.

"Then we backtrack north along the river back to Burgsinn and across."

"We'll never make it," said Stiller.

Baum grunted. "You might be right, but there's no way we can head back the way we came in. They'll be ready for us in force by now. Our only chance is to find something to the south, or at least get them off the scent. We spent too damned long in those hills." The captain glanced at Hall. "*It was necessary*, but it was a hell of a delay."

Stiller paused. "I guess it's the best we can do." He looked up at the GIs hanging on to the Sherman in front of them. "We gotta save those boys, but they're going to slow us down something fierce."

Baum shook his head in agreement. "I don't know what Patton was thinking. I've seen some screwed-up plans in this war, but this one takes the cake." The captain shrugged. "I don't have enough brass on my shoulders to worry about that. I'm a doer, and if there's a chance to get us out of here, I will."

Stiller reached out his hand, shaking Baum's. "I know you will. You've done good out here, Captain. It's not your fault we're in this shit show. We should've brought a hell of a lot more firepower."

"Agreed. But let's see what we can do with what's left. Be ready; we're heading out in a few minutes. I just want to brief my boys."

Baum departed, and they sat there for a few minutes in silence. Hall figured Stiller would chew him out now that the captain was gone, but the major seemed distracted and didn't say anything. The lieutenant was thankful for that, but his mind reeled at Baum's plan. What was the captain thinking? The Main was an insurmountable obstacle. They had to have a bridge to cross it. The only known bridge at the time of the attack was the one at Gemünden. That had been destroyed, and only by a miracle had they found another. They were now heading the opposite direction from the bridge at Burgsinn. The chances they would come across another to the south seemed just about zero. He felt doom closing in on the force.

The column lurched back into motion as the task force moved down the ever-broadening road into the valley toward Hammelburg. As the city loomed larger on the horizon, Hall wondered if the commander had changed his mind about the direction they were heading. His hopes were dashed when the Sherman took a sharp left, and soon they were all traveling southwest away from the bridge and from their only hope for escape.

* * *

There was a small chance now that they were at least back on paved, wider roads. This was not quite a highway, but the column gradually gained speed after hours of crawling. Hall felt a little relief as the column finally put some distance between themselves and the Oflag. Perhaps Baum was right to send them southwest. Certainly the krauts would not expect them to head in this direction. If they were lucky, they might even find a bridge over the river somewhere south of Gemünden. If that happened, they might well escape untouched the rest of the way back to the American lines while the Germans lay in wait uselessly somewhere to the west of Hammelburg.

Another half hour passed. They traveled as far from the bottom of the hill as they had traveled over all those preceding hours. The Germans seemed to be nowhere, and Hall started to feel a flicker of hope. At least they were making progress somewhere.

The sound of ripped linen drew his attention starkly away from his contemplation and toward the front of the column. Hall saw first one flash, then another. He heard the sharp clang of bullets flicking off the Sherman in front of them. A POW clinging to the turret screamed in pain, clawing at his arm. Another GI jumped down and helped the wounded kriegie off the tank as the rest of the men scrambled away from the top of the vehicle where they were easy prey for the Germans.

The lead Sherman fired its 30-caliber machine gun, the tracers tearing through the night. The road was too narrow here for the rest of the Shermans to move into position. Hall ripped his Thompson into position, preparing to repulse an attack he expected on either side of them. Moments passed as the fire in front of them rattled away. Hall noticed no increase, however, in the volume of the fighting, and no attack materialized on either side of them.

This didn't seem to be a significant German attack. Perhaps

it was just an outpost with a few German guards. If so, why weren't they tearing through it?

"What's going on?" he shouted to Stiller.

"It's an attack. What do you think?" responded the major.

Idiot. "I know it's an attack, sir, but it doesn't seem to have much weight."

Stiller cocked his head, listening for a moment. "Perhaps you're right, Hall." Even as he said this, the fighting in front of them died down, and within a few minutes, it was silent. Hall waited in the darkness for the Germans to rumble forward again, but for some maddening reason they remained immobile.

In the ditches on both sides of the road, the POWs milled around. They gradually returned toward the tanks, initially placing their hands against the turret, as if preparing to dart away again, and then finally climbing back on board.

Out of the dark, Hall saw a figure strolling toward them. It was Nutto. What was it now? They needed to roll forward and keep up their momentum. The tank commander had already wasted half the night chasing shadows. Now he was stopping again to confer with Baum. He needed to be replaced. Couldn't Baum see that? The lieutenant had obviously lost his nerve. Perhaps Weaver and the light tanks would evince a more aggressive spirit.

Baum appeared near their tank, and Hall could hear the two men conferring. Nutto kept pointing behind him, and the task force commander listened, nodding his head now and then in agreement. The captain stepped over to their jeep.

"Looks like we're going to have to turn back," said Baum.

"Why?" asked Stiller.

"Roadblock."

"But they stopped firing," protested Hall. "Can't we just push through?"

"Nutto doesn't think so," said Baum.

"How will we know if we don't try?" asked the lieutenant.

Baum shook his head. "No telling what's ahead, Hall. We don't have enough left to fight the Germans head-on in the dark. One more misstep and we're toast. Nutto thinks we should head due west toward Höllrich, where we can hit Highway Twenty-seven. If we can find a route there, I agree. The nice part about that town is we can go north or south, and once we reach it, we will be moving fast along the river. It gives us better options." Baum paused and wiped a handkerchief across his forehead. "Frankly, I should've thought about that in the first place."

Hall didn't know what to say, so he kept his mouth shut. How would they get anywhere if they jumped back like a rabbit stung by a bee every time they encountered the least resistance? If only he were in charge of this operation, he'd handle things differently. He would've left every last one of those POWs back in the camp and got the hell out of there at full speed. He'd have pushed right through the hills and right on to the bridge before the Germans knew what the hell was happening. The POWs were better off back at the Oflag. Hell, the war was practically over; it would be, at most a few days. They'd be safe in the camp until the real army got there. Instead, they were out here slowing everything down like a bunch of sheep herded by Nutto and Baum, the dumbest sheepdogs on the planet.

A few moments later, he heard the engines of the Shermans firing up again as the column lurched into reverse, making its way slowly back down the road until they found a flat patch where they could awkwardly maneuver the task force around and start the slog northeast, back where they'd come from.

Another half hour passed before they found a road that turned due west. They took this path, another narrow gravel roadway, and rumbled along as quickly as they could manage. Hall kept checking his watch, cursing to himself as they meandered through trees and countryside toward Höllrich. Finally, in the distance, he could make out another road passing perpendicular to their own. He hoped this was a larger arterial that would allow them to speed up again. As they drew closer, he noted something strange about the roadway. Shadows flickered behind the branches of the bushes and trees. He tried to understand what he was looking at, and, with horror, he realized the danger they were in.

"Christ!" he screamed.

"What is it now, Hall?" asked Stiller with annoyance in his voice.

"Look out there!" Hall pointed in the distance.

Stiller peered out and swore. Even as the major saw what Hall was looking at, the lead Sherman erupted, firing a shell at the moving shadows. They'd ran right into an enemy armored formation, passing rapidly in the night. Hall lifted his Thompson even as the first enemy fire rained down on them.

Chapter 26

Koehl cranked his neck around and saw with horror the American column knifing up through the middle of his convoy. Even as he watched, the lead Sherman fired its 75mm cannon. There was an explosion behind him. He turned fully around in the turret and saw one of his Ferdinands disappearing in a ball of flame. The armored vehicle rolled forward for a few yards and then stopped, directly at the bridge of the T where the two roads converged. He watched in despair as the behemoth burned, hoping to see someone escape from within, praying for a miracle. But long moments passed with nothing. The flames licked away, erupting out of the top of the turret and through the machine-gun slits. Nothing could be alive inside.

The other Ferdinands were maneuvering to fire. Unfortunately, the armored anti-tank vehicles were not designed with a wide-ranging field of fire. The two in front of the burning husk, including Koehl's, had no chance to turn in the confining space near the road; only the vehicles behind the ruined anti-tank unit could come into play now.

Koehl wanted to scream in frustration. The chances that the Americans would converge at exactly this point, in both time and location, were virtually zero. Was he cursed? His destruction seemed ordained as if from God, and he shuddered at that moment, wondering if his rage, his betrayal of orders, and his loss of control were being punished from above. Colonel Hoepple's warnings lashed at him. He had told Koehl he was being reckless, that he was gambling with his men's lives. The *Hauptmann* had ignored this. He'd been so sure of himself, based on his past, and perhaps more so because he wanted this vengeance more than anything he'd ever desired. Now his commander's predictions had come horribly true. He *had* caused the death of his men through his careless actions or through bad luck. He wasn't sure which, but the result was the same. He'd already lost one of his Ferdinands in the attack, and he was out of position, with limited room for maneuver. He knew there was every chance he was about to be annihilated.

Then something inexplicable happened. For some reason that defied rationality and reality, the Americans failed to press the attack. The Sherman ground to a halt and started to back away. The enemy tanks kept up a steady barrage, but the shells fell wide of their marks. His own vehicles returned the fire, but no further hits were made on either side. Within a minute or so, the Americans disappeared, backing into a copse of trees a hundred yards or so away from the T of the roads.

Koehl's emotions rapidly changed from amazement to a renewed determination to press his attack. The Americans had miraculously appeared just where they could destroy him, and just as unbelievably, they had fled. He didn't have time to consider this further but turned to the reality that he *knew where the Americans were. He could destroy them.* He immediately ordered his remaining column to reform and pursue the enemy.

The difficulty now was maneuvering his column around the burning Ferdinand. Maddeningly, the fiery husk had come to rest in exactly the wrong spot, blocking the apex of the T.

This would not be a problem except that the road at this point was bounded by deep ditches on both sides. Koehl was not sure he could successfully navigate the embankments without lodging yet another of his vehicles into a ditch and reducing his already critically low forces even further. He attempted to direct the first Ferdinand behind the burning armored vehicle to squeeze between the flaming husk and the ditch.

He did this on foot but had tremendous difficulty in the darkness, and he quickly realized, as the Ferdinand approached the gap, that it would never make it through without rumbling into the ditch itself. He looked at the other side of the road, hoping there was more room to navigate, but the burning vehicle was equidistant, as if fate had placed it there to block all attempts to reach his foe.

He considered pushing it out of the way, but it was so completely engulfed in flame he feared another explosion might damage the vehicle attempting to move the Ferdinand.

Precious minutes ticked by. In anguish, Koehl realized it was fruitless to pursue the Americans directly. However, there was room for the rear vehicles to move to the right of the burned-out Ferdinand and continue in the direction he was previously headed. Examining the problem for precious minutes, he realized this was the only option available to him. Better to be moving in the direction of the Americans and hope to find them at another location farther west. Again, he thanked fate that he had previously trained so much in this area. He was familiar with the local geography and the network of roads. The thoroughfare he was currently on continued west for a few more miles, before eventually meeting up with Höllrich. The city was critical as it sat astride Highway 27, the main arterial road north and south along the Main. It appeared the Americans were attempting to circumvent their original route, just as Koehl suspected they would. If they were also attempting to make it back to the original bridge at Burgsinn, then Höllrich would be the perfect place to intercept them. Koehl thought back to the route the Americans had taken in retreat. About a third of the way to Bonnland, there was a narrow gravel road cutting off to the right. This road eventually led to Höllrich as well, but it was winding, and the uneven surface would restrict the Americans' speed. If the enemy task force took this road-way, he would be able to make up time and arrive in their path well ahead of them. If not, well . . .

He ran through the maze of his fears again. What if his column had scared them off and they did not take the first road? What if they headed south to Bonnland and attempted to find a bridge farther south? Were there any? His regiment's territory did not extend significantly to the south down the Main. It was possible there were additional bridges farther away. He cursed himself that his actions had cut off all communication with Colonel Hoepple. If he was able to use his radio, he could call and obtain on-the-go intelligence and also find out if anyone else had spotted the American column.

It could not be helped. He would have to go in blind and trust to his instincts and to luck. He gave his orders, hastening up and down the line. Within a few minutes, the column was under way, rumbling slowly around the burning Ferdinand. Koehl checked his watch; they'd lost another half hour here. Still, with luck, they should arrive first at Höllrich. He shouted at his driver, ordering that he push the accelerator as far as was reasonably safe. Soon the force was rumbling down the road again and making excellent time.

As they sped toward the ambush point, he was just able to make out in the distance the sloping form of Hill 427. This prominence rose a few hundred feet above the landscape; along with an adjacent, lesser hill, it would give any force during the day an outstanding view of the surrounding countryside. As the hill grew larger on the horizon, a deeper dark barely discernible in the starless sky, Koehl ran through his head the necessary turns and the route the column must take to reach Höllrich.

As he considered this, he was surprised to feel his Ferdinand lurching and beginning to slow. What was it now, he wondered? The *Hauptmann* was beginning to lean down to shout at his driver, but he drew himself back up when he realized the problem.

His heart sank. Resting in the middle of the highway was the bulky mass of a Tiger tank, its 88mm cannon aimed down the road at the column. Even as he attempted to shout orders to stop and begin to reverse, he realized it was too late. They simply had not had enough warning in the darkness. Koehl could hear the shouts of the Germans in front of him now, and he knew what they were there for and what was surely to happen.

As his vehicle rolled to a stop, a squad of soldiers rushed out of the darkness, rifles raised, screaming for the *Hauptmann* to raise his hands. Baumann emerged from the blackness, a smug expression on his face. It was over.

Hauptmann Baumann stood just behind the soldiers, hands on his hips. "Well, well," he said, "what have we here?"

"*Hauptmann*, I've seen the Americans," said Koehl, trying to find some way out of the situation. "If we hurry, we—"

"Sorry, Koehl, but I have my orders. I need you to come down immediately."

Koehl's hands were still in the air. "Before you do anything else, Baumann, I want it known that I acted alone. The men have followed my orders without knowing I disobeyed Hoepple."

Baumann raised an eyebrow. "I find that rather hard to believe."

"It's true."

The panzer commander paused for a second and then shrugged. "Well, that's not for me to decide, Koehl. I'll take your word for it now as an officer, and we can sort that out later."

Koehl wasn't willing to leave it there. He had to look after his men. "What's to become of my crew?"

"For now, nothing," said Baumann. "I need them, you see. Despite your belief, we are still trying to capture the American column. I have my forces spread out all over Hill 427. Your men will join mine."

"But the Americans aren't coming this way," protested Koehl. "They're on their way to Höllrich, or perhaps even farther south."

"What makes you think that?"

"My force was surprised by the American column barely two miles back."

"Where?" asked Baumann, his eyes flickering with interest.

"At the T on the Höllrich road. Do you know it?"

Baumann nodded. "What happened?"

"They took out a Ferdinand. We returned fire, but they backed away. Unfortunately, our armored vehicle blocked pursuit. They are either heading south toward Bonnland or east on the back roads toward Höllrich."

"They aren't headed south, that's for sure," said Baumann.

"How do you know?"

"Because they've already been there. The Americans ran into a roadblock about an hour ago just north of the town. There wasn't much there, just a few troops and one MG 42. Fortunately, the enemy turned around and headed north. The patrol called it in to the colonel, and he contacted me. That's why we moved here, to head off the task force. I was also ordered to take you into custody if we found you. Trust me, it gives me no pleasure."

"*Hauptmann*, I'm begging you," said Koehl. "The Americans aren't coming this way anymore. If you're right and they won't head south, then they will have turned off on the gravel road a mile or so back down the T, and they will be headed east toward Höllrich. If we leave here now, there is still time to attack them."

Baumann shook his head. "The colonel's orders are to stay here. We have a commanding position. If the Americans come this way, we will decimate them; if not, then we will avoid any casualties." He looked at Koehl sternly. "Casualties you have already taken through your reckless disregard of orders."

Koehl was overwhelmed. "If you're going to arrest me, fine, but please at least go to Höllrich. We have them right where we want them."

"No, *Hauptmann*. Unlike you, I'm following the colonel's commands."

"Can you get him on the radio? Tell him what I know?"

Baumann shook his head. "It wouldn't make any difference. The colonel is done listening to you. He doesn't care if this column escapes. It's a few hundred men. He has to think about the defense of this entire sector. We have nothing left to defend it with except my tanks and your Ferdinands. That and a few companies of infantry. We're low on fuel, ammunition, even food. We have to preserve what we have." He stared at Koehl again for a moment, his face growing harsh. "You've lost your way, Koehl. The war is almost over. You should be protecting your men. They have families to go home to. I understand you've experienced tremendous recent losses and that this enemy force is directly responsible, but that doesn't give you the right to gamble with the rest of your men. Are their lives worth less than yours? Than your friend and family?"

Koehl was stunned. Baumann was right. He realized he'd fought for so long, with death such a constant companion, that he didn't see that the end of all of this was so near. He hadn't considered that in seeking revenge for the loss of his sister and his dear friend, he was taking away the future of others under his command. How far he'd traveled from his service to church and community. What had he become?

"You're right, *Hauptmann*. I've thought only of myself. I've gone too far with this. But—"

"But they killed those closest to you," finished Baumann, understanding in his eyes. "I know that. If there were a way I could let you have your revenge without risking my command, I would do it. But now it's too late. You've gambled your own life in this. I'm afraid the colonel will have no choice but to have you shot for disobeying his orders."

Koehl knew he was right. That was justice. He deserved it. After all he'd seen and done these past years. After the lives he'd sacrificed and the ones he'd taken. His own life would pay the price in return.

Baumann motioned to a couple of the guards. They stepped forward, taking Koehl into custody. He was walked past the panzer and up through more men and equipment, eventually reaching the top of the hill, where a group of Germans had erected a command tent. Koehl was directed to a folding chair, and he sat down, flanked by the two guards.

He sat there over the next several hours, watching and listening to events unfold. The radio was soon installed, and Baumann arrived. The panzer commander was in constant communication with the regimental headquarters as he gave and received updates on the operation to capture the task force. Despite Baumann's comments about "waiting," Koehl noted the commander's intense interest in the progress of the American force, and he gave swift orders in return. Koehl strained his ears, trying to pick up and understand exactly what was going on, but the radio was on the far side of the tent, and he was able to grasp only bits and pieces.

As the night wore on, he noticed an almost imperceptible lightening of the sky. Morning was just beginning to dawn, he realized. Daylight was an advantage to both hunter and prey.

The Germans would be able to utilize their spotter plane again, assuming the Americans didn't send fighters to blot it out of the sky. They would also be able to spot the column from a long way off. However, the Americans, who did not know the area, would be able to see the Main and orient themselves on the river. They would also be able to pick out any ambushes before they reached them.

That assumed the Americans were still anywhere nearby. If they'd reached Höllrich and turned south, they could have passed Gemünden and perhaps found a way back across the Main somewhere down the way. They could already be back in their own lines by the time dawn broke.

As he considered this, Baumann set the radio receiver down. He turned and walked across the tent, looking down at Koehl.

"What is it?"

"Miraculous news," said Baumann.

"Tell me."

"The Americans ran into another roadblock near Höllrich. My roadblock."

"But I thought you said . . ."

"I didn't tell you everything, Koehl. I'm not going to piss my command away, but it doesn't mean I don't want to bag these bastards. I put one tank and a platoon of men at the crossroads in Höllrich. They exchanged fire with the Americans and destroyed a Sherman, capturing a few men in the process."

"Wonderful. What about the rest?"

"They're here."

Koehl was shocked. "What do you mean?"

"They drew back from Höllrich, and they've taken position on the adjacent hill. I suspect they are waiting for first light. I've issued orders, and in the next hour or so, we will have them surrounded. They don't know we are here. As soon as they ignite their engines in the morning, I'm going to blow them to hell."

Koehl couldn't believe it. He was going to have his revenge after all. He looked up gratefully to the commander. "Thank you, *Hauptmann*. You've given me a last gift."

"Not the very last."

"Will the colonel pardon me?" Koehl asked, a flicker of hope sparking his soul.

Baumann shook his head. "Your fate is in his hands. I'm supposed to send you to Hammelburg now. But I'm afraid the tactical situation is going to create a delay." The *Hauptmann* looked at him sternly. "This is what you are going to do, Koehl. You are going to return to your Ferdinand. I've restored the radio. You will command that vehicle, and that one only. You will follow every command I give without question. You will participate in the attack in the morning, and then you will immediately turn yourself back in to me. If you agree to those terms, then I am releasing you for duty. Do you agree?"

Koehl stared up at the *Hauptmann*. "I do. Thank you. You are a true man. I will never forget this."

"Good luck, Koehl. Both this morning, and at Hammelburg. I will speak to the colonel when this is over. If there's anything I can do, I will do it. For now, you will have your vengeance."

They shook hands, and Koehl walked away, heading in the darkness toward his crew.

Chapter 27

Near Höllrich, Germany
March 28, 1945, 0200 hours

Machine-gun fire ripped through the column in the darkness. Hall whipped his Thompson around and fired a short burst. This was his last clip, and he couldn't afford more than a couple pulls on the trigger. An enemy vehicle exploded in a massive fireball directly to their front, the view blocked by the Shermans. To his right up ahead, in the flaring light from the burning tank, Hall could see German vehicles turning into position to fire at their column.

"We've got to get the hell out of here!" he screamed to Stiller.

The major was already throwing the jeep into reverse. Hall turned behind him and saw that Baum had had the same idea. The tanks and half-tracks to his rear were beginning to back out of the firefight.

The jeep jerked rearward and rolled away from the German column. One of the Ferdinands fired a shell that flew high past a Sherman and crashed into the field to their left. Hall fired another burst toward the tank, not sure if he hit anything. He pressed again, and the Thompson failed to respond. He was out of ammunition.

Shells flew in all directions, but there were no hits on the tanks in front of them. As Hall watched, trees materialized to his right and left, embracing the task force in the protective shelter of the forest. The firing in front of him blazed for a brief time longer, then faded away. They'd escaped. However, they were backing up slowly, and there was no room to maneuver. The Germans would be after them in no time. They had to get turned around and find another route.

The column ground to a halt. Again, Baum was stopping the force when they needed to keep moving! Hall swore to himself, his heart ripping through his chest. He kept his eyes on the front of the convoy, expecting the Germans at any moment to crush the lead tank.

Baum appeared, moving along the vehicles, heading to the front to confer with Nutto. He disappeared in the darkness for a few minutes, then returned.

"What's the deal?" Stiller called out, as the task force commander passed them again.

"I just talked to the lieutenant," responded Baum. "The Germans haven't followed up in front of us yet. He figures they may be blocked by that bastard he took out. That should give us a few minutes at least."

"To do what?" asked Stiller. Hall noted a little impatience in the major's voice. Perhaps he had emotions after all.

"We passed a road a mile or so back to our left. I didn't take it because it was gravel and narrow as hell, but it's heading west. We're going to backtrack and see where it leads."

"What if it doesn't go anywhere?" asked Hall.

Baum looked up in irritation. "I haven't taken us all this way just to flounder out here in the middle of nowhere, Lieutenant. We won't know where it goes until we take it. Don't worry, I've been in worse scrapes before. We just have to keep our heads and stay on the move." He looked up. "We still have half the night. With any luck, we will hit Höllrich in the next hour or so. Once we're there, we can decide north or south."

"How do we determine that?" asked Hall.

"I don't know yet. We get there, and we'll see. Maybe we grab a citizen and interrogate them. They may know if there is a bridge to the south."

Baum sounded desperate to Hall. It was clear the convoy was running out of options. He was right. They'd spent too much time in the hills. They'd been stopped cold south and north. West was their only avenue of escape. And if that turned out to be blocked as well . . .

"Let's get moving," said Stiller, ending the conversation. Baum nodded and turned away, hurrying back down the column.

The convoy continued in reverse, unable to maneuver or turn around on the narrow road hemmed in with trees on both sides. Hall still worried about an attack from the front, but as the minutes passed without any incident, he began to relax a little. Finally, he made out in the darkness the small gravel road to their left as it whisked by in reverse. The jeep kept rolling backward another hundred yards until the lead Sherman was behind the turn. The column stopped and then began to lurch forward, each tank making the sharp turn onto the road and moving west.

The convoy moved forward in the darkness. Hall saw, to his frustration, that they were advancing at half speed on the winding, narrow road. He feared that this track would wander off to nowhere, or end abruptly, but the task force kept rolling forward as the minutes ticked by. Hall's spirits rose slightly. Perhaps they would make it to Höllrich after all.

Another several hours passed. Behind them, Hall could see the edges of the sky just beginning to lighten. He checked his watch. They weren't far from dawn. He shook his head. They were a full day behind schedule. They were nowhere near the

American lines, and they still had the Main to somehow cross. Still, if they could reach the highway, they could at least move out at full speed and, with any luck, find a way across the river and on toward home.

The column reached a crossroads and halted again. Hall could see the lights of a small town in the distance. They'd made it. This had to be Höllrich. But why on earth were they stopping again? They should plow through now and get the hell out of there while they still could. Instead, they were going to have another damned committee meeting and work out their feelings. If only he was in command. He'd have had the force back already, and they'd be eating breakfast in safety . . .

Stiller stepped out of the vehicle, stretching his back and yawning. Hall joined him, shaking his head to try to kick out the cobwebs. They'd been awake for forty-eight hours now. He'd never stayed up this long in his life, even in the heady party days at Washington State College. He wanted some hot food and a bed, but he knew it would be another day before he'd see either. Even if they somehow made it over the Main, they were far away from friendly lines.

Baum appeared with Nutto. "What do you see?" the commander asked the lead tanker.

"Looks like Höllrich dead ahead," he responded.

"Any signs of resistance?"

"Who knows? In a couple hours, we'll have full light, and I can tell you for sure."

"Maybe we should wait," said Baum.

"No!" interjected Hall, his impatience boiling over.

"Lieutenant, you have exactly zero right to be opening your mouth right now," said Baum, glaring at him.

"I'm sorry, sir. I just think we should get out of here while we have a chance."

Baum grunted. "Perhaps you're right. But I don't want to lose the whole show when we are this close. We can't move fast with all these POWs, and we're dangerously low on ammo and fuel." The commander rubbed his chin, thinking things over. "I know what I want to do." He turned to Nutto. "Take the three lead Shermans and head into Höllrich. If the way is open, let us know; if not, fight your way back here, and we'll wait for daylight before we decide what to do."

"Sounds good, sir," said Nutto. "But you want me to waste all that fuel sending a Sherman back?"

"Let me go along," suggested Stiller. "We can report in a jeep a hell of a lot faster than a tank."

Baum nodded. "That's smart, Major. You follow Nutto, and let us know if the coast is clear."

Hall couldn't believe his ears. Now they were going to split their force? And that idiot Stiller had volunteered them to go along on some suicide patrol? He wanted to scream in his frustration, but he knew there was nothing he could do. He stepped back over into the jeep, sitting silently as Stiller slid in beside him. The major reached in and pushed another wad of tobacco into his mouth. "This better work, Hall," he joked. "This is the last of my chaw."

Hall didn't respond. He held on to his useless Thompson, his fingers white. The lead Shermans jerked into motion, relieved of their POW passengers, who remained behind so the patrol could move at more speed. Stiller pushed the jeep into motion, and they rolled out, following Nutto toward Höllrich.

The patrol advanced toward the lights in the distance. At least they were moving at a decent speed now, and on a paved thoroughfare with a little room to maneuver. Hall was still angry over Baum's decision. It made no sense to him. If they ran into an ambush ahead, they wouldn't be able to fight through it. They might be killed outright or captured. On the other hand, if the Germans were not there, there would be at least an hour's delay while they brought the rest of the column up. Didn't Baum understand anything about tactics? He looked over at Stiller. As usual, the dolt was chewing away at his plug, paying little attention to the details. They should have brought the whole column up now, blazed through any resistance, and moved on toward the Main. It was their only chance to escape.

"Something eating at you, Hall?" asked the major, not taking his eyes off the road.

Hall was surprised. How did Stiller know he was upset? How to answer? Finally, he responded: "I think Baum's wrong. We should have stayed together."

Stiller chuckled. "Do you know how much combat experience our commander has had?"

"That doesn't mean he's right."

The major shook his head, spitting to the side before craning his neck toward the lieutenant. "Hall, you don't know shit about right and wrong in a fight. All these months I've been waiting for you to figure out that you're not special, that you don't know a damned thing. Some people take an awful long time to learn something."

What was Stiller talking about? What did the major know about war? About life? All he could see was what was right in front of him. And he barely understood that. He wanted to argue, but there was no point. He couldn't risk his reward. He'd try humility. "You're right, sir. Baum knows more than me, and so do you. I just want to get out of here."

"I know," responded Stiller, his voice softening. "We all do." He looked over and patted Hall's arm. "I was too hard on you just now. I know I've been tough on you all this time, but I did it for your own good. And I didn't lie when I said you've done good out here, Hall. I'm proud of you."

"Thank you, sir," he responded, keeping his voice as subservient as he could muster. He smiled inside. The major was so easy to manipulate. *I don't give a damn how you feel about me, but I'll take what you're in a position to grant.*

The lights of Höllrich grew on the horizon. Hall knew the

highway ran north and south beyond the west side of the town. He tried to see the line of the roadway, but the morning light was still far too dim. Well, it didn't matte;, in a few minutes they'd reach the town, and they'd either make it through or they wouldn't.

They rolled on. Hall could make out individual houses now. The road they were on seemed to travel right through the town on the way to the highway. He couldn't see any movement in Höllrich. He felt elation rising. They'd beat the Germans here. They could storm through the town and on to the highway. He cursed Baum again for his foolish caution. If the whole convoy was here, they could make their escape now instead of letting the krauts have a chance to play catch-up.

Thunderous explosions rattled the patrol. Fire rained in on them from what seemed every direction. The lead tank was hit and burned before Hall could even react to what was happening. He saw Nutto leap out of the tank and roll into a nearby ditch. Figures emerged out of the trees, rifles raised.

Stiller swore, ripping the gear shift into reverse. He gnashed the clutch and jerked the jeep backward, tearing away from the Shermans as a second tank exploded under the point-blank fire. Their vehicle tore away from the battle, whipping rapidly back out of the conflagration. The last Sherman was following them at a distance, attempting to escape from the German ambush. The major did not wait for the tank but found a patch of level ground near the road and backed into it, turning the vehicle around and then storming down the road at full speed back toward Baum and the rest of the force. They were about halfway back when Stiller pulled over.

"What are you doing?" asked Hall, his eyes darting behind them, expecting the Germans to arrive any second.

"I gotta piss. Jump in the driver's seat, Hall. I'll be right back."

Hall climbed over the seat, putting both hands on the wheel.

His mind was reeling. South, north, west. They'd been blocked in every direction. They were trapped. The Germans were going to kill them all. At best, they'd be captured, and he'd spend the rest of the war as a POW. All he'd wanted was one patrol. A safe jaunt into the countryside followed by a promotion. So many staffers had done it. His father had assured him that Patton would give him the same. How in the hell had he ended up in the middle of this? He felt his panic rising. He looked over. Stiller was turned away, doing his business. Hall reached into his jacket, pulling out the flask. He unscrewed the top and tipped the metal to his lips, gulping deeply, finishing the rest of the schnapps in a couple deep pulls. He needed this warmth, the courage to go on.

"Hall, what the hell are you doing!"

He turned and saw Stiller striding rapidly back toward the jeep. "Give me that damned flask." Hall handed the empty container to the major, who sniffed it, his face in a deep furrow; then he tossed it into the field. "Where the hell did you get that?"

"I pulled it off a dead German. There wasn't much in it," Hall lied. "Just a swallow."

"Jesus Christ, Hall. What did I tell you before we came on this mission?"

"Sir, it was just one drink. Surely that doesn't matter anymore."

"You bet your ass it matters!" shouted Stiller, pointing a finger. "I'm a man of my word, Hall. I told you, you'd done well, and that you'd be rewarded. But I also told you before that if you ever took another drink on duty, that'd be the end of you." He shook his head. "I don't get you, Hall. You're not like anyone I've ever met before. I figured you're above all the rest of it. Smarter and better somehow. Well, I'm sorry to tell you that you're just like the rest of us. And you have to follow the same rules. I have no choice but to . . ."

"I'll tell."

Stiller's forehead creased. "You'll tell what?"

"I'll go to the press about Waters. About Patton."

Stiller took a step back. "You wouldn't think of it. Have you no honor?"

"I don't give a damn about honor or about your sacred secret. I'll tell everything to anyone who'll listen. I'll bring Patton down and you with him."

Stiller was speechless. He moved closer, and Hall thought for a moment that the major might strike him. His face was a splotchy red, and his hands were balled into fists. He stood there for a few moments, then he spat on the ground. "Fine, Hall. You can have it your way. I'll keep your secret if you keep Patton's. You'll get your precious promotion."

Hall smiled. "That's all I ever wanted. You keep your word, and I'll keep mine."

"Don't you worry about me, Hall. You worry about yourself. You've lost something today. Something maybe you never had. You think you're getting your way, but all you've done is sell out your last chance for salvation. You did something out here. Something maybe you don't even realize. You took one step toward becoming a man. A real man. Now you've given all that up. You're going to go on being the little worm you've always been."

Hall laughed. "You can keep your honor, Stiller. You and Patton. I want what's mine, and I'll be on my way."

"You'll get it. Not that it will do you any good."

Stiller walked around the front of the jeep and stepped into the passenger seat. Hall was surprised at the major's movements. He seemed an utterly beaten and defeated man. Was he mourning Hall's loss of honor? Or was he angry that Hall had defeated him? The lieutenant didn't care. He was getting everything he wanted.

He shifted the jeep into gear and moved forward, returning

to the task force. They made contact within a few minutes, and Stiller passed on the news in a quiet voice. Baum waited for the last Sherman to return, but it did not. It must have been destroyed or captured like the other two.

Major Stiller said nothing to Baum about the flask, Hall's threats, or the deal they'd made. Baum gave new orders, and the task force turned to the northeast, making their way up a hill where the task force could regroup and await the coming dawn.

Chapter 28

Hill 427
March 28, 1945, 0700 hours

"Fire!" screamed *Hauptman* Koehl. His Ferdinands belched into action, pouring shells into the midst of the American task force, lying helter-skelter on the lower hill to the southwest. The captain watched the attack through his field glasses. The first volley hit a half-track and a light tank, exploding them in a roaring blaze of flames and onyx smoke.

"Keep it going!" he commanded. The second volley flew, then the third. The Americans were sitting ducks hit by a murderous barrage from multiple directions. Another tank exploded, then another. Koehl could see the green figures scrambling for cover, abandoning their vehicles as they sprinted for safety among the trees. A Sherman got off a shot, firing wildly, but then was hit and blew apart. The scene before him was one of annihilation. One of the half-tracks made it into motion, driving clear of the convoy and heading toward the trees. Koehl thought it might make it for a moment, but the Tigers must have tracked it, as shells fell around the fleeing carrier, and then a direct hit stopped it cold, burning everyone alive within. Koehl could only imagine the curdling screams as the men writhed in their death throes below him.

"Infantry forward!" Baumann's voice crackled over the radio. The two companies of ground troops were moving now, spreading out in the trees, sprinting down the hill, and beginning to engage the enemy. In a matter of minutes, he could hear the ripping chatter of small arms as their forces laid fire on the retreating American soldiers. His Ferdinand rumbled down the side of the hill to the base of the lower prominence. There were no more targets above; they had decimated the armored component of the task force, but he might lend the weight of his 88mm cannon to the firefight that was now developing in the woods before him.

Koehl could feel the thrill of victory and revenge coursing through him. These bastards had killed his sister and his best friend. They'd taken away the last two cords of sinew holding him to the world, to a future life after the war. He was left with nothing now but hot hate and the humiliating specter of defeat. For this one last, blazing moment, he was victorious, he had control over his destiny, he was a warrior and a man. He relished the last bright burning flames of his service to the fatherland.

His Ferdinand came to rest at the edge of the woods. Visibility was low here, and he struggled to see the combat at the edge of his vision, even with his field glasses. He realized immediately that his cannon was useless here. He could not make out targets easily, and if he ordered the weapon to fire, he was as likely to hit friend as foe. He stared out at the trees for a few moments, then started to climb out of the turret.

"Sir, no!" shouted Jaeger.

"You stay here in charge!" he ordered, not looking back. He climbed out of the Ferdinand and hopped down to the cold, hard grass of the field. Outside the steel blanket of his vehicle, he felt vulnerable and out of place. Still, the thrill of combat embraced him. He didn't want this moment to leave him, and his revenge was not yet complete. He fastened a *Stahlhelm* to his head, drew his pistol, and moved in among the trees.

Once in the forest, he quickly lost his grip on reality. The trees had an isolating effect, and as he worked his way up the hill, he quickly lost sight of his Ferdinand. He'd not yet made it up to the fighting, and for a few moments, he could have been on a Sunday stroll through a city park. In the distance, he could hear the ripping linen of submachine-gun fire, but with that exception, the morning was eerily quiet. He kept moving forward, darting from tree to tree. The trunks were too narrow to offer any real protection, but they provided partial cover and a sense of security. He moved up, yard by yard. The clamor of fighting grew now. In the distance, he could see the backs of a few comrades, huddled behind trees, darting around for a moment, taking quick aim, then moving back again. One of the men took a round and was spun out from behind a tree, falling face forward down the hill and tumbling a dozen yards or so before coming to a silent rest. Koehl hastened to the soldier, rolling him over, but his eyes were glazed and stared up at the heavens. He'd taken a round directly through the heart and was probably dead before he'd hit the ground.

Koehl laid the soldier gently back to the ground, covering the man's face with his helmet. He moved forward and picked up his Mauser rifle, a much more effective weapon than his pistol, and started back up the hill toward the sound of the fighting.

He passed a cluster of trees and reached one of his men. The soldier was firing and did not see Koehl coming up behind him. The *Hauptmann* placed a hand on the man's shoulder, and the private jerked and turned in surprise, before letting out a deep breath of relief on seeing Koehl. A bullet chipped the trunk of the tree he was resting behind, then another.

"Where are the Americans?" demanded Koehl.

"That way up the hill," said the private, waving a negligent hand.

"How far?"

"*Gott* knows. Maybe a hundred yards."

Koehl crouched behind another tree, moving his head around the truck and staring up the hill, trying to make out the Americans. A bullet hit the dirt near him, and he jerked his head back around, taking a couple of breaths. He fumbled with his rifle, pulling the bolt back and moving a round into the chamber. He cocked the bullet into place and then whipped the weapon up; spinning around the trunk, he took rapid aim up the hill and fired. He returned quickly to his cover, moving the bolt in and out again as he chambered new rounds. He repeated this process several times, unsure if he was hitting anything. He felt alive, excited. He hadn't experienced combat on the ground before. He felt so exposed and vulnerable.

"Let's go!" he screamed at the private. He whipped around the tree again and sprinted up to another trunk a few yards up the hill. The private seemed to hesitate, then followed. Koehl scrambled up again, firing once as he advanced on another trunk, then another. Soon they had advanced thirty yards up the hill.

The bullets were whipping around them now. Koehl looked to his left and right, trying to make out the rest of his men, but he could see nothing. He was in his own little world, just he and the private, and their nameless foes above and ahead of them. He could taste the Americans. They were close, less than fifty yards now. He wondered how many of them there were, how much ammunition they had.

He darted up another few yards. He heard a groan and a crash behind him. The private was down, hit in the leg by a round. He kicked and thrashed for a few moments, and then rolled to his left, pulling himself behind a tree. "Are you all right, Private?" called Koehl.

"I'll be fine," said the soldier through gritted teeth. "It passed through my calf. Hurts like the devil! I can't go on, *Hauptmann*. You should stay here with me. You're going to get yourself killed."

"Nonsense, Private. We've got them right where we want them. I'll be back for you."

"Good luck!" the private called.

Koehl turned and shuffled toward another tree. Rounds danced past him. Someone ahead had a submachine gun. He would have to be careful now. What about grenades? He hadn't thought of that. The American pineapples would roll nicely down this hill and blow him to bits. He would have to keep an eye out for them.

He found a wider tree trunk and rushed forward to crash against it. This time, he thought he saw a flash in the trees ahead. His first glimpse of the enemy, of *his* enemy. *Let me kill the man who killed her*, he whispered in prayer.

Bullets crashed against the tree in rapid succession. The hero up there with the machine gun was giving it his all. But he was a fool, wasting bullets. Koehl waited until there was a pause, then he rolled to his right, spinning over a few feet, then laying his weapon out carefully and firing—one round, two; he rolled again and fired, always at the same cluster of trees where he'd seen the flashes. A bullet hit the dirt in front of him. Another bounced off his helmet. He saw a flash and aimed carefully, firing another round; then he rolled back behind the tree. His heart was exploding in his chest. He was delighted, alive, and coursing with the moment. He smiled to himself, enjoying the rapture and passion of the fight.

His rifle was empty. Damn it! He hadn't thought to take ammunition off his dead comrade. He pulled his pistol back out. It was suicide to engage them with it, but he didn't care. He was fighting them. The killers of his dreams. He rolled out again, to his left this time, and rapidly emptied his pistol as its yippee bark spewed bullet after bullet at his enemy. The machine gunner was back at it again, and a line of rounds crashed past him, barely missing; he rolled over behind the tree, fumbling for another pistol clip in his equipment. He looked over and was delighted to see three more comrades, one with an MP 38. That would even the odds. The soldier nodded approvingly at him, apparently having watched the last exchange with the enemy.

He spun out and started his wild, rapid firing again. This time, two grenades rolled down the hill directly toward him. He continued his turn, spinning away from them and toward the small cluster of infantry to his left. He reached the men as the first grenade exploded. He expected the white-hot burning of shrapnel, but he wasn't hit. The second detonated, showering them with dirt. A fragment cut his cheek, but he'd survived. He looked over at the rest of the men. They seemed okay.

His blood was up, and he wanted to finish this. "Let's get these bastards!" he shouted. He rose to his feet and charged up the hill, not waiting to see if they were following him. He moved from tree to tree, sprinting, firing his pistol at the cluster of bushes above him. Bullets whizzed around him but did not find their mark. He felt invincible, shielded from harm. He was closing in on them now, twenty yards away, then ten. He fired, screaming, waiting for death to take him, but still storming ahead.

He could see them now. A cluster of GIs. He fired at them, and his shot found the chest of one of his enemy, the man jerking backward and hitting the ground. He fired again, grazing the shoulder of another. A few shots fell short of him as he closed the distance where the Americans stood, their arms in the air, attempting to surrender. He ran in to the cluster, knocking one of the men to the ground with the back of his pistol to his face. His breathing came in rapid gasps; he was winded, and images flashed back and forth before him. He heard the footsteps of men behind him, and he knew his small unit had followed him.

There were six Americans here, two wounded. He shouted at them in German, screaming, feeling the fire of his loss and frustration. The private with the submachine gun stepped quickly forward, pulling their weapons away from them and tossing them to the ground at a safe distance. An American was saying something to him, with pleading in his voice. He didn't want to hear them beg for his mercy. He wanted his revenge.

The private pushed the men down to their knees. Their hands were still in the air. The other two Germans were up with him now, rifles pointed at the Americans.

"All over now, *Hauptmann*," said one of them. "You are brave. Or crazy."

Koehl didn't answer. He stared into the faces of these Americans. They were full of apprehension. They didn't look like the killers who had taken away his future. He didn't want to see them. He wanted to take their lives as they'd taken away his. He stepped forward to stand in front of the first one. He raised his pistol and aimed it at the soldier's head. He wanted his vengeance.

"*Hauptmann*, no!" shouted one of his men. "They've surrendered. You can't do it."

"Quiet, Private!" he screamed. "Did they show mercy to my sister? To Sergeant Schmidt? No. They killed them without remorse."

"I don't know what you're talking about, but you can't shoot them in cold blood. Their war is over. Look at them."

The words beat at the flames of his fury. He didn't want to hear them, but he couldn't force the truth away. He looked at the man kneeling before him; his eyes were closed, he was shaking. The other Americans were watching in horror. Behind them, the GI he'd shot was rocking back and forth, screaming in his death throes. The other wounded soldier was lying back, clutching his injury.

He spit on the ground, his anger returning. Was he to be denied this last satisfaction? He had lost everything. Germany had lost everything. He wanted one last vengeance for his family, for his nation. He raised the pistol again.

A hand gripped the barrel, pulling it upward. He whipped around, staring into the face of one of the privates. The one with the machine gun. He pulled and twisted, trying to free his grasp, but the soldier would not let go. He looked at Koehl with a grim sadness and shook his head. "Not like this, *Hauptmann*. Don't end the war like this."

Koehl struggled for a few more moments and then stopped. He let go of the pistol and turned, walking briskly away. He took a few steps and then collapsed, burying his face in the dirt, his hands ripping into the earth until they were cut and bleeding. He screamed, hot tears burning his eyes. He didn't want to let go. They'd taken everything from him. There was nothing left for his future. He lay that way for a long time, sobbing. Nobody disturbed him.

Finally, he felt he'd had enough. The private was right. He couldn't kill these men now. They were prisoners. Their war was over, and so was his.

He rose, stepping back toward his men. The Americans were standing now, and as he moved toward them, they huddled together, afraid for their lives. He stared at them for a few moments, then turned and walked back down the hill and up the higher prominence toward his Ferdinand.

He felt nothing. A hollow emptiness smothered his soul. He was a shell, a shade, a specter. Like Germany. A nothing with only darkness ahead.

Chapter 29

Hill 427
March 28, 1945, 0700 hours

Hall turned the jeep's ignition, and the vehicle coughed and sputtered in the crisp morning air, fighting to come alive. Around them, he could hear the tanks and half-tracks battling to life as the task force sprang forward on their desperate dart to freedom. The next hour would tell whether they had made it. Hall was anxious to complete this disastrous raid and to distance himself from Stiller. The major sat glumly in the seat next to him. In this last hour before dawn, he'd refused to look at or speak to the lieutenant. No matter, Stiller was trapped, and the dolt knew it. He would cooperate when the time came, whether he liked it or not. Like any dog, he'd sacrifice his own desires to save his master.

He felt the explosions before he saw them. A pressurized wave of stifling air washed over him from behind. Even as he struggled to recover from the shock of the sensation, a tank in front of Hall exploded in a cloud of fire, then another. He turned toward Stiller, trying to speak, but the words would not come.

Another moment passed, or was it more? The sights and sounds around him overwhelmed his senses, rendering him unable to act or even think. A hand landed on his arm, pushing away from him. He fought to move the grip, but the fingers pressed in on his upper arm with an immovable force. He turned his head and saw Stiller, shoving him out of the jeep. He blinked, trying to understand what this meant. Then it occurred to him: the major was trying to help him. They had to move, get away from the exposed vehicle before it was too late.

He turned away from Stiller, dragging his feet out of the car and willing them to the ground. He started to rise, but he was shoved with massive force up and away, and he flew through the air, landing hard and tumbling down a few yards. His whole body felt scorched and battered. His ears rang, and his mouth tasted like bitter metal. He rolled over, opening his eyes to look back at the jeep. It was gone. Torn completely apart by a shell. He looked down at his arms and legs. They were a bloody mess, and he felt throbbing pain burning through him. He examined his wounds more closely and realized with relief that they were superficial, caused by dozens of glass and metal fragments tearing along the surface of his skin.

He tried to rise even as the artillery rained down on the task force. He was dizzy and unable to stand. He turned away from the thunderous, burning mess and crawled, moving his hands and knees over the frozen earth, trying to shamble away from the ambush before he was struck and killed by the shrapnel that tore this way and that all around him. In every direction, he could see the soldiers of the task force and the POWs running toward the woods sloping down the hill. Some had weapons, but very few. There was no organization, nobody appeared in charge. Everyone was running for their life.

He felt hard fingers on his back, and his shirt was jerked back. He turned and saw Stiller, who mouthed something at him. He couldn't understand the words or hear them over the screaming clamor in his ears. The major frowned down at him, apparently grasping that he could not understand. He reached down with his other hand and pulled Hall up to a standing position. The major tucked his arms around the lieutenant's back and began walking him out of the clearing.

Each step was an agonizing crucible. They moved slowly, Stiller pulling him, his hands an iron cuff on his back, holding him upright and dragging him away from the fire. Step by step, they moved closer to the trees. Hall had no idea where they would go, or even why, but he wanted desperately to get away from the burning tanks. The eye of the task force held only oblivion now.

They reached the trees. The hill sloped sharply down. The going was even more difficult now, as Stiller was forced to brace them with each step downward, gravity threatening to tumble them freely down the decline and into the waiting arms of God knew what.

Hall saw bullets chirping off the dirt. He looked down the hill but could see nothing. Perhaps they were simply spare rounds from the fight at the top of the hill, but he knew it was likely the Germans had them surrounded. Perhaps they should just sit down and wait for the end. He wanted to say this to Stiller, but he couldn't make the words come out, and the major was not looking in his direction, instead concentrating on moving them farther and farther away from the hilltop.

In the distance, they could see the flash of fire and gray forms moving up the hill. They continued on, moving now this way and now that behind the trees, trying to minimize their target. A small group of infantry caught up to them, and they moved on together. Hall supposed they were trying to fight their way out, but he didn't know the purpose, at least for him. He was too badly hurt to make it very far. Then again, if they could make it through the Germans and hide for a day or two, he might regain his strength.

Bullets scuffed up the dirt at their feet. The small unit returned the fire. Hall had nothing to fight with and wasn't sure he'd have the courage to do so if he had. He wallowed in despair, wishing Stiller would just drop him so he could surrender.

One of the GIs was hit and fell backward. The men paused, a couple of them trying to help the wounded man. They worked away at him as another soldier sprayed the hill below with his Thompson, trying to keep the advancing Germans at bay. Another GI pulled the pins and threw his last two grenades in rapid succession. Twin flashes exploded down the hill thirty yards or so away.

The men moved back into position, firing their M1 Garands as rapidly as they could depress the trigger. The soldier with the Thompson paused to reload his clip. Stiller pulled Hall up against a tree. Their small group blazed away for a few moments, but one after another, they ran out of bullets. Hall could see the major yelling at the men, motioning as if telling them to run. A GI shook his head, then another. Stiller lowered his eyes to the ground for a moment, then nodded. Hall rose, struggling to his feet, wanting to see.

As one, they raised their hands to the heavens, dropping their weapons. They were surrendering. Thank God! But their battle wasn't over. One of the men was hit and dropped backward to the ground, then another. The Germans were killing them. It wasn't going to work. Hall was going to die after all. *Oh, God help me.*

The krauts closed in on them, a small group of enlisted men with an officer. The commander wore the black uniform of a tanker. They stormed up to the men, and while the officer held them at pistol point, the infantry quickly disarmed them, shoving them to their knees. At least the shooting had stopped. They were going to be dragged back to some godforsaken prison camp, but Hall knew their stay would be measured in weeks, months at worst. The war was over.

The officer stepped forward. He had a strange expression on

his face. He raised his pistol, aiming the weapon at Hall's head. The lieutenant couldn't believe it. *Why me?* He was going to die anyway, here in the middle of nowhere. He would never see home, his family, his future. Why didn't the bastard shoot Stiller? His time had come and gone.

The officer hesitated, looking Hall up and down. He started to lower the weapon and then seemed to gather new determination, and he raised the barrel again. He closed his eyes; he was going to die. A moment ticked by, then another. He opened his eyes and was surprised to see one of the German privates grappling with the officer. The pistol was pointed away from him, half raised to the heavens. The struggle continued for a few moments, then the officer released the weapon. He stumbled away from them and fell to the ground, sobbing. Hall lowered his head, his own tears falling freely down his cheeks. He was alive. He was going to make it after all!

They sat that way for a half hour or more, kneeling in the dirt, halfway down some forgotten hill in the middle of nowhere. They were the last remnants of a broken and useless task force that had gone nowhere, accomplished nothing. Eventually, more Germans arrived; they pulled the men up to a standing position and led them down the hill, Stiller continuing to help Hall as they limped down and out of the woods. They were met at the bottom by a convoy of large gray trucks, and Hall was pushed and pulled up into the canvas-covered back of one of them. Soon the trucks were rumbling and jolting down the road.

"Hall." He heard the voice over the ringing in his ears. He knew the sound. He didn't want to look up. "Hall," the voice repeated. He turned to face the major.

"Can you hear me?"

He hesitated for a moment. Should he lie? What was the point? He nodded.

"You did okay up there. Don't you worry; they're going to patch things up. You'll be all right."

"Where do you think they're taking us?" Hall asked.

"Probably right back to the same damn place. At least if we're lucky."

"And if we're not?"

"Deep into Germany. But don't fret none. In a few weeks, this whole show will be over. Hall . . ."

"What?"

"I want you to reconsider. Do the right thing."

"What do you mean?"

"I want your word that you'll keep the secret."

"I gave it already."

"Yes," said Stiller, turning toward him. "But you want something in return. There's no honor in that, son. You violated my direct order. That's not worthy of a medal. But I'll do you a favor in return. You've done well on this mission. I will agree not to bring up your actions to Patton. There will be no court-martial, no dishonor. You go your way, I'll go mine. You've earned that."

Hall couldn't believe his ears. The major wanted him to keep Patton's secret in exchange for nothing? "Why would I do that?"

Stiller leaned in, looking intently at Hall. "Because, son, there is a hell of a lot more out there at stake than a promotion and a medal. There's honor, integrity. I gave you my word that if you conducted yourself correctly on this mission, I would give you the things you seek. But you broke the rules. I can give you one more chance to do the right thing." He put his hand on Hall's arm. "Please, Lieutenant. For your sake, not for mine, do the honorable thing. It will carry you through the rest of your life, a hell of a lot further than some useless ribbons."

"I don't understand what you want from me. I told you to take care of me, and I'll take care of you. I meant it. I won't reveal Patton's secret. But if you're offering me nothing in return, well then . . ."

"Then there's nothing I can do for you, kid." Stiller's eyes were filled with sadness. "You'll get what you want, and you'd better keep your end of the deal as well. After we are done with this ride, I don't want to talk to you or see you again. When we get out, I'll take care of things on my end. I wish you the best, Hall, but I won't have any part of it. I hope someday you learn what I'm talking about."

Hall nodded, turning away. He was on his own? Fine. Why did he need this old bastard's help anyway? He couldn't believe what he'd just heard. How stupid did Stiller think he was? He turned his head, smiling a little to himself. He'd keep the stupid secret. Who cared about it anyway? At least for now. He'd talk to his dad about it and see if they could wring any more profit out of things later. For now, he was going home a hero. Sure, he'd face a little pain while in the camp, but then he would get everything he'd ever wanted.

Strangely, he felt a little knot in his stomach. He'd experienced it before, now and again. Weakness, he realized. His dad had told him about it. Most people were sheep. They were afraid to do what they needed to get what they wanted in the world. He wasn't. He wasn't going to let some sentimental crap dictate his future. That was for saps and simpletons. Like that poor imbecile sitting next to him. He could go back to being Patton's lapdog for all Hall cared, or he could go to hell. As the truck jounced along, the lieutenant imagined what the accolades would be, and how far he could stretch that capital when he got home. He couldn't wait to get out of this stupid war. Back to his future, his family, his father. He chuckled to himself as he thought of Stiller, heading home to nobody and nothing.

The truck bounced onward, carrying them to the Oflag and beyond, to his destiny.

Chapter 30

Oflag XIII
March 28, 1945, 0700 hours

Curtis woke with a terrible thudding in his head. He couldn't remember where he was or what he'd been doing. Then it came to him. The hospital, Knorr. He opened his eyes slowly, just a crease at first, trying to gauge if it was safe to look around. Finally, he risked it and opened them wide, darting his head to the left and right.

He was lying on a cot, chest up, his eyes blinking under the brightness of a bare bulb above him. He could hear the bustle of men moving here and there in the hospital. They were still in the ward. He turned his head to the right and could see the familiar doctor, working away with one of the wounded. He moved his arms, struggling to rise. He could not move. He realized, to his surprise, that he was restrained at the wrists and ankles with what felt like rope. He looked down, his chin resting on his chest, and verified that he was tied to the cot tightly.

Knorr must have done this, he realized. He looked again to his left and his right. There were German guards posted at all the entrances, machine pistols in their hands. Yet the orderlies and the doctor continued to work away as if everything was fine. How could that be? He needed to warn them. One of the men was nearby to his right, and he called to him. He knew him slightly, and the soldier came over, a neutral expression on his face.

"What is it?" he asked.

"What the hell are you doing?" asked Curtis, his voice louder than he wanted it to be. The man's face furrowed into a frown.

"Keep your voice down!" he demanded.

"Don't you realize what they did? What they are going to do again?"

"Shut your mouth!" the man insisted.

"They killed all the injured. Didn't you know that?"

The man moved closer. "I said to be quiet," he responded, putting a hand on Curtis's chest. "Yes, I know what happened."

"Then you have to help me. Can you untie my hands and feet?"

The orderly shook his head. "It wouldn't do any good."

"What do you mean?"

"Look at you," he answered. "Even without your restraints, you can barely move. Look at them," he said, his head nodding toward the guards. "They have machine guns. Yes, I know what they did, but it doesn't mean they will do it again. If they do, they do; we can't fight them. Most of the men in here can barely move. If you cause a ruckus in here, you will get them all killed."

"At least there'd be a chance."

"Nonsense. The only chance we have is to sit and wait." He edged closer. "Listen, I've heard them talking. The appearance of that raid has them rattled. They know the end is near. Do you seriously think they want to add to their crimes?"

"Knorr does. He doesn't care. He's coming to kill Waters and me."

The orderly stiffened. "He's not allowed in here again. You were probably passed out and didn't see it. General von Goeckel came in and chewed the sergeant out. I don't know what he said, but the Ferret was as angry as I've ever seen him. At the end, the general pointed toward the door, and Knorr stormed out. I don't think he'll be back. At least we can hope."

"He'll be back, and he'll kill us all."

"I told you to shut your mouth. You're wrong. And if you're not, there's not a damned thing we can do about it. I'm not going to let you endanger the lives of all of these men."

"At least untie me," Curtis pleaded.

The orderly shook his head. "I'm sorry, Captain, I can't help you." He started to rise.

"What about Waters?" asked Curtis. "Is he awake?"

"Not yet. He should be anytime, though. Don't worry, Curtis. I think they're done. You focus on getting better. We'll all be home soon."

Curtis closed his eyes and didn't respond. He knew there was no point in trying to convince the orderly. He was clinging to a desperate hope. The man was right. There were at least a hundred Germans in the camp. The hospital constituted the last of the POWs. They were unarmed and injured. If they fought, they would all be dead for sure. The only chance they had was to hope.

But that left Knorr. No matter what the orderly said, the Ferret would be back. He hated Curtis with something akin to religious zeal. He was going to get his revenge on the captain and on Waters, whatever the general wanted. He had to get free and find his pistol. He had to protect Waters. How to do it, though? He didn't have any idea how he would break free. Even if he did, where was the pistol now? He didn't know which cot he'd been in before. He had a general idea, but he would need time to search. Even if he somehow had that time, there was no guarantee the Germans hadn't already located and confiscated the weapon. Without it, particularly in his condition, he didn't know how he would possibly fight back.

One problem at a time. He had to figure out how to get free of the ropes. He tried to work his wrists and ankles against them, feeling if there was any weakness in the knots. He couldn't see any of them clearly, and after a few minutes, he gave up. He didn't sense any way to untie the knots by himself. He considered flipping himself on his side. The cots were light, and he could probably manage it. But what would that accomplish? The guards would be alerted immediately and would investigate. They might move him at that point or secure him somewhere even more impossible. He couldn't think of anything he could do. He continued to struggle, trying to work through the bonds that held him, but he was growing weaker and lightheaded. His head and back burned. Finally, he gave up in a haze of exhausted frailty and drifted into sleep.

He woke in the darkness. He must have been out for hours. He felt confused for a moment until he remembered where he was. He felt a tugging at his hands, and he pulled away, groaning.

"Quiet!" whispered a voice he recognized.

"Waters?"

"Keep it down," the lieutenant colonel said. "I'm trying to get you untied."

"How can you even be up? You were near death."

"I'm a little better now," said Waters. "But does that matter? We've got to get out of here. They'll kill us if we don't."

Curtis was relieved that someone else echoed his thoughts. "I tried to get the orderly to help me, but he said we should sit tight."

"He's a fool then. They did it once, they'll do it again. At least Knorr's dead. He was the ringleader last time."

"He's not gone. He survived somehow. He threatened me when you were unconscious . . . and you."

"More reason for us to get the hell out of here."

"But where can we go? The camp is full of Germans."

"If we can make it back to the headquarters building, we'll be safe. It's a long shot, but we've got to try." He gave a final tug, and the rope fell from Curtis's right hand.

The captain pulled his arm up, flexing his fingers and trying to push blood through as he worked his wrist around. "I don't understand," he whispered. "What good would it do to reach the HQ building? Surely they would search for us."

Waters leaned closer, his voice the lightest whisper. "There are tunnels below. We were working on an escape plan. There's plenty of room and a little food and water stored there too. If we can make it, we can hide there for days, maybe longer. Hopefully long enough that the Germans will leave, or that our friends will arrive again, this time for good." Waters pulled and twisted the ropes on Curtis's left hand, and after an extended struggle, they too dropped away.

Curtis pulled himself up, ignoring the dizzy vertigo and the gnashing pain. He set to work on his right ankle while Waters worked to free his left. There were no guards inside, and the other men seemed to be asleep. *Tunnels.* Curtis had never heard about them. He wondered why the secret was not shared with the whole command team. It was probably best it had not been. There were snitches in the camp, perhaps even a German plant or two. No, it was wise of Goode and Waters to keep that information to themselves. Still, it would likely do them little good. The headquarters building was only a hundred yards away, but Curtis could barely walk, and Waters must be in even worse shape. There were likely German guards at the entrance to the hospital and more on patrol in between. The chances they would make it were next to nothing.

Curtis chuckled to himself. Did it matter? Die in the yard outside or in here tonight or tomorrow. The camp had been evacuated. The hospital patients were the last POWs left. They would be in danger even without Knorr, and the sergeant had sworn his revenge. Waters was right: a fraction of hope was better than no hope at all.

He managed to work the rope free around his ankle, and Waters pulled the line away a few seconds later. He was free. Curtis worked his legs around to the floor, twisting his ankles and stomping his feet a few times to restore circulation. "Keep it down!" warned Waters.

"What's the plan?"

"We make it to the door first and crack it open as little as possible. If there are no guards, then we sneak out and tiptoe our way across the yard."

"And if there are guards?"

"We find something to neutralize them with."

"I've got a pistol."

"What?" Waters asked, forgetting his admonition on noise. "What are you talking about?"

"When you were out, a couple of the raid members came in. A major and a lieutenant. You were in surgery. The major left me a pistol. Come to think of it, he was asking for you, specifically."

Waters's eyes narrowed, and he became thoughtful. "A major, huh? Fifty, medium height, and a leathery face?"

"I was pretty out of it, but that seems about right."

"I wonder if it was Stiller? That sounds like him." Waters's face paled. "Jesus, I hope the old man didn't send this whole thing in here just to get me."

"What do you mean?"

"Patton."

"Why would Patton send a raid after you?"

"I'm married to his daughter."

Curtis widened his eyes in surprise. "Why didn't you tell anyone?"

"Nobody's business, and that's not the kind of thing a real

man brags about. Goode knew, and a few others." Waters shook his head. "It would be just like my father-in-law to sacrifice a bunch of men on my behalf. Christ, I hope I'm wrong."

"The pistol . . ."

Waters shook his head as if driving out the thoughts. "Yes, that's more important right now. Where is it?"

"It's right over here," said a voice from across the room.

Curtis's blood froze. He looked up, and through the semi-darkness, he made out the form of Sergeant Knorr, standing near the doorway, holding the .45 pistol aimed at them.

"Imagine my surprise when your good doctor brought me this. He said he found it in your cot, Curtis. Tsk, tsk, that's very poor behavior for a POW, don't you think?" The sergeant took a few steps toward them, a sadistic smirk flooding his face. He looked at Waters. "*Und Sie*, Lieutenant Colonel. Out of bed so soon after surgery? You'll catch a nasty infection."

"We're not going to play your game, Knorr," said Waters. "You're in a room full of witnesses. You can't do anything to us here."

"A room full of witnesses can easily be dealt with, Waters, as you are well aware. Don't you worry about them. They will be well taken care of. It's yourself you should be concerned with."

Waters spat. "Do what you will, Knorr. I'm not going to mince words with you. Do your business or shut your mouth."

The sergeant took another step forward. "I'll certainly take care of my business tonight, but I would like a little more privacy and some space for the fun." He motioned with his pistol. "Let's step into the operating room, shall we?"

"And if I refuse?" asked Waters.

The sergeant pointed his pistol at the head of one of the patients. "Then I'll take steps to assure that *this* room is fully private, immediately."

Waters hesitated a moment and then turned, stepping toward the operating-room double doors. Curtis could see now just how frail the lieutenant colonel was, as he dragged his feet and shambled slowly away.

"You too, Curtis. I told you I have something special in store for the two of you."

The captain turned and followed Waters. Despite the frosty room, he could feel driblets of sweat rolling down his forehead. He wanted to talk to Waters, to try to figure out what they could do, but the sergeant was close behind him, digging the barrel of the .45 into his back.

Waters reached the doors and pushed his way slowly through. Curtis followed and entered the operating room. There was nobody else inside. A set of bloody instruments lay unwashed over a crimson-stained towel on a tray near the operating table. A little light emanated from a window set high up to the left. As they entered, Curtis was struck in the back of the head, and he went reeling forward, crashing to the ground near the base of the operating table. He nearly passed out but clung desperately to consciousness.

"On the table, Waters," he heard Knorr command.

"I won't do it."

Curtis heard the .45 hammer cock back. "Now, or I'll shoot you."

There was silence for a moment, then Curtis saw Waters step up to the table and lower himself down onto it. His feet swung up and disappeared over the edge.

"Now, Waters, a moment I've been looking forward to for a very long time. Have you seen my SS dagger? I showed it to Curtis earlier, but I'm afraid you were indisposed during my presentation. However, we'll have the opportunity to resolve that right now. Where are your stitches? Here they are. What a poor job the doctor did. We'll have to fix that."

As Curtis watched in horror, Knorr drew his dagger from his belt. The steel weapon flashed, and Waters gave out a dreadful moan. His feet kicked up and down on the table. The captain couldn't stand the sound. He had to do something. He looked up. Knorr had the pistol in his left hand, still aimed at Waters. The knife was in his right.

Closing his eyes and muttering the briefest of prayers, Curtis spun himself over, rolling until he crashed into the sergeant's legs. He hit Knorr hard, and the German fell backward, toppling to the floor. Curtis continued his momentum, both hands grabbing for the pistol. He grasped the barrel with one hand and Knorr's wrist with the other. He struggled with all his might, trying to dislodge the weapon.

A fire burned his back, then another. Knorr was stabbing him with the dagger. He could feel the knife ripping through his flesh, in and out. He screamed in agony, but he refused to let go. With superhuman effort, he tore the pistol out of Knorr's hands and reversed it, struggling to aim. He felt the dagger plunge into his back again. He was losing blood rapidly and was terrified he would lose consciousness. With a final effort, he pressed the trigger, and the weapon bucked. Knorr's head snapped back, and a froth of blood exploded on the ground behind him, splattering him with hot liquid and brains. The sergeant went limp below him.

"Curtis, are you okay?" Waters called weakly from the table.

"I got the bastard," said the captain quietly. He felt an almost dreamy sleepiness. He lowered his head onto the sergeant's stomach, the light already dimming around him. As he watched, the door of the operating room ripped open and German guards blazed in, machine pistols at the ready. One of them took in Curtis and Knorr, a look of terror in his eyes. Curtis pulled his weapon up to aim. It didn't matter. He'd fought his enemies. He'd saved his friend. There was a flash, and he was gone.

Chapter 31

Major Stiller sat in the back of the room watching as the reporters barraged Patton. Nearly every hand in the room was up, but any semblance of order had fled as the journalists lobbed their demands for answers at the general.

"Why didn't you announce the raid ahead of time?"

"Did you know your son-in-law was in the camp?"

"Do you feel responsible for all the dead and wounded?"

Patton held his hands up, forcing the din in the long, bare room to finally die down.

"One question at a time now. I'll try to answer every one of them that I can. I didn't announce the raid ahead of time for obvious reasons. We don't publicize our military operations. You know better than that."

"But did you know that Waters was in the camp?" the reporter repeated insistently.

"No, I did not," said Patton. Stiller shifted uncomfortably under the weight of these words. But he said nothing.

"Why this raid then? Why to that camp?"

"Look," Patton said, his hands raised as if he could push the questions away. "I'd been looking for a chance to liberate some of our boys for a long time. You saw what those damned Germans were doing in the other camps we occupied. This Oflag was in range, and I took a shot at it."

"Yes, but you failed," said another reporter.

Patton's face flushed red at this. "Yes, I failed. I don't know if you've noticed, young man, but war doesn't follow a recipe. You throw the ingredients at it and hope you bake up something you can eat. Sometimes the batch gets burned. That's the way it goes."

"Would you have done anything different if you had a chance?"

Patton paused. "Yes, I would. I should have sent a whole combat command. I thought about it, but I wanted a fast, tight raid. That was a mistake."

"You're sure you didn't know Waters was in there?" It was the young reporter again.

Patton turned on him. "Listen here, puppy. My word is my honor. I didn't know he was there, and that's the end of that. But if you need more proof than that, here are my personal and official journals. You're welcome to read them. You'll see there isn't a word about my son-in-law being in that camp." The general held up a couple of leather-bound books. "I'll circulate these after the conference is over. I can only let you look at the relevant pages. Too much in there that's confidential. I'm sure you understand.

"Now, if that's enough about that, I'd like you all to meet my son-in-law. John, can you come out here?"

Lieutenant Colonel John Waters stepped up on the stage; he still had a distinct hobble, and he moved with measured, stiff movements, but he was there, alive, liberated, just like Stiller and the rest of the survivors of the doomed task force.

The reporters erupted in applause as Waters took the stage. Patton embraced his son-in-law, then took his left arm in his right, lifting his hand into the air. The clapping went on for a good while. Stiller took the opportunity to step out of the building.

He took a walk, past tanks, trucks, and the busy hive of an army headquarters. Here and there he was recognized, and he gave salutes or brief greetings, but he didn't stop to talk. He was flushed with his own emotions. He had spent a good portion of his lifetime serving Patton. The general was a gruff, obnoxious prima donna at times, but he had a heart of gold. He'd made just about every mistake a man could make, usually with what came out of his mouth. The people loved and hated him for it. Stiller had never minded. His friend seemed always in the end to seek what was right and honorable. Besides, he was Mars himself on the battlefield, in Stiller and many other people's opinion, the greatest field general of the war, at least on the American side of things. Wars needed men like Patton.

Something was different now, though. Stiller had never seen Patton lie so directly to reporters, to Ike, to anyone who would listen. He'd acted in self-interest, and that bothered Stiller. Still, who didn't want to protect their own in time of war? But to deny he'd done it was something else. *My word is my honor.*

What would he do about it? Nothing, he realized. He would keep the secret. His own honor demanded it. He'd done everything he could do. He'd gone on the raid. He'd tried to rescue Waters. He'd protected Patton's reputation, even at the cost of rewarding someone he found despicable. Perhaps that's what really rubbed him the wrong way. He wanted to punish Hall more than anyone he'd ever encountered. Not out of spite; that wasn't in his nature. He wanted the young officer to face consequences for his actions, to learn that the world wasn't here just for him. Hall needed that desperately. Instead, the lieutenant's deceit had been rewarded in order to protect Patton.

Stiller had fed a growing monster. Well, it couldn't be helped. God's will be done.

He continued his walk, already feeling a little better. Stiller eventually made his way back to Patton's office, where the general sat with Waters, enjoying a glass of eighteen-year-old scotch. Patton nodded to Stiller when he came in and poured the major a glass.

"Come on in and take a seat, Alex."

Stiller stepped in, sat down, and accepted the glass, tipping the container back and enjoying a sip of the deep, fiery whiskey. "Thank you, George."

"John was just telling me about the raid. Hell of a situation. Did he tell you about this Knorr fellow?"

Stiller nodded. "A real bastard. Although not the only one we've heard of. These Nazis have a real sadistic streak. Good thing we whipped 'em good."

"What about Curtis?" asked Patton. "He sacrificed his life to save John. I want the Medal of Honor for him."

Stiller shifted uncomfortably. "Sir, you realize every one of those requires a detailed inquiry into the facts of the medal. I think we want to let dead dogs lie on this little trip."

Patton thought about that for a second. "I guess you're right. Let's get him a Silver Star then, at least. And I want something for Baum, Nutto, and the rest of the boys. They didn't make it, but they gave it a hell of a run."

"What about my recommendations for Hall?"

Patton looked at Stiller sharply. "I thought you didn't like the little prick?"

Stiller kept his face straight. "He did his duty on the raid. He fought bravely." *You better keep your word, you little shit.*

Patton grunted. "It seems excessive to me that he gets a promotion and a medal, but if that's your recommendation, I won't fight it. How about you, Alex? Surely you deserve something for going along."

316 James D. Shipman

Stiller grunted. "I don't need nothing, sir. It's just my job. All I did was sit in a jeep and ride along."

"We all know that isn't true," said Waters. "You're a hell of a leader and a lousy self-promoter."

"I followed orders, nothing more."

"Well, I may do something despite your protests," said Patton. "The war is all but over. You've been a hell of a friend and staff member. I'm not going to forget you."

"How'd the meeting with Ike go?" asked Stiller, wanting to change the subject.

"He was pissed as hell about the raid," said Patton. "I don't think he believed me about Waters, but he let it pass." The general chuckled. "In a way, I've been in so much trouble already that this seemed like small potatoes. I do worry with the war over they're going to want to find a back shelf to shove me on. I've never been much of a peacetime officer. Too much hand-holding and brown-nosing for me."

"They can't get rid of you," said Waters. "You're a hero."

"Watch them," said Patton. He turned to Stiller. "Well, my friend. This thing's almost over. Thank you for going in to get John. I'm sorry it turned out the way it did."

Stiller wanted to say something to his friend, tell him how he felt, but he let it pass. There was nothing that could be done about it. The past was the past. Their friendship was bigger than this. The war was over. The dead from the raid could as well have perished in the general offensive that occurred on the heels of the failed task force. War was messy. He'd let it lie at that.

For the first time, he allowed himself to think of home. His beautiful Texas. The trees, the streams, the humid summers so many people couldn't take but that he relished. It was time to go home.

*　*　*

A month later, a train slowed down at a station. Heat radiated off the platform on the sizzling June day. He looked out the window, recognizing the buildings, the roads, the station. He'd been absent for so long, and now he was back. The car lurched to a halt. He stood, gathering his gear, and ambled down the narrow corridor between the seats. He stepped down the stairs and onto the wooden platform, the heat rising up to meet him.

As he stepped off the train, he heard an excited clatter. He looked up, and there was his family. They rushed forward to greet him.

"Look at my hero!" shouted his mother, embracing him. She stepped back, admiring his uniform. "A Silver Star and a promotion to captain. We're so proud of you! I'm so happy you're home. When we heard about the raid, that you'd been captured or killed, we feared the worst."

Hall's father stepped forward, shaking his hand, his face beamed. "Congratulations, son. I'm so proud of you. You did everything you needed to do, and now the future is yours."

Hall smiled, beaming under his parents' approval. They walked away from the platform, his mother going on and on about how proud everyone was of him; he was the talk of the city.

"Sounds like you worked out things with Stiller," said his father. "I never cared much for him. He had a pretty big stick up his butt most of the time. None too smart either."

"Nothing's changed."

"Well, if he found it in himself to praise you in the end, he's okay in my book."

"He had a reason for supporting me."

"What do you mean?" his father asked.

"I'll tell you later," said Hall. "It's something we need to consider."

"Why can't you tell us now?" asked his mother.

"It's not for you."

He saw his mother's face flinch, but she didn't say anything else. She knew better than to stick her nose into the male business of the family.

The car whisked through the streets of Spokane, starting up the south hill toward the family's historic home.

"Mary Alister was asking about you," said his mother. "You remember Mary?"

He did. A young woman he'd known a little from the neighborhood. She was beautiful and from an influential family. He wasn't sure he was ready to settle down just yet. He'd like a little fun first. If he chose law school, he would be busy for three years, and he wasn't going to go through it with a wife. Still, Mary might make a fun distraction for the summer. No, he would seek his entertainment elsewhere. Her father was a little too important, and they lived too close by. There should be plenty of entertainment from other local girls he could afford to ruin. There would be plenty of time for Mary when he was ready.

"Did you hear me about Mary?" his mother repeated.

"Don't trouble him about that kind of thing," his father chastised her. "He just got home. They'll be plenty of time for that after we've mapped out his future. Have you done any thinking about that, my boy? About what's next?"

"I have," he said. "I'm thinking of law school. Then perhaps politics."

He could see his father practically crowing in the front seat. "That's my boy. When we get home, let's take a look at options. I can land you an internship with the firm, then a judicial clerkship. I'll get you an appointment with our congressman too. Plenty to work on."

Hall sat back in his seat, his mind planning out his future. He thought of the raid, the fighting, the dead, Stiller's words of admonition. Image by image he burned away the memories. They had no hold on him now. He had the world in his hands. Nobody could stop him. He still felt the onyx pit—the hollow of his heart he couldn't fill, the hole he shared with no one. He shook his head, shoving down the guilt, the shame, the loneliness. *I won't think about that right now. Once I have everything and everyone in my power, I'll be content. Wealth and power are all that matters. That's all anyone cares about. Then I'll be loved and respected. Then I'll be happy.*

November 1945

Stiller stepped out of a decrepit bus onto a dusty street in Texas. There was nobody there to greet him. He'd planned it that way. He wanted a little time to just exist, to walk the simple streets, breathe the air, rediscover the civilian world. He wasn't far from home, no more than an hour by that same bus. He'd jumped off a few stops earlier.

Stiller wasn't in uniform. He'd changed at the airport, carefully folding away his blouse and trousers. He didn't want to make a fuss. He'd paused only for a second, to glance at his newest medal. The Distinguished Service Medal. He grinned slightly, rubbing his fingers along the second-highest medal awarded by the US Army. He'd looked around to make sure nobody was watching. He tucked it away, where it would remain. Nobody needed to know about this.

Now, hours later, he strolled through town in a simple shirt and tie, a nobody from nowhere. He found a diner and stepped inside. The waitress smiled at him as he sat down. She brought him a menu, chatting away about the day. She was friendly. Her eyes told him she might want to carry on this conversation later. He thanked her politely, disengaging from the chatter, and looked over the menu. She seemed like a nice woman, but his thoughts were on home and family. He sipped his coffee and

closed his eyes, remembering the war, the battles, the raid. He
thought about the future. He'd get a little place. He didn't need
much. Maybe he'd start a garden. He'd always wanted one. He
imagined the soil, the plants, wiping away the sweat on a humid
Saturday afternoon. He smiled to himself. That's just what he'd
do. He looked forward to the future and to the here and now. A
simple, contented life.

Author's Note

Task Force Baum

Task Force Baum was a forty-eight-hour raid behind enemy lines ordered by General George Patton for the specific purpose of liberating his son-in-law, Lieutenant Colonel John Waters. The force was made up of just over three hundred men commanded by Captain Abe Baum. Major Alexander Stiller, a staff officer of Patton's, went along on the raid to identify Waters.

The column was held up initially at the front, and then again at Gemünden when German forces destroyed the bridge over the Main. The convoy reached Oflag XIII well behind schedule on March 27, 1945, and fought guards and some reinforcements until the camp was liberated. During the brief battle, Lieutenant Colonel Waters was wounded by a German guard while attempting to secure the surrender of the camp. He required emergency surgery and was too badly hurt to be evacuated by the task force.

Baum discovered immediately on liberation of Oflag XIII that the intelligence on the number of prisoners was grossly underestimated. He had resources to evacuate only a fifth of the POWs, and the rest of the men either broke into small groups and attempted to escape or returned dejectedly to the camp.

Task Force Baum left the POW camp at about 6:00 p.m. on March 27 and was bogged down for hours on winding roads heading back toward Hammelburg. The convoy attempted to escape to the southwest but was stopped at Bonnland and then at Höllrich. Down to a handful of tanks and short on fuel, Baum brought the force to Hill 427, where they could regroup and await the dawn for a final desperate attempt at escape.

In the meantime, the Germans closed in from all directions. When the task force ignited their vehicles to leave, the Germans attacked from every direction, wiping out all of the remaining vehicles and wounding more of the men. Within a few minutes, the vast majority of the Americans involved were killed, wounded, or captured. The prisoners were returned to Oflag XIII or other camps, where most of them were moved farther into Germany and liberated a few weeks later.

General Patton was questioned carefully by the press when news leaked that his son-in-law had been in the camp. The general denied any pre-knowledge and showed his official and personal journals as proof. General Dwight Eisenhower also admonished Patton over the raid. General Patton later said that Task Force Baum was one of the greatest mistakes of the war, and that he should have sent the entire Combat Command Force instead of a mere reinforced company.

The secret of Patton's knowledge was kept for another twenty years, despite numerous individuals having knowledge of the truth. This was a different time.

Twenty-five men were killed under Baum's command, and another thirty-two, including Baum himself, were wounded. All of the vehicles were destroyed, and the vast majority of the rest of the command was immediately captured.

General George S. Patton

General George S. Patton is considered by many to be the greatest tank commander and tactical ground commander produced by the United States during World War II.

Patton gained valuable combat experience in tank combat during World War I, where Alexander Stiller served on his staff. In the years between the wars, Patton was a critical component in the US development of armored combat theory.

With the coming of the World War II, Patton commanded significant forces in North Africa and Sicily. After an infamous episode in which he slapped a soldier suffering from PTSD, Patton was removed from command, but he served in a vital role as the commander of a "ghost" army allegedly preparing for an invasion across the narrow portion of the English Channel at the Pas-de-Calais.

Installed in command of the 3rd Army after the actual invasion of Normandy in the summer of 1944, Patton streamed through France and southern Germany. He was pivotal in the reversal of German fortunes at the Battle of the Bulge in December 1944.

Patton ordered Task Force Baum in late March 1945, only six weeks short of the end of the war in Europe. After the war, he was assigned to command the military district in Bavaria, where he was killed in an automobile accident.

Lieutenant Colonel Creighton Abrams

Lieutenant Colonel Creighton Abrams was in charge of Combat Command B of the 4th Armored Division in March 1945. When Abrams received the orders from Patton to form a task force to go after Oflag XIII, he lobbied hard to send the entire combat command. Patton refused, and Task Force Baum went forward with a few hundred men instead of well over a thousand.

Abrams was a top commander. Patton said of him, "I'm supposed to be the best tank commander in the Army, but I have one peer—Abe Abrams. He's the world champion."

After the war, Abrams served in staff positions before serving in Korea. Abrams was promoted to full general in 1964 and played a prominent role in the Vietnam War. He was the proponent of the "Hearts and Minds" strategy. Abrams was the chief of staff of the US Army from 1972 until his death. He was instrumental in the creation of the Rangers. He died in 1974 at just 59 years old.

Captain Abraham Baum

Captain Abraham Baum was the commander of the task force that carried his name. He was an officer under Creighton Abrams in Combat Command B. Baum was a respected combat commander and was selected by Abrams because of his abilities and experience to lead the desperate raid behind enemy lines.

Baum carried out a brilliant expedition, despite the horribly under-armed and undermanned mission. He carried the forces all the way to the camp, despite a lack of intelligence and an imperfect knowledge of the terrain and road system. He was captured along with the rest of the raid survivors on March 28, 1945.

Patton had promised that Baum would receive the Congressional Medal of Honor if he was successful. However, any award of the top US medal requires a full investigation of the facts. Likely because of the secret element of the mission, Patton instead awarded Baum the Distinguished Service Medal.

Baum was ultimately promoted to the rank of major, and he retired to become a garment manufacturer and salesman. He wrote a non-fiction narrative of the raid called *Raid!: The Untold Story of Patton's Secret Mission.* This book was published in 1981 by G. P. Putnam's Sons of New York.

Baum passed away at age 91.

2nd Lieutenant William Nutto

Second Lieutenant William J. Nutto was commander of a company of Sherman tanks of the 37th Battalion, 4th Armored Division.

Nutto commanded the medium tank element of Task Force Baum, with 59 men and 10 M4A3 Sherman tanks. He was wounded at Gemünden but bravely continued to serve throughout the expedition, including hours of start-and-stop groping in the darkness when the force attempted to escape Oflag XIII through the winding hills near Hammelburg. Nutto's tank was ambushed, and he was captured when the force was attempting to find an escape route near Höllrich.

William Nutto became an attorney in Corpus Christi, Texas, after the war.

Lieutenant Colonel John Waters

Lieutenant Colonel John Waters was the son-in-law of George Patton, having married Beatrice Patton in 1934. Waters attended West Point, graduating in 1931. He served in North Africa, where his force was captured by German forces at the city of Sidi Bou Zid, in Tunisia. Waters was in a prisoner-of-war camp in Poland when the installation was evacuated before the oncoming Russian invasion. Waters and others were marched in a tortuous journey across Germany to Oflag XIII at Hammelburg in January 1945. He became the camp's executive officer under Colonel Paul Goode.

Waters had no idea that Patton had sent a raid to rescue him. When Task Force Baum attacked the camp itself, Waters led a small group under a flag of truce to try to compel the German forces to surrender. Badly wounded by a German guard, he underwent lifesaving surgery by a Serbian doctor (there was a large Serbian POW camp attached to Oflag XIII).

After the war, Waters became the cadet commander at West

Point. He served in Korea and eventually commanded the 4th Armored Division, the V Corps, and the Fifth US Army. He was promoted to full general (four-star general). He retired in 1966. Waters died in 1989.

Major Alexander Stiller

Major Alexander Stiller was a staff member of Patton's who had served with the general during World War I, before returning to Texas and working as a Texas Ranger. Stiller rejoined Patton to serve with him throughout World War II.

The major was sent on Task Force Baum for the express purpose of finding John Waters. He knew the secret and refused to reveal this information, even after Patton died in 1945. Stiller was awarded the Distinguished Service Cross for heroism during the raid on Hammelburg.

Richard Koehl, Sergeant Knorr, and Colonel Hoepple

Hauptmann (Captain) Richard Koehl was a Catholic priest who commanded an anti-tank armored company during World War II. His force tracked Task Force Baum and engaged it on several occasions, including the final attack on Hill 427.

Although the death of his sister was fictitious, Task Force Baum did gun down a convoy of women antiaircraft troops on the way in to the Oflag, sickening many of the GIs. Koehl's experiences mirror the feelings of so many Germans at this desperate point of the war: a desire for one last victory mixed with a wish for safety and a hopelessness about the future.

Sergeant Knorr also was a real character, a skulking and dangerous guard nicknamed "the Ferret."

Colonel Hoepple, commander of the German forces around Oflag XIII, orchestrated the destruction of Task Force Baum. He committed suicide shortly thereafter.

Captain Jim Curtis

Captain Jim Curtis is a fictitious character, but his experience certainly was not. Oflag XIII was filled with officers from the 106th Division, a fresh force with no combat experience that was overrun by a massive German offensive at the Battle of the Bulge. The men who survived and were taken to POW camps were angry and disillusioned, feeling they'd been betrayed by their commanders, who had not prepared them for the attack. They shared a collective frustration that they had trained for combat for years and then, amid all the massive American victories in the summer and fall of 1944, somehow had been placed in exactly the wrong place at the wrong time and suffered a crushing defeat and humiliation during their first trial by arms.

Lieutenant Sam Hall

Lieutenant Sam Hall is also a fictitious character, although, like Curtis, he represents a class of soldiers during the war. A number of staff officers, sometimes well connected, were given plum assignments for short patrols or other limited combat experience, afterward receiving accolades and promotion. Stiller, a simple, hardworking, and loyal soldier on Patton's staff, would have balked mightily at dealing with a wealthy son along for a free ride.

Hall also represents, sadly, a more "modern" view of the world. While Stiller would never reveal Patton's secret (in fact, many carried the secret for years), Hall sees the information merely as something he can trade for his own selfish advantage. It is difficult to believe that many of our leading politicians—or, for that matter, many people we know today—would be willing to steadfastly hold a secret for decades, on a point of honor. There are clear reasons these men and women were known as the Greatest Generation.